OUR STRUGGLE

PUBLISHED by Influx Press
THE Greenhouse, 49 Green Lanes, London, N16 9BU
WWW.INFLUXPRESS.COM / @InfluxPress
ALL rights reserved.
© Wayne Holloway 2022

FIRST edition 2022. Printed and bound in the UK by TJ Books.

PAPERBACK ISBN: 9781914391194
EBOOK ISBN: 9781914391200

EDITOR: Kit Caless
COVER design: Keenan Designs
INTERIOR design: Vince Haig

OUR STRUGGLE

WAYNE HOLLOWAY

In memory of my friend and neighbour,
Jerome Samuel 1953-2021
and my Nan,
Winnie Pallen 1917-2021.
All our stories will live forever.

Smrt fašizmu – sloboda narodu!
– graffiti, Yugoslavia, 1944

CIRCA

Prologue 2016

Clowns? Were they even a thing anymore? Rosa and her friends pointed them out to each other.

A line of clowns shuffle right and left in sync with the police, each wearing a skewwhiff toy helmet. All poker faced 1000 yard stares gently mocking the no eye contact police regulation before shifting to a theatrical eyes left/right pose and finally bowing to the crowd, effortlessly working through the gears of mimicry.

Now the clowns swagger to-and-fro gesticulating like monkeys behind the Britain First bovver boys, who also ignored them because they didn't know how to respond either.

Are you taking the piss?

Piss taking cunts.

The clowns aped gestures of guile and secrecy opposite a group of very angry anarchists pulling out bright shiny hankies to cover their faces and pointing and mouthing slogans, all of this executed in silence. One clown pulled out a cartoon like fizzling bomb whilst the others put their fingers in their ears and scrunched their eyes shut.

Bomb voyage!

The anarchists didn't know what to make of them.

Have a wash you dirty cunts the bovver boys shouted at the anarchists.

Fascists out! Fascists out!

Student wankers.

On closer inspection Rosa noticed that behind the uniform face paint that designated them 'clowns', of the nine in this group three of them were women.

The clowns never spoke. They were a mirrored to what was in front of them. Not just what they saw but also their emotional response to seeing it. They somehow condensed, summarised the spectacle before them observing every detail and offering it back up to the players. The clowns had discipline, training. They were guided by foresight, practicing the art of knowing. A twisted reverse, a flopped mirror image.

A sea of white faces.

Hands in the air.

God save our gracious queen.

Like you just don't care.

Long to reign over us.

Bella ciao bella ciao bella ciao ciao ciao.

From a small contingent at the back, smoking roll ups and singing out of tune, mumbling words they don't know beyond the chorus. Out of place, embarrassing.

Confound their politics, Frustrate their knavish tricks.

Which nobody ever sung.

As if we are a ship and not an island, the problem being they conflate the two.

All aboard the skylark.

It starts to rain.

Union Jack Brollies.

Grotesque.

The clowns dance like it's a scene from the Umbrellas of Cherbourg.

Carnival.

Let it rain.

Pinched home counties faces, heavily made up female faces, fingerless gloved rosy cheeked young faces, flat caps and kagoules, labradors and pit bulls. The dogs alone tell you the story of this march, it doesn't need people.

An unholy canine alliance.

Who let the dogs out?

They want their country back.

Now when Gerry Gable came to talk at Essex, we put him up in Colchester and stood guard all night outside because the NF had threatened to kill him.

The National Front? Who's Gerry Gable?

He set up Searchlight.

Searchlight? Come on dad don't be lazy, explain!

Ok Ok sorry, Searchlight was an anti-fascist magazine that kept tabs on all of the bastards. That's standing up to Nazis, calling them out letting them know we're watching them.

And we don't? The good old bad old times, Essex University this that and the other, God it's so boring.

Nothing boring about history.

You used to go on marches, you, and mum. Come on the march with me Saturday, come on, you'll love it.

He didn't go, he was too busy.

Rosa will leave for Lebanon three weeks later.

His loss.

Some things stand out. Expensive sports jackets stand out, silver trident badges stand out, a brisker gait and sense of purpose stands out. Camouflaged trousers tucked neatly into 18 hole Dr. Martins stand out. Marching in step stands out, wolves in sheep's clothing stand out amidst this day out atmosphere, inclusive of blue face painting dappled with EU stars in gold and French Beret wearing older middle classes, this very English affair. The clowns smell the wolves, and start prowling.

Stand up to Brussels.

A different energy marching to a different beat. Take back control. Standing *For Britain* under the sign of the Trident.

This stands out, badly scribbled on card and held aloft.

SECOND REF? YES SURE HANG OR SHOOT THE PM?

Alongside this.

IF IN DOUBT PULL OUT!

A home counties ribald humour, more Terry and June than 'Die Sturmer', more a Good Life script than an Alt Right discussion thread.

Kenny Williams, in or out?

Bitter lemons.

A Union Jack flying on the same pole (above) an Israeli Flag. A country that opted out of our mandate generations ago.

They got their country back.

Rosa was exhilarated to be out and about in central London, with other young people, other women, breathing in the crisp winter air. Only on days like these, demo days, did she feel safe on the streets, felt the city was hers or at least that she had a shared right to enjoy it. Red banners, black flags, green banners, rainbow banners, Momentum banners, misspelt banners, home-made banners raised by quirky awkward republics of one. The outsiders, the marginal, the individual, the gay, the trans, the no idea, but all of them against hate, Davids against Goliaths. Jewish groups of all leftish persuasions, a small, fragile hand drawn and a wonky coloured in Menorah with the legend 'Jews against Nazis' pencilled in over it, held together by masking tape and held aloft optimistically.

The Anarchists were chanting Spanish resistance slogans, 'No Pasarán' 'anti Fascistsa', teachers, care workers, hippies, nurses and ambulance drivers, some adapted pop songs; anti-Tommy Robinson chants of the 'Mrs. Robinson/Tommy Robinson variety...'

Funny joyous moments.

Rosa knew what her dad would say.

Blah blah blah.

She rolled a fag as she marched, a new skill she was pleased with, tightly bound rollies that didn't die after one puff and a filter that didn't fall out either. Neat.

She knew she would miss this, miss home.

To manage these diverse British groups we get Police Liaison officers with white and blue baseball caps. In one crowd buckets are being shaken for donations. Coins rattling in plastic buckets for 'Our boys'. Help for heroes, Homes fit for heroes, 1918, 2016, same, same. Bringing up the rear, a country gent type until you look closer to see a more hard bitten face, haggard and quite possibly unhinged, shoulders draped in a Union Jack, camera gripped in one hand and a pony tail flowing down his neck, this disappointed man in his late fifties holding aloft the only gun on display, in a laminated cartoon of Theresa May with the Brexit gun in her mouth.

In the pub later, the Chandos off Trafalgar square, marchers from both sides were having a drink, no flare ups since the landlord stepped in to a shouting match at the bar and said any more funny business I'll close the pub. They backed off, back to their tables.

Rosa was debating Brexit strategy with friends and neighbours, Corbyn the hero, Corbyn the villain, but her mind kept coming back to the clowns. She zones out of the chatter and types into her phone's browser, well she doesn't know what to type, clowns at

demos? Left wing clowns? Serious clowns? Anarchist clowns?
    Anarchist clowns.

The Clandestine Insurgent Rebel Clown Army returns in one of the searches. She scrolls through their wiki.

    Horizontalists who engage with people without the need for leaders.' she scans down the page, Tactical frivolity, charivari, Mikhail Bakhtin, Towards a philosophy of the act, the role of humour in political confrontation, the world turned upside down, King for a day, Morris men, and on and on.

Did you see those clowns at the demo? They were proper funny.
Yeah who were they? Kind of odd, they didn't speak to anyone.
It says here they are some kind of anarchists.
She takes a big gulp of London Pride.
Taking the piss weren't they?
Middle class wankers.
Maybe it is all a bit of a joke?
What are we doing?
Not clowning about.

Fuck off, they're smarter than that, proper taking the piss out of the coppers and the fash winding them up more than we were. You never heard of Mikhail Bakhtin?

You sound like your old man Rosa.

Her friend Ted had met her dad Paul, they'd gone out for a few months and dad gave him a proper grilling about his politics. She had been mortified at the time but...

Bolshevik mess.

For some reason Ted was spoiling for a fight. It had been his nickname for her dad.

You never said that to his face, wanker. Whilst thinking I bet dad has read this Bakhtin, I'll check his bookshelves. He loves anything Russian, bit sad really, everything he likes is dead.

Sorry, I didn't mean it, shouldn't have said that, another pint?

Rosa nods, offering him a wry smile. Not such a wanker. She had mainly finished with him because she had decided to leave, better not to have any ties.

I'd never heard of him either.

Ted smiles, taking their empties to the bar.

Perhaps one last fling?

Dad should have come today, grumpy bugger, he would have liked the clowns despite himself.

THE LABOUR THEORY OF VALUE

1961

Michael Feeney, spade man out of Ireland. Fifteen years of six a.m. pick-ups from the curb outside the Crown Hotel Cricklewood Broadway until 'You, you, you and you' no longer included him. His wife, Caitriona, a nurse, before, during and after nursing four of her own; She the powerhouse, the earner, pulling rabbits regularly out of hats and onto the table, the one constant in the flux of their new English life. Him taking work where he found it, tarmacking mainly, on the new Westway coming out of Paddington, now there's a job with a short work life expectancy. Michael back and forth to the old country, elderly parents to visit, then to bury and a few acres to sell, a country empty of people but full of politics. Fenian bastard muttered at every border crossing, taig, paddy, bog trotter mick and everything else each time he returned to what he bitterly referred to as home, all of this swallowed silently, tamped down with Guinness, never a word to the wife, not once, anyway she could pass better than he with a respectable NHS job and a soft Waterford accent besides. Him being from Sligo marked him out, chalked him up soon as he opened his mouth.

Two daughters and latterly one son, delivered to the soundtrack of Bobby Vee's cover of 'How many tears' blaring from the nurses station and boy did she cry a river of those welcoming all ten pounds of baby Paul, her final child, the son and heir and Michael only being employed for his first three years, his body betraying him at forty nine, the stations of his cross consisting of a crushed right hand from a bastard mallet, a pair of tortured knees (but never capped), a clicking and worn right shoulder blade and shooting sciatic pains up and down both legs that could only be assuaged, begged off, by codeine and Guinness (he said). No longer able to dig holes or fill them in for the man, it was the back of his useless hand that saw the most work raising his son in the eight years it took him to drink himself to death.

When at his funeral his wife said of and for him that he could handle a spade, his son aged 9 swore silently never to touch one.

1979

Paul Michael Feeney, London Transport employee since leaving school at the age of sixteen. 'Tall Paul' as he was known (there being two other 'Pauls' working out of his depot, neither of them tall) stoops apologetically, looking down at his feet instead of over the heads of the rest of us, as befitted his moniker. A muscle or sense memory of all the flinching he did when his dad got home from the pub, his whole being finely calibrating the speed and reach of a drunk's hands.

The first time he stood up to him had been right at the

end after he raised a hand to his oldest sister Siobhan who had come home wobbly and with the smell of cigarettes and spirits on her, no smell ever escaping their sitting room it was so small, like an interrogation room.

'Don't you hit her dad. I'll tell ma.' Her seventeen years and Paul's nine against him. If he had been five years older perhaps it would have just been a flat, threatening 'Don't you hit her dad.' without recourse to their mother.

Perhaps.

The mother exhausted upstairs after a double shift, thankfully oblivious to the world and its violences. That is at least what sleep can deliver. The father slumped back in his armchair without saying a word, already finished as a violent man, just a residue of such, a pathetic shell of the bully he had been glaring back at his renegade children fists clenched.

Paul was glad he got to do this at least once before his father died however depleted the threat had become. It was a child's victory. He wished he had been born before his sisters. To protect them. To have been the eldest. Only later did he find out that Siobhan had already pulled a kitchen knife on the bastard when she was fourteen. Marion, apple of her father's eye, turned a blind one of her own to his outbursts although by then he had mostly petered out, just going through the motions. Although her silence had alienated the two sisters from each other. His mother had learnt how to manage his anger, diverting it from the children into the privacy of their bedroom, (or so she thought) comforting herself that for the girls at least, their childhood had been full of better memories, a father with a wage, most of which he brought home along with some self-respect. Take that from a man and you get clenched fists with a stranger behind them always getting poked by the wrong end of every stick.

But Paul hated him the day he died, or felt what he thought was hatred, it being a strange emotion for him to understand with very little to compare with, to measure what he felt by. So, he hated until that faded leaving him diffident in the company of men, and the stronger he got, the taller he grew, the more withdrawn he became, scared of his own fists and what they might be capable of. As if it was something he carried inside him, a virus inherited from his father.

Please don't make me angry

Like the Incredible Hulk, whose comics he hoarded, he hated confrontation.

I wouldn't like me when I'm angry.

Looking up to his face you glimpse bright steel in his blue grey eyes, flashing at you with a fierce geometry, a light speed awareness of his place in this world and yours. An ability to triangulate. His quiet demeanour can't hide a mischievous intelligence which he does his best to distract you from noticing. He was a strange one. A young man who thinks, reads and listens before venturing his own observations, tempered in the fires of his imagination before plunging them into the icy waters of other people's opinion.

Constantly rolling or smoking cigarettes Pauls long fingers dip into his wallet of Golden Virginia for fat pinches of moist tobacco. Thumbs and index fingers roll the Rizla tight, a delicate tongue tip swiped across the glue strip, loose tobacco strands rubbed from his fingertips back into the tobacco tin, a flick of the zippo lighter, a whiff of paraffin, thumb grinding the flint, flame and inhale, the long first draw and flecks of tobacco constantly being brushed flicked or picked from trousers, lips, shirt or Donkey jacket. Fags you have to properly puff to keep alight drawing his already sunken cheeks inwards further like the inhaling bellows of a squeezebox, an instrument you could easily imagine grasped in his large hands hunched over as both it and he wheezes.

Quite the performance, a smoke and mirrors of distraction. Fags that when finished you smeared the end off onto the lip of the ashtray rather than stub them out. Unconsciously drying your sticky-stained wet fingers on your jeans so moist they were, like the peat bogs in the Ox mountains, where the heavy wet turf had been cut, turned and stacked by a grandfather Paul never knew wielding a two sided spade, thirsty back breaking work.

Paul drank pints methodically with big gulps spaced out by the metronome of his Adam's apple. A slow inebriation withdrawing him further from the cut and thrust of the mostly male banter he encountered at work. Time passed more slowly for Paul, his clock was wound to a lesser tension and the gaps between the words he softly spoke yawned a little wider than those uttered by others. Tick. Beat. Tock. But when spoken it is with a surprisingly upbeat Camden accent, grafted over his father's voice, which up to his death was still thick with the sound of Sligo.

Paul would be the tortoise in any race. Shaving cuts, some tissue papered, occasionally blood spotting his collar but always whatever the cost, clean shaven. And always wearing freshly dubbed black Dr. Martins in which he would walk apologetically into any room or situation and would be gone, not there, before you knew it, despite the amount of vertical space he took up but not before weighing it all up, each and every situation, taking it all in for later rumination. He was thin as a rake and could fold himself unobtrusively into any room no matter how small, him and his black donkey jacket and khaki knapsack in which he kept his notebook, pens and most importantly his books, usually used Penguin classics, well thumbed copies of Dostoevsky, Nietzsche, Flaubert and Gogol. Given the opportunity he would happily disappear into any sofa, armchair or even, latterly, beanbag. He had the uncanny skill of being able to literally absent himself from any situation.

Until he wanted to be noticed, which came later and then it would be, 'Fuck, how did we let such a big bastard in here?' by which time it would be too late.

Despite being seen as 'a little loopy' Paul is accepted without much comment by his fellow workers. Perhaps he was just lucky or the size of his fists warned some off, his quietness seeding disquiet, whatever the case his co workers and Union comrades chose to defend and explain him to outsiders remarking on his dry sense of humour, the books he read, a man brought up by three women no less, enough to turn any man half crazy they would snigger and therefore his demeanour, how he set himself against the world, the cut of his jib, was understandable. That's just him, Tall Paul, mardy bastard but ardent Trade Unionist. Paul went to all his branch meetings voted on all the motions, not his bag some might have thought, the procedural line dance of branch politics. This assumption reinforced by the fact he hardly ever spoke but sat at the back taking notes. On what, who knew? Who were they for, these notes? Bent almost double adding words to his notebook with the fervour of a medieval monk illuminating a manuscript is what it actually looked like. Pencil gripped and hidden in the crook of his left hand, pushed across the page with a disproportionate effort his hand crabbing along to keep up with his train of thought. But this same hand would fly up pencil first when it came to every vote as if on cue yet without once looking up. He knew his mind which held his opinions as tightly as his fingers grasped the remnant pencil stub, bitten though it was down to a splintered soggy fag end.

His London accent protected him from what his father had got, this at a time of war in Ireland and the mob baying for Irish blood.

To the world he was Paul Michael Feeney, Northern line guard and National union of Railwaymen member in good standing, Golders Green branch number one.

But what was his inner purpose? What was he scribbling down with such fervour, what indeed were his opinions? In short, what was the why of this gentle giant? There had always been clues, like the red and gold Lenin badge on his donkey jacket lapel, pinned next to a 'Pogo on a Nazi' button and his subscription to the *Morning Star* but this was common stuff, run of the mill, the affectations of a tried and tested belief system that had served his class so-so since before the Great War. More interesting, surprising even, was his close friendship with the burly wannabe firebrand Bob Crow; a lowly drain rodder ganging and gagging his way up and down the 'suicide pits' between the tracks, clearing the drains, coming on shift when Paul was usually finishing his. A cup of tea, coffee from a shared thermos and later pints down the social. A friendship forged from the simple pleasures of union life but also passionate conversation and shared belief which placed themselves and not without an element of absurdist vanity, firmly in the Internationalist vanguard of World Socialism.

Bob exhibited an outward energy, his heart on his sleeve, a Viking in his passions. Paul was tamped down hard, his fire inside, smouldering behind his eyes, a trickster perhaps, Loki to Bob's quotidian Thor, yet both advocates of the same struggle. Paul was happy to listen, Bob loved to be heard. Bob smoked Embassy Number 6 and Paul smoked roll ups, yet these two unlikely comrades imagined a future where robots would do the hard work, the repetitive factory line jobs, the night shifts etc. and allow workers the freedom to pursue their creative passions. Robots didn't need the wages. For sure a deal would have to be done with the capitalist bastards that developed them, to reimburse the bloody leeches for their investment; up to and until a revolution, a pragmatic compromise would have to be made between classes. This was a practical solution that threw Utopia into the future but not out of the window. Solutions now creating the conditions for the future to mature in. In Yugoslavia they had worker owned factories and businesses competing against each other in a free market where the fruits of their labours went to their benefit, now wasn't this, this market socialism a pragmatic third way? A way to socialise profit, a path that leads beyond the first necessary stage of nationalisation?

Bob was good at upsetting the applecart and became a union representative after his gang leader complained he wouldn't take the shifts he was given. He soon got branch meetings to change from their traditional Fridays to Wednesday because Friday night was going out night, when any self-respecting young worker would be spunking his wages up west in the clubs and chasing the girls. Paul enjoyed this ability his friend had to change the status quo, to get things done. A word here, an observation there, snappy sentences summing up a mood, a sense of humour, Bob was easy to like.

After the shift to midweek meeting attendance figures went up dramatically.

For Bob politics was all about common sense. Simple organisation, the kind of quiet revolution from below that Paul understood and felt he could contribute to. He grew up in a home where keeping everybody clean, fed and clothed was done with a determined unfussy female energy. His mother and sisters organised the wash, the drying, the ironing, like clockwork, a rota written down and tacked to the back of the kitchen door. Not just the chores that needed doing but a fair rotation of them, combined with an efficient allocation of resources, washing powder, boiling water, scrubbing board, washing line, these three women in sync so to speak and everyone immaculate come the weekend and his father out to work every morning in a clean shirt although somewhat frayed at the neck and cuffs. Sewing machine, thread, needle, cotton, cut offs, roll ends from the local haberdashery, hand me downs, make do and mend, pattern cut, going out threads, everyday shirts, darned socks, let out jackets, taken in waists, runs and snags repaired on stockings, shop bought surprises for birthdays and holidays with the money saved in weekly instalments to a Christmas savings club.

From the age of five Paul ran to the pub and back at 6pm on pay day Fridays to beg the wages off his dad before he drank them and out of shame an amount (variable) was handed over, with or without a cuff across the back of his head to sign for it.

This the home that Caitriona built, as intricate in its apparent smooth running as any fancy watch, a complex domestic movement in which Paul was but a small cog, an achievement he grew up in awe of.

When there was a sing along night down the social, it was always Bob up first, belting out his favourite, 'Sweet Caroline', much to the mirth of Paul and the rest who enjoyed his voice for what it was, all heart and full of fun. In his room Paul listened to John Peel, an eclectic mix of reggae, punk and older prog rock. His favourites were the introspective rock of Soft Parade (the Softs) and Kevin Coyne, the tension and style of The Specials. He recorded his own mix tapes accompanied by meticulous liner notes. The festive fifty was a highlight of the year, carefully hitting play, pause and record, un-pausing in the beat John Peel allowed between his voice and the start of each track, enabling young men and women up and down the country to erase him from their precious recordings.

Bob Crow brought Paul out of himself, he was a man who lived his life in public and later in the glare of public attention. He got married young, his energy encompassing work, politics, family and going out in one great rush of personality. Paul struggled with a public life but wrestled with his withdrawing nature as he was attracted to the flame of company, of belonging to something bigger than just his family and his thinking mind alone. Paul wanted his ideas to become flesh, to see if they would flourish outside the petri dish of his scribbled notes and ruminations. The social side of being in the union was much more than idle gossip and subsidised beer, it was all part of his experiment.

Ideas and action were fast friends, the praxis of revolution right there in a shake of hands, a nod of heads and a downing of pints. Collective bargaining, motions proposed, seconded, passed and carried, international worker solidarity, funds raised and messages of support sent, literacy, leisure, nationalisation. A society based on co-operation and shared wealth in opposition to the extraction of surplus value as profit by the boss class. Not just dreams but real aspirations shared in meetings. Hands raised, the public acknowledgement of agreement amongst fellows, health and safety working practices, holidays, over time, wages, shift rotas, all of this, little by little built something.

Radical bureaucracy is what Paul scribbled down in his notebook, doubly underlined, and underneath the bullet points of what this meant; The skill in knowing everyone's name, asking after family, weighing people up, strong points, weak ones, who to ask to do what, who to leave alone, the right peg for each hole. All of this possible because of direct and open contact with other workers, no gatekeeping or vested interest, the sharing of contacts as important as that of things, knowing how to evaluate people for the common interest, to collectively decide who to be put in charge of printing hand-outs, of speaking to men and women on another shift, to negotiate with management, to forge agreement, including when necessary to compromise.

Who were the firebrands? Who was better with their fists than their tongues? This element to be kept in reserve for away days against the fascists but not for meetings with bosses. All of this information, all of these names, traits, personalities 'Top Trump' statistics to be kept close to your chest in the endless war of position between the classes.

WOODBERRY DOWN AND OUT

2016

The summer before Rosa left Paul made almost daily calls to the Mike O' Hara show on LBC. It got to the point that Mike would greet him onto the show with relish, egging him on, to perform, to entertain 'us' on air with his struggle, the anger of his worldview.

You're a proper warrior mate.

Mike would sign him off with a smirk, although what war he was fighting wasn't clear any more.

Paul bowls down Stoke Newington Church street, shouts into his mobile.

Hello Mike, It's Paul from Woodberry Down.

Mike smiles on camera, leans into the mic.

Good morning Paul! A London legend from Woodberry Down estate in Hackney, always a delight to hear your opinions Paul, what would you like to say on the issue of Gentrification, the good the bad or indeed the ugly?

Paul is walking past a long queue at the local butchers, Meat 16. He nearly trips over somebody's dog drinking from the silver bowl on the pavement provided by the butchers. He gives the owner a wanker sign.

Thanks Mike, likewise. Well, as you know we live in what used to be called a council house.

Mike vigorously nods his head.

..and just like a fine wine you were decanted..

That's just it Mike, we're not moving. We are resisting the CPO.

That's the compulsory Purchase order right.

Yes. Berkeley homes are pulling a fast one. Selling most of the new development sight unseen in the far east, leaving us on our toes. It's a joke. Decant us to where? A CPO needs to prove that it's in the interests of the community, not profit. It isn't and we're not moving.

Mike takes a beat, he knows the way around these calls, the flow of a debate that he controls. He glances down at his notes.

But some tenants want to sell, others want to move back into the next phase of the development and you're stopping them.

Paul has come to a standstill outside Foxtons estate agents. He's eyeballing the people inside. Puts the palm of his hand on the permanently shiny clean glass and keeps talking.

There's a net loss of 300 social houses. In whose public interest is that? It's classic tory tactics of Divide and conquer.

The receptionist stares at the odd bloke on his mobile with his grubby hand leaving marks all over her window. She looks over her shoulder for support from the estate agents working the phones.

In my notes here Paul, it says that the next ten years of development will deliver 2000 affordable homes, subsidised by front loading private sales in the first two phases.

Come off it, There will be no roll out, as soon as they've flogged the flats overlooking the wetlands, they'll pull out.

They run down this estate so people would beg to sell at knock down prices, or take the council's offer of rehousing out in the bloody sticks. One neighbour had to move to a flat in Ipswich. She's 75, lived here all her life what she gonna do there?

And all this from a Labour council Paul.

Labour? don't make me laugh, they're all crooks. You walk down Church street, only black owned business is the funeral parlour, that tells a story in itself. Where have all the West Indian families gone? Home or Hatfield, that's the reality of gentrification, it's ethnic and class cleansing if you ask me.

Mike nods, pulls a face in agreement. (For his YouTube audience.)

And I'm glad I did Paul, speak again soon, always a pleasure to have you on the show, now moving on to our next caller, Sandra in Hainault...

A young estate agent approaches the door, with a leave it to me hand gesture for the receptionist and ventures outside.

Paul finishes the conversation by himself, with his nose up against the glass.

'In the far east a flat built by water is meant to bring luck. For us on what's left of the estate it's a fucking curse.'

The estate agent hesitates by the door.

'Can I help you sir?' Paul turns round rubbing his nose.

'Do I look like a sir to you?'

'No sir, I mean no, did you want anything, are you looking...

Paul gives him a long beat of menace, tuned from elsewhere into the frequency of the right here right now and abruptly walks away. The estate agent gathers himself and walks back flashing a 'I told you I'd sort it' smile to the visibly relieved receptionist.

In a movie there would be a beat before a brick came flying through the plate glass window. In real life..

Paul walks home through the park, hands deep in his pockets. He always felt a bit uneasy after phoning in, a bit antsy. A bit of a phony. It's a guilty pleasure, a way of keeping his blood pressure up or down but he would freely admit a bit sad, phoning up a daytime radio show, a middle aged and under employed activity if ever there was one. Walking down the street and wanting to put in the windows of Foxton's the estate agents is another.

I'll come back with a brick later. He thinks every time he passes it but on eyeballing all the CCTV in the street he always decides against it.

That night at supper.

Rosa: Dads been on the radio again mum.

Oh God Paul, how embarrassing. At least use a different name.

Paul is a common name. They'll never know it's me.

He smiles at his daughter.

Who dad. Who are *they*? Who actually cares if it is you?

Sarah rolls her eyes.

I care Rosa, Christ, God knows what he's been saying this time.

See, your mum cares. He sniggers.

All I'm saying is the truth, that's all. Painful for some though that may be.

You pompous arse, listen to yourself!

The two women start laughing and Paul sips his beer and joins in.

You can laugh all you like...

Sarah steps behind him, hugs him round the neck, his head turns and kisses her arm.

Paul did have *phone in form*. A few years earlier, when he had a job as a park ranger, he once phoned up Vanessa Feltz calling himself Herschel from Waltham road Synagogue, which got him through to the shows guest, the writer Howard Jacobson.

I've got a question for Mr. Jacobson.

Vanessa : Go ahead Hershel.

Celebrities, radio, TV hosts etc always like emphasising the fact they have remembered your name by repeating it. As if names are what we share in common, possibly with the implication that they are (sadly) the only thing.

Howard: Hello Herschel, call me Howard, what would you like to ask?

You're a shit version of Phillip Roth aren't you Howard?

...

He's cut off.

Vanessa: (Clears her throat.) Sorry for the language from the last caller listeners.

A couple of coughs and a glass of water gulped later and a red faced Howard Jacobson is answering the next question about table tennis.

Paul gets a call back from the show's producer. Young female and middle class.

You should be ashamed of yourself for swearing on air and talking to our guest like that.

Paul snorts.

Piss off.

And swaggers down the road.

He loved Phillip Roth books and Mickey Sabbath was his hero, an avatar for all the things Paul wasn't (and didn't even want to be), a chest thumping gorilla railing at the world. A king kong of class and sexual anguish was something to be.

A nurse friend of Sarah's called her up that afternoon, just as she came off shift.

I'm sure I heard your Paul on the radio the morning, claiming he was a rabbi.

In the park later on his shift with his work mate Simon they share a spliff and a giggle, he tells him the story, as they bounce around the park on a ranger's buggy picking up bags of rubbish.

I never even heard of this Howard Jacobson fella.

That was my point Si.

After lunch Rosa does the dishes, turns to her mum who is drying and putting away,

Anyway they record that radio show, you can listen to dad on Youtube, thousands of views, he's famous.

Jeezus no girl. And where is the rascal, why we doing the washing up?

The last time Paul dialled in to any radio show was the day Bob Crow died.

Why can't a working class person stay in their council house? Have a holiday, wear nice clothes, ask your listeners that Mike. Bob asked again and again, a simple question. What do people do? You automate this, that and every other thing, not just on the underground, Bob always said that, the system, technology, advances, it came for him first, came for his members, who's next and what do they do and the next lot until we are all the problem?

Well, it's a good question, but what's the answer Paul, that's the problem. There's no simple answer to any of this?

Bob had an answer, we figured it out years ago. Let the robots do the work, everyone gets a national living wage and we can liberate human labour and creativity. Who knows what we will come up with, what problems people can solve, how many old people they could look after, the sick too, help out, community work unpaid when we live in a society where manual labour is done by robots. That's a decent future for everybody.

That simple eh?

Yeah it's that fucking simple.

Paul hung up before he could be cut off.

resin, Lebanese, Turkish, Patchouli, Brut 'Splash it all over' the unisex choice of skinheads, Napthaline in the collars of old men, 'It will be the greatest and we will call it Opium', on the necks of the gauche, and the rest, Brylcream, High Karate, Anais Anais, Leather, Dubbin grease, floss, reflux, Denim, Vicks nasal spray, Aniseed, toothpaste and strawberry milk kids breath, curry, fish, meat, decay and the Ammonia and Play Doh smell of hunger and despair, for the bodies that fed on themselves.

Public smells.

Only later in life did Paul read Michael Moorcocks *Mother London*. Fragments that constituted a non-linear timeline from the Blitz to the late eighties, as told by the four main characters, outpatients of a mental hospital, (the mind itself whether troubled, healthy or somewhere in between, ironically and fundamentally always already a natural disrupter of Linear time, expressing a high modernist fervour in every flight of fancy.) Stories which elicited in Paul a revelation, by which he came alive to his part in the dance. Up to that point he had been a man without irony; every shadow he threw a fresh one with sharp lines moving forward. A man subject to but also creatively summoned by the shifts he worked, subject to the clock which told everyday time and tried to hold us to it.

Shift work in the capital stretched time out like pizza dough, then kneaded it into different shapes. For a porter at Smithfield market an after-work drink might start at 6 am before stumbling home to bed before midday with the prospect of a good day's sleep ahead of the next shift. Cleaners own the city at night, crossing paths with their daytime shadows at the bus stops and tube stations triangulating the Golden mile. Liminal stress points of transition. The awkward shared workspace moment of the trader and the cleaner.

Shifts that *ideally* shouldn't overlap, glitches in the system of shifts patrolled by security guards, the third point of this panoptic triangle. Workers rhythms of life were dictated by these schedules that framed each and every day. We are infinitely malleable. The constantly warm bed has been a reality for many workers since before the industrial revolution, one person in, one out and never the two shall meet other than in halls or doorways.

Efficiency.

Turkish guest worker hostels in Berlin. The company store. Accommodation deducted from wages. Other deductions. Miscellaneous. Time and motion infringements, lateness, docked wages.

Paul lived by the rota, this is how he moved through time, alongside others. The gaps between shifts filled themselves in. Home, football, politics, music, books and drinking.

Those without *jobs* have other routines. Unemployed workers (short and long term) looking for work sit above the elective unemployed, the shift less, the grafter and the full-blown criminal. All members of the same class however they sought to categorise us, to divide and conquer us through the deification of labour and the hard working family. The shift worker would still buy stolen meat down the pub, or bent bikes, cars, fags and booze off the back of a lorry, this was common sense, if not in reality common cause.

Being a jobless punk or skin or Dread, dealing a bit on the side to keep you in booze fags and gear gave you the freedom to roam, to rebel openly. This was sub culture amplified by class; you got to cock-a-snook at everything. Almost like the wreckers of old it was the system they threatened. Petty crooks, con men and benefit cheats, what they really steal is time, no different other than in scale and consequence from that hoarded by fat cats lounging on villa terraces along various Rivieras, the latter being time extracted as surplus value from the labour of their workers, or from trading shares, bonds and funds in exchange for luxury.

Living off the fat of untaxed time, the sweetest commodity, time out of time. And if you were caught? Well then you had to do time. In prison you are theoretically meant to have a lot of time on your hands. Time to kill or time to write notebooks or to celebrate the very facticity of 'naff all', the two fingered salute of the bored, throwing *nothing* in the face of the screws, themselves bored out of their minds with routine and regulation, two sides of the same coin keeping themselves, aka the working class, at bay. Cerberus licking its wounds, counting the days till retirement or parole.

From Dick Turpins cry of 'stand and deliver' on top of Buckhurst Hill through the two century reign of Bermondsey's female forty elephants gang to the louche gait of a West-Indian pimp on the drab fifties dockside of St. Mary's parish of Southampton, a working class hero was something to be, they all tilted at the moon.

First in the pub when it opens at eleven thirty in the morning, straight down the bookies for the early races and if you had a winner back in the pub by 2pm, drinks all round. Members clubs, Shebeens, lock ins and after-hours drink ups, lolling at street corners or dozing on beaches, hair of the dog or a night at the dogs, all of these samizdat times of day and places where you enjoy the extravagant visibility of your own time. The time on your hands is literally that, a gold watch, a suntan, a manicure, time drips off you, you can smell it.

Workers are those with no time or only time bitterly fought for where ten-minute breaks are a victory. Time like cuts of meat late turns, early turns, incremental pay scales, duty rosters and the much-prized overtime (big time!) with its flip side of wages docked for infringement, shoddy work and lateness, time circumscribed by warnings written and spoken, escalating to union mediation and the threat of strike action. In effect the war over time.

A world in which children see their dads once a week, kids who have to tiptoe around at home after school because mum or dad was sleeping, couples that left notes to each other on their pillows, such was the pricelessness of your time. The year in year out slog for job protection, health and safety and wages that kept pace with inflation, the fight against flexible rostering, the further atomising of work schedules parsing people into units of labour was of a different order of commitment than any slogan on a T-shirt. It had to be.

Work and class struggle was as serious as the cancer it invariably gave you.

In the 70's and 80's everywhere you could see youth in revolt. A revolt of style and politics, of the self in society. How many times would union reps have to defend a members dreadlocks or Mohican, crepe soles or tattoos from a regulation book written back before the last war, or even the one before that? Pauls polished DM's, his donkey jacket, his stay pressed shirts, the way he made eye contact, the way he walked, was all part of a great war of position, a subconscious way of being, a celebration of the impossibility of the individual. The impossibility of Paul as both himself and a member of his class. And there is no irony in this, none whatsoever.

You got to fight for the right to party.

Rebellion was on display in the playground; home made compass tattoos decorated the inside of bottom lips names of boyfriends usually, teenage secrets flashed to shock and bitten off whenever, (whenever chucked), nail varnish black purple other, rows of ear piercings, boot lace ties, skinny school ties fat loose ones red/yellow/green shoe laces done up in singular patterns, tight trousers, short trousers even shorter skirts, shirts untucked, wide collars sub cultural belts (!?) inappropriate bras, Reggae socks, lapel badges of all flavours hearts on sleeves, bell bottom trousers, a la carte footwear, Blakeys.

On the street at work in prison skiving school at school watching telly playing sport we would not be reduced.

There is nothing like a union or a prison yard swagger (a chain gang swagger goes one step beyond, is more like a dance, madness), they perform the same function in different keys, the playground swagger being the inchoate first of these 'keys of life'.

The self-confidence of belonging to a tribe, the implicit insistence that you are as good as anyone else, that your uniform however configured, however mixed and matched with who else you were, was worn with an insouciant pride in display; because behind it, behind the complex system of perks and promotion, pay grades and overtime, what wing you were on, what category you were in, if you had privileges, first dibs, or were at the back of the queue, if you worked bank holidays, took double bubble, had exercised your right to buy or not, the simple fact was that there was pride in in both your tribe and your class.

Day trips, sponsored secondments, regional committee meetings, summer schools and International solidarity conferences; this was the life, the flow, the daily bread of a being an activist worker, and it had a flavour all its own.

In photos of the time, in the handshakes and fist bumps of members at shift change, on fag breaks, in the social or down the pub, at the football, passing on stairwells and walkways, on the estate, we exist 'in common'.

In 'Discipline and Punish' Michel Foucault explores and delineates this outsider linkage; the explicit 'fuck you!' of the school/exclusion/unit/prison/hospital ward ecology. A class at bay but also at existential loggerheads with society and always with revolutionary potential.

Teacher / doctor / screw. The system. Teacher / doctor / copper / screw / landlord / the boss class. A patient sneaking a quick fag outside the hospital in her pyjamas, saline drip trundling along beside her. A legend.

Nose cut to spite face we persist.

Fuck all of it.

This is the granular pushing back against the state, against the man that Gramsci wrote about from his prison cell on the island of Ustica.

This is what hegemony is all about, a quotidian civil war.

Laying in wait for us was our 'Hyperstitional Future'. Pixar this, from Gramsci to beyond. Distilled from our collective imaginations, a willed future mapped out in countless notebooks, at the back of countless meetings, jotted down on the back of fag packets and untold numbers of beer mats, drawn and held in the mind's eye, outlined on black boards in dusty lecture halls, published in obscure journals, summoned into being, by being summoned, a zeitgeist waiting to translate itself into the future, to accelerate, to achieve light speed, an already utopia, replicating itself on an as yet uninvented quantum media...

Everybody out.

THE
PERMANENT WAY

Paul's notebooks were filling up, each page a wall of words made up of his tiny, meticulous and intermittently joined up writing. His own calculations for the labour theory of value as it pertained to his own experience and the surplus that could be extracted from future worker automatons to feed the hungry and emancipate the human slaves of capital. In the margins he drew doodles and diagrams expressing a Fordist machine organisation in the service of mankind in the style of 2000 A.D. his favourite comic as a kid (which he still read).

Post war Government had to cope with a generation of men and women (heroes) who had liberated Europe from Fascism and come home to what? So they voted for a Labour government which founded the NHS, promised a new dawn of social housing and carved time out of the working week for the pursuit of leisure.

Now the establishment had to deal with the children of that generation and their kids across a class divide blurred by a much vaunted (culturally) but numerically lesser class migration; the expansion of new lower middle classes, designed to 'bleed from both ends' a system of opposition and naked class hatred. We had spent time together in the trenches, but not really, we had spent time together on

45

D-Day, in Burma, at Anzio, scrabbling up Monte Casino, but not really.

Not really.

Not for nothing are the lower middle classes seen by sociologists as the glue, the everyday bonding agent of our society. Everyone else either hates or blanks them; the under appreciated ex-working classes, because they never actually arrived in the middle, only ever approached it from below, leaving behind one class but never being accepted by the incumbent middle classes, trapped right there with mortgages, new cars, holidays in Spain, working class parents who were an embarrassment. Parents who were impressed by, but at the same time resentful of your newfound prosperity and detached housing.

The lower middle class exhibited startling small business acumen. They could be anything from car salesmen to middle management on salaries and with prospects. Unsentimental hard-working families, new men and women, modern, agile, masons, active members of the round table, the Lions club, golf clubbers, Bungalow Bills, Thatcher fanboys and fan girls with newly minted accents, high street hawkers, estate agents, the kulaks of suburbia.

Those left behind, the working-class beneficiaries of post war recovery, strong unions and decent pay, were seen as a right shower of shit by the red top rags owned by the boss class. Bone idle, ill mannered, uppity, still not knowing their place, but above all too bloody clever by half.

Paul kept scribbling. Unorganised labour was wage slavery. With every strike of his father's spade, somebody else had profited. He broke earth for others to eat. Paul had managed to exchange the spade for the train, casual day labour for shift and overtime employment. He had scrambled out of one hole and into another.

Crow was elected to represent the 'Permanent Way', the workers who tended the infrastructure, maintenance and renewal of the underground system, the rails that sat on the sleepers on which the trains ran, in which people travelled, the material foundation of everything.

Six months after Paul made driver a young woman threw herself under his train just as he was coming into Tufnell Park station. A blur of green knitted coat and wild blond hair, his foot stamping down on the floor in a useless braking reflex as she flew under the train. He never even saw her face until afterwards, what was left of it. Another 'One under' the guards would mutter to the clippies and the signalmen. 'Person under the train' came the more neutral announcement from the station tannoy. Staff and passengers alike would slump, like after a fatal air raid, survivors and witnesses, stunned, automatically lighting up to calm the nerves, bonded momentarily by their shared experience of somebody else's demise, nervous laughter about nothing in particular distracting each other.

In his knapsack that week was a secondhand copy of the Brothers Karamazov. That morning he had read the following:

'You must know that there is nothing higher, or stronger, or sounder, or more useful afterwards in life, than some good memory, especially a memory from childhood, from the parental home.'

Nothing particular came to mind, and if it had, a special day out, a gift, a holiday, how would this prove to be useful?

Paul highlighted this with a green marker pen.

People threw themselves under trains. It was a known method, on the list of possibles like overdoses or wrists slashed in a hot bath. Most want a painless solution, others are in so much pain that the method of ending is never evaluated for its painlessness. In a cold and wet Turin, Primo Levi threw himself down the stairwell of the building where he lived after forty years of not throwing himself down them, finally succumbing to the idea of ending his life without consideration of the method. That, or he slipped.

Suicide on the underground had its drawbacks. Jump too early and you might fall into the suicide pit between the tracks where you may survive horribly disfigured or otherwise disabled. Too late and you would simply bounce off the sides of the carriage back onto the platform, possibly with not much harm done at all, a front tooth knocked out, a fractured cheekbone. But in falling, you would deliver yourself into the arms of the state and the legions of do-gooders who would try to dissuade you from attempting such a selfish, wasteful, desperate act again with the full weight and range of social and other services at their disposal.

The train was fastest entering a station, so this is where the serious jumpers congregated. (On a dot density map, if you were to draw one up, they would, over time, appear as a massing of red dots, reminiscent of the bowling ball pitch dots peppering a cricket wicket; blood red dots marking the location and frequency of where you literally delivered yourself to the incoming train.)

The driver, blinded by the light of the platform coming out of darkness will barely register you. You will aim for the front of his cabin or just below it and somewhere in your mind hope to be killed outright by the impact and not mangled under the wheels. With electrification came the added possibility of being fried to a crisp.

Progress.

Tufnell Park. One of the way stations of the London Irish diaspora. It was here, in the Boston Arms, near his father's bitter end that he had to pick pocket him of his dole money the day he signed on. Easy to do, drunk as he was and slow. His father slid out of his seat onto the sawdust floor attempting to twist away from his eight-year-old son's nifty prying hands, the pains in his legs forcing him to cry out as they buckled under him. The names he called his son out of embarrassment for being covered in stale beer and sawdust are not worth repeating, rubbish words yet seared into Paul's memory.

Having to break hard coming into the bright light of each station unnerved Paul. This polarity was what got under his skin, marking him as a man from underground way beyond his last shift. There was no light in the driver's cabin, beyond the dull glowing tip of his roll up.

Years later, on a rare beach holiday in Mallorca the light triggered him. Shielding his eyes coming out onto the terrace from his hotel room, he lost balance and grasped the railing, a cold sweat running down his back. Like an acid flashback, the surprise of bright sunlight put him back underground. Memories of his 'sweat day', the first day in charge of the train and the experience of being on your own, the responsibility of that, made him giddy, responsibility for all of those people behind you, and those in front.

Paul Michael Feeney. Tube driver.

Four hours fifteen minutes with your hand on the dead

man's brake was enough to earn a 15 minutes rest in the middle of an 8 hour shift. Out of your knapsack a Thermos of tea, a kit-kat and a pack of salt and vinegar crisps, your hand involuntary flexing its fingers as you tried to roll a fag, the pleasure of it after all that sweet and savoury, a slight light headedness, a low dopamine buzz, one of the best of the day.

You could forget where you were, zone (1,2,3,4...) out. It happened to all the drivers at some point. Some of the stations were so similar, driving so consistently it was easy to forget which direction you were travelling in. Your hand gripped the dead man's switch, your body sat up straight, eyes ahead, but *you* were elsewhere. When this happened to Paul he would joke that at least it made the shift fly by and Taff, his guard, warned him he would get a rocket for it, management and unions being super sensitive after the disaster at Moorgate only a few years before.

But Paul had a manner that seemed to absorb anger, to neutralise any animosity. Not just gentle, although many saw him as such, but detached, absent, somehow otherwise occupied, so that haranguing him was immediately sensed as a waste of time, talking to yourself. But you couldn't put your finger on it, figure out what his game was, indeed if he had a game, was he perhaps simple in some way you asked yourself, making it harder to call him out.

Once, after coming back up from Kennington Paul was met off his shift by the station manager.

You have any trouble at Finchley central, driver?

No Guv. Said Paul.

Oh. The manager replied, thinking he was onto something.

I had a report you didn't stop there on the down.

That's right. Shot straight through. Replied Paul.

I thought you said you didn't have any trouble.

A short silence in which Paul picks at his fingers.

I didn't. It was the punters who had the trouble. I forgot to stop and they had to go on to East Finchley and get one back. So what?

The manager falters, but recovers to challenge him further.

You thought you were on the fast road, it being dark and wet an' all.

Yes said Paul, thinking.

That's it.

An unproductive pause, maybe he's not the full ticket.

Thanks Guv.

Well, be more careful next time. His manager capitulates.

Right you are, thanks Guv.

Paul says again, without implied assent, just victorious flat repetition.

This happened a lot, zoning out between stations, running through, the guards couldn't do much about it, knew you were dozing, they just called through on the intercom or maybe jogged the emergency brake if they were feeling edgy, jolt you, and everyone else, a few breakfasts, coffees spilled in the carriages, some spilt milk up in the cabin, a dropped fag but so what if that's what it took to keep you awake.

Running through wasn't the worse that could happen. Moorgate was a dead-end terminus. The train had accelerated past the stop signal and smashed through the buffer, the first carriage and driver cabin pile driving into the concrete wall concertinaing the cabin and carriage up into the ceiling.

The second carriage drove under the first as it rose up also slamming into the wall. The third carriage hit the back of the second and rode up to meet the first. 156 feet of carriages mangled into 60ft. 41 dead, 82 injured. The driver's body was found 4 days later with his hand still clutching the dead man's switch and an open copy of London Underground train regulations somehow surviving intact in the debris. Witnesses said they saw the driver sitting bolt upright accelerating into the tunnel, his hands not reaching up to protect his face, which is assumed to be the reflex reaction you would make if you lost control of the train and were facing imminent disaster.

In the dead driver's pocket was the three hundred quid he had saved to buy his daughter her first car. Not an argument against possible suicide, but a fact none the less.

A month after the Paul's suicide (it was referred to as such by his colleagues as 'your suicide') Paul's guard Taff lost his head hanging out of the rear cabin eyeballing some talent on the number two platform at Bank. Taff was one of his best work mates. They paired you up on the same shift rota, so it was hard not to be mates with your guard. He was one of the other Pauls. Welsh Paul they called him, or Taff, Taffy, the Taff. They were also collectively called the Pauls. As in, 'See if the Pauls fancy a pint Friday after work.' The third Paul, originally from St. Albans, was simply *the other one*, had not enough story or character to warrant a workplace nick name, however prosaic. Welsh Paul was the first person in his family to get a job above ground. A family joke. Not ending up 'down that bloody black hole' was seen as social climbing. He had escaped the pit in the same way

Tall Paul had escaped the shovel.

That morning the two Pauls had shared a fag by the guard's door at the rear of the tube.

Got a light mate, I'm gasping.

Sure, here.

Paul leans in. The match flares, startles them both.

Fuck me.

Wake you up?

They snigger, Taff draws deep on his fag.

Right, let's get started.

Taff nods and swings back inside as Paul waves and ambles back to his cab.

Hanging out of the door was all part of the swagger of being a guard, just like clippies on the buses, hanging from the pole, watching the world go by, whistling a popular refrain, (I remember Duke Basie blowing his harmonica slouched at the back of the 38 bus out of Mare Street. He even released a single, a soft reggae version of *My girl lollipop*, billed as the 'singing bus conductor'.)

Clippies would always be keeping an eye out, being seen, tipping their cap to the regulars, a man and bus in harmony, at speed, something special, that swagger again, not so far removed from David Essex in 'That'll be the day' a roustabout hanging off the dodgems, the lights, the music, the speed. Was this the workers futurist dream brought down to earth? From outer space to the inner deck of the Routemaster bus, ticket machine riding low on a leather strap from the shoulder, the alchemy of exchange between punched ticket and money, the magic jangle of coins pulled like flowers from a hat at speed, conductors feet, torso and shoulders wedged in place, no bumps or bruises below or above decks for the experienced clippy. The kinetic duress of the fairground or the high street, constant movement, twists and turns, braking and acceleration, the fluid conditions of labour...

For the train guard this was all about territory, the guard rail demarcating 'his office'; the cup of tea on the stow away table, his pull out seat, the intercom with the driver, (on which you could rarely hear what anybody said), his fingers on the buttons, a jangle of keys and tools, the opening and closing of doors, announcing stops if he fancied it, banter with both the regular commuters and the tourists. After his road training Taff put in for the Piccadilly line because it was fancy and got the Northern line which definitely wasn't.

His death was emblematic, despite being an accident. It meant something. Paul was sure of it. Later he would write down what he felt, a private commemoration, for it was not something he could say at the funeral to Paul's friends and family without being assaulted.

Taff's death, his hanging out the back of the cabin, was an example, however subconscious, of the workers nonchalance in the face of regulations, a rebellion against rules and a two fingered salute to society in general. Implicit in this visual display, is a seething class consciousness that given the right conditions will express itself as revolutionary. Off with their heads! (NOT HIS!) Behaviour you can see across the public sector, an expression of latent energy as yet untapped. (BY US!!)

Paul had to reverse his train back into the station so they could clear up the mess. The station closed for three hours as they removed the body, washed the claret out of the rear carriage and got a replacement shift from the emergency roster. Paul was ushered outside by station staff and the police, given a cup of tea and a fag then sent home but not before he had seen what was left of his mate.

The routine failed them that morning and they had failed the routine. The guard blew his whistle for the driver when all the doors were clear and the train could move off. The last thing Paul heard was Taff's whistle. First, he knew something was wrong was a couple of minutes later when passengers started banging on his cabin window, screaming for him to stop. That spooked Paul, it really did, more than what came after. Those faces jammed up against the glass, their fish eyes made him feel suddenly claustrophobic. The glass wet with saliva, smeared there by hands and faces.

Later in the social, the most he said all night was this:

He come down the Arsenal a few times, yeah, I mean he was a Cardiff City fan, but when in Rome, I remember him saying that. When in Rome. Yeah. He enjoyed it. Came to the quarter final replay against Southampton, yeah he loved that, Alan Sunderland's two goals, great day out he said, great day out. He loved his football. Cardiff was only a few hours away on the train, but he didn't bother going to many games. I said to him, give it a year and you'll be a Gooner. Told me to piss off. Funny bloke. Yeah.

The inquest came to an end, the things you could say petered out and his workmates drifted off. Paul sat there, drinking.

Bob Crow came in after his shift, put his arm round Pauls now swaying shoulder.

You just sit there, mate, sit there, you've had a bloody shock.

Bob didn't know Taff hardly at all but nonetheless he

was one of them. Paul silently sank his pints and rolled his fags. In his head he was talking to himself ten to the dozen, reliving the moment, the moment he was violated; Hands banging, screams leaking through to him in his cabin. His window. The smeared saliva left on it. His space now that he'd made driver, somewhere private, his space. He never knew the suicide, it shook him up, but that was part of the job, you didn't expect it, but you heard about it, it had happened before, and would again, life went on. Why did that fucking Welsh bastard have to go and ruin it? They weren't even words just inchoate feelings, his truth, the understanding came before words, which weren't needed anyway as he would never talk about it.

Each round Bob bought was sunk and duly appreciated, Bob doing all the talking as he usually did, the unions responsibility, the compensation, the insurance, taking care of the family. Only at this did Paul come round, out of himself, observing bluntly..

He didn't have a family. Of his own I mean, no wife or kids. He had a mum and dad, don't know about brothers or sisters he never said. Dad's a miner.

Bob nodded at that, concluding

Well, the funeral will be taken care of, that's for sure.

Paul fretted over his fag, his hand shook trying to light it, matches flaring out one by one. Bob lent over, steadying Paul's hand in his so he can finally get the thing lit, an instinctive kindness.

Filthy habit that, it'll kill ya. My older sister Ann killed herself in her twenties. Suicide. She looked after me and my brother after my mum died. I was 8. I'm getting married this summer, would have loved to have them both there, but what you going to do? Life goes on mate, we go on, we smoke, we drink, we laugh, and we fight. Sit tight, I'll get us another.

Paul remembers *The Brothers Karamazov*. It bubbles up into his consciousness, he slurs it to himself. *It's the great mystery of human life that old grief passes gradually into quiet tender joy.*

Bob places two pints on the table and sits back down.

I wouldn't go that far mate.

Paul's mind drifted back to football.

His dad loved the Arsenal, even took him a few times, when he was on a promise not to get too polluted, as his mother and sisters called it. Stamping up the huge stone stairs freezing cold, chapped hands, six years old burning his fingers on a mug of Bovril, his dad's sore lips worrying the rims of a four pack. Paul inherited his North bank season ticket when he died. Our end his dad called it. 'We're the north bank High-bur-rey' the fans chanted on the way down the concrete steps and out. His father never went that far, was never that exuberant and neither was he, they didn't chant, although Paul always wanted to. Finally did when they won the 1979 F.A. cup. Pat Rice, O'Leary, Jennings, Brady. Now that's a team from the old country his dad would have said triumphantly. But here are a clutch of memories he thought he didn't have, something small and common, like other people's. Memories, not bad ones.

Football like everything else was a private pleasure for Paul, one he shared awkwardly, decanted as it had to be into the sinewy machismo of the times.

It was an age of protest, like any other. Marches, demos, sit in's, factory occupations. 'Everybody out!' on the streets.

Workers and students, the most awkward of temporary alliances never forged anything more reliable than protest. Anti-Apartheid, Cuban solidarity, campaigns against pay freezes and compulsory redundancies. Students passionate about the former, workers resisting tooth and nail the latter. It took the energy and native intelligence of a Bob Crow to bridge the gap between the two, constantly (re) negotiating a common ground on which to share his vision for a bigger and better world.

And it took place in public.

Paul's most flamboyant moment was to come at an anti-Apartheid demo a year after he left University, when he joined a splinter group storming into the South African Airways office on Regent Street and liberated the large scale model of an SAA Boing 737 out of the window display flying it into a line of riot police. Like kids flying a kite. The plane crashed into the coppers, fists flailed and riot shields wielded, Paul decking a constable, his fist glancing off a chin strap. Then he had to leg it chased by the coppers, he flew, adrenalin pumping, into the safety of the crowd, one of many limbs attached to the body of resistance, a voice in the choir of solidarity, Paul Michael Feeney, Tall Paul, the quiet one, the shy one, now fled away with the rest, draining themselves back into the faceless mass, back into the pubs in ones and twos, lighting up a fag, hand shaking with more than just his usual tremor, heart beating a tattoo in his chest, stooped over a pint, the froth of which was running down his hand, as the cops raced past, looking for a mob who had melted into thin air. His hand started to throb, hurt like fuck, then swell up tight and by ten PM he was in A&E strapped up and on the painkillers, just another drunk mick injured in a pub brawl.

Bob is back at the bar filling up a tray of drinks and crisps, talking ten to the penny at the barman as he works the pump. London Pride, what else.

They'll use this poor bastard as another reason to get rid of guards, you'll see, they'll twist it, turn it on its head, so that it's a health and fucking safety issue, to protect their employees, to run the whole train from the cabin. Driver only.

How's that work Bob, two sets of eyes are better than one surely.

How will they do it? Mirrors, smoke and bloody mirrors. Cheers Kev.

At the end of the night just before last orders the union rep popped his head into the bar, but by this time Paul was already well pissed. Again, a final round bought, that being what was called for, seeing the table full of pints the rep opted for brandy chasers. A serious drink for a serious occasion.

Time off Paul, that's what I'll recommend, time off on full pay, if that's what you want. You should talk to somebody.

This stopped Bob dead in his tracks, he laughed. Good luck with that.

The Rep shrugged, shook hands and made his excuses.

Before Paul was helped out and home, Bob reminded him again that life goes on. Paul was so far gone he didn't remember the story of Bob's sister Ann, a kindly attempt to trade a fresh sorrow for an old one.

Paul muttered, with a smirk on his face.

Life goes on Bob, very insightful, I like that.

Outside Paul disappears into back of a black cab, Bob paying the driver an extra tenner as insurance against his passenger throwing up in the backseat.

Goodnight mate, try and get some sleep.

That night Paul was so pissed he literally couldn't remember anything that happened between the accident and being woken up by his mother the next morning brandishing a strong cup of tea. He didn't have the heart to tell her.

Paul, Paul you've gone and got yourself polluted again, what are we going to do with you coming home every night like your father, and we thought those days behind us, oh Paul.

Her hand shaking the tea all over the saucer and dripping down onto the carpet, his sister scowling at the door.

Thatcher and (Sir) Peter Parker were to turn the screws on the railways, over and underground, in 1982. Flexible rostering, spurious productivity targets meant renegotiating shifts and contracts which would lead to sackings and breaking the 8-hour day that had been agreed in 1919. Ray Buckton had no choice but to defend his workers. ASLEF with 24,000 members were the first out on strike. Footplate men and engine drivers, came out that summer.

The great British public responded in kind. ITV news lapped it up, this from a bus stop outside Golders Green Tube station, an irate woman who will be at least an hour late for work, but gives up the time to have her say.

I think it's absolutely disgusting, it's the same old story, Its minority rules OK. Stopping decent people doing a decent day's work. It's disgusting. I'm over an hour late as it is now, I'm even wondering if it's worth going in.

Ha! That's it! She too dreams of a life without work, a day stolen, clawed back to work in her garden, walk in the park, or just be mean in her own time and to blame the union for it, the perfect scapegoat for her own twisted dreams of leisure or perhaps a nightmare of leisure, staring at the wall dreaming of work.

And this from a journalist goading an ASLEF picket line outside Kings Cross station in his clipped public-school accent.

And you, you've got driver written all over you, what would you be driving today?

To which, in a spirited, wary, shrugged response the young driver replies, his accent all stressed vowels and fuck you consonants.

One of those trains.

With a slight louche nod of his head towards the tracks behind him and an unsaid you cunt tacked on the end.

He had Richard Beckinsale written all over him. Not somebody afraid of a bit of Porridge either. Journo / teacher / cop / screw they were all same. His shirt the same as the one he would have worn at school a few years previously, the V neck jumper likewise the same, darned by his mum.

And this from (Ex Sir) Tony Benn, jostled amidst the crowd of strikers, press and coppers, on Thatcher's attack dog.

When Norman Tebbit says on your bike he didn't mean it, he meant on your knees.

TV crews hunt in packs, they smell blood with a driver who broke the picket, wanting to turn him out as a hero, sitting up there in his cab, all awkward smiles and fidgets, where once, a few days ago he had been comfortable and at ease in his own skin.

How have you found passengers have been reacting?

A boss class answer neatly wrapped up in a boss class question, like all lackey *Journos* deliver and the driver is meant to swallow it. But he's not having it, up against the ropes as he is, this class traitor can still muster a rear guard action.

Well pretty favourably, well naturally they would do wouldn't they? Why wouldn't they?

It hangs there. He hangs in there, claws back a little...

Mind you I've not enjoyed doing this one bit.

No? Almost inaudible, the journalist wants more, his eyes widen, he wants all of it out of him.

No. I'm only doing this 'cos I'm not losing me 'ome.

Bingo. In one. Bullseye.

So, you're going against union rules? Gleefully prodding the mic towards him, smelling blood.

Whatever he had left has drained from his face.

Well, I'm going against it because I'm over a barrel. They put me in this position, I'm behind with my mortgage, no fault of anybodies but it's the last straw.

His naked truth.

Have any of your colleagues been getting at you? The follow up, as per playbook.

Not yet no, not that it bothers me. Still be more tea in my pot when it come to me break time. As I say it's up to them, cheerio.

He sounds the horn somewhat half heartedly, almost apologetically, as he pulls away. No bang, just whimpers.

This reaction from another passenger.

Marvellous isn't it, shows there are some good people about int there? Train people see, they're not all bad.

Another driver stalked by TV cameras as he walks down the platform, willing him to be another strike breaker. Plastic carrier bag in hand he mutters a shy *No comment.* when asked if he's going to drive the train, asked if he was an ASLEF member, a little more forthcoming *I didn't say that did I?* Then he sits with the passengers as if waiting for the driver.

A wolf amongst the sheep? Or a sacrificial lamb?

But he is the driver, the passengers look to him awkwardly, all too aware of the TV camera, guilty of their complicity in his unmasking.

The camera keeps rolling on him through the open doors of the still stationary train until finally he gets up, walks through the carriage and opens the door to his cab. He nods to the cameraman apologetically and drives off, to the delight of the camera.

Bringing in driver only trains took ten years from 1984 as the Unions, latterly led by Bob Crow bitterly resisted the move. It would take CCTV and curved mirrors to finally replace the eyeballs of the train guard.

All of this background noise to Paul's personal misfortunes.

He'd had enough. Part of him felt that his life had been stolen from him. He loved his job, the camaraderie, the politics, the feeling of being at the heart of a big city, his city, one that his family had come to and however hard it was made their home. Deep down Paul knew he couldn't do it for much longer. The anxiety, the night sweats, the fear. Holding his hand up in front of him in the bathroom mirror he could see the tremor running through it. Some of the staff looked at him differently, he was sure of it. A suicide, a fatal accident. What next? He was marked out, a jinx. Exiled from the many, he felt singled out, he felt one, alone.

A few weeks later it was the depot foreman at Golders Green who repeated the idea that Paul should talk to somebody. Not about depression but about getting out of the bloody job for good.

All those books you read, them notebooks you got, put it to some use. What good's all that here? Union will sponsor you to go to college, what you been through. We need people like us up there.

Paul just nodded, felt relief, as if somebody had opened the door for him out of a crowded room.

He never drove another train.

Late summer 1983, a farewell send-off down the social club.

I just got married and you're going to University. Life, we got it covered.

Bob presents him with a gift from his fellow branch members. An Olivetti typewriter.

Never could read your handwriting.

People like us.

HARMOLODICS Nº1

Melody is singular in the way it seduces us, think Hitler, the Pied Piper and Ancient Greek sirens. The tune hungrily commands the ear.

Beyond this dualism of tension and release lies freedom. If the tonal centre is terror then we must free ourselves from it.

Between the 16th and 18th of September 1982 Christian Phalangists entered the Palestinian refugee camps of Shatila and Sabra in southern Lebanon and began slaughtering the innocent.

All the millions of words thought but never uttered, scribbled down or shouted across a crowded street, typed up and sent off or memorised and passed on. Fragments, sentences crafted into stories woven from scraps of other stories half remembered at suppers or in bars, overheard turns of phrase, tall tales and quiet asides, but also well plotted thrillers and commercial love stories, notes to self-remarking on events and feelings, auto fiction waiting for its moment, private diaries and public poetry composed from notes taken as we pass through our lives; the ecstasy and the agony we all experience, the wages we enjoy, the unfair shift rota's we resent, the pleasure of holidays and fresh experiences, mountain air taken, the best Shawarma eaten, the smell of recently turned earth or the surprise of flowers given and received, the thrill of money won and lost on the dogs, the horses, the football and whatever else we did with our precious free time, the boredom of work, the boredom of home, of love, the not knowing what to do, the late nights, the early nights, the thoughts you might have had, did have, never had time to have, the drinks, the sex, the laughter, the forgetting yourself, the coming to, the remembering, slights taken, slights given, punches on the nose, sore ribs and glorious wanks, the searing pain of a kick in the balls, a punch to the tits, the endless gasp of the winded which finally ends, the pleasure of that moment, lungs flooded with oxygen, life, the natural high of that, the joy of breathing, the simplest story we all have in common, the beating of hearts in chests.

The text is free. We (word matrices) kill the author to escape.

After the slaughter the melody lingers on. What remains is the grief of those left behind, the prosaic statement of witness, a righteous tragically familiar monotone.

Yet a single typewriter can raise the dead, make space for them in the world all over again, slaking its thirst on words from the well of what might have been, words with the ability to undertake hard work to show us the things that will never be, the world we have been denied. Words laid down by hard finger work on the keyboard of this explosive device, words slingshotted into type, each one a giant killer.

Crank the black knob, feed a new sheet into the inky black and pliant Platen. A pleasing tight resistance, as the paper winds up under the hammer.

Hit return.

Polish Christian Karol Józef Wojtyła, AKA Pope John Paul clasps the hand of Palestinian Muslim Abu Ammar, AKA Yasser Arafat, whose hand breaks the shake first? Israel turns a blind eye to Christian terror in the camps of Shatila and Sabra.

Tap, Tap, Tap. Return, replace ribbon. Fingers now flow across the keyboard, is this the automatic writing that we have read about?

The permutations of 'Murdah!' are seemingly infinite. They line up, they loop and repeat, they interlink, tucking themselves into our history, myth, fantasy and brutal everyday reality; changing along infinite lines invoking parallel destinations and geodesic patterns of global probability, to only then shift once more, diverting us elsewhere, a Rubik's cube logic driven by our insatiable bloodlust. Bad shit happens everywhere, the song of the siren, the persistence of the tonal centre.

Bloodlust which is more and less than hate an almost chemical, bodily function we share in both minor and major keys across all of time, from Zion to Babylon.

Tap, tap tap tap, pause, tap tap tap tap tap, pause, return.

(Insert link to Olivetti Lettera 32 sound effect.)

Candyman.

Words conjuring the dead and the silent into life, weaving the shapes of life from the dance of time.

Candyman.

Words are proof of all of their rights to return, letter by letter. Fag ash falling like snowflakes, words inches deep. The tap tap tap-ing muted by Johnathan Richmonds broken ecstatic voice singing Roadrunner on the record player, high up on the 12th Floor of Rayleigh Tower, University of Essex, windows levered open, restricted to nothing more than a crack for fear of student suicide, but wide enough for these sounds to escape and join the flow, of words, letters, typed, sung, spoken, whispered.

I'm in love with the modern world.

Candyman.

LIFE AND FATE

At the bingo Winnie knew they were laughing at her, the other mothers and not a few widows, as her homemade Tombola spun, she knew what they were about, her old man, Albert the bin man, unmanned, unhanded, and the dirty sniggers, what they got up to with it, the stump, and how much compensation he got. Her hand picked a ball.

Lucky Seven, seven!

It was not as if he was the only one mutilated with so many worse than him back from the war. Enough stumps to go around. To buy that flashy car, driving it with one hand en all, what was he thinking of drawing all that attention?

Came out of France without a scratch on him, God she had been proud when he jumped off the train in one piece and they both smiled like loons at his good fortune. She grabs another ball.

Numbers up. 56. Was she worth it? 56.

Every penny!

The cows shouted back at her and then one at the back screams as if her life depended on it.

House!

Eyes down.

Paul was finally leaving home. He couldn't help feeling that it was a mistake, that he should have stayed at work, with his own people. He felt like he was jumping ship. At

69

twenty-six it all felt vaguely childish, piling all his things into a suitcase and a bloody great rucksack on his back. But the world had conspired against him. He was never working underground again. He got a tremor when he imagined clutching the dead man's brake so what use was he any more as a driver? He plunged his rebellious hands deep into his donkey jacket pockets.

A last breakfast cooked by his mum before her shift; bubble and squeak, bacon, mushroom, grilled tomato and black pudding, a feast in honour of his departure.

Who'd ever of thought a child of mine would be going to a University!

She was proud and that embarrassed him, the awareness of another's feelings towards you.

Not good enough for you are we? his sister Marion joked, her sore bird like hands bleached by her job at the Broadway laundrette, darted across the table top for the brown sauce.

It had been just the three of them for ages. Paul sits back and smokes.

No sis, just fancy a change of scene. Don't you? She scowls and leaves the room. Their mother shouts after her.

Your brother's not been well Marion, he's, he's been through a trauma.

Mum, I'm fine.

He pinches the tip of his dying rollup between two fingers, pockets it and gets up.

He needs to get out, *to take the air* as his father used to say on his way to the pub and heading for oblivion. Shouldering his rucksack, he pecks his mum on the cheek.

There will be lots of young ladies at University, I suppose, from all over.

Mum, I'm going to study.

Philosophy, I know! Well think about this, maybe one day you can bring somebody home for me to meet. She beams at him.

Yeah, maybe, I might surprise you.

She pulls him close, on a rare impulse, because for whatever reason it has never been a family ritual.

Don't be lonely son, it's not healthy.

An intimate silence fills the space between them. She breaks it.

Now is that all you're taking with you? She eyeballs his rucksack and the small suitcase by the door.

You rented my room out already?

His mums eyes flash up the stairs, more emotional distance covered over one breakfast than well, than...

She'll miss you, you know, despite what comes out of her mouth, go up and say goodbye. I'm off to work. I want to know all about this University malarky, so don't be shy of the phone. I love you son.

I love you mum.

They share a small, relieved smile, complicit in thinking that wasn't so hard to say after all was it.

She slips out. Reluctantly Paul puts the rucksack down again resigned to the fact it will be heavier the next time he lifts it.

He pulls out his hanky and wipes his face before taking the stairs. A hanky that he habitually uses to dab at his nose, which is long crooked from a teenage punch up and prone to dripping.

Marion sits in an armchair by her bed reading. Paul stands in the doorway. She reads harder.

What you reading?

You're not the only one with a brain in this house. She jerks up the cover on which is an illustration of a dour faced Chinese child cupping a bowl in both hands. The surface of the bowl reflects a sweeter rosy cheeked face.

Marion reads aloud.

In Lily's experience there was no stand-still in life. Families rose and fell. There was deadly rivalry between them. Their members were united against a hostile conspiring world. If one generation didn't climb, then the next declined, or the one after that. Sound familiar?

Paul smiles.

We swap books at work, get all sorts in there, old books brand new ones like this, it's like a people's library sort of. Amazing how much you can get through working at a launderette. This one's about a family who run a Chinese restaurant.

Timothy Mo. Never heard of him. Must be a Chinese fella. She nods. Paul bends at the waist to give his sister a kiss before she can complain, be rude or ward him off with the book. She sighs instead, or to be precise expels the air inside her lungs with utmost control, quietly.

I'll be off then. Take care sis. I'll be back in December; we'll go down the Boston Arms tear it up, Christmas eve. Look after mum.

I always do.

Whispered softly from behind the book as if speaking through the pursed lips of the child on the cover.

This he allows with a sharp nod of the head and a thin smile as he ducks out of her room down the stairs and out of the house.

A bus, a train and a thumbed lift transported him to the margins of the city. One last obligation before heading off to Colchester.

Paul leaves his bags at the Worlds End pub by the old fort and sinks a swift half before meeting his friend Len outside. A last walk along the estuary from Tilbury. Now retired, Len Mc Clintock had worked the docks all his life finishing up as a foreman at Bostroms, one of the last cargo companies. He got a gold watch out of them. Thin as you like on the wrist, white gold, name engraved on the back. The firm had closed earlier that year, its headquarters at berth 26 was in the process of being knocked down to make way for a new railhead to facilitate containerisation. Twenty-seven jobs saved from a yard that once employed hundreds.

Paul started walking after the accident. He had trouble sleeping so got up early and started walking, his thoughtful lope taking him further than you would imagine. Urban walks up Willesden Lane to Brent reservoir where they went as kids for a day out in the countryside. Another day he followed the river through the old docks and past the two power stations, along the broken down and yet to become heritage shoreline of the Thames. He first met Len slumped on a bench by Tilbury Fort. They shared a light and started talking. He was only sixty-five, but looked ten years older. Len perked up with the sudden company, sat up straighter. Over the next few months they met up a few times out on the estuary for a walk and more often than not for a few beers afterwards. Two trade unionists separated by more than a generation – what they had in common had to be renegotiated. Len had lived to see his way of life disappear. How to rationalise this change out of the ruins, to carry on? Len came to see Progress as a force of nature he had no way of controlling, sod it if you didn't see it coming, everybody was at its mercy. Paul wasn't resigned to fate, you had to make your own fortune; he wanted to de-naturalise *Progress*, bringing it down to earth to harness technology and innovation to serve people not profit. This was a big part of the socialism he shared with his Union, a no-nonsense approach and a set of ideas you could explain to anybody down the pub. A set of working beliefs. A fairer world that was achievable, this is what he and Bob Crow had been passionate about. Had been? Nothing had changed for Bob but how will Paul be now, how will he be a socialist outside of his union? What will the framework for his life as a student be like? A clumsy way of thinking about it but he was out of sorts, confused, on the brink of the unknown.

Len snorts, bringing Paul back to the little time he has left in the present.

Don't make me laugh. Wasn't that what we fought Hitler for? To make the world a better place? Fighting our way across the bloody desert, then up through Italy and for what? I lost a lot of mates fighting for naff all.

Paul was lost for words. He knew what he couldn't say, that all wars and the nation states that wage them and the capital that funds all of it and makes vast returns in its execution were the real enemy. Len had been mugged off, along with all the other returning heroes. Freedom was a trickier kind of good, that's for sure, much like the pursuit of happiness. Paul didn't say any of that, because he sensed that Len was also proud of his service, of having done his duty for something bigger than himself, as big perhaps as the progress that was to ultimately make him redundant. His bitterness was fruitless, it went nowhere, didn't lead to any understanding of the why of it, just visceral resentment, more than that it was an act of self-harm. Len never wore a poppy, he never attended any regiment reunions, yet he had joined up with the same regiment that had taken his dad to Flanders, caught up in the melody of it. Len couldn't help himself. For years he was unfit for work but they kept him on making tea and sweeping up so he could make his retirement and get his watch a year before they went under.

Problem with Len was…

He was an old git.

And anyway Paul didn't have to say anything, Len wasn't fishing for a response, he saw things as they were and that was that.

Len was a twitcher (a practical response to being steamrollered by progress) and had spent his spare time documenting the wildlife up and down the estuary as far as Benfleet before his chest gave out, conscientiously sending in his observations by postcard to the RSPB every Spring and Autumn. Out walking when Len didn't agree with something Paul said he would pass him his binoculars, with a gruff 'Have a look' and pointing with his thin fingers.

See it? Black tailed Godwit, quite rare, numbers been on the low side for years.

Out on the mudflat a long beaked orange looking bird was wrestling with a worm. Paul peers through the binoculars, grunts an acknowledgment and satisfied in some small way they move on.

A family of ducks threads it's way single file through an oil slick to reach open water. A stragglers feet are caught up in a plastic bag that drags tar. It swims hard to keep up, but for how long? Will it make it across?

Paul didn't want this last walk to be consumed by following the mindless mini dramas of wildlife, he wanted to talk to Len about the old days, the graft and the labour down on the docks, the craic of it, to salvage a sense of the past from the ravages of the present. They stopped right by the old Bostroms dock.

Best tea in London! Len chirped, eyes glued to his binoculars.

We drank it in the Clan line canteen, right off the boat.

The smell of tea and rubber coming off the bales was long gone. Now the shoreline smelt of nothing much and was strewn with used johnnies and empty bottles of cheap spirits.

They had both been on the same picket line during the winter of discontent, a cold day of solidarity on the 22nd January 1979, solidarity with the lorry drivers, the bin men, the NHS workers and the gravediggers amongst others.

The smell of barrel fires and thermos flasks of coffee. A brother and sisterhood of workers that replaced the internecine domestic squabbles of family life for the young punk rebel in Paul. For Len it had been the final straw, one last defeat that gave way to 'I'm alright Jack' self-interest, slim pickings for a man to be left with.

He had been born in Poets Corner, Tilbury on Thackerey Avenue, growing up alongside the 'Colemans', the 'Strongs', the 'Sharky's', local families as thick as thieves and some of them that as well.

Young dockers with a few bob in their pockets joined up with Kitcheners army on a day out to Grays in 1914. Lens dad Albert first in the queue, cocky as. His mum Winnie remembers Albert home from leave.

Coming round the corner, pale as a sheet, mud from the trenches all about him, like a muddy god he was!

It was in those four days that Len was conceived. He didn't meet his dad until he was nearly three years old, born as he was in 1917. In his nursing home Albert told his son that he had put a bullet through his army issue hat before leaving the front, the better to butter them up at home, heroes got all the perks and that's what he wanted. He could point to the hole and say, *that was a near one all right.*

Remember that bullet son he sniggered.

Ighty iddley ighty/Carry me back to Blighty/ Blighty is the place for me/ Put me on the train for London town/ Drop me anywhere/ I don't care if its Piccadilly, the Strand or Leicester square/all I want to see is my best girl and a cuddling up we soon will be!

Back on the stones and Albert lost a hand to a cable winch in 1928 and got a job as the local binman, with a one-handed technique that flipped the bins up onto his shoulder and into the dustcart before putting them back again.

Came back from France without a scratch, would you believe it? He pointed out to those that asked on the doorstep, slurping his tea without a saucer.

That's life!

In 1980 Poets Corner was demolished and Len moved to Grays. His mum Winnie had been dead fifteen years, his dad in a home for the last five. After the second world war Winnie had worked in a local shoe factory for twenty-five years, then part time as a bingo caller in a church hall with an Asbestos roof. Fit as fiddle she was, never took a day off sick he would tell anyone who asked. Paul wanted to ask

Len why he had never got married but he could never find the right words.

All that last morning Len coughed before and after he spoke making him even more cantankerous. In between the coughs a rattle, a tick and a wheeze accompanied his words, at times overbearing them.

Paul couldn't bring himself to ask him to say that again, whatever it was, instead he just nodded.

Killed my mum and now it's going to get me.

Thirty odd years later and they are still trying to document the use of Asbestos in the company warehouses, to bring those responsible to court, to chase the money through holding companies, the winding ups and sell offs, and finally a much delayed and much protracted inquiry to determine responsibility and eventually compensation. Meanwhile the docklands development corporation dreamt of airports, high rises and railways. Len had kept all the correspondence for years but chucked it away when he moved. Why bother? He'd never live to see a penny.

Lapwings, look up there, a pair flying south! Curlew Sandpiper is it? Nope, Little Tern, a pair.

They stop to roll themselves fags staring at a huge container ship being unloaded mechanically. The only human in sight was the man operating the crane. By the scruffy water line birds seem to thrive blissfully unaware of the noise, the rubbish and the effluence.

A Merlin flying upriver.

Len gurgles something about the dockers tanner, the strike way back when the Tilbury lot came out with all the rest for a wage of 6D an hour, when most stevedores only worked three hours a day. It was 1889, a non-violent strike, with orderly marches that impressed the middle classes and aroused their sympathy. A strike that gave birth to the union.

How much you reckon he earns that docker up in the sky? Gesturing with his already dead cigarette up to the cabin of the nearest shuttle carrier.

Paul shrugs. Ton fifty a week?

A bloody clerk is what he is.

They cross a field with six skewbald Romany horses grazing in it.

You have to pay to go to that University?

No, get a grant, I get some money from the union as well.

They gonna retrain you there? So you get a job when you come out.

A job? I'm studying philosophy for fucks sake.

More fool you. Watch out for the horse shit.

Len rolls up the sleeves of his jacket. His arms thin from age but still corded from a lifetime of lifting.

You see these scars sunshine? His arms are crisscrossed with raised weals, gouges and scar tissue. One of his thumbs is more like a nub, permanently missing a nail. Every bale and crate we took off those bloody ships is written right here, on the legs and arms of every man that worked the docks. We're the walking book of it all. But nobody wants to read it, us standing on the stones at sixteen to beg a day's work.

Jack Dash was a reader. He knew the worker's story.

A clumsy gambit, but Paul couldn't think of anything better.

Don't you give me Jack bloody Dash, Communist bastard.

Come off it Len, the union tripled your wages because of those strikes, you'd still be on the bloody stones without it. Fuck me mate you're a contradiction.

What I earn is mine, I never borrowed a penny from

nobody, nor lent a penny neither. Jack Bloody Dash wants the coppers out of all of our pockets, not just the bosses.

He passes the binoculars, waiting for a comeback.

Iceland gull out there on the mud. Have a look.

Len was ambushed by a series of wheezing splutters interspersed with tidal gasps for breath. His mind flashed back to his mum, running the bingo out of the red hut youth club until she could no longer walk. Seventy-eight, Heavens gate.

Take it easy Len, take a seat, get your breath back.

And let's not talk about the bloody war what he skived out of.

Len! For fucks sake!

The path ran past a long low concrete wall behind which sat one recently mothballed coal fired power station next to one belching smoke. The blank surface of the wall was soon to blossom as a message board for pro and anti-miners strike graffiti sitting alongside sub cultural pop band affiliations and other youth in revolt signifiers:

Scabs!

Fuck the miners, NUM wankers!

The Merton parkas

The Miners must win!

OH No! Whats happening?

Tories out!

Rocky 3

Purple Hearts

Thick as thieves us we stick together for all time and we mean it

The Lambrettas,

Growing Mod Revival Survival.

In a few years the wall would read like a visitors book for 1984 when Poison Ivy tightened its grip on the hearts of a nation.

For now it was blank, yet to be discovered by Mod, Miner and Tory alike waiting for the future to fill it in. Len and Paul walked beside it, Len constantly looking up and around, his bins never far from his eyes.

Nothing of interest, just some Pigeons.

They rest their backs up against the wall, watching the crane unload a coal ship.

They used to call overtime plus money. If you unloaded a ship pronto that's what you got. It was their incentive. They never knew back then when a bloody ship would turn up and then they'd all come at once. All the dockers lining up to be taken on or be sent home it was a fucking shambles. Some docks cut plus money to make their dock attractive, well I mean cheaper to dock at for the ships coming in. We all came out when they did that. Piss takers. 140,000 workers from all departments, rope makers, lightermen, firemen, porters, the lot. Just like the match girls did before 'em. All we wanted was to work and get a fair day's pay for it.

Paul chooses his words more carefully this time (or so he thinks). The system never pays fairly. What's fair about the distribution of wealth in our society?

That's that Bob bloody Crow talking. He's another one, his sweet talk, well we heard it all before. Just like Jack Dash, pretty words.

Fuck off. I make my own mind up. Jack bloody Dash, you make me laugh. He's yesterday's news, a bloody pensioner, like you. Paul's long bony index finger points at Len, the wreck of him.

Watch it. Len cracks a smile, he's got a rise, he's happy.

Bob's alright, you wait and see, we ain't gonna roll over, not after what they did here, it's going to be different.

So you underground fellas, you RMT boys know something we don't?

Paul shrugs. What's gonna be left for us to do Len?

Len gets back up with some difficulty, blowing hard and wiping the saliva from his mouth. Paul offers him his arm as they head back.

I won't live long enough to see your glorious revolution, if I live to be a fucking hundred.

And so it goes as these nature lovers, mudlarks of a different feather amble amongst the weeds and black sand of the scrappy shoreline each armed with a notepad for observations, the odd sketch, a pleasure which none of their bluster can derail, both reclaiming the estuary, inscribing their lives into it as they go.

Jack Dash.

Len hawks up and spits.

Auxiliary fire service, you gotta laugh at his front, along with all the spivs and the bookies, good company, chancers, leaving us to fight his precious fascists for him.

Oh my God mate you've really lost it, hahahaha.

What? I was bloody well there, wasn't I?

Paul rolls his eyes and Len starts a chuckle, a wet roiling churn of sand from deep in his forever fucked lungs.

Number ten, Maggie's den. Number ten!

Up goes a cheer

House!

BOAT AND
OTHER PEOPLE

What did I learn at University? No answers, that's for sure but God by the end of it we knew the (ontological) difficulties involved in asking a question.

Over a period of five years I took a joint Degree in Sociology and Literature, a Masters in Ideology and Discourse analysis and abandoned a PHD on Language games and class struggle when the grant money ran out and I was literally (and to be fair, reluctantly) escorted from the building with three boxes of books. One of the admin secretaries had a tear in her eye as I passed by the office. I swear.

There was another year or so when I just hung around dossing on friends' sofas, lining up cigarettes to be smoked each day on the kitchen table but I can't be sure for how long, if this was longer than a year or not. When you measure time in cigarettes, drugs and alcohol, larger events become tricky to recall, or at least put in sequence. You can lay out the jigsaw puzzle pieces of the 1980's and try and put them together but the thing is they fit more than one way. There is no definitive picture just variations on a theme. Truth bleeds as much as fiction and both occlude the precise recollection of events, if that is what any of us are after.

Sometimes it feels like University and the people I met there took up most of my twenties. In many respects we took it with us when we left for the city, indeed many of us lived together or *in the same area until our late twenties. it has never left me, an experience of a time and a place against which I gauged the rest of my life and the things I did with it.*

There is some slippage or compression in the following pages, Laclau for example never gave lectures to first year sociology students but in the next chapter I have him explain radical contingency to First year students in order to put me in the same lecture as Paul Feaney. But maybe I was, I have a recollection of sitting next to him but can't be sure where or when that was.

Everything, even the most mundane details of our lives is mysterious. It can't be helped.

I was there for years whereas Paul came, did his degree and left. He either did a bachelors degree for three years or a masters which would have been two. Or he didn't finish either, I don't know. Either way I didn't see him again for thirty-five years. Except once, maybe. I think I saw him on a demo, probably the Anti-Apartheid one where the crowd broke into the SAA office and took the plane, or it may have been North London Poly during a sit in late in the 1980's. Other people reported seeing him on the Underground during this period or maybe slightly after, back driving a train. But I doubt he would have done that.

It all boils down to people and places, now and then and the cracks in between. They disappear, return, haunt us or hover just out of the reach of our consciousness, all of them, the ones you remember and the places they were in and the ones you don't and the places they never were…

Coat man, or coke man, we called him as he wore an odd trench coat with a raggedy fur collar which was always filthy but he also dealt a bit of coke, so maybe it was either depending on the context in which you knew him. Years later I was in Dorking magistrates court for the only war crimes hearing to take place in the U.K. and this old man, Syzmon Serafinowicz (his grandson is a comedian) shuffled into the courtroom wearing exactly the same fucking moth-eaten fur collar coat I swear, and I flashed on Coat man as this deflated monster sat down in front of me. This was the second time in my life that I had come face to face with a (suspected) Nazi or collaborator, the other being in Vienna on an inter-rail trip before going University in a seedy bar where I picked a fight with some old men with SS tattoos...

Anyway, Coke man was an Iranian refugee and along with his brother, whose name escapes me, turned up in Colchester in 1982, the year I started University. I can still see them clearly, unruly black hair, jaundiced complexions, one with pitted cheeks, from teenage acne or something worse, his face, now I conjure it, the brother's face, leaping across a thirty-six year chasm. He might have been called Amir. One memory unlocks another. Both of them had such bright almost tearful eyes, slotted under coal black brows set in sallow druggy skin. Coke man was affectionately referred to as Monkey man by his occasional girlfriend Shayna, a typical North London Beck, as Jewish girls of a certain type were once called. He was in love with her, she lived by her own rules of engagement and, from my own later experience, 'love' wasn't something she shared easily. It was always a possibility until it wasn't and you then realised that it probably never had been. She existed on a different plane to everyone else and the illusion of sex was all part of her attraction.

The brothers became part of our set such as it was. Despite not being students they fell in with us, fellow somethings in the years after the Iranian revolution had made them stateless.

We accepted them as two exotic brothers, who took coke and speed but also smoked resin, sometimes even opium, which would make sense, there being a big opium smoking tradition in Iran. Squidgy balls of it have been rolled and pinched out into the bowls of antique pipes for centuries if not longer, ritually heated until bubbling like Muscovado sugar, both a cultural tradition and a growing social problem. Indeed, Amir especially I recall, loved joints of all kinds, effortlessly rolling them off his fingers in tight pencil like spliffs you could sell in packets they were so regular in shape. He reeked of the staleness of tobacco and narcotic, teeth stained and chipped, sometimes dipping cigarettes in coke powder, or making tobacco spliffs sprinkled with coke – these joints the most special of all and the most expensive, fine white powder sprinkled with utmost care over the tobacco, then licked and sealed. Coke man had a monkey like mischievousness, his coat sweeping glasses off tables, sending chairs flying, always on a mission, to go somewhere, do something, whilst Amir was more laid back, just had that hippy vibe coming off him. A hippy who blew precise smoke rings from his spliffs, and if you were lucky enough, close enough to risk his death breath, resin blow backs to die for.

Coke man was more like Wally Hope, a magical whirlwind who created a (literal) snowstorm from his coat in the garden of Dial house to the applause of his host Penny Rimbaud. Back then I hadn't heard of either of these people or of the existence of Dial house. Only now do I imagine the resemblance, a similarity of surplus energy.

Coke man played the guitar (badly, mostly bum chord noise, with an occasionally recognisable riff, usually Hendrix). Amir played bass (well) which figures, coke and guitars being an all too obvious melody, whereas spliffs, opium and resin spoke to a deeper harmony.

They had money, as many of that first wave of exiles must have had to get out of Iran so quickly. There were no Iranian boat people that I am aware of. They came by way of Heathrow. I have a sense of frustrated and concerned parents or family members at the end of bad phone lines but maybe this was just my projection.

Mad Mike sold drugs to Monkey Man. I remember that, or they had drugs in common, passing them to-and-fro in a complicated barter system whose rules only they knew.

Mad Mike was a character in a panoply of many that we knew only by their nicknames, which were usually riffs on the themes of mental health, sexuality and hygiene, intelligence or lack thereof, relative height, weight and predictably, presumed social class; Legends such as Spiv, Spider, Salmon, Filthy, Dwarf, The Finch, The Taff, Big Kofi, Clever Thomas, Smelly Mike, Bigger G, Fast Eddy (he was a bit slow) and Jesus (This for the leader of the student SWP society, and yes he did have flowing locks of (red) hair, but was from Lancashire).

Mad Mike was a huge speed freak and if he could get hold of any, coke sniffer. Greasy black hair, wild eyes, fucked teeth, pockmarked cheeks, matchstick limbs, patchwork clothes and worn-down Cuban heels. Some people called him Catweasel, most people ignored him. A mature student or fellow traveller who gravitated to campus and the oddballs who had collected there since the 1960's. He might have been an ex-patient of Severalls, the local loony bin, (of which more, later).

One summer Sunday morning I was woken up by the noise of the front door being kicked literally off its hinges. I thought it was a break in, (God knows what they expected to find worth stealing) but as I stumbled downstairs grasping a broken tennis racket, the opening riff of Neil Young's 'Sugar Mountain' came on the stereo at full distorted volume and I discovered Mike hunched over the coffee table chopping lines on the open triptych of the album cover. A mountain of coke, a pyramid of coke rising. It was 4.45am.

'*You can't be twenty on Sugar Mountain.*'

Mad Mike was probably in his forties, but looked way older, weather worn, almost a figure out of time, a sailor even, an old tar, an ancient mariner, his lined and sweaty intent and salty face and clothes that didn't do the job of categorising him. Back when thirty was the new fifty and he couldn't leave his sugar mountain. Hippy/Townie/Student/Squaddie. Oddly he could have been any of these. An LSD burnout from mid-sixties Ibiza, a parka wearing townie kicking doors in at dawn, an earnest in your face mature student asking too many questions, or a seasoned whip thin Infantry officer suffering from PTSD.

Mad Mike who famously (in the micro mythology of that time and place) played cricket for one of the local village teams.

That morning he offers me a rolled pound note as if it were a bacon sandwich or a glass of freshly squeezed orange juice at the Sunday brunch he was hosting.

In off campus years we variously lived in damp falling down houses in Colchester or the surrounding villages. We read books and wrote our essays, but spent as much time in the bookies and the cafes, the pubs and clubs as we did studying. Most students got accommodation in the new build estates off the Boundary Road that led up to Campus. Lecturers and Graduate students gathered at the Rose and Crown in Wivenhoe, quaffed real ale and mumbled their critiques of the real, but us, we outliers, chose to populate the blasted margins in far flung places like Jaywick, St. Osyth or Brightlingsea.

Brightlingsea, a small town at the mouth of the river Coyne on the Thames estuary across from Mersea Island. Once an oyster town, a thriving fishing port, still serviced by the Black Buoy pub, a watering hole that serviced what was left of the locals.

One particularly harsh winter we were snowed in for what felt like months, so we spent our days chain smoking 'Red Band Superkings' and playing Konami's Karate Champ arcade game for hours on end in the local caff. Each new game was heralded by the dojo master's vocal prompt '*Begin*', delivered in a heavily digitised yet still recognisably Asian accent, one of the first computer game voices I had ever heard. The owner swore at us occasionally for leaving fag burns on the console as our fingers wore themselves out on the kicking, punching, blocking and jumping buttons. I would go to sleep at night bone cold and damp, the flashing *insert coin* screen owning my mind's eye until the moment of exhausted oblivion.

This isolation worked both ways, because in the years spent on campus we rarely ventured off it. This was us at 18,19,20, 21. How we lived and what we lived for.

With hindsight Monkey man and Amir's parents were

probably part of the problem in Iran, not the solution. Members of a Persian elite that had bled their country dry ever since, well, forever. In Colchester they came and went. Our only rule was they couldn't take their shoes off because their feet stank. They didn't wash much but then neither did anyone else. Perhaps it was their drug use that made them stink. Shoes on, I don't remember them being that bad. I think drugs make your feet sweat, especially opium. Either way, this one rule they accepted with humour and they were more than welcome, because their company was at the very least different, especially to 18/19/20 year olds from the home counties.

They were stateless. Persian as opposed to Iranian. Like the Persians I would later meet in L.A. arriviste to the max, schizophrenic lovers and haters of their revolution. Bitter exiles of two places simultaneously, one superimposed on the other, the hated palimpsest of a once and future paradise. Tailors, limo drivers, Jewellers, restaurant owners, businessmen, their wives, children and extended families, students, doctors, writers, musicians and artists. They clung onto their identity through politics and food. To be precise – the topology of cuisine becomes the politics of food; regional delicacies endlessly argued over, secret recipes, handed down dishes from mothers, grandmothers, uncles, cousins, food is the gateway drug for most immigrants. The moment when Bolognese becomes meatballs, Italians become American, famine becomes feast, the comfort of the familiar weaning you off what's missing and onto what's additional. Kitchens and restaurants, food trucks and supermarkets allowing you to maintain enough of a connection, the taste of home in a new land. More is the new less, surfeit is proof

positive you made the right decisions. You are what you eat
becomes you eat who you are. Like a hand full of dirt in
the pocket of a jacket, food becomes what home becomes,
a heritage reduced and reduced and reduced, simmered
down to an essence, the living taste memory of home right
there on your palate.

But what now thirty plus years later? Revolutions
consolidated, what are exiles now?

Where they are from is no longer forbidden. Vietnam,
Iran and Cuba are places we have been able to visit for
years, places that now feature in magazines like the *FT
Weekend*'s 'How To Spend It', elite destinations along with so
many other places that once created exiles. Tehran now the
happening spot for a certain class of world traveller. (Mosque
for mosque, world class architecture, food, friendly locals,
textiles to die for.) Authentic, Boutique, bespoke, exclusive,
tailored, off the beaten track, the destinations of supermen
tired of well-trodden places and ordinary people. Albania
(unspoilt Mediterranean, cabanas on the beach) Eritrea
(Futurist Italian 1920's architecture and cinemas, world class
coffee), Lebanon (an endless list of delights), Georgia (World
class wine, hill walking, nightlife, cuisine), Kazakhstan
(immense/unspoilt deserts and mountains plus post-Soviet
frisson) Chile (Post Allende frisson (descending arpeggio, but
with a late as of writing reprise!) and Columbia (Post-*Narcos*
frisson, Atlantic, Pacific and Caribbean, one country, three
oceans. Post-conflict, a safe time to experience the music, the
food, the women, the falling Medellin crime rate...)

Who knows if the brothers ever went home, or went to
America, or became British citizens or are indeed dead, an
option I've included due to their proclivities back in the day

that I have no doubt were continued after their stay with us in Colchester. This was their authenticity, a bohemian agency which we admired. Cut loose from their past they lived without knowing or caring about their final destination or so it seemed to us; boisterous flat earth sailors blithely under full sail day and night.

Their status is one of being half remembered. My mind fills the gaps of their personalities and back story with its own obsessions, borrowing other things that have passed through it and grafting them onto whatever remained of actual memory to fill them out.

I do, however, vividly remember the huge turd that blocked the downstairs toilet story. Nobody admitted to doing it and all of the housemates suspected Coke man or Amir of laying it. After three days lying untouched somebody (the culprit?) had removed it, cut it up into segments somehow and flushed them away, possibly at night. It couldn't have been one of the slight women who lived with us as the thing was over two feet long and as thick as your arm. We had all stood around the bowl shaking our heads, holding our noses and laughing hysterically. The magical disappearance of the log proved it wasn't the Iranian brothers, who couldn't have cared less. Their appearance in this story is one of absence and possibly our own prejudice.

We never found out who did it. It wasn't me.

I don't know what telly they liked because we never watched any together. They loved Hendrix I remember that, an easy guess to turn into a memory but not the books they read although I do remember them being stuffed in coat pockets. Iranians have a rich tradition of Persian poetry, Rumi and others they may have enjoyed or not. Sport was a foreign country to us in those times. In 1982 only fascists did sport. So we didn't have that in common.

They manifest as characters. Two Iranian brothers set adrift in Colchester in the early 1980's. Later on in London, I met a Chilean refugee, Federigo Cruchaga Medes, a name that could only be one of exile, or if not, one of those in power, a grand personage from a revolutionary committee, kindred in name and spirit to the likes of Lucie Simplice Camille Benoit Desmoulins.

Fede had been a supporter of the murdered President Salvador Allende, a student communist leader, obsessed by the injustice that had befallen his country and now lived an ex-patriot life in Chilean circles, somewhat of a mystery, a political, an exotic, in a way that the Iranians were most definitely not. His feet also stank, which is an odd coincidence and after a while in another house with other people, we wouldn't let him take his shoes off either. Like most exiles of the time Fede smoked constantly.

Women flocked to him despite his breath and feet because of his revolutionary aura, which I imagine faded over time and he fattened up, had kids and became like everyone else, an ex-exile, a post refugee, a no longer political.

Chile Libre!

Again a country that now probably offers air b'n'b bargains, with high and low tourist seasons for expat and tourists alike. Time in this case isn't the hunter, far from it, it farms out our self-importance with blind disinterest.

The list of exiles grows exponentially with a concurrent increase in refugees. Countries expel them from the body politic or they flee on pain of death or incarceration. Other countries absorb them out of strategic calculation or rare acts of compassion. ANC people, Sudanese Communists, members of the Polisario, the PLO, Indonesian revolutionaries, German, Spanish and Italian Anarchists, Soviet exiles, Yemeni leftists, the list grows to encompass the dispossessed from around the world. I have seen empty tented cities in the UAE awaiting (what remains of?) the Palestinians. There are also defectors, people who chose *the other side*. Spies traitors or heroes take your pick, from Kim Philby to Anthony Blunt, with George Blake in the middle. They had changed colours, swapped one country for another, traitors in the eyes of their Patria.

Lord Haw Haw the most infamous of the lot – a stateless fascist, foot soldier of a new world order that would subsume all under its thousand year mandate. Like Ezra Pound in his nuthouse, perhaps the only way you can come back, be taken back 'home' is to be incarcerated, cordoned off from the state you spurned. Toxic. A quarantined return, lest you infect the polity, the sanctioned discourse of State and society. Poet/traitor is the most unusual chemistry to contain, the most hazardous and least understood.

Flash on a military graduation parade scene in Narcos in which the Columbian President leans in to one of his commanders and whispers 'the greatest sacrifice you can make is for your country', your *Patria*. This word again, Paesa, Patria, Paisan, Partisano, Pristrastnyy, words for all seasons.

Pound paid a lesser price than the firing squad. He wasn't even tarred and feathered. His head neither shaved nor nicked but cut as per the regulations of his temporary mental confinement. Note that it's fashionable in certain writerly circles to mention Ezra Pound in an early chapter of your 'work', amongst others of the (white/European) literary illuminati, (Cendrars, Lispector, Duras, Bernhard etc), I'll point them out as and when. On reflection, Pound is also a moral exile to a set of liberal values we are all beholden to and take for granted, so by referencing him, to place ourselves adjacent to his transgression allows us to question our own conformity.

Victims.

Then

The dispossessed, the defenestrated, thrown from helicopters into the ocean; drug dealers, radicals, students, opponents.

Now

A trim bearded Afghan Uber driver works two jobs, cabbing at night, Pret a Manger during the day. Much to the consternation of his co-workers he had just taken his wife and new baby on a trip back to Kabul to see his parents. His dad was a grocer on Chicken Street. He told me they had a great time.

We didn't hear a single bomb or gunshot for the six weeks we were there.

His right to remain allowing him to visit Afghanistan as easily as a trip to Spain. Easyjet doesn't fly to Kabul, but you get my point.

Now

Range Rover Evoques loaded into containers and shipped to Eritrea. Coffee sipped and hands shaken in the crumbling Art Deco cafes of Asmara. Secondhand luxury for the brand new middle classes of Eritrea and Southern Sudan, new wealth augmented by U.N. service personal spending power in the hotspots and war zones of sub Saharan Africa.

Sell a house in Maida Vale, buy a hotel in Juba, the penthouse leased for ten years to peacekeeper generals.

Don't be stupid be a smartie...

Then

The '90's, New York.

Fantasy Shtetl food lovingly prepared and eaten in Duplexes on the upper east side after Yiddish classes. A Ghetto fantasy. Kasha, Buckwheat noodles, wild fermented pickles, Cholent the sabbath stew, Kugel, coconut milk chicken broth, Matzos, Kiske, Latkes in the land of plenty.

Then

1930's Lithuania.

It was all about potatoes (Bulbes) and if you are a greedy nosher you had bread to eat during the week. A standout, a show off, probably an American visiting nosher, who could hear the children sing...

Sunday we have bulbes, Monday-bulbes, Tuesday and Wednesday-bulbes; Shabbos, thank goodness, we have bulbes kugel, Sunday its back to Bulbes.

And to think these children would live to eat soup made from leather belts or shoes, sawdust, pocket dust, carpenters glue, birds, cats and dogs.

Now

The dirty Havana trilogy. Miami migrant blood boils at the dilapidation on show in the old country, shame for them, pride for those that remained, untainted by running away, by being kicked out, exported, expelled/thrown up onto mainland America, to beg, deal, work hard but all the same fester in exile. Flash on the 1970's 80's desperate counter insurgencies across Latin America as documented by James Ellroy; Mob/CIA Black Ops/Diamond funded despots/

drug and people trafficking/explosions at oil refineries/ black flag mercenary insurgencies/white hand death squads and people being thrown from...helicopters.

Whup whup whup.

Now

Everywhere

Uber designate their drivers 'the other person in the car'. Internal exiles. West Coast big ideas surf the crest of globalisation with the goal of washing away borders that inhibit profit. Or as they would argue freedom.

Borders that inhibit profit freedom.

Now

London

The O.G. 20th century boat people, the Vietnamese, now populate East London and after an invisible thirty or so years of hard work and higher education, their children and grandchildren have emerged as super entrepreneurs, graduates, hardworking businesspeople who have opened a rash of delicious authentic restaurants all over London and other metropoles. Buns, baguettes, summer rolls, street food, Vietnamese French fusion, celebrating communist iconography and social dining, the fear of which drove their parents into the sea, into precarious junks and other rusted out pirate hulks in the first place.

Salvation in Noodles. Uncle Nam's. Hanoi beers and Saigon rocks.

Ho Chi Minh chic is everywhere and now, more so than Iran, an admittedly niche holiday spot, (yet safe, ever so safe and civilised, the birthplace of weaving...), Obama visited, he even drank beer from a bottle with Anthony Bourdain, they shot the breeze, they chewed the fat, ate with chopsticks and fingers. Vietnam was back although Tony also went to Myanmar, which didn't work out so well. Vietnam is the go-to destination for gap year pack packers, post Uni English language teachers, mid-life adventurers and the wealthy retired of almost all 'developed' Western countries. Not to mention adrenalin junky, sex crazed demob happy post national service Israelis, not to mention them at all.

And to take a break from it all there is always Laos, with its laid-back capital Vientiane, a back water chill out zone for western youth before returning to the fray of full moon parties and more Anthony Bourdain inspired destination hopping, his signed photo adorning restaurant walls up and down the continent.

Follow that cat baby!

So the ex-exiles, these Vietnamese Brits with boat people heritage, whose refugenes are in the process of being mangled, put through the ringer of the dietary mores of an advanced industrial society, bear their norse like sagas of who they are and where they came from in the face of so much multicultural homogeneity. When these foundation myths appear as fiction, in novels with accolades, then the cycle is complete.

Yet outside of 'fiction' the cycle is incomplete.

We holiday in countries still blighted by unexploded ordnance. We fire automatic rifles at water buffalo instead of children, pet drugged up Tigers for photos instead of shooting them for trophies, we fuck more sex workers now than we did in wartime.

The skinny Vietnamese or Chinese guy selling shnide DVD's on the street out of a low slung heavy bag which drags down his shoulder, is hardly the enemy within (although perhaps an enemy within Capitalism, think of all the people whose job it is to make those movies; the producers, actors, directors not to mention the gaffers, the make up artists, the catering staff, the set dressers, the teamsters all with lease cars and mortgages to pay for, not to mention their pensions to pay into and the health care plan to be kept topped up), yet his Asian-ness implies a foreigner not playing by the rules, something that the Chinese (in particular) are seen to be too good at, ripping off, copying, (even at times admittedly improving on) our originals at knock down prices.

North Korea revives echoes of Fu Manchu, this *bad fiction* returns to stoke *real* racism.

Way back when

London 1922.

White girls hypnotised by Yellow men.

We imported the yellow peril panic from Amerikkka.

Bland, inscrutable, impassive — as typical an Oriental as any novelist ever pictured.

Brilliant Billy Chang, dope king of London. The East and West (ends) collide.

White female flapper drug death caused by Chinese hoodlum in sex for drugs scandal.

Obey Fu Manchu or every living thing will die!

Limehouse knocking shops, opium dens and Chinese laundrys. Chang transformed into the Limehouse spider, spinning his web of sex and narcotics. At the height of this panic Thomas Cook staged promenading player style fights for the entertainment of Charabanc tours of the Limehouse causeway, featuring yellow men with pig-tales shouting in Mandarin and waving machetes in the air as the incredulous tourists were driven by...

Chinks out.

...As a female hand runs its fingers longingly through the pomaded ebony hair of Billy Chang in the moments before he is deported...

Now

A confident, swaggering working class channelling Saturday Night Sunday Morning, clock on and off for work down the print under the names M. Mouse or D. Duck. Supervisors look the other way, shop stewards take the credit, profit share by other means in the class stand-off that characterised most of the post war period up to Thatcher who snatched more than the milk, so much more.

Indigenous graft, like selling knock off meat down the pub, 'Wanna buy a watch?' 1940's spiv style micro capitalism, dodgy off the back of a lorry tellies and other assorted electrical goods, duty free fags or booze brought back on innumerable white van man booze runs, none of this is seen as being Un-British. Even lighthouse wreckers got away with it.

This is working class pay back, parallel graft to the bigger scams the rich pull off, invisible stocks and shares, non-executive chairmanships, buy to let mortgages. We are all in on it. Capitalism invites an open season on itself. It has an anarchic beat, embracing those that take it to heart. Jobs for all the boys. That's who we are, or who we consider part of us, a working class who knock off, sell on and take a cut of, all the things they have been disenfranchised from. Double bubble. That's what makes the status quo. From meat raffles ala 'Raining Stones' to Lidl and Aldi's unbeatable offers on cases of Prosecco, we've come a long way since the days of hanging our poor for hunting rabbits in the King's Wood, but not far enough for the recently arrived.

By a long chalk.

Chinese, West Indian, Irish, Vietnamese.

Then and now

Boat and other people.

The dogs are set to run as well as the Gun boats.

No blacks. No Irish. No dogs.

And repeat.

More blacks, more Irish, more dogs.

Paul and I were coming at this from different angles, headed in the same direction, caught up in the jumble of history, or more precisely the coincidences thrown up by it, that washed us both up at University. Universal grants, Trade Union sponsorship, Free Tuition. Was this a new found land to be discovered or just the end of history? Was any of it worth it? Did we get a pass from work or were we exiled from it, were we an experiment? Did we escape from or were we expelled to, decanted into something called campus.

* Sax Rohmer author of the Fu Manchu series of novels (20m books sold during his lifetime) died after catching Asian Flu in 1959.

FRESHERS

The first night at University everybody got off with everybody else. Whoever was to hand. You got off with people in the same flat as you, those you talked to awkwardly in the shared kitchen over cups of tea, exchanging potted life stories as parents lingered, unable to let you go. You had a good idea of each other's social class by observing them, single, double or absent. You got off with each other because you went to the bar together for the first time and got pissed with them.

It was an unreal moment in time.

The cool ones didn't have parents drop them off and were automatically more fancy-able, and one could argue, had a head start for the duration of University, if not for life. You never spoke to these first night stands again, nor they to you, as soon as it became apparent that you belonged to or wanted to belong to a different tribe. Over the next few years you ceased to recognise each other. There were horror stories, cautionary tales of people who met that first night and stayed together forever, having a kid on campus in 'married quarters' in their third year or even sooner. A match made in heaven. Or Hell on earth.

Sex aside, flat mates bonded if they were 'on your level' which meant name checking the same music, the same books, having a shared sense of humour. Some people bonded because they came from similar backgrounds.

Class identity can fast track you to friendship in this type of situation, at least in the short term. Other people, perhaps more intuitive, less guarded spirits, read different books and listened to different music and came from different backgrounds but recognised a similar energy, were tuned in to the same frequency or affected the same attitude, or just had a chemical attraction, an inquisitiveness, a camaraderie born in those first tentative moments that somehow survived what came next. It just so happened that they could be found in your flat on that first day, that first afternoon after the parents had left. How they walked, how they laughed, how they smoked a fag. The people who put their perishable food in (labelled) Tupperware boxes in the fridge and the ones who didn't. For boys also, how hard you came across was also calibrated from observation. Coming from *London* also gave you an edge, *Northern* made you 'potentially interesting', home counties invisible (so you had to shout louder, get more pissed than the others) West country, exotic (kind of) and foreign was interesting.

When I woke up, mouth tasting of stale cunt, (hers of stale cock) the immediate task ahead being to get the fuck out of there. To return a few doors down the corridor to your own room, a million miles away, evacuating the scene of the tiny death of a shambolic orgasm. I did not wake as if from some marvellous voyage. We had not descended the mountain together but I had managed to get back to my room, to sprawl amongst the unpacked things I had brought with me from home. Books, records, record player, a suitcase of clothes, bedding, two pillows, some posters, and thank

God some toothpaste.

Freshers week, where we got to meet other first year students, the second years and beyond, old hands who already knew the ropes, who were already part of the student body. We also signed up to student societies, as part of the getting involved ethos of 'going to University.' We didn't meet or become aware of mature students until lectures started, because in the main they didn't involve themselves in freshers week, were curricular as opposed to being extra curricular, besides some of them were too busy sorting out visas or accommodation for their families. Parent type stuff. They were semi invisible, not of interest, they were reminders of what we had come to University to avoid, and if only we realised it at the time of who we would (shortly) become.

How did I find my friends over the next few weeks, how did they find me? It all boiled down to funny, who had funny bones, saw how funny the world was, and added their own humour to it. Humour provided a clarity of vision. How we linked this to our politics, how irony, satire, piss taking, out of ourselves out of everybody else, ran through our lives like a seam of precious gems and was directly related to how (un) reliable politically we were.

To photocopy leaflets, to paste up posters, to arrange transport, to hold meetings, pass motions, write up minutes, arrange strategy, all of this was pretty dry, humourless work. We did bits of it, but didn't throw ourselves into it. We did turn up at opening nights, the big demos and rally's, the set piece run ins with the cops, we were always good for the spectacle. The hard work of organisation, campaigning, knocking on doors was always going to be done by others.

Give me a song to sing and the romance of a lost cause to champion and the drink to toast it with, for we were still young and living in an advanced capitalist social democracy for fucks sake!

'I, I, IRA, fuck the Queen and the UDA!' we chanted with gusto (and for the first time) at a knees up held by 'Troops out!' in the Student Union Party room. This is where I noticed Paul for the first time. Definitely not a typical fresher. He sneered when I rattled the fund-raising bucket under his nose, smoking silently at the back of the room as we all staggered to our feet for the Irish national anthem, his teary eyes drilling each and every one of us as the ash fell from his fingers.

The troubles. A united socialist Ireland. A socialist Ireland united. Nationalism. Sectarianism. Bloody Sunday. Revolution. The Workers party. H blocks and Hunger strikes. Class overdetermines race and religion. Class overdetermines gender. Resistance. War. Freedom. Housing. Jobs. Social security. Abortion on demand! A people wronged. Other Peoples wronged. Somalia, The Somali salvation democratic National Front, the Luta Armada de Libertação Nacional in Angola, the war in Western Sahara, support The Polisario!

Never ending Internationalism, the war of the world.

I had grown up in Woking, where a night out was smashing up bus shelters with empty bottles of cider, smoking fags, listening to trains passing by on the way to somewhere else. The road home littered with glass from naked phone boxes crunching underfoot like gems spilt from a heist gone wrong.

Whatever University offered I wanted it.

Freshers were moths to each of these flames, each fanned

by their societies and clubs, causes on sale, sold from behind wonky trestle tables laden with merch, pamphlets, lapel badges, stickers and flags, sold by the already converted, the blissfully aware, the cadres, the acolytes and that rare beast, the stone cold revolutionary.

Who wants to play British bulldog, no girls!

The rocks upon which idealism foundered. Hard rocks, soft idealism. The cheers that went up after the Brighton Bomb, the scuffles on campus between 'sides', provocation, anger, outrage, disgust, revenge, fit for an incendiary Ancient Greek comedy soon to feature Norman Tebbit and his wife in wheelchair sex jokes, full throated and word perfect renditions of Kinky boots and My little Armalite, marches, sit ins, more fund raisers and resolutions passed by a show of hands; all this in the future, but seeded there in that party room.

All join on to play kiss chase!

This was the rapture that captivated us, barely a year out of the playground. A potency we were to treat with careless abandon, thinking ours the only one, the inevitable one, whereas we were just one possibility, one set of vibrations that fed into a sea of many.

Later the same week, Paul was waiting for a lecture in the sociology common room. He was ruminating on a postcard turning it over and over in his hands, it was from Bob Crow, a jokey card celebrating the fact that they had both finally got out, got out of working for a living by becoming its advocates, and ultimately its abolitionists. Paul the brains, Bob the muscle. The picture on the front was a cartoon line drawing of a hole in the ground and the blade of a shovel appearing over the edge, earth flying through the air.

The caption read: The only job where you start at the top is digging a hole.

Paul was thinking of the holes his father had dug, trying to visualise them as if imagining what all the food you would eat in a lifetime would look like lined up. A line of holes.

Since he had arrived he had held himself apart, observing, trying to figure out if he had made the right decision or was it all a mistake, a detour, a dead end he would have to back out of?

Paul didn't recognise himself anymore, Bob's postcard seemed to be addressed to somebody else. He wasn't familiar with the new Paul yet, or even comfortable with the idea that such a thing was possible. If he gave himself up to *University* then perhaps the impasse would be broken. From what he had seen so far this was a place of imaginary identities, made up people, fictions, fragile egos, lonely 'I's clashing in febrile conditions to no obvious advantage. A human petri dish, to what end?

Wolves circling sheep with a few tricksters in the middle, scattered amongst the wingmen, the seconds and the secular clergy; handmaidens to the wolf. Too clever to be sheep, not vicious enough to be wolf. Loki. Trusted by neither, but tolerated, entertainment for the wolves, (for sheep are poor company), a stay of execution for the sheep, momentary respite from the wolves inevitable attention.

Paul watched me scoop up the change from the coffee percolator honesty plate, with perhaps a flicker of a smile on his face. His hands were big, as if stretched by labour somehow, and the skin was rough, cracked, his nails broken, bitten and dirty. Something we had in common, that dirty habit, a common bond of affliction; we both bite our nails down to the quick, signature spots of dried blood along the edges of our cuticles; Skin peeled back by our teeth from the top of the fingers, parsing out the troughs and peaks of our subconscious obsessions, trails in the snow, plotted paths through high seas, a shared fear of a flat earth and the cliff edges that no doubt awaited us.

Anxiety blood brothers. What other reason was there for biting your nails and the skin of your fingers until they bled?

Bad drugs and boredom.

I slump into a chair. Paul was listening, head cocked, to some students discussing somebody called Ornette Colman over the bitter hot coffee which I had just taxed. Too hungover to speak, I throw him a knowing smile instead. On his lap I clock a much-thumbed copy of Curzio Malaparte's 'Kaputt', a book which enters my life at that moment. On my lap my fingers rifle through the pages of a stolen, pristine edition of Lacan's 'Ecrits.'

When you bite your nails habitually it never occurs that they might run out, that the supply of Keratin was finite, for you always managed to worry, tear, peel or scratch yet another sliver of something, nail flesh, cuticle or skin, from whatever finger, little, index or middle, there was always more, the habit was voracious rather than particular. A lack, a lack that fills a void momentarily. Just like cigarettes. The imaginary phallus that is definitely not a penis, although self-evidently the phallus allows itself to be represented as such. This operates as a kind of trick to hide its power, but 'it' is so much more than 'just a penis' which is precisely its phallic *destiny*, to go beyond the penis itself, to dominate the imagination as an exquisite supplement to the real. I smirk at all of this French drivel I have been reading, riffing on it playfully to pass the time.

We step outside for a quick smoke and an exchange of essential information. I flick my stub towards a flowerpot. It misses, wastefully fizzling out on the concrete, a few drags left in it. Paul grinds out his fag end, two quick pivots of his steel toecap and we go back inside. It's 11 a.m. and the coffee drinkers eagerly hustle forward to get the best seats. We hang back instinctively to be the last in and first out. Paul nods to me curtly as I worry the swollen corner of an index finger against my thumb and we file into the lecture theatre for an introduction to the Enlightenment.

THE
EASTERN FRONT

A couple of weeks later we sat smoking in the 'Hex' Sandwich bar situated on the top *Quad* of the University campus. It was the fag end of October, cold, wet, drab.

Paul is irate.

There's a fucking vicar in my flat, can you believe it? I'm at University for fucks sake, I'm meant to be having the time of my life and I've got to share a fridge with a fucking vicar.

I bet he keeps it well stocked. Bottles of milk, Tupperware boxes full of cheese slices, sausages, all with his name on them. Feel free to expropriate.

The cunt drinks poxy cider can you believe that? Cider for fucks sake. And guess what he's studying?

I shrug, smiling. Paul's flat was in Wolfson Court, a low-rise block of flats adjacent to the towers where they put a lot of the mature students, most of them dull as fuck.

Fucking theology. I said to him aren't you putting the cart before the horse there, fella? Shouldn't you have studied fucking theology before deciding to become a vicar? Take the whole idea for a test drive, like. Discover if the whole cosmology of it was for you or not.

I cracked up. Paul hissed through his teeth like Muttley.

God give me strength.

What did he say to that?

I'm a vicar by vocation, and now I'm here to learn the tools to help me deliver on the message. Christ on a fucking stick it's like he planning to go out there selling shiny new bloody cars.

Poxy priest.

Not even. He's a vicar, church of fucking England.

Paul starts coughing, wipes his mouth and nose with his hanky whilst I order two *Steakwiches* paid for with liberated money from the Modern languages common room. (I farm the honesty plates, one day sociology, the next Linguistics and so on.)

My treat. Crispy beef strips on lettuce, slathered in red hot salsa and piled in a bun. Delicious but very messy.

Before I forget, here.

I give Paul back his copy of Malaparte's 'Kaputt'. He nods, checks it over and carefully puts it away in his knapsack before we tuck in, starving.

He actually checked if I had creased his fucking book! And not even surreptitiously. Anal bastard.

Between hot mouthfuls...

Rommel visited him at his house once, did you know that? The house he built on Capri overlooking the bay of Naples, the one from that Goddard film *Contempt*. You seen it?

I shake my head thinking we don't have Goddard in Woking mate, swallowing a big hot bite at the same time. My tongue tossing it too-and-fro like a hockey stick. It gets momentarily stuck at the top of my throat before going down scraping my tonsils as I relish the umami flavour. Pleasure and pain in one mouthful.

Have some water, fuck me.

I gulp some down.

Fucking hot!

Paul gets back on subject, answering his own question.

Great movie. Saw it at the Renoir a few years ago after work.

Never heard of it.

I pat my streaming eyes, trying to focus. *The Renoir.*

The house is a red ziggurat shaped spaceship crash-landed from the future, teetering out over the sea. Like this.

Paul scribbles a shape in his notebook. He swivels it towards me. I am none the wiser.

I'll look it up in the library.

Casa Malaparte. Built just before the war, a vision of modernist optimism, or arrogance, either way it's a unique building. During the war after he gets back from Russia and his book is banned because it pissed Hitler off, Malaparte is just sitting it out here, out of favour with Mussolini, but protected by his son in law, fuck it what's his name? Ciano, yeah, Count Ciano, well he got his in '44, shouting 'Long live Italy!' at the firing squad. Boom! So Malaparte is expelled from court, exiled but not put back in prison. Rommel visits him in 1942, he's also out of favour having fucked up in North Africa. He'll be dead in two years, his ticket to ride a no way out suicide. They're like a pair of Fascist lepers having a last supper on the roof terrace overlooking the bay of fucking Naples or whatever it's called, and he asks Malaparte if he designed the house. Malaparte shakes his head...

No, no, I designed the view.

...

Get it? 'I designed the view.' Genius cunt. I mean think about it. Pure fascist vertigo.

...

113

This was Paul at his most voluble, passionate about things that not many other people knew or gave a shit about, leaping from subject to subject, never getting to the end of one thread before starting to unravel the next, jumping from branch to branch of this great tree that was his brain like a monkey hunting for coconuts that were always just out of reach, higher and higher he went constantly on the move, chattering to himself, going God knows where but always hungry, reaching higher, searching for some kind of epiphany, a moment of gestalt in an ongoing and unstoppable conversation that sometimes spilt over, needed grounding or just was him reaching out for company, to be in the world, to be listened to, to be acknowledged, to achieve immanence.

He was already flying, a force of nature, already this entity, I had to grow into mine, at 18 I was mainly just potential, playing catch up from a cold start, *one hundred miles and runnin'*.

Paul focused totally in whatever moment he found himself in. I think that was what he valued. In between these moments he was at a loss. Anyway, we became friends, friends in the moment and for a time we became very good at creating these moments and being in them.

A trickle of relish ran from the corner of Paul's mouth down to the stubble of his chin where it clung, suspended over the table. I couldn't take my eyes off it, hanging precariously like that fucking house he was rabbiting on about. *Steakwiches* were notoriously messy things to eat, no wonder he put his precious book away before eating. But Paul didn't care he let it drip, he was on a roll.

These Gods of cinema, Bardot, Jack Palance, Michel Piccoli. Fritz Lang is in it fucks sake.

Fritz Lang, I'd heard of him.

Playing himself, an ageing fucking director in thrall to a starlet, the writer selling her to him, her contempt of his servility when confronted by the dollar, and driving it all forward the consistent vision of Lang to complete his movie, his vision beyond sex, beyond money, beyond human almost. A God like tenacity. The cliche of it, fuck me, but this reverberates with the coining of the cliche in the Odyssey, when it was fresh, this original text could have said, been about, described anything, these were the first metaphors, brand new, literally novel. All of this stuff comes together at Casa Malaparte. Gods literally descended onto the stage to force a happy ending, to resolve an impasse. In the film, a car crash kills the two protagonists, the money and the sex taken out of the equation, Palance and Bardot kaputt. It's perfect. A piss take of sterile macho creativity. Fucking Godard...Deus ex Machina.

Paul took to University like the first ever duck to water. He even picked up the lingo without missing beat.

My tongue was burnt, I worried it against the inside of my cheek.

I was going to say something about the penis being *less than* the phallus but fumbled it in preview. Or was it that the Phallus was more than just a penis, which might have something to do with the movie or movies in general? I hadn't seen nearly enough of them that was obvious.

I'll get it out on video.

Was all I could muster, struggling to literally parse the words spitting from his mouth, so much ticker tape to process. I watched the movie at some point after this and, well, let's just say I didn't see what he saw.

All I could think about was why the fuck did this guy need to come to University. That, and I would definitely hesitate before getting on a tube train driven by him.

Afterwards, when he had gone back to his flat to take a shit, (he wouldn't do it anywhere else, the idea of using the student union toilets filled him with disgust) his absence made itself felt as a continuing presence. One moment he was hunched over the table talking, or staring intently at you as you spoke excepting more, the next he was gone. It was like a squall had died down, there was a relief, a silence. Background noise flooded back, you could almost hear the cosmos ticking, a moment in which you could collect yourself, decompress and then play catch up.

Rommel never visited Casa Malaparte. They never met. For a writer it was too good a story not to invent, not to will into existence. Malaparte had invented so many others, spinning his experiences (literal and imaginary ones) into grander narratives. Who would question a story like this? On the one hand so inconsequential, on the other...

Malaparte described his house 'me as a house.' The design an echo of the prison cell he had been (briefly) put in by Mussolini. There was no *other* for Malaparte, everywhere he went, everything he did was an expression of his will, which, given the things he witnessed was mythomania par excellence, yet probably what kept him going. A sardonic self-mythologisation in the face of horror, of living through the world at night. Which he did twice, in both wars, writing '*the character called I*' over and over again.

Paul lived fully in moments which expanded to contain him. Malaparte lived in himself as a house. Now I can see the similarity. Then I was barely taking notes.

Contempt adapted from the Moravia novel of the same name, climaxes in the inevitable denouement of a car crash; speed, technology, death, the three tropes of Italian Fascism. No wonder Godard wanted it to be shot at Casa Malaparte, the house summons its dead creator in each frame. His vibrations concatenating so that *we* 'take offence' *(Predere in Mala parte).* Today the house is dedicated to creating an environment in which a visitor feels that Malaparte has just left each room, his books, paintings, objects all in situ as he left them. It is forever *his* house.

At the end of the original Odyssey, after all the action, the trials and combats Ulysses endures, Homer prioritises Penelope's psychological struggle against the suitors over his exploits in the summing up of the saga. The power of woman over man before, maybe in the moment of becoming, the cliche at the heart of the movie.

'The royal pair mingled in love again
and afterward lay revelling in stories:
hers of the siege her beauty stood at home
from arrogant suitors, crowding on her sight,
and how they fed their courtships on his cattle
oxen and fat sheep, and drank up rivers
of wine out of the vats. Odysseus told
of what hard blows he had dealt to others
and of what blows he had taken-all that story.'
All that story.

In the film it is the producers secretary Francesca who has to literally translate between English, Italian, French and

German but to also parse the egos of the three magi; producer, writer and director into the conception of the movie, almost to give birth to it but failing, for the contempt between each was compounded by the dubbing of the movie into Italian thereby erasing, silencing her role in the story, erasing her translation, taking away her power. The film is *really* about her silent suffering, she is the films true Penelope.

This is how we used to think and write at university, intoxicated by our own arcana.

Technical words, French ways of thinking, the use of inverted commas (for almost everything was now thrown into parentheses), ~~Strike throughs~~, _underscores_, hapHazArd caps and later when computers arrived the (extensive) use of *italics*, the use of brackets, [(brackets)] within brackets, long convoluted sentences, endless commas, algebraic even, to dispense with transparency in order for us to interrogate the text *in and of itself* the brickwork behind the trelliswork of story.

To be frank we had become 'book smart'. It was indeed an insult. Drunk on ideas and obsessive about how we saw the world and the things in it we found important. Paul was always already in overdrive. The rest of us mostly avoided his fate by being recruited into already existing academic intellectual traditions. We swam in lanes. Paul remained on dry land. He resisted systems of thought for their own sake. What was behind them? Solid ground or thin air? He dismissed academic disciplines as just another middle-class straightjacket. For Paul postmodernism, as it came in to being 'in front of our eyes' during the 80's, could never spirit away the realities of class war, at best these ideas were a new rhetoric, nothing more than signs taken for wonders.

Perhaps this was talk without consequence but just like the language and rituals of football it was our banter, the terraces from which we experienced life as a lived and thought experience. For Paul being able to share however incomprehensibly the things that spoke to his inner life was liberating. He didn't have to keep it all to himself, hidden by the unassuming grunts of agreement and curt shy replies that passed for his conversation in the world at large. What we came to share was nothing less than fragments, clues and resonances of an implicit knowledge of civilisation.

How far this took him from the common-sense advocacy of a fairer world he shared with Bob Crow and his union comrades would only become clear after his incarceration.

Yet we also shared in good faith (which is no mea culpa) a fascination with something essentially bankrupt and phallocentric, a nihilistic melody that we couldn't shake, it had bored into us, an hypnotic ear worm.

War and revolution.

Satisfied and all talked out, Paul smoked a roll up and finished his cup of coffee, burping *Steakwich* reflux under his hand. Behind him I watched Gary Finch (The Finch) bowl across the square, trench coat flapping at his sides as he exited the supermarket and headed straight towards us. Gary Finch, another working class mature student, Chelsea hoodlum, his dad a hard as nails army sergeant, Gary a Tommy Steele look alike with Dickensian teeth, exuding total energy, an unputoutable personality. He came right up to the window and flashed the customised inside long pocket of his trench coat where we spied the glistening rear end of a supermarket chicken he had just pocketed. Grinning from ear to ear the Finch had sourced that evening's supper.

The Bill Sykes of our generation, instead of a dog, he had a budgie on his shoulder. What a legend.

I am sure Penelope grew sick and tired of bloody heroes, but in the winter of 1983, at the apex point of my childhood, I had yet to learn my lesson.

FROM WOKING WITH LOVE

My beat surrender...

Since my early teens I daydreamed about being Lenin. I put myself in his shoes. I lay in bed fantasising about being the Bolshevik mastermind. My dreams played fast and loose with what I knew, which was very little. I was a better faster tougher and sexier Lenin.

I never wanted to be either Tortsky or Stalin despite the latter having a certain youthful cache, a street fighting man robbing banks for the cause in oil rich Baku, unlike others who talked themselves into the history books.

I must admit to having previous form. From the age of ten or eleven I projected myself as an RAF pilot recovering from his wounds in a makeshift field hospital, (possibly first world war, a magnificent man in his flying machine) or recuperating in the vale of Kent or somewhere coastal in Suffolk, a scene lifted straight from the edits of the technicolour movies we were spoon-fed as children, with me in a wheelchair, blanket folded over my knees pushed along the gravel paths of the manicured gardens of some annexed country house by an attentive blonde or brunette nurse, who bent down to catch my every word. (Spoken softly, my lungs probably shot from exposure to mustard gas, the confusion of which war I was in colouring my fantasy). In the next frame so to speak I found myself up and out of the wheelchair and back in the thick of it, as if the injury had never happened, I was recuperating and falling in love and fighting simultaneously; In the trenches, all sucking mud and gnawing rats, but at the same time circling hedgerows from above, the POV of vertiginous dog fights alternating green fields and blue sky, flipping like the paddle opticians use during eye tests, contrails like crossing blades flashing overhead, as I look up from the trench. Smoke clears the whistle blows machine guns start rattling, on earth as it is in heaven, torn fuselage fabric, broken struts and leaking oil wiped from shattered goggles. In dream time I was legion, past present and future all lived at once, as a fever. I dreamt on all fronts.

'*After all what is time. A mere Tyranny*'

The upshot in these dreams was I now had a sweetheart to come home to but the relationship was never consummated.

'*Yes June, Im bailing out, I'm bailing out. But there's a catch I've got no parachute.*'

I was probably no older than sixteen.

Reviewing the above I notice the software or the keys on my seven year old laptop auto-spelled or miss typed Trotsky as Tortsky. I flash on a commissar obsessed by cakes, getting cream all over the lower part of his Lenin specs just like Paul with the runnel of tomato sauce escaping from his juicy *Steakwich* and down his chin. A human touch, the pleasure of food, a moments gluttony; the masks slips. Blaise Cendrars' nose is another example, seeing it you can't help but think 'What a ludicrous Shnozz!' bringing this high modernist God right back down to earth, details from this mortal comedy.

'He once was alive but now he's notski, who we talking about? Leon Tortsky!'

Again, sung with relish and spat with venom in the face of the Socialist Workers Party members who sat at a table opposite us in the Student Union bar. A game but also not a game, there were consequences to our behaviour, to this word 'Trotsky' and our role play which in this case meant starting a bar brawl with the Swizzers to the soundtrack of Bonnie Tyler singing 'I need a hero, I need a hero till the end of the night.'

Yes we are all carnival, nothing is outside the big top. Nothing at all.

Fucking students! as many Kent miners would soon observe whilst drinking our booze and dossing on our floors. Also, something their wives had cautioned them against or else they'd be out on their ear.

My childhood had tuned my radar to phenomena in the world that disturbed the people who brought me up, things which prompted flashes of irrationality in my guardian's behaviour. We lived in a cul-de-sac, literally. The family car was parked on the gravel driveway. My dad's cars went Alfa Romeo, Rover, a gold Citroen, Renault (the one that talked, the first car to talk in fact, with a female voice, A top of the range 'Boccara' with express up and down electric windows), then I left home. Holidays followed a similar trajectory, Isle of White, Devon, Spain, Mallorca, Mallorca, then I left home and they took my brother to America, to Disneyland.

My dad got angry when I asked why the miners were striking as he sparked up a brand new shiny red generator in 1974, 'TO KEEP THE LIGHTS ON' as if to answer my question would acknowledge their grievances in some way, give credence to something he was scared of. The question invoked the Miners into his life, Candyman style as if they were about to march on Woking. He banned me from listening to Monty Pythons *Life of Brian*. When I bought the book I had to hide it. I didn't get to see the film until I had left home. When I blasted 'Arseholes bastards fucking cunts and pricks' on my stereo he went potty and snapped *New Boots and Panties* in two in front of my face. What was it? What else gave this irrational fear a face? What other demons lurked behind the everyday story of my mostly normal 1970's childhood?

Percy fucking Topliss.

Reading *The Monocled Mutineer* in Sixth form was dynamite. Later I remember watching it with my parents, a hammy yet 'moving' (when parsed as telly) adaptation starring one or more of the McGann brothers. Drove the Tories potty I seem to recall. Especially Norman 'on yer bike' Tebbit, who, as we know, was extremely sensitive since the IRA put his missus in a wheelchair. The story blew the doors off so much of the history we had been taught at school. Taught, who am I kidding, we had it stuffed down our throats, war poets, poppy day, honourable sacrifice, play up play up and play the game, the white feather, heroes who died for our country we shall remember them they lay down their lives for us no less to protect our green and pleasant land, and the empire, the red map of empire that seamlessly evolved into the Common/Wealth, that's a send up in itself, right there in your face, all of this *ideology* was everyday rations in post WW2 UK. *The Monocled Mutineer* on the other hand was an incendiary opening into a parallel universe, a through the looking glass moment that sent me and my purple three speed chopper zigzagging straight down the local library for more. The idea that there had been revolt and anarchy in the trenches, British as well as Russian and German, (French?) that 'No man's land' provided more than just the location for Paul McCartneys 'Pipes of Peace' video, (the tentative handshake and ensuing game of football on Christmas day between combatants, 'they're the same as us fellas, and we are the same as them', (with dog eared photos of wife and kids to prove it), but had been a literal haven for soldiers (workers) refusing to fight each other on behalf of their shared class enemy, wanting instead to fight for themselves as a class, for bread, land and freedom; the freedom to not die for a system manifested by the nation states that ruled them. And this served up on the BBC just after the Miners strike!

My parents enjoyed it I think, as something to watch on telly, defanged of its revolutionary implications, flattened out as *Television*, a good historical yarn unconnected to their lived experience, 'The McGanns are very good, aren't they, did you know there are four of them, all actors, amazing isn't it?' Oh the soporific power of the horror box, the flickering screen in the corner, for it does contain unknown pleasures.

This workers war was all new to me, mutineers shot at dawn 'pour encourager les autres.' To stop the Russian rot dead in its tracks. It was from here that I dived into another past and came up for air imagining a different future.

It was cultural Nazism, the exotic horror of its manifestation rising from the embers of the Weimar Republic that doubled down on my fascination with the world at war. The devil plays all the best tunes and for boys in the 1970's, the siren song of Nazi Germany was too strong to resist. The first world war paled by comparison, an Ancien Regime European stand-off literally lacking blitzkrieg. The A team were the main draw, Hitler, Goebbels, Himmler, Goring, Hess, Heydrich and Eva Braun. Pantomime villains to many yet also playing at something much darker, stars of a snuff movie we watched without blinking; The Beer halls, street fights, storm troopers and plebiscites, the faux folk glamour of the SS, modern uniforms, Pagan insignia, runes, rings and the brutality of Kristal Nacht, (turning against your own people, your shop keepers, your tailors, literally turning the Jews out by the magic trick of smashing their windows, summoning the ever present logic of the pogrom), the purging of Ernst Rohm and his supporters/ the night of the long knives, revealing the interior workings of a political party as violent and eruptive as its exterior behaviour, igniting the glowing embers of the Weimar Republic into a conflagration of excess, taboo breaking, amorality and violence, a stiletto demos revelling in the sheer existential thrill and horror of the knife itself; torch lit processions, burning book pyres, blood seeped soil and sex, lots of sex. Its theme tune an ode to a pimp killed by communists. The Third Reich peeled back the thin skin of civilisation to expose the bloody body of a middle Europe unchanged since the dark ages.

Achtung Tommy!

As children in the aftermath, the vacuum, the slipstream of all this, from the moment we flicked through our first copies of comics like the *Eagle, Sgt. Fury, Battle* and *Commando* and watched movies like the *Guns of Navaronne, The Dam*

Busters, Escape from Colditz, we were sold, right up to the surprise ending; We won the war and they, fuck 'em, lost it.

But it was the supporting cast of Nazism, the foot soldiers, the minions, the bureaucrats, the banality of their evil that brought a second, deeper wave of rapture. Every detail of that regime became fetishised by a swath of disaffected male youth, from Sven Hassell novels to Joy Division records, the horror became a compulsion precisely because the details took over the horizon of our perspective like Malaparte's phantasmagoria of frozen horse ice sculptures rearing up from the surface of Lake Lagoda.

Over time we came to know too much, as too much became known. The precise table manner etiquette of mass murderers like Himmler and Hans Frank, the cold blooded careerism of Kaltenbrunner and Franz Six. Their cars, their mistresses, their collectors habits, diets and health regimes. The day-to-day pharmacology of a Nazi lifestyle. The day-to-day Thanatopia of a Nazi lifestyle. Field reports of the logistical problems facing each of the A,B,C,D Einzatgruppen, mobile death squads operating behind the front lines as Germany pushed east. Arthur Nebe (operating out of Minsk as head of Group B), ex Berlin Kripo chief (and later to be one of the stars of Phillip Kerr's Bernie Gunther novels, Bernie, the ultimate not so good German). Nebe's scrupulously detailed reports of each Aktion, collated by historians. How to kill so many people without affecting your morale. (Gas chambers and ovens, over executions and mass graves, an industrial process supplanting a cottage industry, a machine greased by a lot of booze, a lot of prostitutes, strict shift rotation, regular home leave and an abundance of already laid in Ideological superstructure.)

The grammar and style of the Holocaust, as it happened and not just in the final numbers, the camps and the chimneys. It was this forensic accounting that gave meaning to the figures, a granularity up close to the true horror of it, like watching all the ISIS videos or the footage from inside Bataclan, the Helmet-cam go pro footage from Christchurch, Norway, Orlando but dressed up as academic research, illustrated with photographs, supported by copious footnotes, references and pages of bibliography. Primary source materials being the holy grail of this need-to-know voyeurism, this time travel by other means to bear witness, startlingly fresh and as yet unexposed to the indifference of mass reproduction. The information just kept on coming.

A Lithuanian crowd watch a man attack an old Jewish man with a baseball bat and laugh and cheer in the background as others walk past on their way to other things. The old Jewish man collapses under the onslaught, dead at the feet of his assailant, the swagger and superman derangement of the man with the bat, who then proceeds to do it again, to kill another, pausing only to hike up his trousers held up by a thick white belt, pose and have his picture taken.

I google this story/memory to double check the facts. I type 'Lituanian man beats Jew to death with baseball bat' into the box. Again my keyboard doesn't register a letter, this time the h in Lithuanian, but the algorithm recognises the mistake and answers me with a question 'Did you mean **Lithuanian** man beats Jew to death with baseball bat?' The machine code response time is 0.65 seconds. Lightning quick. 1,870,0000 answers.

I flash on chess programmes that take ages to mull over your move even though this delay is fake, (to encourage the others) like the shutter release sound on camera phones that you can leave on for nostalgia sake (the sound effect is for now still the default, a remnant of a remnant), or disable this function for, well, practicality, a modern sense of digital tidiness, of cutting back the clutter, an excess of bytes, of memory taken up by unnecessary code, of excising an albeit tiny ghost in the machine.

My enquiry was immediately rewarded with the information that it wasn't a baseball bat the man used, but a metal pipe. Another task the algorithm has undertaken, a calculation that compensates for my mistake. I almost typed lead pipe, which is also a metal, but not mentioned by name in Wikipedia or any of the other search engines. The man was also given a nickname, 'The death dealer' but this must surely have been retrospectively bestowed, so therefore not a name he had on that day when he was captured in any of the photographs (taken by a German soldier, so novel was this murderous activity that it had yet to become censored, or the soldier himself had not thought 'I better not film this' He had just got his camera out as this was part of his experience of the new war, of the early days of Operation Barbarossa. It was war but also a great adventure, something to take pictures of and send home.) This nickname, 'death dealer' an oddly nondescript handle given the specifics of the context, how many others could share it? Too vague, to have any purchase on his identity, or indeed the possibility of his later apprehension. Definitely a not-getting-nicked name.

Imagine this scene in Kaunas, Lithuania, 1941 brought to life as a diorama, figurines posed on Papier mâché backgrounds,

*in a 360-degree scale reproduction of what happened in those
photographs but also extending beyond the frame of the images, to
both the foreground and background and also to the sides where all
stories really take place.*

Perhaps cameras never tell a story. (Which is self evident.)

This also happened. At school we had an Art teacher who
introduced us to the wonderful world of Tamiya scale model
kits and their exhaustive collection of World War Two soldiers
and equipment. These were 1:35th scale perfect moulded
replicas of real troop formations (detailed down to the angle
and thickness of creases in their uniforms) and *materiel*, tanks,
armoured vehicles, artillery, subs, destroyers, the whole
shooting match, embedded in paper mâché rendered topology.
Environments we adapted to the historical scenario we had
chosen. These dioramas reflected moments in time, of retreat,
or attack, of trucks being bogged down on the Eastern front in
spring, racing across the steppes in summer or frozen in time
by 'General Winter' with all the concomitant deleterious or
otherwise effects on our figurines that we diligently cut from
their frames, rubbed down with super fine grit sand paper,
painted, accessorised, weathered and 'historicised'.

A machine gunner with a makeshift eyepatch, wounded
men on stretchers missing limbs, stumps wound with
bloody rags, a decorated sharpshooter with modded Kar
98k and turret mounted scope, an 'Elefant' tank commander
perched on his turret in a very satisfying matt black boiler
suit, modelling that reflected what we imagined were the
combat and field repair improvisations of *actual* warfare.

The paintings on the box rendered the inert plastic figures
staked out on rectangular frames as hyper-real action men
in moments of war film poster style combat idealised in full

colour against an abstract white background. We adapted, altered, burnt, scarred scalded to fit the moment which we desired to recreate. Out of action Flak 88's, an overturned, burnt out Kubelwagen, strafed tanks and bogged down motorcycles, modded weapons to fit enemy munitions, broken down engines for part replacement. A mischlinge of materiel abandoned on the battlefield. Our art teacher never said a word about politics, or the war, or Hitler, none of that crossed his lips. His (revealed) obsession was historical accuracy, paint, turps and the drama of the piece in itself. And this years before Lego Aushwitz. His other passion were military engagements from ancient history involving Mesopotamian Spearmen and Elephants ranged against a weakened late Roman phalanx. Morale, lines of supply all being added modifiers to dice throws. All of this took place after school in the an extracurricular war gaming club.

Nazism jibed with our late 70's nihilism, which when we grew up delivered us eventually to Bolshevism. (At the time we were unaware of and would have been disinterested in the Soviet Tamiya model range, which was also less exhaustive, reflecting the Nazi fetishist bias of the times, not to say the military sympathies of the Japanese owned company itself.

The death dealer beat 45-50 Jewish men to death with his lead/ metal pipe or crowbar. He then retrieved his accordion and played the Lithuanian National anthem whilst standing on a pile of corpses.

Somebody has remarked in the comments below one of many websites/blogs, forums (from the 1,870,000 responses to that initial search) that this type of savage killing was

'Rwandan in its intensity.'

Think about that sentence, it certainly knocks my fact checking Google search into a cocked hat.

Follow the money, gold mined deep in the comments below YouTube videos.

Leaping ahead as if through a wormhole, bypassing university, (so at least a third of this book you are reading) through to the conclusion of both a formal and informal education the following are some of the opinions that came to hold sway (became hegemonic) in my friendship group by 1988. (Except number 8, see below).

This was our headspace heading into the last decade of the 20th century.

1. If Hitler hadn't hated Jews then some German Jews would have been on his side and he would have won the war. Many Jews in Germany were WW1 veterans, patriots. The waste of manpower and focus on the final solution contributed to the outcome of WW2. This thought leads to darker thoughts. The relationship between German Jews and their Eastern European counterparts would fill another book or two.

2. Hitler could never have won WW2 because of materials and production. As soon as America entered the war and Japan didn't invade Russia it was already over. Which kind of negates point 1.

3. The civil war in Russia 1917-1922 was to define the direction of Soviet development, a turn towards practicality and survival, industrialisation and militarisation. In effect the problem solving skills

needed to defeat Hitler twenty years later.

4. 1917-1930 in the Soviet Union was the most inventive decade in human history. A unique experiment, the birth and childhood of a new society.

5. The rise of Nazism again curtailed this 'freedom' and focused Stalin on preparing for confrontation with Hitler. A childhood denied its adolescence.

6. 26m Soviet citizens died defeating Hitler.

7. The shit that went down in Yugoslavia was off the scale and reverberated right down until today through the Balkan war and beyond. Tito was a mensch. In 1982 I went to his birthday party celebrations in Dubrovnik where the whole town sat down at trestle tables laden down with barbecued lamb, each place setting marked by small pyramids of salt. Then there were fireworks over the sea. He had been dead for two years.

8. 'Red Plenty' by Francis Spufford read all these years later, totally validates (some of) these points linear programming for one, willful dreaming another.

9. All the bad things we know about the Soviet Union are the context for the above and vice versa.

10. America as Imperial power post WW2 is also context for the above to the extent that capitalism and communism had devolved back into nation state antagonists. Which was the point of the SWP, which was the point of Trotsky, (spelling win!) yet wider context for the above.

We were drawn to what was a secret history, the truth that nobody else knew or cared about, we were the true believers, like the Illuminati who are now devotees of Tupac, Biggie Smalls, Elvis and Aliyah, Nipsey Hustle, and so on and on.

For us it was Yakov Sverdlov and his radical bureaucracy, literally birthing the Soviet Union by sheer force of chairmanship! Isaac Babel on a horse, Budyenny's Red cavalry, Nestor Mahkno's anarchists, Mayakovsky's suicide note, Karl Radek's compromise, Khruschev's Chauffeur (and the tale of the dodgy car tires) Rosa Luxemberg, La Passionaria and on and on, our people killed by their people in a head-to-head death match, a war that rages on the page and in the imagination and spills occasionally onto the streets; Our Gods versus their Gods.

This was our secret Odyssey.

At University Paul and I had somehow boarded the same ship, although I sensed even then we would disembark separately.

Listen to the beat. Surrender.

THE
HAPPY MAN

'A drumming sound woke me up. I saw a warm flickering light reflected in the windowpane. Outside people were passing by to the beat of a drum. It was a procession. People carrying candles, men and women dressed casually some with headscarves. Two big torches led the way lighting up the features of the people carrying them. Everyday faces same as the ones you see in supermarkets, schools and hospitals. London faces. They didn't make much noise just footsteps and a single drum coming from behind, marking the pace. In the middle of the crowd was a coffin shouldered by four people. Others held up placards with a man's face on them a smiling man with a moustache, stencilled on a yellow and green backdrop. They all wore black armbands and something I couldn't make out was draped across the wooden box. You didn't see night funerals, they weren't a thing, were they? I didn't want to be seen watching so I crouched down. As they went past the kebab shop opposite the men that worked there stood at the door smoking and watching. Later I found out that this was a mock funeral to echo and amplify the night funerals happening in Rojava where Kurdish fighters had no time to bury their dead during daylight hours. Draped over the coffin were the names of fighters killed in combat. And the marchers held aloft images of Abdullah Ocalan who I had never seen before that night.'

Rosa's diary, recovered 2018

Rosa would regularly come to fetch her dad from the Happy Man not to drag him out because lunch or supper was ready but because they had arranged a trip out, to go for a walk or to a gallery or the cinema. This holdout locals pub had always fascinated her. There was an old plane tree outside and she would often lean against it watching who came and went before going inside. Paul would always jump up out of his seat as if surprised to see her, not even finishing his pint first before ushering her back outside. He was always caught unawares. Planning his week was not something he did.

Remember me? Your only daughter?

I thought you looked familiar.

She shook her head.

Where we going again?

You wanted to go to the Monet exhibition remember?

Oh yeah, that will be good. Your mother coming?

No dad, she's at work.

Shouldn't you be in school?

It's sixth form. Flexible hours. I am a responsible young adult.

Come on then we'll be late. He winked when he delivered this line, she rolled her eyes, it was one of his 'jokes'.

Rosa lived with and between her parents in a fine balancing act. Sarah fed her with common sense, Paul fed her with books that didn't make sense. An unconventional family yet seen from another perspective this 'balance' reinforced the conventional division of gender relationships between sensible hard working mothers and wayward loveable fathers. The nuclear family always came at a price, usually paid by women.

On the bus into town Paul told Rosa about a new addition to the Happy Man fraternity, Jack, an American veteran of the war in Afghanistan in '07 on disability benefits.

Says he's now writing a thriller set in Kabul.

American? What's he doing living here?

He married somebody off the estate. She left him, he kept the flat.

Weird. What was he doing in London in the first place?

How would I know that, Rosa?

I'll ask him. From Afghanistan to Woodberry Down. Interesting.

Anyway, now he's writing a novel.

Paul emphasises an imagined slug line with his fingers quoting the cover blurb.

Drugs, forbidden love and the fight against the Taliban. The real story. Gonna make him a fortune he reckons. Proper character. He sinks a pint, goes out front for a ciggy, comes back sinks another, then another ciggy out front. Never appears drunk. Sits down, reads the paper. Always keeps his jacket on, always sits with his back to the wall eyeballing everyone who comes and goes. Jack in the box he is, wound up tight as a spring.

Sounds like a proper fascist dad. He could go postal at any minute.

Well, he might be a fascist, who knows, but he's black, so maybe not.

Paul Chuckles, Rosa frowns.

Interesting.

You could always see Rosa thinking.

I know what, I'll interview him for a project I'm doing at school about the people who live on our estate.

You can ask him! First thing he says when you talk to him is *I haven't got PTSD*.

Which is odd.

You will have to get past that.

Rosa's class were doing a project with the memory shop the council had opened on the estate. In the face of massive changes and development this was a sop to those who wanted things to stay the same or at least move more slowly. It was an attempt to co-opt opposition into the idea of change, a place for lived experiences to be turned into archived memory. People were literally being decanted elsewhere but uploaded right here; the stories of the people who lived on the estate were to be preserved for posterity.

A few days later Rosa turned up at the pub to meet Jack. She was so open, direct and sunny in her disposition that people felt comfortable in her company. She soon had Jack conspiring with her over drinks and between fag breaks, her phone recording everything during the consumption of half a pack of Marlboro lights, four pints of Pride, and three visits to the toilet.

We were out on a routine patrol, and then all this incoming, pinning us down behind a berm. Had been quiet for weeks so this kind of took us by surprise. So we radio for QRF.

What's that?

Quick reaction force. The cavalry if you like.

Rosa nods.

Anyway, the closest unit is a Brit Armour company. Fuck it the CO says why not, I remember our sarge shaking his head with the shame of not having the balls to fight our way out, him sitting there loaded with rounds and grenades and itching to unload, to fuckin' do it, but fuck him he had a death wish or something, the rest of us grunts backed the CO calling up the armour, anything that meant I didn't have to risk my shit and I guess everyone else agreed other than the sarge, so we calls them up. We sit and wait for their unit to show. Sit tight until the radio crackles, all the time under sporadic small arms fire. Something like a bus horn comes over the radio, like what the fuck is that? All type of strange shit happens out in the desert so comms calls them back to check their ETA, and now we were not just getting small arms incoming, these fuckers had RPG's and we didn't want to wait around to see if they brought up mortars and walked them in on our LOC. Does my language bother you? I'm sorry I get carried away.

No not at all, you should hear my dad, it's fine, carry on.

Jack hesitates but gets right back to it talking faster, as if being on pause for even a few seconds made him want to play catch up.

Ok Ok. So guess what now comes over the radio in reply from the red coats, that stupid song from six flags with the old dancing guy, you know the one. 'We like to party, we like to party party' full fucking blast these clowns are blaring out the Venga fucking boys but now the music is playing from the battlefield, I nearly pop my head up to see that, two armoured vehicles have turned up blaring 'Party bus' from jerry rigged speakers blasting the Venga boys whilst they laid down hate on the enemy. Thank fuck one PKM lets a belt loose and takes out one of the speakers, so now we get to hear it at half volume. The Brits hate that though, it fucking riles them so they let off a heat round into the MG pos, taking them out, drawing down mucho rocket fire in return. Instead of laying down smoke to shield themselves these guys fill the battlefield with Chem lights for fucks sake like a disco, hundreds of fucking glow sticks raining down on the enemy who fucking run away in confusion. Saved by the Venga boys, never saw a one of them neither, the Hajis got routed by the English boys who were probably brewing up a cup of tea in their fucking tanks.

So, how did you end up on the Woodberry Down estate?
That topic is off limits.

You like living here, in London?
Cops don't carry. I like that.

Paul and Rosa stood in front of a painting of the houses of parliament, bathed in the dark furnace orange of sinking sunlight reflected on the surface of the Thames and burnished by being refracted through the smog.

Paul took a bite out of an apple.

It's good that.

The smog protects the city from the heat of a burning sun in some future eco catastrophe.

You see that?
Why not?

When her teacher shares her students interviews with the memory museum they rejected two about local drug dealers (one who gave away free fruit when delivering weed) along with Rosa's interview with Jack Masters born 1980 in Bovina, Wisconsin. The rest were curated online.

That's not the sort of memory we are looking for said the Hackney council archivist.

Perhaps you should try the Imperial war museum.

RADICAL
CONTINGENCY

Paul channels *Lie dream of a casino soul*, head bopping as if he was listening on a pair of as yet to be invented earbuds, his memory (programmed with John Peel's festive fifty) as good as any future device. He's on his way to a lecture on Radical Contingency, his mind speeding spitting lyrics and attitude. His body deceptively shuffles into the back of the lecture room and folds itself onto a bench. He coughs discretely into a hanky, having for breakfast liberated three quid from the coffee and biscuits honesty plate in the Modern languages common room to buy tobacco. A trick he learnt from me, out of the corner of his eye. Paul has taken up his usual perch near as possible to the exit, nodding imperceptibly, to the professor already pacing up and down in front of the audience, chasing his thoughts whilst stroking his moustache.

Ernesto Laclau was from Buenos Airies, in his late forties, raffish, professorial, in threadbare brown woollen suit with worn leather elbows, his salt and pepper hair worn over the frayed collar of his check shirt. Traces of tobacco tinge his moustache yellow, which he fondles as a concentration fetish, a prompt for his thoughts, punctuating his stream of consciousness, his incisive dialogue mumbled from under his top lip. 'Take your hand away from your mouth when you're talking' is what my mum would have told him. He could have done with having sub titles.

An as yet unlit liquorice paper roll-up or occasionally a darker still cigarillo clasped in his fingers, Laclau prowls the rectangular space in front of the chairs. In front of him, but behind ontological bars, thirty mostly young faces look up with dewy eyes. His thick, soft consonants, to Anglo ears lisping and strong accent struggles to penetrate their inner ears. They hang on every word of his English in order to comprehend it, the difficulty of what he is trying to communicate being subject to this twofold amplification.

Laclau still keeps an old pipe in his jacket pocket, worrying it for comfort, sometimes tamping it into his palm, whist his eyes bulge behind the thick lenses of his glasses. A pipe, dark cigarettes, glasses, a head of hair constantly fussed, these were his props.

Between the logic of complete identity and that of pure difference, the experience of democracy should consist of the recognition of the multiplicity of social logics along with the necessity of their hegemonic articulation - an articulation which needs to be constantly re-created and renegotiated. If negativity is radical and the outcome of the struggle not predetermined, the contingency of the identity of the two antagonistic forces is also radical and the conditions of existence of both must themselves be contingent.

Paul scribbles, his mind racing forward. 'Contingency subverts necessity.' Shit happens. Not that this would bother a bookie. *Underlined.* You lay some bets off. Others you fly by the seat of your pants with, tilting at glory. *Struck through.* Necessity only partly limits the field of contingency. *Question mark.* That's usually enough. Chance is interior to the system of rationality. *Underlined.* Objectivity is made up of this inclusion. *Arrow to:* Heisenberg. You can only ever predict one of the two variables of proton behaviour at any one instant. Their reality is a blur, unpredictability built into their physicality; location or speed, never both at the same time. They are always moving so you posit them as a wave, which is their radical contingency. Paul doodles in the margins of his notebook, he shades them in wave after wave, right to left facing waves, aimed to crash on the shore at the crook of his left elbow. He smudges the thick traces of pencil lead with his thumb, creating a blur.

He zones out back to his cabin, train driving. Laclau catches Paul up, overtakes him.

On the one hand each difference expresses itself as difference; on the other hand each of them cancels itself out as such by entering into a relation of equivalence with all the other differences of the system. And, given that there is only system as long as there is radical exclusion, this split or ambivalence is constitutive of all systemic identity.

Snapping back into the moment, back into time. What the fuck does that mean? A radical ambivalence between equivalence and difference? The fuck am I doing here? Am I different, (like all the other differences, so basically the same) or am I radically excluded from any reckoning?

Bakhtin argues that there is no outside that everything is interior to carnival. Carnival being his notion of a disruptive discourse, an energy which shapes our reality overcoming thesis and antithesis, heaven and hell, good and bad. Carnival is how we flow in whatever we want to call 'The Real World.'

Laclau presses on, Paul rambles further behind, mumbling to himself this guitar kills fascists.

The precariousness of every equivalence demands that it be complemented/limited by the logic of autonomy. It is for this reason that the demand for equality is not sufficient, but needs to be balanced by the demands for liberty, which leads us to speak of a radical and plural democracy.

You got to crack all the eggs to make more than one omelette. Paul smiles to himself, he's conscious of his eyes blinking, blinks them some more, controlling his experience of time. He falls away, shears off into inky interiority. The lecture recedes, zooms out, until it becomes Universal Background Noise.

He is lighting Taff's fag before his last shift, the match flares and in doing so births a universe which lights up his face in the slow motion of eternity.

In fact if differences were related strictly by nothing, the result would be total segregation or equivalence, and by no means the complex web of relationships thematised under the label of hegemony. In Heidegger's vocabulary, which to be sure has to be employed cautiously.

Sniggers from the front row at this, boffins delight at any reference to the Heidegger debate.

Paul's long distance radar still picks this up from wherever he is.

Pogo on a Nazi, Spit upon a Jew, vicious mindless violence that offers nothing new.

Crass saw a radical equivalence of Left and Right to be sure. He didn't agree but they made a great racket.

Paul had grown up in a world where you took sides. More than that, you were born into a side. By taking sides you doubled down on your birthright. If you are not for us then you are against us. A practical sometimes brutal world built on this polarity. A world where the gulag was different from the death camp and political prisoners segregated from common criminals. The heroes and villains of the old country, patriots, traitors, Hun or Tim, workers or bosses, all of these oppositions made sense of the world wherever you went. Here, at University he was confronted by shifting sands of perspective, a fluidity of identity and a redefinition of agency.

Different elements in order to enjoy a relationship are linked to the level of 'being' a term denoting a non objective type of matrix in which positivity and negativity, ground and abyss are peculiarly intertwined.

Paul imagines pogoing on fucking Martin Heidegger.

If in Leninism there was a militarisation of politics, in Gramsci there is a demilitarisation of war, although the reformulation reached its limit in the assumption of an ultimate class core of every hegemony. Once the latter assumption is dropped, Gramsci's notion can be metaphorised further in a manner compatible with radical democracy.

Bobby Sands weaponised his body, escaping its prison and the body politic holding them both. Gramsci, writing secretly from prison, cocooned from and subject to the world at night. His body unlike that of Sands betraying him.

Paul imagines the demise of action, of agency in all of this theory, the seduction of words, the indulgences of tenure, all that's solid melts into air, no eggs ergo no omelettes.

Flash forward   Abdullah Ocalan, incarcerated leader of the Kurdish workers party (hereafter The PKK) pens the feminisation of Islam from his island prison of Imrali. The diary of Bobby Sands was translated into Kurdish, and quoted by James McClean, Irishman and Stoke City striker all in the year 2018, and if this isn't the laughter of our children...

'They have nothing in their whole imperial arsenal that can break the spirit of one Irishman who doesn't want to be broken.'

Bobby Sands.

The Fall were the cauldron, the subjective matrix of cause and effect in which everything was Kaputt yet everything made sense, a world view that energised Paul in the binary totality of his troubles.

'Good evening, we are the rip tide of integrity monkeys' flashes through his mind, this barbed obscurantist Mark E. Smith's opening salvo at a recent Fall gig. Students, local punks, different but the same, equivalent punters, neither group a Prole art threat.

Man with chip: I'm riding third class on a one-class train
I'm cranked at nought like a Wimpy crane.

The pleasure in words dripping off a sharp tongue, the cascade, the rap of it, the swagger, the rasp of it, as dense in places as this Laclau fella, but sexier, grimier. A class perspective that wasn't binary Smith invokes the pure crystal-clear experience of the street, of where he came from, his life in each moment of being lived.

'Non Binary Flux!' could have been one of his repetitions, with his voice rising up over the last vowel to smash the consonant, the letter X being important to him elsewhere.

How to harness polyphony?

Good vibrations...

Surely only Gods have no need of popularity? They don't win landslides they create them. They are the authors of their own destiny.

We will thus retain from the Gramscian view the logic of articulation and the political centrality of the frontier effects, but we will eliminate the assumption of a single political space as the necessary framework for those phenomena to arise.

Frontier effects. I hand't yet read much science fiction, which must have been what this alluded to; a layered, subtle universe of shifting affiliation and synchronicity, personal and political (dif)fusions, fluid gender, post gender machine / Biological identities, degrees of Artificial Intelligence and the resulting contingent allegiances, that were to resonate in the Iain M Banks culture novels that were coming down the pipe, subconsciously primed by the Ideology and Discourse analysis Masters Degree run by Ernesto Laclau.

This wormhole exists! Explore it! Liberate this text from the monologging influence of the author! (Which is not the named 'author' of copyright but the matrix combine which lurks behind every word, into which 'the author' has always already been inscribed.

Paul standing with his back to the wall in the Andromeda night club.

Watching.

Students, squaddies and locals eyeball each other, seething with hatred to the beats of 'Maneater', 'Pass the Dutchie' and 'Forget me Nots'. An unlikely combat medley as you could imagine. Female locals thread themselves through the eye of all this needle. When it did go off, with the expansive, exquisite inevitability of the end point, the rightness, the completion fetish of reaching this pre-ordained climax set in motion earlier in the evening when you pulled on a relatively clean pair of pants, (the butterfly effect of this action) Paul potted a couple of squaddies from the shadows, sending them sprawling from outside the roving circles/ deranged dance floor patrolling of mirror ball reflections and strobe lights, his arm and bottle hand flashing down from the inky darkness off stage. Fag drooping from his bottom lip, glued there as only roll ups can be, smiling eyes, amused at this intervention, his being in their time. And the rightness of it, the godliness of participation. And always the donkey jacket, skinny enough that he wore it like a shirt so nobody ever mentioned its ever presence, so much like his skin was it, this yet to be broken Irishman.

To assert, as we have, the constitutive nature of antagonism does not therefore mean referring all objectivity back to a negativity that would replace the metaphysics of presence in its role as an absolute ground, since that negativity is only conceivable within such a framework. What it does mean is asserting that the moment of undecidability between the contingent and the necessary is constitutive and thus that antagonism is too.

The match un-strikes itself and Taffs face disappears for a millisecond into blackness,(the absence of so much unexpected light from the match head.) The iris of Pauls eye not quick enough to dilate, to compensate, to let more light in, to see Taffs face, and in that millisecond time stops, holding the light in like a breath, like a drag on a fag. Pitch black and counting...

Sunday Morning, nursing a hangover and a sore hand with a four pack of Breaker on the beach at Jaywick. October. Freezing cold. You finally manage to light a ciggy for the wind to smoke it. Tears streak down your face. Backed by mobile homes and 'vans on cinder blocks as if somebody had stolen them. Paul and Mad Mike sit and watch the waves, one of them twitching from the speed still in his body, the other hands full of cuts and fresh swellings, numbed by strong lager, his tremor calmed, his face as blank as it ever gets.

They watch a man digging for worms, his spade and fork melting into the wet sand, turning over black oil tar stains, the odd crab and lugs by the handful. He fills his bucket, sifting through his catch, chucking back small and severed worms.

Cunt. mutters Paul.

Yes, yes. Fucking worm. Chatters Mad Mike.

They laugh like drains. The fisherman walks past them, laughs tamped down to insolent sniggers.

Wankers.

Paul releases his breath hard, looks up from his notebook. Laclau was still talking, stringing along his sentences with seemingly endless soft, mesmerising, lisp like consonants. He finds it hard to focus enough to be a spectator...

For, if something were mere, unchallenged actuality, no ontological difference would be possible; the ontic and the ontological would exactly overlap and we would simply have pure presence. In that case, Being would only be accessible as that which is the most universal of all predicates, as that which is beyond all all differentia specifica. And that would mean it would not be accessible at all. But if nothingness were there as an actual possibility, any being which presents itself would also be, to its very roots, mere possibility, and would show, beyond its ontic specificity, Being as such. Possibility, as opposite to pure presence, temporalises Being and splits, from its very ground, all identity.

Laclau checks his watch, it's 12.47 pm, time to wind up, a psychoanalysts hour. He coughs.

Next week a visiting colleague from the University of Llubjana, Slavoi Zizek will explore the Hegelian roots of radical contingency and its implications for Marxist theory. See you all then.

A muttering of surprise from the front row disciples, muttering the name of this guest speaker, passing it back and forth amongst themselves like a hot potato, the amplification of a name thereby increasing its valency. Especially such an exotic one, a name with two Z's in it. They jostle round Ernesto eager for intimate exchanges, to be recognised by him in a personal capacity. To his credit Laclau is rather more interested in lunch than the adoration of teenagers, his pipe dowsing a path through the crowd to the door.

PARROTS AND BUDGERIGARS

In November Paul got another postcard from Bob Crow. On the front was a picture of Fidel Castro with 'Cuba Si!' printed across the bottom. On the back Bob filled him in on the new rostering agreements they had negotiated and his thoughts on the unemployment figures (*14 million mate, its not sustainable, we got to bring these bastards to their knees!*) He also wanted to know the name of a Scott Walker album they had listened to before Paul had left for Uni. Scribbled at the bottom, overspilling the designated writing space, he added that Sally who worked in the canteen was asking after him.

You can't fit much on the back of a postcard. Paul had no idea who Sally was or what she could be asking after. The Scott Walker record he referred to was a Julian Cope compilation. '*Fire escape in the sky: The godlike genius of Scott Walker.*' Paul loved the Teardrops but he hated compilations not least because they fucked up an artist's discography.

I love going to gigs, I love listening to records. Two different things. Live albums are shit versions of both experiences.

He would say.

Worse than that were the extra tracks that sometimes appeared on Japanese releases, it drove him fucking mad.

Don't get me started.

Bootlegs were an exception on political grounds. He liked them, just as he did mix tapes.

Bob had sung 'It's raining today' at last year's Christmas do. He murdered it, getting as far as the first chorus before he gave up, stumbling off stage to quench his thirst, cursing the stupid song and not his shit voice.

Paul wrote back.

He didn't mention what he was doing at university and Bob hadn't asked. Even on a postcard the centre of gravity was still up in London.

Fuck that compilation, get hold of Scott 2 and 3.

He ran out of things to say signing off

Who the fuck is Sally?

The glossy picture on the front of his card was of a Robin which was all he could find in the campus shop. He dropped it in the post box on Quad three.

He needed to get off campus, walk into town, get something to eat, get a haircut, go to a record shop, do something normal. The things he did at home before coming here.

He smoked a fag at the bus stop on Boundary road. It was a two and a half fag walk to be fair but he couldn't be arsed, it was about to rain.

He found a caff just round the corner from the Minories Arts centre. He put his tobacco pouch and lighter on the red Formica table and ordered a cup of tea, eggs, bacon, mushrooms and tomatoes, two slices. He took out a book of poetry from his jacket pocket and read whilst swirling the teabag around the mug with the spoon.

'That night was to decide
   if she and I
   were to be lovers.'

Paul squeezes the teabag against the inside of the mug with a spoon and removes it to the saucer. He takes a gulp, puts the book down and stares out of the window. His eye can't help but follow the rivulets of rain as they work their way down.

When the food arrives he eats it quickly, mind blank, then picks up the book again, half reads, scans the words, until the punchline.

'Passion's a precipice –   so won't you please move away?   Move away,   please!'

Paul pays and comes outside. The rain has stopped. He goes into a newsagent and on a whim buys twenty Bensons. After a number one flat top at Rodney's on Church Walk Paul lopes into Parrot records feeling fresh.

Rifling through the seconds bin, he picks out a white label of the Jimmy Castor Bunch single 'It's just Begun.' He takes it up to the counter.

Give it a spin for ya? Wheezes Martin the owner.

Paul shrugs, he just wanted to buy it but couldn't be bothered to say so. He didn't want to have to listen to a record in front of other people who would expect him to say something or make the right gesture, head nod, smile, whatever. It was awkward. Sometimes the song and dance of buying records got on his tits. Martin places the record on the turntable. A big brass sound fills the small room, announcing itself just as a young black woman comes into the shop as the drum and bass kick in. A punk with jet black spiky punk hair.

She immediately responds to the music, her feet, legs and head caught up in the rhythm. Paul's head nods imperceptibly as he studies the sleeve. The woman approaches the counter.

The three of them listen to the rest of the track in silence. Martin takes it off the turntable, sleeves it and hands it back to Paul.

What a tune.

Yeah I'll take it.

What is it? The young woman asks.

Paul shows her the record.

It's a boot, a bootleg, off a reissue I think, look he's scratched his name in the run out, see? 'The kid' was his handle kind of... I collect them. People who love the music so much they make it their own, put it out in small numbers, ends up selling for more than the originals. What it's all about really. There's not much money in it for them, just enough to keep them doing it.

I mean the song, who is it?

Oh sorry. Sometimes the music. It, distracts me. Here.

He passes her the cover.

Jimmy Castor Bunch. Never heard of them. Good though.

She stares at him.

You a student?

Sort of, you?

Fuck off.

Paul smiles back.

'Sort of', what does that mean? She asks.

It's a long story. You come up for gigs?

Sometimes yeah, you get some good bands, and cheap drinks.

Yeah, true that.

He hands Martin the money.

Thanks, keep an eye out for more of those.

Sure thing, cheers.

She eyes him up and down.

Somehow you don't look like a student.

Paul shrugs.

You smoke?

What's your name?

Sorry, It's Paul, nice to meet you.

Paul the maybe student. I'm Sarah.

Sarah the adamant townie.

She bows. They both smile, connect somehow.

He bites off the cellophane from the new packet of bennies, pulls the silver paper away from the tightly packed bank of filters and offers her one. Her black lacquered finger nails delicately draw a cigarette.

I have to use my teeth to get the first one out. He flashes her his bitten down nails.

Sarah's face is like 'urgh'.

Classy.

Usually smoke roll ups anyway.

Right.

Not in here folks, I got asthma.

Paul nods at Martin as they step outside to light up. It's cold and they both stamp their feet, smoking in silence.

Back on campus Gary Finch had just punched somebody out during his audition to play Tybalt in a production of Romeo and Juliet.

He came at me with the sword, what you expect me to do?

The director is speechless.

He's a fucking nutter! screams 'Mercutio' from the floor nursing a bloody nose. Gary looms over him snarling.

Get up you wanker.

The director has had enough.

Gary, it's a play, you are meant to be pretending. The swords are a prop. For god's sake.

This deflates Gary, momentarily. He glances over at his budgie Eagle shuffling sideways back and forth on his perch and fluttering his wings in agitation.

I knew that, that's why I punched the cunt. You want it to be real yeah?

The others shake their heads in disgust. Gary's head swivels about, re-assessing the situation.

So, I got the part or what?

Paul bumps into Gary back on campus. Gary is wired, his jaw working, muscles tense, unconsciously stroking Eagle who is as always perched on his right shoulder.

You alright Gary?

Yeah, fuming, didn't get that part in the play, middle-class wankers.

What part? You want to act?

Yeah why not?

Paul shrugs.

Didn't want him on my shoulder did they, I thought it would be authentic right, something different, Romeo and Juliet is old hat, bit of a snooze. Only trying to help, what do all the luvvies say, 'bringing something to the role? So Eagle had to sit there on his little perch, poor bleeder, look.

He pulls out what looks like a small wooden stick on a stand, Eagles perch.

Paul chortles. Their loss mate.

Got a fag? Gary shuffles about on the spot.

Paul shakes the pack in his pocket.

Yeah.

Bennies. Posh!

Gary pops the fag behind his ear. Flashes Paul an ear-to-ear grin. Paul thinks fuck me he looks like Tommy Steele, as he does every time he sees him.

Cunts. Gary mutters and with that he is off, his gait more of a bowl as he's a short man with bowed legs.

Paul finishes his fag, glances into the empty packet, the last of the Bensons and crushes it thinking about Sarah. Her mum was from Grenada, her dad a squaddie. 'Everybody asks me' she said.

I hadn't. Must get a lot of stick for that. She was nice. Bold as you like. Be good to see her again, should have said something.

GOD BLESS US EVERY ONE

Sarah's father was a military policeman, a redcap. A copper and a squaddie. *Shame guy*. He swanned about regardless, king of shit mountain in a racist, backwater town.

A mixed-race girl in late 1970's Colchester, Sarah walked about with a target on her back, despite and because of who her dad was. Because of what she was. In the early 80's *what* had *who* on the ropes. Colchester had always been an army town and was full of military police because of its glasshouse. The only Military prison in Britain, all the bad apples were kept in this barrel and their families came to visit or to live nearby. More bad apples. Her mum warned her not to visit Dad at work.

So I'm an embarrassment now, we are an embarrassment?

With a haircut like that? No dear, not an embarrassment at all. And the rags you wear?

Listen to yourself mum.

Her mother pointed a dripping wet finger (she was doing the washing up).

You listen. You are a black girl in a white town, never forget it.

In a different town would I be a white girl in a black one?

What nonsense you talk, girl.

Flicking suds at her breaks the tension.

Mum!

They both laugh.

They lived in a nondescript 1970's box house. Thin walls. Her mum and dad probably only had sex when she was out. Thank God. On her bedroom wall she pinned a photo of Maurice Bishop, the revolutionary Prime Minister of Grenada. She had never been to the island where her mother was born. She had never been anywhere.

Don't let your father see that, the man's a communist you see?

She wanted out, but didn't yet know how to get out.

Forever forward! Backward never!

Bishop spoke to her through the walls of this temporary home.

She remembers bouncing on Uncle Jerome's knee when she was little, big bounces because he was tall with long skinny legs. He was a soldier and loped down the street. 'A spade around town' was what jealous white people called him. He had a flash car too, an old red Jag with leather seats, his pride and joy no matter how many times he got stopped in it. He was her mum's older brother, whom she idolised, because he looked every man and woman in the eye. It was through Jerome she had met Sarah's dad; they had served together. The idea her dad had black friends back then blew Sarah's mind, because he didn't have any now. Perhaps she was being unfair. Perhaps.

After a second tour in Northern Ireland 'If you touch my hair again I swear I will fuck you up' uncle Jerome left the army and became a bodyguard, escort to the rich and famous. A big man up West, in all the clubs, Annabel's, the Astor, with all the Lords, Viscount Linley, Princess Diana, the colourful scene up there, Chelsea, Mayfair, Kensington. He 'took care of' Andre Previn and his new wife Mia Farrow whenever they visited London. Lunch at Del' Aretusia on the King's Road, tab picked up by clients who desired a little colour as well as the connections. Oysters and champagne. Cocaine. Tramps, Regines, where on-the-make Britain collided with an international Jet set of celebrities and the harder up members of the right families, Princess Grace of Monaco, Peter Sellers, Ringo Star, Warhol, Rod Stewart and all the James Bonds adding their names to a new constellation.

He had a flat on the Lancaster West estate, Grenfell walk, right by the 'Moroccan tower' that had just been completed. Great food, night life, the best Hash all on his doorstep, right there, he took all sorts back to it.

Sarah hadn't seen him for years, all the moving around they did. Before Colchester they had been in Akrotiri. Same type of house but with a small pool. She had loved it. When she asked her mum why they hadn't seen Uncle Jerome she said he was busy, away somewhere, in America, but her eyes told another story. Three years in Colchester and still they had no visits from the family. Something had gone on, Sarah wasn't stupid. Families were stupid.

In the autumn the American marines invaded Grenada, Maurice Bishop was assassinated and Sarah didn't talk to her dad for about six weeks.

Forever forward backward never.

Nobody understood her she understood nobody and was drawn to people like her, like that, the misunderstood. Like the odd, quiet fella Paul she met in Parrots with the disgusting finger nails. Sarah played her mums records, lover's rock mostly and heard in it the same sexist shit she heard walking down the high street, the whistles, the suggestions, the cat calling. Men were all the same colour, most men. Feel you up, touch you for money, knock you up and then disappear, if you were lucky.

Life turned her into a punk, it was natural selection, survival of the fuck offish.

The Colchester scene was small, incestuous. Bands swapped members like partners, everybody hung out at the Affair club, punks, Goths, New Romantics, and casuals, there were even some old Teds there from whenever. Whatever your style there was just one scene, which is probably a good definition of being 'provincial'. Same down the Colne Lodge, another legendary venue which catered for everyone under one roof. Rugby types and students bar on the left downstairs, trends upstairs, (Choc and Gilly on the decks), bikers downstairs on the right. Small town economics put everyone in close proximity, all chugging cheap Swan lager until things got feisty.

'No leather jackets' signs up outside the cocktail lounge, two quid on the door for DJ nights at the Cups and three quid to see Hanoi Rocks at Woods Leisure centre, or a free art exhibition up at the Minories.

The United colours of Colchester.

Sarah's friend Arnie crimped his hair and played bass in a local punk band called Fear of Sex. They were pretty shit but they had got a gig up at the University before Christmas. He also had never tried to get off with her, which is why they were still friends. Fear of Sex had a Thalidomide drummer. Punk shock! So that an attraction, got people talking, jeering, pointing, seeing him smashing the skins from his shoulders.

Paul might be there. He talked like a Londoner, probably was one too. She wouldn't mind seeing him again. She liked going up to the University, it was a different space and there were other people like her, young black students from all over the world. (But not many of them ever went to gigs in the student union dancehall, they weren't kids looking for cheap thrills, they weren't nihilist teenagers, they were serious revolutionaries or hard-working science types, chemists from Malaysia wearing hijabs, biologists from Uttar Pradesh, hydrology post graduates from Somalia, sociology department revolutionaries from Angola. Why would they be interested in her, Sarah, an angry half pint of mixed up and mixed-race townie trouble?

Fear of Sex were supporting Modern English (previously 'The Lepers'), local new wave heroes. 'The Colchester band that made it.' In years to come half the town would say they loved Modern English, the other half hated them. That is two halves that made up a small whole of people who gave a fuck about music that is.

Sarah had once snogged the lead singer at an after-gig party. He liked himself that's for sure. Dyed his hair black, had his hand on her arse after about a minute, fingers probing before she prised them away. 'I melt with you' was their big hit. Yeah right, tosser. Everyone on the scene wanted to snog her and worse, she was exotic. If anyone got too handy she just told them who her dad was. Only thing he was useful for. They ran a mile. At least Bobbie from Modern English had a plan, a way out of town. People said they were off on a tour to Japan in the new year, now that was *somewhere else*.

Sarah felt anxiety building inside her, every day she fought a little harder to contain it, she felt bloated by it, but it also held the promise of what would come after it broke, she was pregnant with the future. Something was happening, a new country was being born inside her. She longed for recognition, to be able to host delegates, receive Embassies, hold banquets; they would all come to celebrate her independence, her sovereignty. To enter into alignment, to treaty with Russians, be in league with Cubans, Angolans, Palestinians, Grenadians, the island of which she was a contested satellite. She wanted to embrace the pan Africans; Egypt, Libya, Kenya, Ghana, Algeria, Nigeria with open arms. She was part of this International, as head of her own state, she was regal, presidential and revolutionary, but this was classified information, nobody knew, she was a sleeper cell of one, top secret.

On the bus up to the Uni it felt quite Christmassy. Sarah and her friends drank cans of special brew, smoked fags, finger painted condensation on the windows; xmas trees, stars, cocks and tits, whilst outside red smears of cars and bikes streaked past in the rain.

Sarah rummages around in her bag for her hairspray, twisting up her black spider spikes, fixing them in place, wet sticky spray cold drying on her neck.

Fuck me, not on the bus Sarah, it's like a fucking gas chamber in here. coughs Arnie. She pointed the spray at him, he dove for cover. They were both a bit pissed. The bus driver rang his bell to warn them to stop fucking about.

Sarah got her lighter out a lit the nozzle. Flames leapt down the aisle.

Happy Christmas Arnie!

Arnie and Sarah leapt down the stairs and ran off the bus chased by the drivers threats to call the police.

You nutter! gasped Arnie. They fall about laughing.

In the foyer of the Students Union bar Paul has trouble hearing his mum on the other end of the pay phone. He cradles the receiver, awkwardly hunches over it, his free hand frantically rummaging in his pockets for more change.

...Yes I'll be home next week, end of the week, yes, for Christmas, of course mum. Sorry I didn't get a letter no, the post here is, what's that mum? Len, yes my friend Len. What? Dead? Oh dear, well that's sad but not unexpected with his chest an' all.

Paul feeds the phone.

Does it say anything about a funeral?...Mum? A funeral?... Last week? Well, looks like I missed that. The lines terrible... Not your fault mum, letter from you must have got lost. What's that? The flu? You're seeing a lot of it on the wards? I'm wrapped up well, bitter cold it is yes, for those poor bastards out of work mum, worse off than us. What? It doesn't matter...Christmas? Yes, well, I'll see you both then...I will write to his family, yes, did they give you an address? Good. Don't you worry, I better go, yes, am keeping up to date with my studies, goodnight mum, love to Marion...

Paul smashes the receiver against the wall.

Poxy fucking phone.

Nobody notices and he leaves what's left of it hanging from the frayed lead.

Len was dead, no surprise there, to either of them. He hadn't thought about him since leaving but now his voice came flooding back.

After defeating Rommel (his words) *I took a piss in the Nile*. Len's division, (1st Infantry) later landed in Anzio.

'...*too many Scottish bastards for my liking. Well not for long, Jerry soon took care of that*.

Len McClintock. Paul smiled. Hard man and arsehole.

The chorus of Our House by Madness blared from the bar and the bustle of people coming in for an early evening drink floods the focus he had to sustain for the phone, the crackly line and the voice on the other end.

Time for a drink or two.

A handwritten banner hung limply over the door to the Student Union bar. 'Vote Cushman for Information officer.'

Paul heads inside nodding to Klaus the German bouncer.

Paul noticed a group of townies on his way to get served. The usual mohicans, trench coats, drinking snakebites and black at working men's club prices. The girl from the record shop was with them, small, but with big hair. Sarah. He smiled as he went passed. She smiled back. One of her friends said something funny, probably about him, about him looking at her, *what's he laughing at?* the cunt had crimped hair for fucks sake.

Paul orders a double scotch to chase his pint. Sinks it. *Night night Len* and scans the room from the bar. The place was filling up. Paul was filling up, another double shot and he felt better, bought two more pints of lager and loped across to the table where we were sitting.

Rozzer, Graeme, Dominic, Ashika, Rachel and Wendy were all dolled up for a night out. It didn't matter what band was playing, what music, we had nowhere else to go in our first year, so the dancehall was it. You could look like George Michael, Boy George, Johnny Rotten or Dexys

Midnight Runners surrounded by an old guard of Goths, Teds, Rockabillies or sports casuals all Benetton pegs and roll necks. A fight could break out at any time. Clothes, attitude, make up, social class, tribal allegiance, (in) ability to dance, inferred political opinions, so many reasons to take offence but also throwing up a unique frisson, a charged atmosphere that usually ended up being channeled sexually. Being young was a minefield.

I eyeball Paul and shuffle up. The others nod, they don't really know him as I'm the only one who shares lectures with him.

Alright? Going downstairs?

Yeah, should be alright. You coming?

Paul checks the flyer.

Modern English. Supported by Fear of Sex.

We both smile and drink, share fags, poxy cheap Red Bands that made you hawk like a bastard the next morning, but we had a whole night ahead of us. The noise levels rose as we approach last orders. Queues at the bar were six deep. Talking was pointless so we continued to scan the room, looking for girls, possible trouble, other people we knew. We surveyed the scene.

By Christmas of the first term there was already a sense of political side taking between the left and the left and the left and the right, and possibly the right and the further right, demarcated by simmering hostility and potential violence. Even in the imaginary world of university, the real was present, even if only because in its absence we invoked it. The street, the workplace, the home, in which class, gender race and other antagonisms manifested themselves, were refracted back onto campus. Fascist cunt, Tory scum, Male pig, lesbian slag, commie wanker, middle class cunt, poxy toff, Trotskyite filth, working class scum, IRA murderer.

Ho ho ho.

The enemy had its own camp up in the 'Top bar' situated above another quad. The apolitical drank here, (most of the student body was apolitical, some of them even ventured into the student union bar) people who play sports and do their homework and laundry on time. Civilians caught in ersatz crossfire, unaware of the war. A tougher demographic were the working class sports loving casuals with traditional Labour views on women, national identity and middle-class poofters, who would watch the football, darts and sing their national anthem.

You think I'm making this *eco system* up? This was Thatcher's Britain. Think again.

Last orders and the bar pours itself into the dancehall. Klaus leans in to one of the townie punks.

Excuse me.

He whispers quietly pinching a swastika pin badge from the lapel of his jacket. The punk eyeballs the lino on his way out, Klaus hardly missing a beat as he sweeps the floor.

As they funnel down the stairs Paul finds himself next to Sarah, we catch...

Why you look so sad earlier? Didn't even stop to say hello.

Sorry. Wanna drink?

She nods. He passes her a can. She pops the ring pull.

Mate of mine died, I just found out.

Gulping the fizzed up top of the beer and hiding her (slight) embarrassment behind the can.

Sorry about that. Was he old?

Paul enjoys this, the beer frothing all over her jeans.

Old enough. Was in the war.

Not a surprise then.

Nope. He was a twitcher.

A what?

A bird watcher.

You taking the piss?

Paul smiles. And a proper cunt to be honest.

She smiles back, finally relaxing. She notices his mirth.

She gives him a kiss, a big beer wet peck on the cheek which he sheepishly wipes off.

Bastard. Still sad though, to lose someone.

Paul nods.

Missed the funeral.

What was his name?

Len.

Sarah offers up what's left of her beer.

Well then, here's to Len.

Paul chugs what's left of his can.

'Wanna another one?

Despite his best subconscious efforts to put her off with the Len is dead conversation, Sarah is in the mood, she likes this strange kind of sad but funny geezer. Like a shit Fear of Sex track, the thought of death turns some people on. Paul had no idea. Really he didn't.

RECLAIM THE BEATS

When she says all men are rapists she doesn't mean all men are rapists.

Paul's finger index finger stabs the cover of a book on the table.

Dad, I can't talk to you about this.

Come on Paul, this is ridiculous. Sarah despairs.

What, we're talking about Andrea Dworkin, one of the greatest feminists of all bloody time.

You're talking. I don't want to talk about Andrea Dworkin at Sunday lunch.

It's not a contest, feminists aren't football players, and you do not get to say that anyway, that's the fucking point dad. I've never heard of Andrea fucking Dworkin does that make me a bad woman, a shit feminist?

Don't be ridiculous. What?

Paul looks at Sarah who gives him that shut the fuck up for once why don't you look.

Just read the bloody book. You might just...Paul pushes the book towards his daughter.

Fuck off dad! screams Rosa.

Enough! Can we just have a family Sunday lunch for once without all the drama! Sarah screams and Paul and Rosa shut up.

Eat up people, nobody has touched a bloody thing.

She pours them all wine, serves them all more food, even though their plates are mostly untouched.

Sunday bloody Sunday. Paul hums. Sarah smiles despite herself and Rosa scowls into her phone after taking a big slug of wine, the situation defused for now.

Bono? For fucks sake Paul. Sarah laughs.

He shrugs his shoulders. What? Their first album *Boy* was a great debut.

Great debut. She mouths back.

Paul ignores her.

Very Catholic. They lost God and made a pile of shite if you ask me.

Rosa looks back up. What you on about?

Rosa was in sixth form but didn't know if she wanted to go to University or not. What was the point? So much suffering in the world, so much violence. Her mum hadn't gone to Uni and she was a midwife, something useful. Her dad, well, he never used what he had learnt, that's what mum shouted at him when she was angry with him. Which was a lot and getting worse. But Rosa could sense the affection that filled the gaps between these outbursts, the silences and periods of just rubbing along together. She was in the middle of it, the love and the resentment, fragile youth in the middle of their middle age. Life could be pretty shit, even for those lucky enough to have one, to have a home, somewhere safe to sleep, food and an education. Somewhere, in all of this, Rosa searched for the ingredients of her own life, her few friends asked the same questions, it was what they had in common; what do I like? What makes me happy? What makes me angry? What are my responsibilities? Sex had yet to play any major part in this so her sense of being a woman was of course biological but also speculative, she saw her allegiances in books, in struggle, in the struggle against female genital mutilation for example. They went on matches, organised fund raising and awareness at school and in the community but this was her empathy and her political awakening and not yet anything truly experienced. There was a remove from the circumstances of her own life to that of the lives of other women that she tried to bridge emotionally with fiction. Rosa read and read and read out the distance between herself and the world, closing out the parallax of their lives, towards the singularity of being a woman, a feminist, a human unit.

This expressed itself in class, at school, her English teacher, Miss Banford, the first person, the first woman she knew who took her seriously because of what she said, not who she was. A public space that didn't come with the emotional baggage of family, the claustrophobia of her own small room, her computer screen and the anonymous world of her phone. But you had to be brave nonetheless, a room full of your peers was a tightrope to be walked...

Rosa shook, her cheeks hot with shyness but also anger, as she channelled the rhythm and cadence of the words in her hands. Sweaty hands gripping her crumpled notes. The rest of the class sat silently, the teacher also, you could hear a pin drop between the words.

I want, I say, I want to be treated a certain way, I say, I want I say to be treated like a human being I say and he weeping my name and says please, begging me in the silence not to say another word because his heart is tearing open, please he says calling my name.

She uses poetry, the rhythm of her words to express emotion. How difficult it is to stand up for yourself under the weight of this power relationship. A weight that oppresses the tongue, physically, like a stutter. A war is going on by proxy. These are words thrown into the fray, into battle the unspoken power of the male, which then speaks, mocking her.

I want I say to be treated I say, I want I say to be treated with respect, I say, I have a right I say, to do what I want to do I say, because I say I am smart, and I have written and I am good, and I do good work and I am a good writer and I have published..

To be assertive, to dare to claim anything for yourself as a woman in this or any situation. The repetition here is a self-pleading, she needs to big herself up, get pumped up in order to resist... (through words, as building blocks, one on top of another, the same ones, then adding another as if her claims are outrageous, which in the situation of this man, this teacher wanting to have sex with her, and them being at a party or wherever it is he has cornered her, are even more outrageous as if her claim to an identity other than wanting to be fucked by him is an affront to his sexual needs...

...and I want I say, to be treated I say like someone I say, like a human being, I say, who has done something, I say, like that I say, not like a whore, not like a whore I say. Not anymore, and I say to him seriously, someday I will die from this, just from this, just from being treated like a whore, nothing else, I will die from it. And he says drily and with a certain self-evident truth on his side, you will probably die from pneumonia, actually.

We know, Andrea knows, there is nothing wrong with being a whore, but what is wrong is how men like him, men like all men are brought up in the ways of treating women as whores, of how to treat whores. How prostitution is a danger to women, and not just young writers who have to fend off their male teachers, who have to pander to them, let them feel you up. Now sex workers organise and are respected in the right circles and its almost as if they can put in wage claims, again in certain circles, but in the world of men and not just men who pay women for sex, it can still be a way of degrading women, of exploiting them as sex objects, its not that Andrea has a problem with whores as such. She says it how it is, 'I am a feminist. Just not a fun one.' as a deadly serious joke.

Men will kill women. I might be in a room with those men, or on a bus with them, many of them are in the same family. Men cut up women's genitals and say it is cultural, it is part of who they are. How the fuck! Andrea knows how silky tongued men can be, how they have to be to cover up all of this violence and hate. She gives the most fluid line to the man, the most humorous, the most conventional payoff to a story line to a man because they have always owned that space, in fiction, in life. It's a funny put down. That's how hateful we can be to each other. We can look down on this woman who stutters, who has to almost beg for her own life. She will she says, die from being a whore.

The class sits awkwardly still. Rosa coughs and sits down wiping her hands on her jeans, she irrationally thinks she wants to apologise or undercut herself but doesn't. She could say that her dad wanted her to read Andrea Dworkin and that's kind of ironic, something like that to lighten the room, to make it fun, to be a funny person, but she somehow manages to bite down on that, to stay silent, as if she hasn't spoken enough, her breathing playing catch up, her heart still a little crazy. The teacher smiles. The boys in the room try and make light of it with movement, rustling bags, putting things away, but they all know something has gone down and that this class on feminist writers of the 20th century has gone down.

And I am wary of having a boyfriend, wary of starting a game neither of us control, of gambling on any man to be a good one, although most of the boys I know are funny and kind I'm scared that something out there in the world will change them the moment I trigger their interest.

HARMOLODICS Nº 2

Paul was older than us, but it wasn't just his age. He looked and behaved like he could have stepped out of any decade of the century whereas my generation were purely ephemeral, although we must appear otherwise now, sub-cultural remnants trapped in the treacle of slow time.

He had an old head? What does that me. An ancient soul? Don't be silly. Somebody who doesn't wear his heart on his sleeve. A cliche. A timeless reserve. Closer.

Paul dodged being pinned to the present tense, which was mysterious, but this charisma came with a price. He never (as far as I knew/as far as I know) felt the liberation of giving yourself up to the moment. To live life intensely for its own sake and then move on, left with just the sensation of memory, which was nearly enough to sustain me in the years to come. Ephemeral moments, the montage of life, the atonal beats more data than story; a taste, a smile, a soft breast, a hard nipple, an aching cock, the cold cold sea, a cigarette burn, the nutty smell of a vagina, the salt lick of an arsehole, your heart pounding in your chest, lungs gasping for air after being winded in a scuffle, laughing until it hurts, salty tears and a blush of shame, an ice cold pint, coming up on an E, the sharp mineralogy of a great wine. Sensation without context, the story boiled away leaving just sense memory.

Free Jazz.

The small part of me that wanted to analyse, to understand and change the world took up much more of Paul. Perhaps this was to become his sadness, which seemed sage and mysterious at the time. Because to lose that, to lose the fight and be left with nothing other than bitterness and regret. To give yourself to the moment is the only way to be a part of eternity. To be strictly political was to be squeezed in a vice between past and future with little wriggle room. The now was pure hedonism, the rush of drugs, of alcohol, of self-harm, of sex, of live music and throwing punches and bottles, the rush of adrenalin.

Political action had to aspire to spectacle, the situationist thrill of tumbling down Odessa steps, storming the winter palace, wheeling in the saddle of a steppe pony at the vanguard of Budyonny's Red cavalry.

Charge!

There is only a sequence of nows which immediately become, as part of their own event horizon, a parallel sequence of thens and always beyond us the great unknown, an infinite landscape of not nows and not thens, teeming with tantalising maybe nevers. This is montage. There is only always the now in which you are reading this, living in precarious tandem with the now in which I write it.

This is montage.

Across the two sparks the eternal arc of life.

We are ever present text.

SKETCHES OF SPAIN

> '(The Real is) the essential object which is not an object any longer, but this something faced with which all words cease and all categories fail, the object of anxiety par excellence.'
> **Jaques Lacan**

January 1984.

After Christmas it was fucking cold so me and my friend Paul Evans, who we called Evansio, bunked off Uni and spent our grant cheques on a cheap holiday in sunny Spain. There were a lot of Pauls at uni. Tall Paul was called Vulture (mostly behind his back) and was also referred to as London Paul. As far as I can remember he never used nicknames. In fact I don't remember him ever calling me by name at all.

Tall Paul wasn't the sort of person you would go on holiday with whatever your name was. At a stretch I can picture him with rolled up trousers and a hanky on his head, getting burned, book in hand, unlit fag lolling from his gob on some pebbly British beach scanning for shade or a pint from under those hooded eyes. Flash forward to the last holiday shots of his mate Bob Crow on the beach in Rio like Ray Winstone sunning himself on the poster for *Sexy Beast* sporting budgie smugglers, a British man for all seasons;

tanned, hairy, hot and sweaty, living it large, pot bellied and dying in his council house despite earning 145k plus perks.

I was born in a council house. As far as I'm concerned I will die in one.

God forbid the working class could have enough disposable income for holidays like that eh.

My body never burns because I am a Greek God.

What do you want me to do? Sit under a tree and read Karl Marx every day?

Fond fair wells, Bob's fuck yous.

Me and my Paul found ourselves in Fuengirola.

Once upon a time this place had been exotic. When time still cast its shadow forward. We still lived in the shadow of a century that still had a few surprises up its sleeve. Late reprisals of its major themes, fugues descending.

The road to Fuengirola.

Once people with old rusty or no guns at all fled here on foot, pursued by other people with shiny new guns, driving tanks and flying planes. This became known amongst those who were on the side of the people without guns, as the 'caravan of the dead'. Bad time, the time most people do well to avoid, flowed through this place like a flash flood of biblical proportions.

Let the good times roll.

In the early '80's time share was all the rage and young Brits were recruited from up and down the beaches and bars of the Costas to sell paradise in chunks of two weeks a year minimum leases to their peers. A share of time, accessible to the relatively shallow pockets of the working class for the first time. Finally, their place in the sun. Clip board surveys at the airport were the sites of the first skirmishes, the first line of attack, the tip of the spear, holidaymakers giving away personal details and signing up for on-site presentations where reps would hound them to sign, to give up their credit card details after being made silly by sunshine and cocktails. This new selling culture was only made possible by a boom in consumer credit made available to a Britain soon to be abused of its credit fear and generations old pride in never borrowing a penny. The careful husbandry of income and household purse strings tightly controlled since the industrial revolution unravelled in the sun sea and sangria promises of another country. Why cool off when you can stay hot hot hot? The late 70's and early 80's fucked any semblance of probity out of them. Like the pyramid schemes that later burnt through post-communist Eastern Europe, time share sales ate the British worker alive, like the booze and the fags did, not to mention the sun, Greek Gods exempted.

The sales teams paid runners to hand out leaflets outside the bars and clubs of the resorts. Invented raffle tickets, lotteries, bingo, anything to get the punters to sign up for a tour, a presentation for which they would get X pesetas per person. A top-down bottom up Boston press system for creating an *us*. All of this achieved without app or smartphone, phone call or computer, literally run by line-of-sight intel and bravura contingency logistics. Free booze, free tickets sold by sexy young men and women, upgrades to fancy bars and VIP lounges if you booked in for an hour's tour of Los Apartamentos del Mar, del Sol, Torrenova, Mirabel, Matador etc. Half built, unfurnished flats scattered with box fresh air con units waiting to be wired in, unfinished pools and dirt landscaping. But you get to 'Get in on the first floor' and whenever were 'we' ever offered that?

Soft cash buying hard dreams.

Going up.

We went, got pissed, got comps for a fancy club and left. We had zero credit, zero cash, and were of zero use and soon ushered off the premises, our purely statistical job done.

The sellers made their numbers for the day and we saw them again at the nightclub. They even bought us some more drinks. Fuck it, no skin off their nose. A strange alchemy works its magic on holidaymakers from the moment they sink their first 6.30 am pints at Gatwick and Heathrow (and thirty years later rolled out to Luton, Stansted, Bristol, Birmingham and Manchester in the age of Wetherspoons). They lose all sense of fiscal responsibility and become in fact marks, victims in waiting for flamboyant and at the very least irregular schemes to defraud them.

Now we dress down to be had, in romper suits, onesie's, chalked up with the tattoos by which they will be known, down payment on the winter/easter/summer paradise which is now 'all inclusive Mahoosive', cheaper to go away than stay at home, all you can eat, all you can drink, local spirits, local beers, Brexit bribes in non E.U. Turkey, western Turkey that is, because the east is a war zone, the east bleeds Kurds, Assad and ISIS, the east reels to the beat of that old black magic, in bad time, caravans of death trundling back and forth across the cattle grids of international borders. Whereas in the west, in the shadow of Bodrum, of Milas, of Iasos and Herakleia, the remainder of it all, what's left, is for us, cheap as chips.

A holiday in Spain has become quaint almost, in a post Brexit graveyard for monolingual ex-pats who can't afford to re-pat.

In 1984 you still dressed up to go to Spain, best trouser suit for mum, sports jacket for dad, shell suits for the kids, for this was the tail end of the exotic, packaged extra brightly for those of us late to the party.

In the face of this phalanx of salespeople, who ended up selling hundreds of thousands of hours, days weeks of shared time up and down this and other coasts the world over, the fourth/fifth or sixth Socialist International never stood a chance and looking back we should have taken this glimpse into the future, we should have shared this knowledge going forward into the jaws of the impending miners' strike and saved everyone the trouble. There had only ever been two options and most of us were all out of courage for the latter.

What happened in Fuengirola, stayed in Fuengirola.

We walked into the The *Benny Hill* bar and asked the barman if he knew of any places to stay.

See June, she's over there having a drink. He nodded to the corner of the bar.

June was an ex-pat from the Midlands who took the rent up front on her own doorstep as she was going to drink it that evening. Probably in her late thirties, her legs were tanned pencils pitted and scarred by lack of nutrients and purple bruises from falling over when drunk around so much concrete. Her apartment was up the hill a ways. She tottered there, we followed. We past a boarded up shop in front of which was a post box and she stopped, wheezed, pointed at it and said 'That fucking post box doesn't work.'

On closer inspection we saw that it had had its back ripped off and there were a few postcards lying in the gutter.

Ah shit. One of us said.

The further up the hill you got the cheaper it became. June's was quite a way up. At one point I thought she would slump down, hand us the keys, point up ahead, and expire right there on the kerb but she took her time punctuated by a fag break and made it. She seemed a little abashed to take our money, but she was driven by thirst. We were twenty and this was a great adventure and everything was authentic.

See you boys later. With that promise she staggered back down the hill.

Our apartment. Marble floors with thin walls in which the pipes didn't connect, they gurgled and banged and the taps dripped, punctuated by dry flushing and random gouts of brown water in the sinks.

We were invited to join her that evening, new blood and all that, at a place one block from the seafront called *Screwy Hueys*. The bar had a gynecological theme, although calling it a theme was over doing it; There were a number of risqué 'through the keyhole' jokes hanging on the wall above the bar, cartoons of women in medical stirrups (I kid you not) alongside these. Fleshing out the theme as it were, hung a series of framed fading redtop front pages. Their headlines screamed our National shame down at us from the mid-seventies onwards, reading from left to right.

Gotcha, Gotcha, Gotcha!

Huey himself was an alcoholic, pickled somewhere in his late sixties. A wiry physique, wavy ash white hair sat high atop a sunburnt forehead, tinged with the yellow of cigarette smoke but with fastidiously kept nails and expensive loafers, Huey had known if not better, at least different times. He wore expensive looking jewellery, rings, necklaces and amulets, which he would have had to take off at work if indeed he had ever been a doctor, let alone a gynaecologist. It crossed my mind to ask him, but I never did. At night I imagined a bedtime ritual which involved a slight bowing before the bedroom mirror as the chains came up and over his head to spend the night on his bedside table, and him looking older, guilty somehow bereft of his youthful totems as he got into bed somewhat reduced, such nonsense we can think of in the space of seconds I thought simultaneously of old gangsters and Jimmy Savile.

Amidst all the ex-patriot bonhomie of welcoming rounds of drinks and tips on things to do and places to see (mostly bars and clubs), we were fast tracked like all visitors into the circle of gossip; the resentments, the sexual peccadilloes and the high daily drama of this transplant community, whose life operated on a closed circuit constant loop, a short cut to good times without any other times by which to judge them by other than hospital visits, news from home (usually death) and money problems. It was like membership of a private club with zero waiting list, you were already on the list the moment you arrived. Part of a terrible us, but an us nonetheless, a community in heroic denial of the world outside, the let downs, the failed businesses and relationships back home, the country that had changed, the violence, the crime, the immigrants, the weather of a home that had not lived up to expectations, although neither had this place with all the same problems, the petty local government, the regulations, the bloody Spanish almost as bad as the bloody Labour party, but somehow slightly less so, being here was still for now a better place to be, for the lifestyle, the prices and above all the sunshine.

We were here for ten days, amongst all these lifers, a position which at times I could see they were jealous of, or perhaps this could have just been our age and the undimmed capacity we had only recently discovered for booze, drugs and life. They clung to the climate and the lifestyle they enjoyed as something for everyone else to envy. They had made it, they made a living in a paradise whilst we were just visiting. 'What's not to like?' 'Not bad right' 'Could be worse' and all these *jokey sayings* accompanied by either a hand holding up a pint or a cocktail with an Mediterranean sunset behind them or sitting on the beach or by the pool or posing with the local waiter who had just served them tapas or perched on the cream leather sofa of the open plan apartment with sliding doors leading out to the terrace with sea and / or pool view. These would have been the Instagram posts of the day. Perhaps this resource of imagery the world over is what constitutes our desire for social media, the smiling faces and raised glasses and plates of restaurant food that have denoted good times for a long time. The groundwork had been in place for years; analogue photographs glued in dusty holiday albums stashed away and rarely seen, in cheap frames hung on the walls of restaurants, tavernas, trattoria and bistros and 'wish you were here' postcards from people who had actually been there.

'Happy holidays!' we toasted, clinking glasses round the table. It was clear almost immediately that the lines were blurred between us and them, between home and away, guest and host, prisoner and visitor, as if a strange, shared humanity had usurped, overcome the normal barricades of identity.

This wasn't a holiday it was a sociological exercise in participant observation. We folded into them, effortlessly.

Gotcha!

The summer of the Falklands war had also been a holiday. I went to the Greek islands with mates our first holiday abroad without parents. We island hopped, slept on roofs and beaches, hired mopeds. It was magic.

In the caldera of Santorini we learnt to snorkel and catch octopus, pushing one hand under rocks and letting the whip fast tentacles wind round your wrist before pulling it out and bringing the serrated knife down with your other hand, twisting it and kicking up, kicking up through dark to pale blue, to white spume and sunshine, blood and bubbles trailing below your feet as you gasp for air and throw up a handful of cloudy collapsed Octopus into the row boat, into a bucket with the rest. The suckers from its tentacles peel off like snails poked with hot matches, the octopus becomes a catastrophe out of water, it collapses in on itself, floods with water almost drowns in the air struggling to survive with what remains of its elemental strength. Suckers puckering in the heat, expiring one by one like a sticky soldier figurine cartwheeling haphazardly down a dirty window.

Afterwards, a Marlboro light hanging from my lip I beat an octopus on the stones of the pier, tenderising the flesh before cooking. Cooking it, throwing its corpse back into its element, albeit at boiling point, now the goal being to stop it reducing itself to a rubbery hardness, to keep it tender and moist.

That night under the stars chanting "Las Malvinas son Argentinas!' for no reason other than the reason of youth.

That summer, a holiday saved up for by working double shifts at 'A.P Bessons' the local telephone factory, it cost a quid a night to sleep on roofs under the stars. The summer of Goose Green for some, Belgrano for others, and this, this paradise for us. Even the blue shark we disturbed left us alone, shearing off into the inky black as we kicked for the surface with our plunder.

That summer we were golden.

The first night at Screwy Huey's we met June's sometime boyfriend Tony, tall ginger and seething with psoriasis. On his arms, up his legs and through his thin red hair we could see patches of it like dried seaweed across his skull. Tony, ex two-para, had served in Ireland and seen 'terrible things'. These new friends let it all hang out, never mind us the audience. After four pints and a few chasers he told us what he had seen. In the pitch-black night along a stretch of the Irish border a flare goes up and lights up the field catching men running to get across, armed men, suspects now cut in half, severed from themselves like in a magic trick by heavy machine guns manned by soldiers like him. His hand shakes to light another fag, June's strangely delicate hand cupping his lighter to steady it, IRA suspects cut in two by him in a shooting gallery. By him. Border crossings that were killing fields.

Did he have PTSD or was this just alky rambling? How do vets handle their past, or their pasts? Do they talk or keep silent? June didn't appear surprised by it. How many times had he told this story?

Once in a supermarket queue an old guy with sandy coloured hair and a limp starting talking to me after gesturing towards his injury.

Got that in Iran. We'd sold the Shah ten Centurion tanks. Part of the deal was we had to show 'em how to use them.

Fucking Shah I thought, cunt, then out loud; The Shah was a right cunt wasn't he?

The vet just ignored that and smiled, tapping his dodgy leg. Iran.

I got to the front of the queue and the middle-aged woman on checkout whispered.

He tell you he was in Iraq?

No, he said Iran.

Different day different country, he's just making it up.

Really? You must hear it all in here. Should write a book.

She smiled conspiratorially, revealing a mouthful of bad teeth. She leant in and whispered I am!

She taps her head.

But I can't publish until I leave here though.

Checkout stories.

She was very pleased with herself.

Perfect title. I'll look out for it, thanks, good luck.

Bye.

Big Tony (again with the names, so I imagine they must know other types of Tony) scratched himself as he drank, small piles of skin flakes littering the floor below him like discarded fag buts and on the table spilt in and around the ashtray (he chain-smoked also), his index finger punching a line of stitches in the air before him punctuating his war stories.

Unstitched the poor bastards we did, up and down left to right, didn't matter, they just came apart like ripe melons.

Now he was finding his voice.

And the jukebox plays Bucks Fizz 'The land of make believe'.

Gotcha, you bastards.

Malaga, Marbella, Torremolinos, Belamedina, Benidorm. They swung in the sixties. Hotels like the Mare Nostrum were swish and Mediterranean, full of American celebrities, film stars and starlets. Now run down, all peeling paint and staff with worn collars, hounded by 'all in' holidaymakers and winter sun seekers, young families and the retired, generations caught in the flawed mirror of the (when working) elevator.

In 1984 I sat on the beach reading a well-thumbed copy of Sven Hassel's *Wheels of Terror*. A few days later I swapped it with The Taff for his copy of Sartre's *Iron in The soul*. A more challenging read this would see me through the rest of the holiday, filling the increasingly smaller gaps of boredom we found ourselves in between getting pissed.

We gave ourselves up to the random world of the Costas and those that lived there all year round, the lost and found, the what's not to likes and the on the runs. We scored some shit coke from a guy who spooned it out from a baggie with his long, curled over and stained little finger nail in a fucking phone box, then went to a club with fluorescent lights that make all the drinks glow and your yellow teeth look super white and tried to pull some Welsh nurses in ra-ra skirts. Too pissed and coked up to interest them (or anybody) we stumbled back to June's, masters of all we surveyed. Masters of a Universe that seemed to be lying at our feet. The voices and ideas in the books we had read in the supercharged first five months of university imposed a narrative on the world that fitted like a silk glove the energy anger and inexperience of youth. We were awash in signification and the order it imposed on the world as we saw it.

From the swinging sixties to the minging 80's.

A few nights later we visited the *Dalesman* pub owned and hosted by Ronnie Knight a medium sized gangster 'on his toes' in Spain who had been married to Babs Windsor. Dripping in gold bracelets and ingots with a chunky watch on his hairy left wrist clicking and clacking all over the zinc bar top, Ronnie held court to a varied assortment of gawping tourists and more regular hangers on. He loved meeting lads out from England, bought us drinks and got the barmaid to chop us a line of coke on the bar (on the bloody bar for fucks sake) and then started telling us stories none of which I can remember but I imagine we could all make up, back when money, gold and jewellry was moved around by security trucks and trains, and crooks like him still managed to rob them.

It was a mean time out there in the world. University was a shelter from the storm, from coke and the people that sniffed it, a mean unimaginative drug releasing waves of anxiety and edginess in marginal shitty little places like the post Franco Costa Del Sol.

Years later I would spy Johnny Depp at Malaga airport, an acoustic (needless to say Spanish) Guitar strapped to his back, neck facing down, over a coat with a lot of feathers. Knotted through the button holes were loose cloths of bright colours; He looked happily lost, heading for the exit to overexpose himself in the bright sunlight outside. It struck me how odd it was that the world of the news, of celebrity, of movies, can sometimes literally cross your path as if you had been on the same plane that crashed and there would be a register somewhere and on it would be written both of your names. A Venn diagram that may or may not mean something to those inside and outside of it.

This moment of time persists, Depp dissolving into sunlight, the tinkle of bells, perhaps from the sleeve of his coat, a smile on his face a smile for himself, for his moment of freedom although I have no idea what I was doing sharing it, either coming home from or going to a film shoot. Malaga airport. Ricardo Bofill Terminal 2. Modern, stylish, confident, a triumph of the *new Spain*, it photographed well, the only hint of SPAIN the smell of herbs in the air, cooking oil and strong cigarettes.

Flash on a photo of Depp years later covered in tattoos, cross legged on the bonnet of a car at a festival, smoking, blasted, lost, haunted perhaps by the memory of his younger self in Spain that morning lost in Malaga, on the beach, at the Roman bullring, or roaming the market, zooming out to find himself somewhere in England, under a hat with a feather, bangles clinking to remind him of another kind of being alone.

1984.

We stumbled upon a local bar where the youth were dancing Flamenco. Not for show, not for an audience but as authentic as say skipping rope in 1970's Harlem or some other trope of cultural authenticity we over use. Why are things inauthentic when done for an audience? Do we never show our true selves, can we only be authentic in private, secret even and who are the people who can share their authenticity without it becoming a show, a dissimulation? All acting on the stage or screen is by definition inauthentic in and of itself yet perhaps some performance contains (smuggles?) authentic emotion or behaviour or at least glimpses of what these may be like in our own lives but no

I am totally at a lost with this analogy, and perhaps with tropes and analogies all together.

These Flamenco dancers re-energised the last days of our trip, reset the holiday and how we came to remember it. We were flagging after seven days of all the authenticity we could get and the experience rejuvenated us cleansed us somehow by what we should be cleansed with, our own youthful optimism and good times. Casually dressed teenagers dancing Flamingo and The Taff and I who quickly became known as *Dos Cerveza* feeling part of something out of time but something in place, an activity rather than a performance with a terroir of its own. Later we would slump exhausted on the doorstep of the apartment as we had lost our key and June was sleeping the sleep of the dead from which we possessed no spell to wake her.

February 1937. 100,000 refugees on the road to Almeria bombed from the sea and strafed from the sky. 3000 plus dead. More casualties than Guernica forgotten because nobody painted it. Men beheaded in front of their children who were then forced to sing the Fascist anthem Cara al sol. German, Italian and Moroccan troops, the other International brigade, Brigate Nere.

I remember that fucking post box in Fuengirola with its arse hanging off and the scattering of fading postcards in the ditch behind it.

Dear Mum and Dad. Having a great time. Weather is great. Hope you are both well. Lots of love.

The things you write when you are 19 although I could never bring myself to write 'Wish you were here' (did anyone *ever* write that?) *Lots of love* was a stretch. These sentiments perished on Spanish soil like so many others before them. Technicolour pictures of beaches and swanky 60's hotels, traditional flamenco dancers, bullrings and fighters, Toros and Toreadors, blood red gazpacho and the garish colours of paella bleeding over each other.

My handwriting is so loose that there is only ever space for a sentence or two on the back of postcards and I run out of space even then cramming my last words round the corner into the illegible margins.

Kiss kiss.

On our last day we checked out of June's flat in the early afternoon dropping off her keys off at screwy Huey's and saying our goodbyes and the usual lies of see you again were exchanged not without a sad flat sense of going through the motions, of behaving like everyone else does in these situations. We didn't even duck out of the 'one for the road' farewell drinks on the house. Thanks screwy. Pete wasn't there, nobody mentioned him. Hugs all round.

Lovely boys. said June, lost for words.

The flamenco dancing bar was shut so we decided to spunk what was left of our money going out out as our flight wasn't until early in the morning. The big club in town had just been done up in shall we say, a high 80's style. We got there too early and the place was empty. After picking up drinks from a sour faced barman who turned out to own the place he took us back into his office and chopped us all lines of straight off the boat coke. In the back through the office was a brand new fully equipped recording studio. He told us, Ender, was his name, that he was waiting for a British heavy metal band that had toured with AC/DC to 'lay down some tracks.' Fuck me what a throw back. He asked us if we knew them. We didn't. I can't even remember the name he mentioned but the equipment was impressive.

He played Tusk by Fleetwood Mac through the enormous speakers. We sniggered, drank his shit local brandy until the coke ran out and then fucked off to the airport. There didn't seem to be any other guests the whole time we were there. Odd energy. Ender was homesick, but fuck did I know where he came from. A week later he was dead and the lead singer of the band was in prison for murdering him. It was in the local paper.

Sketches of Spain.

Time to rotate back to the world.

Sitting at my desk staring out of the window I think of Tall Paul. How the world must have changed him, for I see no sign of him having changed it despite back then thinking we could change it all in *the what happened next* of all those years ago. (Paul Evans, Evansio I see all the time, he's been like a brother to me since I came home and therefore immune to all of this speculation.)

SEVERALLS

"For the madness of men is a divine spectacle: In fact, could one make observations from the Moon, as did Menippus, considering the numberless agitations of the Earth, one would think one saw a swarm of flies or gnats fighting among themselves, struggling and laying traps, stealing from one another, playing, gamboling, falling, and dying, and one would not believe the troubles, the tragedies that were produced by such a minute animalcule destined to perish so shortly."
— **Michel Foucault, Madness and Civilisation: A History of Insanity in the Age of Reason**

Students stumble out of the lecture theatre into the freezing cold not a few of them wrapped up in 'Echo and The Bunnymen' greatcoats. Paul slouches against a concrete pillar smoking a roll up.

Alright.

Got a light?

Yeah. Paul stoops down to light me. I inhale the first drag, follow that with a sharp cough, rough cheap fags that burn hot.

He peers at me as if at an alien.

You got a fucking suntan.

I shrugged. Costa del Sol mate.

My eldest sister lives there. Fucking loves it.

You been?

Paul shakes his head like I asked him something ridiculous. I change the subject.

What you make of Foucault then?

Yeah, once you get your head round it, I get it.

His considered response.

A vacuum of the real, pushing out all of the others, will implode resulting in the return of all of the others. Mind fucked. Headshot curtesy of my index finger.

I'd call that a revolution, a proper house clearance.

Paul runs his tongue down the edge of another tightly rolled cigarette.

I think with precision, but talk shit. 'Up against the fucking wall.'

We laugh, ice broken as it has to be every time you meet up with some people, that's just the way they are. Perhaps smoking enables him to think before he talks. I note the grammar of its pauses.

Fancy a pint?

Why not? I got a headache.

He pinches off the dead end of his fag, returns what's left back in his tin. He (sad) eyes me stubbing the Red Band out, flakes of unsmoked tobacco smearing the pavement, but doesn't say anything.

What a waste! What a waste!

We walk into the student union bar, Klaus is mopping the floors, back to wearing his year-round short sleeve stay press.

Looking sharp Klaus.

Big smile.

Bit early boys isn't it?

God I love his accent it, sends me.

Aren't you cold Klaus?

Come on fellas, you call this cold.

Like the fucker had been at Stalingrad.

Anyway, you got a tan. Been anywhere nice?

Fuengirola, Spain. Weather was great.

You know I've never been to Spain. One day. Take it easy boys.

I almost salute him as we step over the bucket and head for the just un-shuttered bar.

Klaus shakes his head with a smile. *These guys.*

We order our pints, a bitter and a Snakebite.

Cider is a cunts drink.

Bitter is a bitter drink.

Fucking Wurzel.

Working class hero.

And don't you forget it.

We clink glasses, sink our pints, wipe our chins with our hands or the sleeves of our shirts. There was a time when this type of drinking felt rebellious, liberating almost seditious.

A couple sit down next to us and start talking about the new R.E.M. record. Some by the numbers punk and I couldn't believe it, Suzanne bloody Humby!

Suzanne Humby was trouble. She had it going on in spades and was years ahead of the rest of us boys and girls in how to work the room, any room. In the first months of uni she was way out in front; Posh, nihilistic, nothing excited her and that excited us, she wore fishnets and very short leather skirts, dyed to fuck black hair, Egyptian eyeliner and white face powder. She drank, took drugs, gave zero fucks.

She was punk sexy and had all of us on the hook to some extent, a proper wind-up artist who apparently left dildos on show in her hand bag. We all wanted to see that, as we had never seen one before.

Well everyone except Tall bloody Paul, he lent over and told them to do one.

R.E.M? Piss off.

Obviously, Suzanne loved that and noticed me for the first time.The plank she was with quickly turned away and changed the subject. Suzanne kept glancing our way, I gave her the smallest of smiles. Our conversation continued at a slightly higher volume.

...Mate of mine from school, Nick Music, all he ever talks about, this record that one, a proper N.M.E. bore. For every record you said you liked he'd say another one you hadn't heard was better. Implying you were an idiot to like the first record.

I like to listen to music not talk about it. At work in the canteen all they ever did was talk about the top twenty, like songs were horses in a race, did my head in.

I looked up and Suzanne had gone but I felt we had started to play a game. Paul was oblivious or so I thought.

What the fuck do you like to talk about then?

Paul's eyes switch on. They had that agility, a minor superpower, on and off, elsewhere or right there.

Good question.

He thinks.

Nothing. Not really. Small talk mainly. Drink, Yeah, and fags. Not talking, no, that's a mugs game.

Paul smiles over crooked teeth.

Piss taker.

Quiet pint, that's me. You talk, go on, go on, pick a subject, how about...books. Let's have it, something memorable you read in a book.

Delivered like somebody who never reads, with two big, fat, taking his time B's for both times he stays book, difficult bastard!

For example, what did you read on your holiday in the costa del poxy sol.

Now this cunt doesn't miss a trick.

Books are too much to like as a whole thing. Hundreds of pages can't be wall to wall perfect, can they? It wouldn't be human. It's bits of books that can be good, images, sentences, ideas. What's wrong with remembering a great word from a book and using that?

'Ark at you. Give me an example.

I don't know, what about Defuncto?

I pulled that out of God knows where.

Meaning dead, got that out of a book about Thomas Mallory.

Good word. Never heard of him.

Exactly my point! Overall stories are disappointing because they are fake constructs that come to an end. Endings are fake. Bits and pieces are enjoyable, fragments, passages, I remember them.

What about your holiday bestseller?

He sniggers, but I know the fucker is impressed, or I hope he is, I can finally string a few sentences together that aren't pure wank.

Iron in the Soul.

Not read it.

It's got some great bits. The main character has to sit up in bell tower shooting Germans, holding them back for fifteen minutes so the locals can escape, he kind of uses every shot to pay off his sins because he's a fuck up, totally up himself, got somebody pregnant, fucked her off, the whole existential crisis thing that is Sartre's philosophy right, anyway, so the book flashes back to all the bad shit he had done at the same time that he finally develops a pair of balls. It's where Warhol got his 15 seconds of fame from. Fifteen minutes in a church bell tower, holding off an attack with a single rifle and a finite number of bullets. This is his chance for personal redemption, each bullet he fires wipes one line of his slate clean.

Paul starts silently clapping.

Lovely. But I don't buy it. Hold the fort like the fucking Alamo. Like fucking Rambo.

You haven't read it!

Existentialism is a middle class lie.

Paul snorts. Bastard. Of course he's read it.

I fight back.

What about the rhythm of the prose, Sartre's repetition of the sentence, *fifteen minutes*. It carries the rest which would otherwise be just so much story.

Your round.

Five minutes later mouth full of crisp packet and hands grasping pints I return.

Paul has had time to reflect.

It's all Catholic hocus-pocus. Sartre could never escape, never free himself let alone any of his 'alter egos'.

Paul did the inverted commas thing with his index fingers. A proper rascal.

Stick to Sven Hassel mate. Now that's a proper piss-take of existentialism.

I down half my pint looking for an answer, clutching at straws.

From somewhere in the inchoate mess of my tiny cosmos, this:

Images held together by the energy of the words used to describe them and not anything else, not propped up by a story with a cast of characters to hold it up under the fake gaze of the author. These fragments are immanent.

Pauls eyes widen ever so slightly for less than a second.

Fake gaze of the reader more like. They wanna believe it from the moment they pick it up. They all love Sartre. It's just dinner party blah blah.

You ever been to a dinner party? I parry.

No.

I finish my pint and slam the glass down on the table. He's had two big sips of his. He usually beats me to the bottom of the glass.

I feel happy to have gone a few rounds and said my bit, to have followed a thought through out loud, to have said something. Paul downs his pint, catching me up, wiping flecks of crisps from his jaw.

The empty glasses sit there, marking time.

Fragments. Sartre doesn't do that, he's like fucking Delacroix, wants the whole war in the palm of his fucking hand. Iron in the soul, arrogant bollocks. More fucking Germans died trying to capture Popov's house at Stalingrad that died in the whole invasion of fucking France.

But this is too good to end here I think of how to sustain it. I've got a fresh fag on and cough through the first words of...

Fiction can communicate truth.

And Paul throws us both a lifeline.

What is the truth? We all make up what we want to believe, even the numbers, Pint?

That word guarantees and underwrites the moment. As if I was ever going to say no. Paul lurches up and heads back to the bar. I've totally lost my thread and stare vacantly about the room.

He returns.

Frozen Soviet soldiers planted upside down limbs, used as sign posts. The words conjure the image, they put a spell on us. But what is the truth of that image how do we break the spell?

We both take first gulps from our beers.

We are entranced

Nazis, Soviets, the war, the holocaust, it's transcendent, we are compelled to not look away. It's bored into our skulls. Imagine what else we could think about, what space we would have to think about something else.

He taps his head, hard, looking mad.

Well, it's not just me and you is it?

We should read something else, there has to be something else. It's pathetic, we didn't fight the poxy war, our granddads did.

Spellbound

My grandfarther was an air raid warden on the Kingsland Road.

How many wallets did he nick?

That's another story. I smiled, swigged my pint, lit another fag.

I'd rather read about that. All the snide stuff that went on. Mine was Irish, only fucking war he fought was against you black and tan bastards. Anyway, why do we need to know all the details, what purpose does it serve to know all about the Einsatzgruppen A, B, C, D, where they were deployed, the names of the towns and villages they raised to the ground, its fucking porn mate, we're addicted to it, the forensic detail of how all that murder happened. How does it help?

I shrugged.

Spellbound

Dunno. Help what?

Bring about a workers state, that's what would fucking help.

I got up, leaned on the table swaying, a bit pissed.

Same again?

Paul vigorously nods whilst focusing on rolling himself another fag.

I returned with pints and dry roasted peanuts.

Anyway, women like talking about books, books, films and music, makes you come across more sensitive.

Paul froze, looked like he'd had a seizure, swallowed a mouthful of beer, smoked the end of his fag down to his fingers and spat out.

Sven or Tiny?

Trance trance trance

I looked up at him over the rim of my pint. He hadn't taken the bait.

Go on, Sven or Tiny?

I banged my pint down on the table, split the bag of peanuts and put them between us. Fuck it.

Legionnaire, the desert wanderer! *Come death come.* I intoned.

Paul stuffed a handful of peanuts into his mouth.

Legionnaire became a muslim. Plus he had no knob, remember that but if you ever motioned his lack of manhood he'd go potty and probably kill you.

That would make you angry, to be fair.

Komm susser Tod!

A Mutley hiss of a laugh emits from Pauls face as he lights another rolly.

Running off at the mouth, plus the pints, had gone to our heads. It was 2.30 pm.

SS sticking grenades up peasants cunts, stuffing villagers into barns, setting them on fire, losing their shit, their discipline, that's the narrative we are hooked on, addicted to the horror, the come and see of it all.

Fucking great film.

That's my fucking point!

Maybe it's because we identify with the Soviets. It allows you to enjoy all the Nazi stuff without feeling like, well like you're a Nazi.

Spellbound

Paul snorts at this, but doesn't say anything.

I continue.

The only good Germans were convicts, in a world that dark led by psychopaths the good people were in prison. Hassel was in a penal battalion, ergo it's O.K. to like reading him. His characters are the ultimate anti-heroes.

Ergo my arse.

A great hulking older man in a muddy trench coat covered in burrs ambles past our table mumbling to himself, giving us the nod. Paul hunkers down into his pint, I smile back but turn away before he can latch onto us. I whisper over the top of my pint.

Vaughn. He wrote an essay on Rousseau and spent two weeks living in the woods as a natural man. Wanker caught pneumonia.

This place is full of nutters.

You know that yank in our philosophy class, wanks on about Ornette Coleman or Kant at any given opportunity. Comes right up in your face proclaiming his thoughts on the ontological arguments for existence in a flat drone of a voice. Has piss holes in the snow eyes. Scares the living daylights out of people because he has had them scared out of him. Evil in his eyes or good, whatever value, is far beyond anything we would recognise.

Fuck off, what's he seen? Other than in his fucking books, he's a proper rich American cunt, I'd like to see him on the trains, when they chuck themselves under. What clever conclusions, what he'd have to say about that? He'd shit himself.

At this Paul lurches to his feet. Fuck me he's tall.

He never talked about his job or how he came to be at university, but now it just kind of spilled out. This was as close as I ever got.

Shit himself he would, shit himself.

And with that he was off.

I downed the dregs of my last pint at a bit of a loss. In a fuzzy blur I thought about books and girls and what's it all about Alfie. In my pocket was a freshly nicked copy of Saussure's 'Course in general linguistics' so I flicked through it, weird small type and heavy on the ink as if it was smudged. Couldn't make head nor tale of it.

I didn't see Paul the next day, he wasn't at the Ken Plummer lecture on narrative pluralism. In fact a week later I hadn't seen him about on campus at all. I was a bit worried after how we had left our last conversation and went up to his flat in Rayleigh seven. The vicar nervously showed me to his room. I knock and there's no answer.

He has no idea where he is.

Keeps himself to himself.

With cunts like you for flat mates I thought. Paul always had been cast as an outsider, whether he wanted the role or not. Cast outside was more accurate.

The cleaner came into the kitchen and told me Paul had been taken to hospital.

First I've heard of it, said the vicar.

She tapped her head to communicate what the problem was, her English wasn't great, she was Spanish I think, and showed me his room, talking about the smell of the other rooms, mimicking holding up a pair of socks or worse. 'Phew wee what a stench' She was funny. She said that Paul was different. She opened the door looking a little sheepish, as if it was her fault he wasn't there. It smelt of Brylcream and tobacco. A grown-up smell not the adolescent stink of body odour and farts. You could sit in his room without embarrassment.

I don't want to cause trouble but he not well, what if he sets himself on fire and the whole tower? When I come to clean to do my job, he's behind his door shouting at somebody and I come inside and there is nobody, just him sitting on the floor rocking like a baby, so thin and always smoking a cigarette. I was scared, for him..

I told her not to worry and that she had done the right thing.

You a good boy like your friend, close the door ok, I don't want no trouble.

A record was still spinning on the stereo. I turned it off and looked round the room. I couldn't bring myself to touch anything or disturb his privacy in any way. There was stuff on his desk, notebooks, bits of paper, but the idea of reading anything made me feel sick and way out of my depth. I felt like the boy the cleaner had called me and that I still was.

I never even asked Paul the details of why he was locked up. It didn't seem to be a relevant question. Anything that happened to us was more of an experience, part of the experiment of being at University.

He just disappeared for 28 days.

Quite a few of the lecturers spent time at Severalls. Rumours of cross dressing, empty prams being pushed in the street, essays thrown up staircases and marked according to which slid back down the furthest, although I don't think either of those 'acting outs' counted towards being sectioned, there must have been other behaviour probably related to their reading material. Foucault, for one, was a rallying cry for anyone designated mentally unwell, recasting them over into heroes, savants and the ultimate sane ones amongst us. So I wasn't that worried about Paul, he'd be back.

Madness is the false punishment of a false solution, but by its own virtue it brings to light the real problem, which can then be truly resolved.

Perhaps Paul would be a happy fool.

28 DAYS LATER

Early morning, Rayleigh tower, floor seven, kitchen. Paul and his plastic bag stuffed with dirty clothes and medicine. Marjory Razorblade was still on the record player. He puts it back in its sleeve.

I rifled through all the pill bottles in his bag.

The fuck are these?

I knew there was a 28 day limit, that I would get out.

Fuck me. These pills are Lithium.

And hey presto here I am. Back in this nuthouse. Needed a break to be fair.

They must have known why you were at Uni in the first place.

Smoke escapes his nose in wisps over an awkward silence.

Anyway what did I miss?

Let's get out of here, I'll fill you in.

The lifts not working so we take the stairs.

There are corridors hundreds of feet long. The inmates cycle up and down them for exercise, something to do. I hadn't ridden bike since I was a kid. Fucking wobbly I was on it. In 1942 the Luftwaffe bombed Severalls and thirty odd patients were blown to bits. I mean they didn't bomb it intentionally – they were just dumping bombs for the sake of fuel efficiency. Imagine inmates cycling like crazy clowns to escape the bombs as they dropped down the corridor, boom, boom, boom, exploding closer and closer till they got you. Imagine that? Indians scattered on dawns highway bleeding.

His fragile eggshell mind. Hippy music quotes, he'd changed but not the flecks of spittle struggling to lubricate a mouth running at 100 miles an hour.

Fuck me I'm out of breath.

Being in there, committed for seeing things, hearing voices, hallucinating, being paranoid, all the things that got you banged up in the first place, in a place like that and guess what? It was all true, it all came fucking true. Hitler was out to get you!

We come outside, thank fuck.

I light us two fags as his hand was shaking too much.

I bet they secretly put bromide in your tea.

We both snigger, although I had never had a conversation with Paul about his actual sex life, something else I sensed was not off limits as such but irrelevant not worthy of discourse.

Cordoned inside jokes sex made us all laugh but we never talked about it for real. Nobody had a *sex life* back then come to think of it, we just had sex or we didn't. People went out with each other, then split up (this term had replaced the school playground phrase 'being chucked.' *Love* was a numbers game, a game of getting off with people, usually down in the student union dancehall at the weekends. Or in the library, that was a good spot too, for chatting up, not getting off with , that came afterwards, after the set up. A sophisticated business. And obviously the bar, the sweet spot of this Venn diagram.

On the sniff, smelly fingers, red and brown wings, wedgies, blow jobs, still this boys playground banter lingered rather than be replaced by the more twisted or truly pornographic. University demanded more of us but this hadn't filtered down to the giving or receiving of sexual pleasure, let alone the sharing of it. Gender rights, women's liberation was something we were more comfortable with, especially all the theory that came with it. We had female friends, comrades and classmates. We all got off with each other at some point, only a few stayed together for any length of time in the first two years. Those that did were seen as being either experimental or losers. Too much else was in flux for any of us to focus on boyfriend girlfriend dynamics. They existed for sure. As a mature student going out with a townie, Paul's relationship with Sarah escaped our mocking censure. .

Paul pulls his trousers up from round his ankles. Sarah's top was up and now she pulls it back down. There's another knock on the door.

I'm coming out with my hands up. He sniggers.

Sarah put his cigarette back in his mouth cupping his face.

He nods to her over his shoulder as he opens the door.

After they explain he goes quietly. Sarah buzzes around them like a fly asking questions. Paul nods and smokes. She follows them down the corridor to the lifts effing and jeffing at the backs of the bastards who completely ignore her.

Fucking pigs fucking police state is what this is.

OBJET PETIT A

'Hello uncle Fedia. Greetings from Magnitogorsk. Uncle Fedia, we arrived at the place safe and sound. They did a poor job of meeting us. We sat and waited a very long time for a bus to take us to the place we were going. They finally brought us to open country and left us. It was night already. They showed us a tent in which there was nothing except the tent itself.'

Letter from Komsomol shock worker, Magnitogorsk, June 1931.

Lunchtime at The Rose and Crown in Wivenhoe. A cold wind comes off the estuary as we bundle inside the snug bar. Paul orders two pints of Abbots. Still shivering I pass him a bag of speed and off he trots to the bog. The pub smells of scampi in a basket so I light a fag to cut through the grease of it. Somebody is eating a pint of prawns dipping them into a side of mayonnaise which makes me wince. I glance down at my sore, bitten, fingertips. The man shelling and eating his way through the prawns obviously doesn't have my ravaged fingertips.

Bastard.

Paul slides back into his chair and palms me the baggie back under the table. Off I go to the bogs, where it was nearly as cold as outside and fumble the whole process. Shit claggy gear, split bank card to chop it a greasy bog top and a crumpled up fiver. Fuck it. I end up licking my bloody index finger, smearing the gear off the cistern and rubbing my gums. I swallow and gag. I flush and bend down to suck the tap to wash the chemical paste down. I cough, choke a little, rubbing my sore finger.

Nightmare.

Back in the warm of the snug it was my turn to talk. First, I gulped down a long swig of my beer savouring the sweet malt taste behind my teeth, cleansing my mouth and my numb gums of the bitter speed.

I lean over the table conspiratorially.

Sign is sin with a G.

The fuck you talking about? Forefinger wiping drug snot drips from his sherbet fountain nose.

Zizek lecture, you missed him, it was on Derrida's Writing and Difference.

I was detained under the fucking mental health act . You missed that! Stretching his neck side to side to emphasise his recent confinement.

Full house mate, he lapped it up, women love him.

The author speaks. That is logocentric. A gooey forefinger stabs towards my chest.

He's got a killer lisp.

I impersonate Zizek for Paul's entertainment.

In short, language is always saying more or less, something other than what it means to say.

Obviously. Paul snorts, killing his pint, bobbing up to fetch two more.

I hold myself back until he returns, all ticks and repetitive gestures, mostly involving the beer mat which is in shreds.

Didn't spend a penny for twenty-eight days mate, I'm fucking loaded.

I nod my thanks and clink glasses before continuing, which I was literally gagging to do.

Derrida argues that the act of writing, *Ecriture*, puts the author in his place. Back in his box. The process of writing is decentered, diffuse, writing swamps speech, pulls it down to earth, democratises it, mutes the power of the symbol, castrates the cock of the author allowing the free play of signs back into the world. The author is silenced, he is dead. He is rewired, re animated into the text itself!

French cunt. Paul says with deadpan respect.

So writing empowers the reader over the writer, more so than the listener over the speaker.

Perhaps it was the amphetamine, the bikers coke which drove the mechanics of talking rather than the subject matter but there were times in this rarified world that we enjoyed talking beyond ourselves, about ideas not in some purist academic way, but playfully and tied into the gist and banter of the lecturers themselves, for there could be no intellectualism without irony. And by irony here I mean the solipsism of the professors whose ego undermined the ideas they espoused thereby making them for us human, flawed and precisely because of that interesting and worth talking about. The ideas were fragile you could just about make them out and to sustain the thought of them in your head let alone be able to communicate them was hard work, so when you did, when it all clicked into place then the fragile beauty or truth of them was sexy as fuck. In these moments, more precisely during these elongated drug fuelled passages of time we could see beyond our own biographies, our own lived experience and participate freely in a world of ideas, both political, philosophical and to some extent sexual way beyond who we were.

Speed loved all of this, it literally bled out of us, like Christ on a stick.

So, in a symbolic universe all is well, Catholicism, Judaism, Hinduism, Islam all traditional religions exist within a symbolic framework. Everyone knows what things mean and what they are doing. The sun rises. The holy ghost, the body of Christ, the five pillars of Islam, the roots of heaven and the sun sets. You know where and who you are, thats the point. As soon as the symbol shifts, looses its footing to become merely a sign, that's where the true sin, the true fallibility of being human creeps in... that is sin with a g.

You're full of shit.

I chuckled, a pig in clover.

Out of the corner of my eye I see the barman watching us. Maybe it was Pauls unkempt appearance, or our excitability but he didn't look too happy.

I lowered my voice.

Transubstantiation meant literally the body of Christ. Right?

Tell me something I don't know.

A world without sin, bound by the invocations of strong magic, a system of belief and worship summoned from the pages of the Old Testament. The modern novel began with the reformation. The ability to write as others. As soon as the blood and body of Christ became symbolic then it was only a matter of time for the whole pack of cards to collapse. And from symbol to sign, well that's just the modern fuck up on top of it. The cherry on a rotten cake.

Paul pounces.

The worm that flies through the night!

Yes! That's why Opus Dei hated movies, exactly that, the Catholic fear of uncontrollable signification in movies, the sign itself set loose, the mocking sign lurking in the dark between each frame of film, the abyss, literally hidden from us by a trick of the eye, which we see only when slowed down, the holes, the gaping chasm from which leaps the disorder, the disordering of meaning.

Paul gets up silently eating his face and orders two more pints. The barman serves him reluctantly and not without trepidation.

And Zizek said all of this?

Mate the cunt doesn't stop talking, this is just a fucking synopsis.

At what point in any dialogue, conversation or lecture do we lose the thread of what it is being talked about? When does anyone listen and from listening change their response to fit what they have heard? We each hang on the other's words only to pounce on the gaps into which we can insert ours. Sometimes oddly, it's the drugs that keep our mouths shut, so busy are we trying to keep control of our bodies, our muscles, to hold ourselves together. And in those moments we can truly listen. Paul nodded for me to continue, the rest of his willpower focused elsewhere.

I jumped in on speed dial.

Jews were the first religion to put words under erasure, so you can imagine what Zizek had to say about them. Right this is the last bit... from the Torah to the Tarot. Language is essentially sinful because it is shifty. That's why the Latin mass was so important. It was a reliable performance, passing on words like stones, each one polished like a fucking gem. To translate the bible into English or any vernacular, well that's asking for trouble, a living language is like a fucking bucking bronco. We fuck in it, haggle in it, steal, kill and dream in it. To worship in that stew? All those Rabbis benching back and forth at the wailing wall, wrapping those lacquer boxes round and round their arms with leather straps like holy heroin addicts. They are athletes performing for their God. His pure words.

I start moving like them, backwards and forwards on my increasingly precarious pub stool. Paul sucks his pint, eyeballing me.

God.

An amphetamine pause.

He's a tough audience, you can't put a foot wrong without pissing him off. Tarot readers perform and we are a very malleable audience, easy to supplicate, because we will interpret whatever the reader says the way we want to. And they don't care, they're getting paid to talk. God isn't open to persuasion, but he's all ears, listening for mistakes. He said his piece a long time ago. He has the ultimate poker face. We can't read him because he isn't there. Gypsy Rose fucking Lee is at every pier on every seafront reading every sad grubby open tearful, hesitant, expectant fucking face and hand she comes across.

Easy money.

Paul starts dealing out an invisible hand of cards onto the table.

Look at the hand I was dealt, what else would you have done with these cards?

Exactly. I said.

And Charlie Manson enters the room. Applause. 1984 was before it became crass to mention Charlie Manson before he had been found out by us, the self appointed counter culture that found him 'of interest' back then.

The barman picks up our empties and brushes up the ripped up strips of beermat from the floor.

Come on fellas keep it down or I'll have to ask you to leave.

Humans are easy to read. This one is pissed off listening to our shit and doesn't want to have to deal with kicking us out. Paul barely acknowledges him. I smile apologetically on my way to the bogs to do another line.

I leap back down onto my stool down having rehearsed my next point whilst stinking out the toilet with amphetamine shit.

It's like Charlotte Rampling and Dirk Bogarde, what's that fucking film called...

Night Porter. Quick as a flash, disdainful, he didn't like that film as much as I did. Shit.

Yes. Max and Lucia meeting up at that hotel in Vienna playing out their symbolic erotic relationships from the Holocaust.

What's symbolic about that?

Because it's 1957. The Nazis no longer have power, because the camps have been liberated. In 1957 the symbols of Nazism have no public value, but instead have become twisted into private signs. The camps are over, but their roleplaying has been liberated into sex play in the very stuffy 'No sex please we're Austrian!' world of post war Vienna. It's the inversion of their symbolic relationship, that's what turns her on, the rewiring of the relationship between an SS officer and a Jewess. Now he's the lowly night porter living under an assumed name and she is the wealthy well known guest. He has become a nobody whereas before he was everybody, and she has undergone a miraculous transformation.

From the gap between denotation and connotation leaps endless imagination, endless evil. Writers are the true sinners, worse than readers they enable sin in others.

Paul nails the conversation. Every time.

That's what you're getting at am I right?

Fuck yeah.

Paul nods vigorously, spittle cornering his mouth, and rummages for a much thumbed book in his knapsack and reads...

'The book is a static product.'

Cendrars.

He slams it down on the table, Some pages already loose from the spine offering themselves like marked cards in a sharks pack.

But text is dynamic productivity.

He fingers the text, prods it, ink lifting off the page onto his wet fingers.

Folk tales are merely symbolic, whereas the novel overflows with potential signification.'

Fe fi fo fum.

I pass him the bag of speed, this time over the table, fuck it. Dib dab doo, lick yer finger stick it in the bag and suck it off.

I grab the book and read from it, my finger searching for purchase on the text which swims before my eyes, a way in.

However, much believers perform their rites, there will always be somebody with a different interpretation, tinkering with the symbols, turning them into signs making the divine symbol human again. That is literally the meaning of iconoclasm.

The farts and shit of Gargantua and Pantagruel! That speed is rank.

The barman comes over.

Thats enough, get out or I'll call the police!

The leg of my stool splinters and I collapse onto the floor in a fit of giggles, swearwords and spittle, soiled by the dregs of my last pint.

Paul unfurls himself and teeters over the barman.

Fucking Wurzel.

I can't get up, debilitated by laughter and dizziness I give myself up to it.

The barman punches Paul on the nose. He stumbles, knocking over a pint of prawns on the table behind us. The elderly couple join in abusing us. He doesn't need an excuse to abuse them back.

C, Coffin dodgers! a childhood stammer making an odd reappearance. I repeat this from under the table, paralytic with laughter.

C, Coffin dodgers, C, Coffin dodgers. Luckily Paul doesn't hear me or doesn't take offence. He backs up to the door, stuffing his hanky to his nose.

My fucking nose you cunt. He mumbles.

My legs beetle about trying to move me towards the door. The barman reaches under and grabs my collar dragging me to the door and throwing me out onto the cobbles of the street outside.

Student wankers.

Fuck that hurts. What about our stuff?

The elderly couple are watching us out of the pub window

as two bags follow us out of the door, books spilling into the puddles. Paul snorts blood from his nose, I give the olds a V sign. We stuff the books back into the bags and scarper. We didn't even want to put the windows in as we would be let back in after a few weeks. Besides the barman wasn't a regular and we'd probably never see him again. Fucking funny tho' I knew as soon as I handed Paul that bag of speed on the way in that something like this would kick off.

It always did.

When I was a kid we used to crash our push bikes on purpose onto the front lawns of strangers. Then we would lie there in an accident tableaux until somebody came out and offered us juice and biscuits or to tell us to piss off. That was the game. It passed the time. Bored kids loved being chased. Destroying peoples front garden snowmen had the same intention. Kicking them over or throwing spears at them. Throwing home-made petrol bombs at trees. Or chucking one at a lock up garage door on the estate.

To make things kick off.

To make somebody mad enough to notice us.

We were always waiting for something to happen, pulling silly little stunts like this and now getting pissed and sniffing speed it was essentially the same. Paul had been a real person in the world or so it seemed but even he was fading in front of my eyes, a shadow of a former self I never knew. Was there anything coming down the line, anything at all that could shake us up, would anything ever actually happen? Would we ever be in danger, experience proper jeopardy, for some malign force to actually take notice of us?

If everybody has their own unique story then society ceases to exist, if every signification is unique, it has no meaning outside an unsharable madness. Society is defined by the sharing of meaning and the struggle for what that meaning is for however many members of society there are. What we can forge in common is the birth of the political.

Later I read that somewhere. My childhood was full of small stories that we forced other people to share, our first experience of politics.

Political is the return of the symbol by way of the sign. Look at the first five-year plan for example. The liquidation of private tradesman strengthened this specific communal matrix of signification, every action now had to perform symbolically. When in the early thirties the first wave of consumer goods came on line in the Soviet Union, spontaneous sausage parades celebrated the end of rationing. Sausages became a symbol for plenty and Soviet prosperity. Soviet champagne became cheap and plentiful, again, a real pleasure with which to celebrate Soviet success in every sphere *symbolically.* So hesitant were citizens to embrace these symbols (perhaps to embrace the future, so wary of it they had become), that local councils had to ban the sale of single glasses of wine, to promote people buying bottles. Anastas Mikoyan visited Macy's department store in New York in his capacity as commissar for food production and realised the power of consuming symbols. Mikoyan cutlets and sausages were the result. He also imported the idea of canned foods to the Soviet union, the symbology of Warhols Campbell soup cans already at work in the 1930's.

Let them eat sausages.

Perhaps.

In reality people couldn't get their shoes mended or a

haircut and the supply of boiled sweets dried up because there was no private enterprise and as yet no five year plan for a short back and sides.

The idea was huge and only symbolism could hold it up. Look at Magnitogorsk for example. A city literally summoned out of the earth by sheer will. Shock construction sites where Hundreds of Komsomol idealists shipped out to help complete the first plan, to build a shining city from the white heat of technology and innovation, which was in reality a collection of tents, the wrong workers at the wrong time waiting for other workers, the right ones, to have been there at the right time to make the whole thing work.

This was reality conjured out of signification, forged into a symbol.

Fuck me.

We sat and smoked by the quay, watching the boats and the birds.

That's revolution for you. I sighed, coming down off the gear and the adrenalin.

What is, what you on about? Gibberish. Paul frowned.

It was modelled on Gary, Indiana. Did you know that?

What the fuck are you talking about? I'm not a bloody mind reader!

Magnitogorsk.

For fucks sake.

A Soviet delegation visited Cleveland in order to copy the steel mill in Gary. To recreate it back in the USSR. Transubstantiation if you like. The body of Christ, the steel mill of Gary. Stalin closed it in 1937, the city not the steel mill, paranoia over leaky signification. The hundreds of foreign specialists went home. The moment for copying was over. Despite the steel being real the symbol had become faulty.

The phrase delegation is part of the incantation. If I had said 'they went to Gary Indiana' it wouldn't resonate within a Soviet narrative as much as using the word 'delegation'. That word empowers, (or powers up like in trading card games). What lies beneath this phrase is what signification is all about. This is where we all fight for signification, how hegemony is gained and sustained, how my world view beats out yours, this war which happens in the undercarriage of language everyday.

The everyday war.

That's what *ecriture* means, the system of meaning that exists before the author. It is diffuse, the woven matrix out of which we conjure meaning and identity. The voice is writing on airwaves, it has no primacy over text in fact it is writing on memory, on recording machines inscribed into the operating manual of language itself. There is no voice outside that, there is no voice in a void. Sound does not carry.

Zizek is obsessed with this idea of the matrix, which when you throw the switch lights up a hyper reality.

Paul grunted.

A German officer views Picasso's Guernica in Paris during the war. He asks 'Did Picasso make this? and is answered 'No you did.' That's a literal war of signification decanted into metaphor. I bet this never actually happened. Go figure. Would you risk your life or freedom for a bon mot?

Boom Boom.

Cold, wet and hungry and with gnashing teeth fit to splinter I observe...

Identity is always an illusion. An effort of conjuring. Yeah. The author sinks into the text like it was quicksand. The book is *of* the author not *by* him. He is lost, at best a spectral presence haunting the text.

This was the last gasp of what had been a great day out. I was running on empty, Paul on the other hand was wired for sound.

Lost in music, feel so alive, my nine to five, I'm lost in music. Rapped out onto the quayside, Paul in full nutter mode on the day of his release from Severalls, providing the soundtrack to his own fragile bill of health.

Maybe it was the drugs, but there was something missing. There had to be. We looked for it everywhere. Was it Ok to be not OK? Always looking for that bit to top us up. Was it actually normal? The empty feeling, the something about to happen anxiety I felt, was just, I don't know, was it just fucking catcher in the rye?

Was I normal? Say it ain't so. I had another explanation.

I chose Lacan.

We were his *Object Petit A*'s. The surplus that can't be inscribed, unobtainable objects of desire, what cannot be talked about must be passed over in silence we can only address them in the manner in which we pass them by. They remain inviable, untranslatable like the phrase itself, an algebraic sign.

Les Autres, the others, always out there, beyond the campfire, where no light falls. Not outside the circle, but right there, interrupting the line of the circle like a breaker in an electrical circuit, always heading off the circles completion, so that there are no circles without this leap across the unknown other which is always calling to us, edging us towards unknowable promises of pleasure.

Nobody knows me but I'm always there.

Paul now in full karaoke mode, mud larking and in need of a long hot bath. He holds up an empty crab shell.

Maybe we were just fucking cool.

HARMOLODICS
No 3

We can only think through language constructs, (words/ sentences etc) outside of this 'house of language' is just nebulous feeling. Time is itself such a construct. It all ends up with us making ourselves up, constantly. People who live in houses made of words.

Saussure says, *Time changes all things; there is no reason why language should escape this universal law.*

Yet time doesn't exist outside language.

I think.

Psychologically our thought-apart from its expression in words-is only a shapeless and indistinct mass.

See how true that is?

But meaning as constructed in language is contested territory, quantum in its peculiarity. The slippage of meaning, how connotation is dependant on culture, who you are, what things mean where you are and that denotation is almost impossible to maintain, to impose your will on language is like catching water, some of it will always slip through your fingers, meaning will overflow the parameters of what something is meant to mean, and all we have is a war of connotation, yours and mine, a minefield of meaning that can blow up in anyones face at any time; this accounts for the rise of Anthropology amongst other competing disciplines. Tribal time, urban time, slow time, thick time, dreamtime.

Which is what we have just been talking about. Which is enough to drive you mad because it is in effect all we ever talk about. That's what all the noise was. We were caught in a no mans land without sides on the battlefield of the connotation wars.

'*Who killed Bambi?*'

STRIKE!

Don't pretend that we have got an army out there straining at the leash – because we haven't ... Some of them [rank-and-file trade unionists] put the Tories into power ... You can't make a backbone out of a wishbone.

Ron Todd TGWU Summer 1985.

Twenty years and you're still a scab!

Football chant Notts County vs Barnsley, Nationwide league division two 31 January 2004. (Sung by Barnsley fans).

Strike!

April, May, 1984

Kent miners start picketing the dock gates at Wivenhoe, Essex, one of five privately-owned ports along the River Colne estuary, where freighters carrying coal from Germany and Poland had begun to unload. The aim of the pickets was to turn back lorries sent to collect the coal. Within days convoys of unmarked trucks were arriving at the two largest ports, Wivenhoe and Brightlingsea, which both relied on non-union labour. The response was immediate. From mid-April every morning before dawn fleets of white police transits could be seen travelling at high speed through north east Essex in the direction of the five ports...

Walking into thick time we marched from campus to the

dock, banners flying at the break of day. There was even a bridge to thicken it further.

Trip trap trip trap.

Miners and students plus some locals. Donkey jackets, Army Surplus Camo gear, flat caps, beanies, Doc Martins and Chinese slippers, Dickies workwear and frayed Nehru collars on charity shop shirts. Happy coppers on double bubble lined up on the other side of the bridge where coal was being loaded onto scab lorries. Banter. The stamping of feet. Rising expectation. The scene more Neo Panto than Neo Realist.

That's the way to do it!

Flashback to the night before; students on their knees in the union bar finishing up '*Coal not Dole*' banners and other factional solidarity statements from Labour party branches, black sections, women's support groups and the inevitable Socialist Workers Party Meanwhile the Revolutionary Communist Party were making a very home-made looking banner somewhere off campus. In secret. Obviously.

Oh no it isn't!

At the head of the march the meticulously repaired, sewn and sewn again Union banner from Betteshanger Colliery; a living antique in faded colours bearing the grandfatherly face of Kier Hardy. We follow behind this quaint legend, made over as minor characters from a Thomas Hardy novel. 'Agitate, educate, organise' it read, as he would have written.

Proud but poor!

Or even at the stretch of the imagination, which is something we were to become very good at, a scene from the ill fated (what else) Kett's rebellion which took place 65 miles north and four hundred and fifty years ago from where we were marching.

Oh no it didn't!

Oh yes it did!

A year later Betteshanger colliery was the last to go back to work, miners marching under the same banner through the pit gates on March 11 1985. Betteshanger had been the only one to go on strike during World War Two. A militant union, with a core of blacklisted miners from the general strike of 1926. In 1985 they successfully held out for the re-instatement of all their comrades who had occupied the colliery during the strike. Eventually in 1989 it was the last of the Kent mines to close, with productivity targets set at an unachievable 20 yards of seam per shift. The writing had been on the wall since the end of the dispute, perhaps before even that.

Trip trap trip trap went the bridge.

A mixture of the hung over and the over eager, workers and students. Miners pushing some students up front soft sacrifice to the forces of law and order. The socialist worker party contingent (Swizzo!) as willing vanguard with a gleam in its collective eye as if this was *a,* (if not *the)* day of judgement. Their leader looked like Jesus for fucks sake, a charismatic bearded and unruly flaxen haired northerner from Rotherham by the name of Stuart, the first to be arrested.

Everyone was buzzed up by the physicality of it all, of being in the moment rather than any bigger picture. We fooled ourselves that anything could happen.

Here we go here we go here we go, here we go here we go here we go O.

Whereas in fact the possible outcomes were limited, the narratives familiar. We were extras in a story that had been told many times before.

Behind you!

Like a social studies field trip, picketing was a practical example of Gramsci's war of position. The intersection of base and superstructure class and culture, a popular front in action as declaimed weekly by our lecturers from behind pedestals and in the tutor groups we had temporarily left behind or indeed, superseded. We lined up, shoulder to shoulder, arms linked, and differences erased. The Miner next to me wore a badge depicting a handshake with the legend: Derbyshire NUM 1880-1980.

We started chanting.

One Arthur Scargill, there's only one Arthur Scargill, one Arthur Scaargill to the tune of Guantanamera...

Who would you have by your side, who would you want to see over your shoulder as the boats hit the beaches of Normandy? Who was staunch? Who a coward?

More memories from the night before. Kent miners dossing down on student floors, farts and belches traded all round in the bonhomie of being on the road, of striking, of being flying pickets, of sharing common cause with people you've never met before like some bloody Lord of the Rings quest. For the miners it was probably the first time on a University campus and finding the beer nearly as cheap as in the club back home and lots of young women too from all over, but keep that quiet from wives and partners back home, manning the soup kitchens, sorting out the day to day, making ends meet, the kids uniforms, lunch boxes, fags, days out, coal for the elderly and for them too since the deliveries stopped and the men away like archers off to Calais, on the road and all the (mis)adventure that entailed...

Maggie! Maggie! Maggie! Out. Out! Out!

Dissolved into the crowd of men and women, liberated and atomised, surrendering our volition to the mass, the joy of being one of many, unsexed, liberated, human. Paul lost his inhibitions in the same way he did when drunk or under the influence of drugs. On the picket lines grey areas of political thought resolved themselves in action. This was true for both sides. These moments (and others later) were a true existential high followed by an emotional comedown that left us jonesing for the next time and still does, punch drunk dreamers of the one true ring.

Isness.

Dasein.

The cops banged their batons on their shields as we surged against the line, those in front on a wave being driven from behind as we pushed, and they pushed before giving way to pull some of us through their lines for arrest and/or a kick in. When the line gave it was as if we were cannoned into the police line sucked through it and out, if you could stay on your feet that is and not get trampled. Insults traded, screamed in faces as the lines separate before surging again. Pickets at the back had stones, bottles and these flew over our heads to jeers from the crowd prompting a baton charge back across the bridge as the tide turned against us.

We ran for cover.

Some of the cops punched women's tits.

The miners united will never be defeated!
The miners united will never be defeated!

The line breaks both ways and we at the front try to smuggle ourselves past the advancing police line evading capture, dodging truncheons shields boots and fists, running through them to get away off the bridge and down into the town. On other darker days the police lines would part to allow mounted police to charge our lines, batons swinging at head height. On this morning there were no horses, so they try and head us off on foot and we run into Wivenhoe, chased by the cops.

This is proper mad! Shouts Paul with joy as we crash into some bins and scrabble up over a fence into a backyard. The age difference between us has dissolved in this *action*, he is no longer twenty something but a youth once more and bang up for it.

A door opens and an old woman gestures us inside. We bundle in and sit panting on the sofa of her sitting room catching our breath, no idea how we have found ourselves here. A minute later she pops her head round the door.

Cup of tea fellas?

We nod vigorously heads between our legs to stop feeling dizzy.

Paul starts coughing up his lungs. Thank fuck he always has a hanky on him. I look up through watery eyes at a framed photograph on the mantlepiece of a young man, same age as me, posing by a Hurricane.

Her son, same age as me, killed in action over the English channel. I assume.

She brings in a tray, cups rattling in their saucers.

Profit before people. That's all they care about. That's what all this is about. We just die protecting it for 'em. That's what my Sam did, flew up in the sky and down into the bloody sea. To protect what's theirs. 21 years old. Loved it he did, flying. He wrote to me about how free he was up there. Joyfully alone he said. Had him where they wanted him in one of their fancy machines, alone.

She looks at us as if for confirmation. We both nod.

There's the kettle, just a mo'.

We smoked and listened and drank tea, what else could we do? There were slices of cake waiting to ambush us from an ancient cake tin already on the table.

She shook with a remnant anger she must have cherished.

Why do you think we allowed the toffs to drive the trams in '26? Not enough of our boys left to throw them off, that's why. Lying dead as they were in the fields of bloody France not 100 feet from their German brothers. Same brothers who shot each other down over the bloody channel.

Whatever we said would always sound hollow when measured against the grief and bitterness of a mother, so we listened in silence. She sat there, her teacup softly rattling against the saucer. After what seemed an age, we poked our heads out the front door to see if any coppers were still about, washed up the cups splashing cold water on our faces to wake us up from the wet heat of the Calor gas. We thanked the old lady and left her sitting on the sofa. We were still wired, adrenalin, fight or flight chemicals still coming off us, energising her anger probably, she picked up on it, hearing us clatter over her garden wall, seeing me eyeballing the photo of her boy and his plane and understanding what had happened in the blink of an eye. Us sitting there in the stillness, invited in to disrupt it, Paul's hand shaking, his essential tremor running across the small room like a cat on a hot tin roof. We ran faster from her than we did from the coppers. She absorbed, negated the flow, her bitterness blocking it and we didn't want to give it up just yet.

Back on Campus in the safety of the bar we heard that

there had been fifteen arrests, mostly students. A protest was going by minivan down to the police station in Colchester. Lorries laden with scab Polish coal had been trundling out of Wivenhoe docks since lunchtime. Rumours of flying pickets from Wales and Durham did the rounds as we drank to our shared experience of strike action and what would come in the days that followed.

Strike breaking Polish communist coal?

Paul swallowed one of his lithium tablets. Chased it with a beer and a whiskey.

Offered me one.

Smoothes it all out. All of it.

He looked down at his shoes, his buzz finally gone.

Snip, snap, snout
This tale's told out.

FOR A FEW DOLLARS MORE

2016

Paul looks up and finds himself in another bar at another time.

How did I get here?

Scattered at tables sat the old, the odd and the decanted, regular customers of the 'Happy Man' last pub standing on the redeveloping Woodberry Down Estate in Manor House North London, where by 2031 Hey Presto! 2000 council homes will be upgraded into 5,000 new flats. The Happy Man. A hold out pub in a changing world like the old guys house in 'UP!' A dilapidated make do and mend building dwarfed by the purposeful, cost-effective new builds, the past haunted by the future. A resident committee resists compulsory purchase orders on their flats in an estate where 42 percent is being sold off plan to Chinese/Singaporean/ Malay investors with a net loss of 300 plus social housing residences and an undisclosed number of flats ring fenced for 'key workers' the new corporate/responsible buzzword for the poor thereby negating, so their lawyer argues, the public good benefit that legally has to underwrite the CPO in the first place. The tenants are picked off one by one with offers of compensation. Fish in a barrel. Slamming the door after the horse has bolted as the decanted would lose out on recanting and so it goes, to the inevitable anti-climax. The Happy Man is also ticking down to its final denouement. The landlady Patsy is not a saint, who is when it comes to offers of money far beyond the scale of daily recompense? The residents meet in her pub, she serves them drinks with the letter from the developers burning a hole in her back pocket.

I mean look at it, it's like a concentration camp no wonder they filmed Schindler's List here, says the developer of the estate he had just 'acquired'. Warsaw wasn't a concentration camp and this estate has been home to thousands of people less fortunate than him since 1948, not a few of them survivors of the camps alongside fathers brothers and husbands back from the war moving into homes for heroes. But he couldn't care less.

Outside, walking briskly under corporate umbrellas the investors are being chaperoned past the pub and onto the estate proper overlooking the majestic Woodberry Down wetlands, not theirs but all of ours. Who are they to know that, with flats for sale that own the view sold sight unseen by glossy catalogue.

Schindler's estate is now a blueprint for urban happiness crows the Times. Back when the original went up the same rag accused Labour MP Herbert Morrison of stealing middle-class homes to build an estate for slum dwellers. Different tune, same song sheet.

A circular walk to clear the head, shiny new towers framing the view, older blocks in the process of becoming new of being re-clad to match the Lego / Ikea inspired visual diktats of *what is new.*

Inside the Happy Man, Meg, seventy something, one of only three left in her block refusing to be moved talks to

Paul's daughter Rosa who is interviewing her for her sixth form school project on gentrification. Paul returns from the bar with two pints of Guinness and a coke.

Thanks darling. Lucky you got your mums colouring, look at yer dad, white as sheet.

Paul sits down. Meg takes a couple of timid sips of her pint. She is a little self-conscious and wipes her mouth. She's got a lot to say.

That thing working?

Rosa nods. Her phone sits on the table in between them, a fleck of foam from a pint of Guinness froths away to nothing on its screen.

They offered Mabel sixty grand to move to a flat down in Kent, and she was gonna take it and give the money to her son, who's had to move out to Edmonton with his family. Most kids would have grabbed it but he asked her what's a black woman going to do down in Kent? Called the council, shame on them for offering, for wanting to dump her with all the migrants and nutters down on the coast, his mum who had worked all her life in the prison service. Mind you they ended up taking the money, who wouldn't? And she's moved in with them, now that will end badly you mark my words. Whole building is empty, security guard long gone, it gives me the shivers going up in the lift, door opens on empty corridors, one on top of the other. Mopping up the piss outside my own bloody door, God knows who done that. Scared to death I am but nobody offered me any money and I ain't got any kids. That's another story, wasn't for want of trying I can tell you. Every day I wake up a fucking ghost in my own home, it's not right I tell ya.

Rosa nods, checks her phone is still recording and sips her coke.

Meg slowly, methodically drinks her Guinness as proof of life by means of the laws of physics and disappearing liquids.

Where does she put it all, skinny as a pencil? A line of foam accruing on the hairs of her top lip trembles as she sucks her teeth and mutters.

Another one Meg?

That will be lovely ta. Who lives in those new towers I ask you, overlooking the fancy pond?' She shrugs and shuffles off to the beer garden for a smoke.

Told you she liked to talk.

What a strong woman. Legend.

Carl, a fifty year old park ranger, whose *sensi* green fingers work their magic on the flowerbeds of Clissold park, lives in Hackney but with kids all over from Peckham and up the estuary as far away as Rochester, always keeping a river between him and his exes, his hand snaking like the Thames as he outlines his philosophy for a quiet life over the top of the table and the cans of Breaker lined up like grain silos.

A pub that serves cans when the glasses ran out and even before, up to you. What's your poison? Mine? Wray and Nephew on the rocks with a spit of coke, thank you kindly.

In (slightly) darker moments he riffs on the Parliament channel and all the conspiracies that lie up on the big tables, Davos, G7, IMF, the World Bank,

Bombaclaat White House and dem places.

But none of these clouds darken his karma enough

to embitter him it's all just engagement, observation, enlightenment, the way he rolls through life his hands deep in the soil nurturing flowers and plants, anchoring him to small things in a big world.

Six spliffs carefully rolled before breakfast, three with filters, three without, a healthy balance for the day, everyday.

At the bar on a stool perches 'Everybody out!' Pete, always scabbing drinks, nicknamed *Laces* when he worked down the print, hanging back doing up his shoes outside the pub to miss any chance of having to buy the first round and then made sure he was in the bogs for the second and ponced a fag outside for the third this was the measure of the man. Pints of lager with chasers after 5pm, Carling and generic whiskies you'd have thought would have killed him long ago. But it was hate that kept him alive, bitter coffee beans of hate, fuel to be ground down in the rituals of devotion and sacrifice on the high altar of his precious beliefs. He offered up his memories to any that would listen. The good old days when the East End turned on the royals during the blitz, crowds booing and chucking tomatoes at the Queen mum, seeing her off and the cops that came with her.

Urcha!

After a doodlebug killed 173 at Bethnal Green, what do you expect? The working-class will only take so much.

He spits the last as if you hadn't got his point. The kind of man that's no use to any class, especially not his own.

Investigating this story you find no record of any of this, no tomatoes thrown, no jeering, there's no trace of this dissent in any of the history books. This disaster took place during an air raid in 1943. The victims died in a crush trying to escape Hitler's wrath underground. But there wasn't any bomb and this the largest loss of civilian life during the war in the days after allied planes had hit Berlin in the biggest air raid on the German capital to date. There was a fear of reprisal in the air. Trepidation on the streets. What you read in the newspapers had consequences. Enough to spook a stampede to escape Hitler's revenge, helter skelter down the stairs of Bethnal green Tube station.

In the days that followed, the Queen was greeted by cheering crowds of fellow Londoners when she visited the area. Solidarity. The East End, The Royals, Londoners.

Pete's mouth twitched as he spat out his version, becoming a tremor that contorts his whole mouth. A story as ugly as the manner of its telling. But at least the lies got shared around. It was officially reported that the Tube station had been bombed which provides a grain of truth for all his rubbish, the false memories of this disappointed man. Only the pub anchors him, magnetic north for his life compass granting him sanctuary from harsher judgement. The Happy man had its own way of world making.

Paul summoned all of these people in this room and wove them into an idea of who they were. Who they were for him, how each functioned in relation to his symbolic order. His chess pieces. And he had invited his daughter into this demimonde. Sarah wouldn't approve, had never stepped inside on principle, having no time to waste.

A room full of losers Paul and you one of them, the worst because that's what you think you are. You think it so hard that it's become true and that's really sad. It's what you want to be. A self-fulfilling prophecy.

Paul returns to the table with two more pints. The residents meeting is about to begin. Rosa pockets her phone and finishes her coke. Her mum is on nights so they will get a takeaway for supper.

Paul raises his hand and suggests in his quiet flat voice that they chain themselves to the diggers and plant machinery surrounding the pub. To the wheels of the cranes, the fucking executive vehicles of the site managers, to the coaches of prospective buyers, to the old Yew tree they plan to cut down. Direct action to slow down the process of development, to make some noise, to attract attention, to capture the hearts and minds of the people. To engage once more in the war of position.

Rosa is impressed with her dad, places her hand over his, partly to quiet its tremor. This was as far as she knew an echo of a younger Paul. Her dad the radical. She would tell mum.

A few cheers (possibly ironic) and the rest awkward silence. There's only fifteen of them at the meeting although online petitions have been signed by a few thousand. An invisible few thousand.

What's it to you? Wheezes Meg, who'll not be helped.

You already live in one of the new flats.

Sarah had said this to him only that morning.

Patsy finishes pulling a pint and says guiltily under her breath 'You see this lot doing any of that? Where's the balls on them? It's too late Paul, too late for chaining yourself to anything.'

Paul shakes his head, ruffles a pile of papers, a printout of the online petition.

Thousands of signatures. He mutters.

Patsy is exasperated.

Where's the people then? The ones that signed it? I don't see 'em. If they all came in here and bought a drink I'd like to see that. This is a public meeting in a public house. Doors open. God knows I could do with the custom.

A few sheepish laughs from the floor. A fag hangs precariously from the corner of Paul's mouth, like in the moment before a western shootout, as the musical pocket watch ticks itself down intercut with fast cuts of downcast eyes in close up.

The locals look away. Meg, Pete, Carl, the few others gathered in the pub did not have it in them.

At the moment of asking.

Neither did Paul. He shouldn't have asked.

His daughter taps his shoulder.

Shall we go home dad? Come on, let's get a Chinese.

THE GREAT PEACE

O Rose thou art sick. The invisible worm,
That flies in the night In the howling storm.
Sick Rose, William Blake.

University generated many different timelines which we lived simultaneously. Academic life, family life, life of the mind, social life, a life in music, a life of drink and drugs and for some (others) a life of sport. And then there was the life of student union politics and beyond that the life of the world at large, North vs South, East vs West, the liberation movement in South America and Southern Africa, the non-aligned movement against capitalism and the struggle for world revolution beyond, encompassing that.

You could argue that we lived in a Venn diagram of many object domains in which the revolution was being won and lost at different rates in each one.

You could argue that.

The winter of 1984 was no different. Like all good foot soldiers, we found ourselves one wet and wintry day in Calais.

Kent NUM President Malcolm Pitt and the General Secretary of the National Union of Seamen Jim Slater were on the dockside to meet the CGT's convoy of lorries as they assembled at the port ready to board the British ferry St. Christopher. The 35 lorries were accompanied by 800 French workers who were given a rousing send-off as they set sail. In a short speech before they left the CGT general secretary Henri Krasucki criticised the British government. Speaking from a platform on the quayside bedecked with French and British flags and a joint CGT-NUM banner supporting the strike, he condemned Margaret Thatcher for cutting off family allowances to punish the strikers.

We all cheered, huddled as we were on the French docks surrounded by French workers.

In this domain, the domain of class struggle, we sung the Internationale.

The police have formed special repressive brigades to unleash violence in the mining communities. British miners no longer have enough food to eat, enough money to clothe their new-born babies, or to bury their dead.

In faltering French, Pitt declared Mrs Thatcher was *the parrot of President Reagan, perching on his shoulder preaching the same militarist and imperialist policies.*

We applauded.

There is blood on British coal shouted Mr Pitt to chants of:

Thatcher is a fascist from the crowd.

We cheered.

On its way to Calais the long procession of lorries had lumbered through the straggling villages north of Arras on a tour of French mining communities.

Villages north of Arras. We have been here before. Another object domain, that of war which shares many objects with that of class struggle. Blood, soil, officers, men and civilians, the call to arms, victory, defeat and medals of honour.

> **Outside the town hall of each mining village with names like Bully les Mines or Billy les Montigny, the convoy stopped briefly to present the local mayor with a gilt medal to commemorate the CGT's generosity. Copies of the medal, complete with red, white and blue ribbons, were later put on sale to union members at about £4 a time as they munched sausages and bags of chips in a carnival atmosphere on the quayside at Calais.** *(The Times, 15.10.1984).*

The Times attempting to insinuate something about both the French in particular and trade unions in general. But carnival was always ours, and couldn't be used against us. The toiling man and woman, the indentured worker, the slave, the serf, the soldier owned carnival gifting us the human comedy.

Ben Battle was a soldier bold
and used to wars alarms
But a cannonball took off his legs
So he laid down his arms.

The lorry send off was done in this spirit of timeless carnival, cocking a snook at all the powers ranged against us from the grand injustice of Fate all the way down to the parking tickets that awaited our vans and cars back home.

The convoy drove on to the ferry to a rousing chorus of the Red Flag and three cheers for the striking miners. The ferry workers clapped the lorries aboard. The St. Christopher left Calais in blazing sunshine, horn blaring under clear blue skies and an atmosphere of convivial solidarity. On the top deck bar, we opened cans and raised glasses to the Miners, the French workers and to the International. Victory was within our grasp.

> **As the white cliffs of Dover came into view, a roar of pleasure rose from the throats of the 800. The French blue, white and red tricolour, the British Union Jack and the red flag of the CGT fluttered in the light breeze.** *(Morning Star, 15.10.1984).*

King for a day was to be as good as it got. It always was. Blake knew exactly how close to God you could get and no further.

That winter I was cast in the role of 'The spirit of the revolution' in a student production of Volker Braun's 'The Great Peace.' This auspicious East German playwright, director of the Berliner Ensemble no less, was to attend the opening performance.

The problem was the play was a turgid Maoist metaphor written as historical allegory to pass East German censors by way of boredom. The story of a village of Chinese peasants rising up against their evil landlord to throw off the chains of poverty and oppression. (I kid you not). It was lifeless and reductive. Staged in the U.K. at the height of a national strike under a high Tory government the play was at best an irrelevance. It took no part in any war of position that I could fathom. The director, James Dudley Brown was also on the U.K. frisbee team. A man of many talents. After the dress rehearsal the cast agreed to drop acid on the opening night as a gesture of rebellion. The play was dead at a time when the struggle itself was still alive.

At a rousing speech in Dalkeith, Midlothian, N.U.M. Vice-President Mick McGahey expressed heartfelt thanks for the financial and material aid striking miners were receiving from their brothers and sisters in the Soviet Union.

We are proud and grateful for it, said McGahey, responding to a campaign that was attempting to smear the NUM for accepting 'Russian gold'.

The Soviet domain or indeed the domain of the Soviets had many objects.

Britain's miners had received from 'our Soviet comrades' a total of £903,000 including £500,000 worth of food and clothing from Ukrainian miners, the remainder being made up of collections for the miners' hardship fund. Literally buckets doing the rounds of mines, factories and other workplaces at shifts end. McGahey emphasised that the solidarity between British and Soviet trade unionists went back a very long way. We were amongst the first to send a delegation to a young Soviet Union in 1924.

We have always remembered the contribution the Soviet miners gave us in 1926. In Scotland it was called the 'Russian hauf croon'. This union is proud of our internationalism, and we welcome and are grateful for donations coming from Soviet trade unionists. (*Morning Star, 19.11.84*).

The climax of the Great Peace involved the peasant hero (this was in effect an East German Panto devoid of any contextual humour) receiving a Sword from the Spirit of the revolution. My role was to swing onto the stage, hand him the sword and swing out again. Symbolically empowered (sic) the hero proceeds to defeat the evil landlord and his henchmen.

Early evening on the night of the first performance I had a drink with Paul and Sarah. She was actually wearing a black dress for the show. Piss taker.

Looking forward to this. Can't say I've ever been to the theatre before.

Come off it, what about school or did you leave there at ten?

Paul sniggered. Sarah gets up, straightens out her costume.

Another round? I want to show off my fancy dress.

We both nodded and she flounced off to the bar.

This is going to be more panto than theatre, you must have seen a panto?

Broadway theatre, my mum took us to see Cinderella.

Well, you get the picture.

I was still dressed in my spirit of the revolution silk trousers with drawstring under my Bunnymen coat. I flashed Paul a leg and a Chinese slippered foot.

Fuck me.

Sarah came back with pints and shots on a tray. We downed them and cheered ourselves.

Right I better be off. See you later.

Break a leg. Paul, always with the last word.

The theatre was packed. There were even some reporters from London sitting in the front row to document the presence of Volker Braun. He'd shaken the cast and crews hands beforehand. Po faced prick. Crew first, cast second.

Fuck knows why he got a visa, perhaps the DDR were hoping he wouldn't want to go back. I dropped my tab of acid in the green room during the interval. The rest of the cast changed their minds.

Come on. I said. We agreed.

Holding out the tabs in my sweaty palm I shook them towards the cast like dice, which they refused to roll.

The hero of the revolution even muttered an apology. In their shifty eyes I could see they were worried about what the director would say. Middle-class wankers. He had them all fooled. From that moment on I have never trusted or become friends with another actor. Meat puppets the lot of them, petit objects of the theatre domain.

I came up in the wings five minutes before my big entrance. The rest of the cast blanked me as if it wasn't happening, carried on as per rehearsals, the fucking director beaming in the front row alongside Volker Braun.

Tripping in the dark is weird, there's not much for the mind to grab hold of just motes of obscured light behind your eyelids swirling about in the darkness. It's not until I glimpsed the stage through the curtains that I realised I was in trouble. An explosion of shifting shape and colour. Rainbow coloured outlines bled off the sharp edges of everything, colours with sound effects exploding against each other. I closed my eyes tightly allowing fireworks to project and fade onto the back of my eyelids. In the dark I felt I had it under control. I tamped down hard and stumbled up the ladder into the gantry. The stagehand helped me into the swing, I couldn't hear a word he whispered, his lips just a wet nibble on my ear. The curtain was pulled back so they could time my flight with the action on stage, I remembered this bit from rehearsals. Somebody passed me what looked like a sword in its scabbard. It nearly slipped out of my clammy cold hands. There were too many straps and buckles on the scabbard I thought they would get tangled and I would strangle myself trying to get it over my head. But I remembered I had to hand it over, not wear it myself so I pulled the sword out held it in my hand across my knees. The scabbard fell to the stage. The stagehand held up some fingers then took them away one by one. I remembered this countdown and held tight with a gloved hand to the swing rope. This was proving to be a very complicated procedure with too many variables. I sweated profusely. I saw no more fingers and glided out into the centre of the stage. Light embraced me, a sharp glare bounced off the sword as we both fell to earth.

Gasps from the audience which I heard as an animal hissing but also as a rush of timpani, a word I didn't even know I knew.

I was eating my face off in A&E, no breaks, a few bruises, apparently if I hadn't been so out of it, it could have been a lot worse. They see it all the time with drugs the nurse said, same as falling down flights of stairs and getting up without a scratch when plastered she said.

Paul and Sarah were waiting for me in reception.

Fuck me you fell like a sack of spuds from the poxy swing mate, almost impaling yourself on that sword. I never laughed so hard in my life, Sarah was fit to piss herself.

A true legend you are, she kept saying, a true legend. Which I liked.

The hero bloke, well he just ran off shitting himself. It was the landlord's serf fellas that picked you up before the curtain fell. The German was the first up on his feet and scarpered. Sarah and me unfurled the Miners banner at the back and the rest of the audience started clapping.

Just a pity you didn't turn up earlier. We had to sit through the first half. It was worth it mind, in retrospect like.

He patted my shoulder, the only time I think we ever 'touched'.

December

A Danish coaster, the Berth Bjorn, carrying 200 tons of Christmas toys and clothes for striking miners' families, docked at Hull after a crossing from Copenhagen. The cargo, unloaded without pay by TGWU dockers, included shoes, winter coats and sweaters, plus 50,000 toys. The gifts had been collected over a ten-day period following an appeal issued by the Danish Seafarers Union. Trade unionists in Denmark established 174 collection centres. The scale of the response to the request for solidarity with the mining communities and the support this had received from children especially, had amazed the Seafarers Union, said its President, Henrik Berlau.

Waiting on the dockside for the Berth Bjorn to dock were Jim Slater, General Secretary of the National Union of Seamen and a large contingent of Yorkshire miners and their families, led by the Yorkshire NUM General Secretary, Owen Briscoe. Mr Slater said the support for the strikers' families from children in other countries who had learned about their hardship showed that the miners' struggle was one that had backing from the *whole international working class movement*. Mr Briscoe praised the support shown throughout Scandinavia which had been *fantastic and second to none.* Yorkshire NUM executive member Brian Conley said the clothes and toys would be distributed among the families of the 53,000 striking miners in Yorkshire, and would help mitigate the effects of the tremendous hardship they faced. *It will put smiles on our children's faces and bring home the fact that our communities are not isolated.*

> **Tom Sibley, London representative of the WTFU, said all its affiliated organisations had pledged to continue supporting the British until the victory they deserve is achieved. International aid is pouring in to ensure that miners' families, particularly children, get a little extra at Christmas.**
> *Morning Star, 20.12.84*

I received a reprimand from the vice Chancellors office for bringing the university theatre into disrepute. There was no interview in the press from Volker Braun, I assume he scuttled off back to the socialist paradise he hated. That was to be the only performance of 'The Great Peace' in the west. A blessing for which I should have received a medal. Instead, the director found me in the student union bar and told me I would never work in the theatre again. I was sitting with some Kent Miners at the time, drowning our several sorrows and it was all I could do not to lay the prick out.

SIGNIFICANT / OTHER

Sam's hair smelt of bubblegum, an odd thing to smell with her bobbing up and down on top of you grabbing her tight pale arse and getting whiffs of childhood from all that hair that didn't move. It was the hairspray on her mohican, keeping it rock hard which in itself is a bit odd whilst fucking, this immobile vertical. After a night caning it we looked a proper mess also, crusty earring holes rimmed with spots of blood and puss, black tar fur balls of make-up rubbed from bleary eyes, crumpled discarded clothes, lipstick smears and skid marks mocking the glamour of our student post punk lifestyle.

Sam was from Westleigh Lancashire. Her dad was a miner and her granddad before him. Her mum was a primary school teacher. Her parents had saved up for her to go to teacher training college, sacrificed holidays, skimped on clothes and she had also been funded by the Union via donations from the Miner's benevolent fund, all of this backstory delivered in a disarming slow and steady delivery of short vowels and flat consonants. Sam was an only child because they couldn't afford to have another, if that is, they wanted to send Sam to University. Her mum wanted her to go one further than she had got. Her dad was all for an easy life so he went along with it which meant for him as much overtime underground as he could get. The amount of foresight and sacrifice it took to get Sam to this point in life was like putting a woman on the moon. And here aw am fucking some southerner telling uz all about Karl Marx and Fidel Castro. It's like being in heaven, it really is.

She was funny. When she was little her dad had tried to kill himself with her and her mum in the house by sticking his head in the oven and lighting a match. He couldn't handle going down 'that bloody black hole' any longer. The funny thing was she wanted to tell you the story whilst you were having sex, especially morning sex.

In th'end bastard couldn't go through wi' it. Why I'm here fucking you, every cloud an all that.

I think this made her feel better. She wanted to shock people, put them off at the same time as wanting to be liked, or at least understood better.

She would tell a variation of the same story or just more of it, more details, when drinking in the bar.

Ma not told him they turned t' gas off day before. Find that funny do ya?

It was her story. These were the facts of her life. She wore a snakebite grin and a speed gurn at the same time which made her look like a demented Batman baddie, which she wasn't at all.

She was the only *girlfriend* I had that Paul acknowledged. He liked to buy her drinks to see what she would say next. She had amazing green eyes, jewels set in the pallor of her face and they burnt with a cold fire. Lighthouse eyes Paul called them, although he'd never seen a lighthouse, not even the one at Holyhead when he was on the ferry to Dublin.

As a kid as he had always been asleep in the car, for they always took the earliest crossing. This detail came out after an exchange of working-class holiday stories between the two of them. Sam's camping weekends up on the moors and Pauls yearly visits to the old country, to his grandparents. She got it out of him, he didn't mind telling her stuff about himself that he guarded from everybody else, mundane details that would lessen his mystery although I doubt he ever thought like that about himself.

Sam threw herself into the Latin American solidarity campaign. She had never been abroad and wanted to volunteer in Nicaragua. She also told a story about Arthur Scargill's daughter (Margaret?) who had been a doctor in Cuba and came home to set up the first ever walk in medical centre in the UK, in Yorkshire, based on 'get this, the Communist Cuban model.' She really loved that irony, it validated her and her background even before the strike. In the years that followed she would become a leading internationalist. She travelled way past what her mother envisioned, coming to University had transformed her life. It would be easy to write that in another life we could have been happy together that maybe life would have been different if we had stayed together longer than the few months we went out for. But I do remember her grin and her smile (two totally different ways of arranging her face, both disarming and vital), her quirky attitude, the fire in her soul and the way she made love almost fanatically to banish her own demons as well as scare the shit out of me. In a book without lies I would wonder why I remember those things so clearly out of a sea of other things I have completely forgotten and a sense of loss would disarm me.

When serious, when looking for the most serious things in your face, in your heart, her eyes would be wet with tears she refused to shed, her mouth would hang open in a small O shape, in expectation of you telling her the truth, whatever the question was.

Her dad told her about the first black man down the pit. He'd moved to the village with his family looking for work. So the women had spoken, the kids had started at the school. 'A very nice family' by all accounts. During his first shift few words were shared, helmets on and coal black faces they all looked the same, but it would take more than that for him to fit in. In the showers at the end of the shift each man rubbed the coal off the others back. That's how it was, the custom was you rubbed each other down as you wanted to walk home as clean as possible, they didn't want to carry the smell of it back home with them.

See a man without his clothes on, then he's just a man.

After that they became mates, pints down the pub, went to the football. The women in the village were another story, how they treated his wife and down the social, what they whispered. The family moved after a few years, away from the pit villages and back to the city. The man would have stayed, it was good wages but his wife couldn't stand it, couldn't stand the other Miner's wives. Jealous cold bitches her mother called them and she should know she had to teach their kids and Sam laughed so hard to hear her mother talk like that.

Int all plain sailing feminism, is it? Not like in books. Wimmin beware Wimmin reet enough.

I didn't have time to think, I listened and looked at her, her sharp eyes, her thin dry chapped lips. Looking back, well we had to laugh, what were we doing? She nineteen going on forty and me, well all I had was just 19.

Paul even told Sam the story of the girl going under his train, which is how I know the details of it. Of his mate Paul the guard losing his head going into the tunnel. She trail-blazed this ability to talk about yourself at a distance. Like a talking cure she wasn't afraid of revealing all the gory details of her life as if she was a character over there in a story, not right here the person telling it and she relished in the telling of it. Her ailments were another chapter in this book, cysts on her ovaries, shingles, 'I still got bloody cradle cap look!' she would bend over and immediately part her not inconsiderable hair to show me, standing there shivering in her knickers.

Last thing she wanted was sympathy and I think it was this that made Paul happy to talk to her in the same register. I remember Sarah hated Sam and I can see why.

Sam truly existed, she stepped out of the crowd. To be seen. The facts of her were unique delivered with a glint in her eye as if life is all one big wind up. You remember things or people that truly exist, they persist in memory, less altered than the rest, unequivocal. And offer up more of themselves the more you think about them. The rest is just interference, flat and predictable.

I loved her, I think. We only slept with each other for a few months and not all the time even then. We stayed friends throughout the rest of our time at university. She had her ups and downs like everybody else. She could lose the plot, throw beers on people she thought were taking the piss, cry herself out over some perceived slight, be vulnerable and aggressive by turns. She always did her course work, handed in her essays whatever state she was in. She carried the responsibility of her families sacrifice quietly and with purpose and she never stopped talking from her perspective as a working-class woman. She demanded to be acknowledged, from lovers, fellow students, lecturers fuck me, even bus drivers. I remember one time...

The story didn't get any better for her old man after the miners' strike. He was a Bickershaw miner, a pit that struggled with its deep seams, where working conditions were 90 degrees, 80 per cent humidity. He worked the plodder seam, hard graft but a 15 foot seam with a 1 in 7 gradient, made harder by a dirt band right through it, taking that out and holding up the roof made it a ballbreaker. He wrote to his daughter giving her the facts with which to set the record straight as if she, the first person in their family to go to university had the power to do so. Which Sam pursued with a passion, reading from this letter and others at meetings and to journalists for months afterwards, wearing the paper thin with her finger tracing the lines she read from until she had learnt them by rote.

She truly represented.

With another tack seam just below it, the Haigh yard seam, our plodder seam had always been prone to overheating and spontaneous combustion. Fire damp had killed men regularly since before the war. Rail transport ran out 60 meters from the face and they had to drag the steel by hand, so this 15ft seam was laughing back at us, we had to half kill ourselves to get at it, we thought we were gods if we made 60 metres in a week. All the money spent and profitability the new buzzword, threat more like, so when the strike came we voted, we voted easily. Other seamers less so, but down on 71 seam, it was everybody out and take our chances. This is underground talk, no paper was interested all they wanted to know about was the begging buckets, and what our wives were doing behind our backs.

And then we find her up in the pit villages (of course she returned home) those green eyes lighting up the corners of a story we all thought exhausted. She was fearless. To go back and down the pit to witness the end of it.

Old men in the corner of the club, in the only armchairs, telling the story of what they saw in '59, of the five men hauled onto the conveyor belt, deadweight, like so much coal going up to the surface, 200 yards 1 in 8 gradient others waiting to drag them out not a burn mark on them, just carbon monoxide, the invisible killer.

And technical notes written down with Komsomol like sincerity, underlined, made bold starred and annotated throughout.

Stoping is the process of extracting the desired ore or other mineral from an underground mine, leaving behind an open space known as a stope. Stoping is used when the country rock is sufficiently strong not to collapse into the stope, although in most cases artificial support is also provided.

The Miners strike was the end for her dad, he never went back down a pit that only stayed open until 1990, working on the pit top on the screens sorting dirt from coal, off a conveyor, like working at the checkout of a fucking bloody Supermarket, for shit pay and his former colleagues disdain, although they would still stand him the odd pint.

What with the investment in the Super pit and our sister pit Goldborne closed in 89 from exhaustion our targets were going up week by week, finally that bloody black hole was closed and I couldn't even get a job in a supermarket.

I can't remember what Sam studied, except that she loved reading. She was always reading, Bronte, Austen she loved, Anna Kavan was her role model she would joke, a posh woman who ended up in a nut house. Sam got me to read Dworkin for the first time, pressing her book *Woman Hating* into my hand, which makes sense as they both burnt from both ends and in fact Sam had clammy hands, even these details come to mind with ease. I imagine Sam now, the easiest person to recollect after all these years, no need for embellishment. She was studying for a degree in literature and sociology, I remember that now, and I only really knew what she did in that first year of ours and less and less after that, her occasionally showing me her research, her interviews with her dad, with other miners, pensioners and the women, which must have been her degree thesis in the aftermath of our great disaster. Her life after that was her own.

JUBILEE

The Queen visited the University campus in the summer that followed the end of the Miners strike. It felt like we were having our noses rubbed in it.

A few days before the planned visit staff brought in (at night) a special Portaloo for her Majesty's convenience and parked it discretely out by one of the lakes. The night before her arrival we rocked it onto its side so that it overturned and came to rest half in the water. Rumours of a gold toilet seat spread across campus but in truth we never got a look inside because as soon as we turned it over we legged it. The Chancellor, or whoever it is that runs the University and invites heads of state like the Queen to visit was apoplectic with rage, threatening to expel the culprits as soon as they were identified. Tory students scoured the halls, the bars and the quads looking to beat up likely suspects, without any joy but there was a level of political tension on campus seeded by recent memory and the continuing war in Ireland, that could reignite itself at any provocation from right or left.

Love was definitely not in the air.

On the morning of the visit there was a lot of security on the ground framed by helicopters overhead. On the rooftops overlooking the quads you could see heavy duty special branch or whoever they were whatever unit it was they belonged to visibly armed and ready to scan the crowds. There was a sense of trepidation, odd vibes as soon as you got up. The state was in the house. The atmosphere recharged us, made us feel important, something was going to happen. Everyone eyeballed everybody else as Campus filled up. Left and right wing students mixed with a crowd of locals and visitors. We had read Elias Canetti's Crowds and Power.

We were the crowd.

When it came to it known troublemakers were discretely taken out of the equation by faceless men in everyday suits, no noise, no fuss, redacting the 'troublemakers' and themselves from the picture.

This way sir. A vice like grip on the elbow, threatening a twist.

Just for the next few hours.

Up and into an unmarked van parked underground.

Not a peep out of you sonny boy.

Finger gun drilling the middle of the forehead.

They didn't come for me and I watched the whole visit from the back of large flag waving crowd mostly bussed in from Colchester. I think I saw the Queen's hat, or at least a hat worn by one of her ladies in waiting or it could have been the wife of the University Chancellor. Bright green it was, like a day out at the races kind of hat. It was a sunny day so I ended up with a little sunstroke after drinking four pints of London Pride.

God save the Queen.

The night ended with a few bottles thrown across the concrete expanse of the quads as the political tribes of campus retreated to their respective bars, the police, secret services leaving as soon as the Queen's visit was over. The state had left the premises.

The crowd hadn't performed.

OUR CHANTY

The first time I took MDMA was in the Student Union bar
in the early summer of 1985. An American friend had been
sent some powder in the post, this was before pills and was
exotic as fuck. All we had ever sniffed up till then were
five pound bags of amphetamine. We chopped lines on the
kitchen table of our tower block flat, did them and walked
down to the bar. Coming up was subtle, a smooth cool
tingling feeling after knife like sinus pain, the eye watering
initial hit fizzed into our tummies down our legs and along
our arms shooting straight out of our hands and feet as we
bounced along the concrete walkways.

Walking on air.

We started to smile in sync as if smiling came first and we
the smilers just tagged along for the ride.

Gravity weakened. We were hyper aware of what was
left. We felt pressure pushing down on us and pushed back
against the weight of its blanket as we moved. In the bar the
warmth, the noise and the jukebox overwhelmed us. Our
skin was no longer resistant to music, it flowed through us
dragging us along in its wake by the hooks it sank deep into
us. Touch! We touched each other. As the high took hold,
deepened, we touched each other a lot. Lubed with sweat it
was effort enough to hold ourselves in, to hold it together, to
control to harness the flow. Kissing was like feeding time at
the zoo, we were inside the cage and didn't want to be let out.

The light pours out of me.

That first night whoever went to the bar spent everything they had on a round of drinks for anybody who wanted one.

Coke, which we started taking much later when it was cheaper and we could afford it was always wrapped up in glossy porn mag paper but never MDMA which came folded in clean white paper, which kind of sums up the two drugs. The excitement of getting handed a wrap by a dealer and whispering 'great, that's a fatty' as you felt the bulging amount of powder inside. The origami like intricacy of the process itself, managing your rising expectations, taking it into the bogs trying not to spill any as you unfolded it already pissed or already on a line trying to slow down be methodical dividing off an amount onto the ceramic toilet top, like Shep in *One Man and His Dog*, herding the gear off the paper with your cashpoint card, or bus pass and then the fucking edge of the paper flips up and spills some of the powder away from the main body of the mound you have sidled off or even occasionally literally catapults a soft rock of it across the floor of the bog and you wetting your finger to pick it up off the piss wet tiles, (or not). Powder waiting to be herded up and then chopped, a tricky business. Roll up the fiver, sniff the lot and mop it up with your index finger, gag, wrap the gear up again trying to put the paper tongue triangle back into its fold like a camel through the eye of a needle it was easier to just do the lot in but you couldn't do that as your character was judged by how little you took of somebody else's gear just as you judged them in turn.

Don't be a greedy cunt. and/or *Leave me some.* as they take your wrap and on returning it *Fuck me you cunt.* and/or *I just had a line mate, wasn't a lot left.*

By the time whatever was left of the gear was back in

your pocket and the toilet wiped down and you came back out into the bar you're desperate for a shit and have to squeeze your cheeks or turn right back round again.

When pills entered the market it cut out all the bloody faff.

After we started taking E's, Paul still slouched against the wall in the kitchen at parties but now would be biting down on the desire to laugh uncontrollably, eyes swimming in his head his natural shyness and reticence under chemical assault. He literally looked like somebody was firing a hand cranked gatling gun at him as he jerked and spasmed to tamp down the drugs inside him. And he kept eating them. Sarah was no better, giggling, coal black eyes shining under all that hair propped up against Paul laughing like drains.

Go on, give us another. Fucking great! And drank a half bottle of wine in two or three gulps to wash it down.

He loved E's.

The light pours out of thee.

In the 90's I went out with somebody who worked as a teller at the Midland bank on the Edgware Road and remember dropping her off outside on a Monday morning after a huge weekend and a Sunday session down the Egg club where she had had at least three pills. Who knows the long term effects of this but in the short term how she held down her job was a miracle and if I had been cleverer some kind of bank heist must have been on the cards as there must have been literally hundreds if not more of youth working in banks who were off their tits all week or at least Monday and Tuesday and probably the best time to hit a bank would be midweek when the huge comedown must have rendered them catatonic and susceptible to persuasion or the threat of violence. *Just pulling down a smiley face mask would have them twitching behind the counters...*

That summer, July 1985, the Womad festival came to Mersea Island and we all camped out on the beach with our beat boxes, extra batteries and cheap two man tents, spliffs, pills and sheets of acid tabs. The Burundi drummers were playing fresh off the back of doing that song with Echo and the Bunnymen, the concert being a mash up of Indie bands and what was then called world music. Toots and the Maytals, Nusrat Fateh Ali Khan, New Order, the Fall, the Pogues and Thomas Mapfumo.

Throwing up underwater after acid tabs chased by scrumpy as the bands played behind the beach and we floated and sank out there, eventually dragging ourselves out of the sea to sway to the bar like mermen ordering drinks by slapping down the new one pound coins on the bar in a puddle of seawater and shouting 'gold nuggets' at the top of our voices which is what the coins had become inflated into by the hallucinogenics, rocks of gold in our cartoon like throbbing hands.

Drink and the Devil had done for the rest.

Most students had already cycled back into the world for the summer; to London, Heathrow and beyond, to summer jobs, holidays, trips back home. We on the other hand were busy playing pirates years before Johnny Depp made the cliche his own. So spangled on tabs of acid so drunk on cider and fortified wine.

Help me somebody help me.

And the headliners were on stage and we came out of the

sea, drawn to the stage by the pulsing synths of New Order. We succumbed to the electronic waves.

That summer, that weekend on Mersea Island did feel like the end of something. Red and white Sandinista T shirts in the sunshine.

The weekend replays itself in moments of slow motion and speeded up sequences to the soundtrack of September Song by Green Day which was released 2004. I have succumbed to nostalgia. Losing the 'Isness' of what I am writing about. Being in that moment, seeing it through my eyes for the first time has been lost.

Summers contain the DNA of how we remember them; the freedom and romance of holidays, the excitement and noise of festivals, endless summer and the inevitable end of summer. Oaths and promises kept and broken. Rich material paid forward. Summers are themselves anthems to be sung over and over which is probably why that song was so popular, so demotic, so familiar, so always already having been sung. Summers are always already over the first day twinned with the last. This is the melancholia of summer.

On one of these last summer nights I was in the back of a car with Paul smoking out of the window. Sarah was sitting up front and Arnie was driving.

We drove out to Brightlingsea, passing a bottle between the four of us. Earlier we had done some mushrooms. It was after midnight and we parked on the quay by the Yachtsman Arms. We unmoored a row boat and pushed off. Under a half moon Sarah sang sea shanties from the prow as me and Paul rowed out into the estuary. Arnie sat at the back playing guitar.

I thought I heard the Old Man say
Leave her, Johnny, leave her.

Tomorrow you will get your pay,
and it's time for us to leave her.

Sarah stood elegantly in the prow. Paul stood up to join in and nearly went overboard. He had no sea legs and his voice was terrible, it was as if the boat wanted to throw him off.

I gripped the oars and kept her steady. Arnie started giggling which was catching. We all were gripped by a fit of giggles and the boat rocked.

Sorry, sorry, give me a minute, managed Arnie slumped over the tiller.

She called them her shanties, (She sang regularly when drunk, at parties and sometimes in the pubs of Colchester and surrounding estuary villages. Her string of pearls she would call them, referring either to the songs she sang or the pubs she sang them in.

We got our giggling under control and Sarah resumed her song a bottle of Vodka gripped in one hand whilst the other gripped the gunnel as she swayed.

Oh, the wind was foul and the sea ran high.
Leave her, Johnny, leave her!
She shipped it green and none went by.
And it's time for us to leave her.

Paul sprawled on the bench and looked up at her silently.

Fifteen years later they would finally have a child long after giving up trying naming her Rosa after the murdered German revolutionary Rosa Luxemburg.

But it was that night before life made a tragedy or an irony or a whatever it is that life makes of the lives we all end up living, no matter how long or short, it was that night, with me keeping the boat steady that I like to think sealed their relationship for longer than the duration of a moment. A song that binds or something memorable like that something to hang all the rest on. If Paul had toppled over the side perhaps it would have been me (via the route of sympathy and a shoulder to cry on etc.). Her voice was so clear singing stories of lives lived that made ours feel dwarfed by the scale of the emotion in them.

I imagine she sang throughout their life together and to their daughter Rosa when she was born almost a miracle and afterwards when she asked them how they met. They probably didn't mention me. Perhaps Arnie earned a place in their recollections, he was after all her friend and played guitar.

I wasn't to see Paul for another thirty-five years.

HARMOLODICS №4

November 1985 was cold and bright as we piloted the South African Airlines scale model Jumbo Jet down Regents Street, bits of its fuselage and tail fin breaking up and scattering all over the tarmac after being liberated from the SAA offices. We smashed the front window with a brick pulling out huge shards of glass with scarfs wrapped around our hands. We stepped gingerly inside the display and up onto the carpeted plinth to seize the prize from its stand. The feeling you get from smashing a huge pane of glass like that, of putting the window in and stepping across the now redundant demarcation line between public space and private property is a trip, is a total adrenalin buzz. The pent-up energy it releases, the almost sensual sense of transgression the taboo broken in so doing is like nothing else; it is nothing less than a narcotic enchantment. The psychic potential of breaking windows is not to be underestimated, like breaking the sound barrier, a psychological Mach One moment, we took off flying that plane down Regent street towards Trafalgar Square and felt free, albeit temporarily and once again on the right side of history. Beyond normal boundaries, literal outsiders yet soon to come crashing back to reality as it was before, tethered as we were to the real.

The coppers just watched from the side streets, smirking. They smoked fags pointing out the odd crusty, more disinterested in us than they had been during the miners' strike but just as happy to take the overtime. We ditched the plane in a side street and joined 80,000 protestors outside South Africa House to hear Jesse Jackson, which made it feel like a global event. Him being American and straight out of the civil rights narrative, it was like something from the movies. Mandela out. Thatcher out. That felt real, that linkage, like the world was listening and speaking at the same time.

On stage people of the moment, heroes of the movement; A young Ken Livingstone all London swagger, the exiled Oliver Tambo, oozing revolutionary reserve both men in their prime before their ignominious futures. And minor characters, local heroes as support act, this was a gig after all.

Our very own Black Panther, Tottenham's Bernie Grant introducing onto the stage Spartacus R resplendent in silver and black tribal face paint, dreadlocks and threads of many colours, hailing from the island of Aruba in the Dutch Caribbean, (the Spanish phrase derived from 'there was gold'), Spartacus R the exiled bass player and vocalist of Afrobeat rock band Osibisa, singing the Pan African Congress dream of a new Azania, of an African man born in the West Indies not an island man an African man of the islands, both Aruba and the British Isles, twice removed twice over an exile.

Paul Boating, young rebel firebrand before middle age shadow cabinet disappointment calling for him to be proclaimed President of Azania a state that doesn't exist, revolutionary words from the mouth of a man who would get used to speaking social democratic ones but at that moment heady notes of positivity and future thinking bubbled up in all the things we heard, said, repeated, argued in a potent atmosphere of idealism and action.

Spartacus R, Truthsayer, early internet mass communication adopter in the service of the liberation of Africa, died in 2010. Hounded by the police who exerted violent and non-violent harassment on his person, business and reputation, he had also led one of the first grassroots anti-Apartheid campaigns in Brixton. Spartacus thought global and acted local. Stopped and searched, undercover infiltrated, vexatiously harassed perhaps stemming from the moment the possibility of him being made President of Azania was born on stage that day in Trafalgar Square marking him as a man who would be king.

His memorial service was held in Lambeth. The speakers noted with much fervour his Pan African identity and his advocacy of more local and immediate challenges facing the community. One talked about African children killing African Children on the streets of London and citing the brutal statistics from this invisible war waged by knife and by gun, his voice weaving together his South London accent with West Indian patois, this modern African language Sparatcus spoke, this hybrid dreamer.

Right now we're fighting a war in Afghanistan, the Taliban they make bomb, sniper bullets fire after them over three hundred of them (youth) dead in ten year. They fighting a war. Whose definition of a war do you follow?

To a ripple of applause punctuated by a handful of 'That's rights'.

Spartacus was a soldier in a pan African war that

crisscrossed the continent of Africa, the Caribbean, North America and Britain, (The band claimed 'Osibisa' means to crisscross between rhythms that explode with happiness, literally an adaptation from the Fante word for highlife, Osibisaba.) His music fashioned weapons from the rhythms of roots, rock and folk. Spartacus summoned the we and we of all African peoples.

African people not island people this island that island, so much fuckery to keep us all down and not rise up as African people.'

It was in Libya that the Azanian People's Liberation Army, literally an army without a state, was to train with Gaddafi's blessing, somebody else who dreamed of Pan African Unity north and south of the Sahara. Libya, that pariah state, was visited by Mandela as soon as he was freed. *Umkhonto we Sizwe*/spear of the nation, the armed wing of the ANC also trained here. The cuddly Mandela the west wanted to defang, death by a thousand chants of his name, was in reality a lion of Judah and if you really want to free a Lion and she gets out, watch out for her bite. In 1990 Mandela went with his first wife Winnie, a state visit to condemn the American air strikes of 1986 and again, under U.N. air embargo in 1997 Mandela travelling by road at night, with his soon to be second wife Graca Machel, her own first partner, Samora, revolutionary leader of Mozambique having been murdered, shot out of the sky by South African mercenaries. They took the coast road from Tunisia to Tripoli under the heavy manners of the western powers, his new allies in the wake of the triumph of his election feted by Time magazine as their man of the year, Mandela repaid his fickle allies with his very own three chords and the truth...

How can they have the arrogance to dictate to us who our friends should be?

Roared Mandela, President of South Africa.

The echo of this roar ringing in our ears winds back to Spartacus R, Trafalgar Square in 1985, Mandela still caged on his island and reverberates forward to Spartacus R lionised at his memorial by the likes of Mandingo and Cosmo, African men in exile.

We a man, Lion, and we talk loud, we fierce. He never lose being a man.

A roar that pays forward to that other Pan African lion, Gaddafi, a different African colour, chairman of the PAC that put the fear in America and its passenger planes in the sky, Libya the richest country in Africa, Tamoil the gem in its crown, dealing the west its liquid obsidian fix, put fear in the West, the East, North and South, yet by 2011 Gaddafi, his ego burst, his body defiled, paid in full for warning us about them Talibans coming for Europe next if we let him fall during his phone calls to Tony Blair.

It is not their tactic to have demonstrations. They are not the type.

Terse through the static, perhaps a tone of resignation almost fear, but lots of delay, cut out, so it's hard to tell.

Libya, Jihadi staging post to Europe, Gaddafi a lion at bay still proud but crazy, his teeth pulled leaving only the solace of a resigned clarity of perception.

Like in the day of Barbarossa and during the Ottoman Empire. They want to control the Mediterranean and then they will attack Europe.

Snap crackle pop, but a prediction none the less.

And all that came to pass.

Come here and see the reality.

Gaddafi exhorts Blair before the line finally goes dead, Zion pleads with Babylon.

We spiral down, back to that cold bright winter of '85, pregnant with the future, intoxicated all over again by the beating of drums, the growing pressure of the 24-hour vigil outside South Africa house, the beginning of the non-stop protest that was to last five years until Mandela's release in 1990, the momentum on the streets and skirmishes in the early winter dusk. Rocks, bottles, batons, the romance of running battles with the police against a backdrop of barrel fires, cars alight, smoke billowing in the air, all rendered in low contrast flat light that held it like fog, the fog of war no matter how phoney and into the night playing cat and mouse in the side streets of power and elsewhere in Notting Hill outside the Mangrove, the Tabernacle, righteous Rastas blazing, perched on their carved swagger sticks entertained by a white riot and Socialist Workers raging.

Black man gotta lotta problems. But they don't mind throwing a brick. White people go to school. Where they teach you how to be thick.

We spiral down the looking glass to Dorset in '44, white American soldiers shooting a black soldier from the 761st for fraternising with a local white woman. They fell in love dancing the jitterbug in the back room of a village pub.

A ten-day love affair. She was pregnant. He never knew. Instead, was shipped home in a combat coffin bound in silence. She had the baby and after the war married a white man from the Isle of Wight, a secondhand car salesmen recently returned from Europe who had seen more than enough refugees and worse and willingly took the boy on who now as a grown man has black American second cousins who visit.

Churchill called Roosevelt and told him on British soil Americans had to follow our rules and customs. They couldn't bring their Jim Crow ways with them and this during the secret build up to D-Day and the defeat of Fascism, all too little and too late for the dead man Sergeant Moses Ballard and he was not the only one, coming out of a country pub in Devizes or wherever, on leave, a night out in the Horse and Hounds, The Nags Head, the Barley Mow, The Pilchard Inn, Ye Old Jolly Sailor in the early summer of '44, dancing, listening to music, an object of exotic interest on so many levels but not for their fellow but separate White Americans trapped as they were by the rules of an old and bitter game, a line across which you danced with death. The comrades of Moses Ballard had to carry his loss into France, into the fire under their motto 'Come out fighting' past the D-Day landings and beyond, to Bastogne and onto tainted victory as if there were any other kind.

Buffalo soldiers.

> *If one day you wake up to see,*
> *That I'm not where you think I should be.*
> *Please,*
> *Spare a thought for me.*
> *I might be*
> *Where I want to be.*
> **Spartacus R**

Moses Ballard, say his name.

A FAREWELL
TO ARMS

On the fourth floor of the library (history and philosophy), I remember the last time I saw Gary Finch. You couldn't really describe it as a farewell. He was crushing graphite into the blank pages of his dissertation, pressing hard enough on his pencil that every so often he had to blow or wipe away the accumulated detritus that smudged and occluded the words that he had inscribed there. The title of his dissertation was 'Evolution of combat tactics in the French Foreign Legion, 1945-1962'. Gary looked up at me with Golem eyes. He'd been up on speed for three or four days. Speed was not a drug that Gary Finch needed to use. A fountain pen would have exploded in his hand. The deadline was 5pm that afternoon to be delivered to the department secretary, so we didn't talk much. Gary loved the Laurel and Hardy film 'The flying deuces' in which they join the legion and much hilarity ensues. He knew the dialogue by heart, especially the bits about joining the legion to forget about love, something that highly amused him.

He handed his thesis over as if it were a matter of life or death, sealed military orders delivered on the eve of battle *under fire*. Apparently he told the department secretary that he was off to join the Legion, as if that was the obvious next step for him to take. Graphite powder rained all over her tidy desk. Gary held her eye for far too long before relinquishing his work. A surprise tug of war that shook even more graphite out from between the pages. He set ambushes everywhere he went. Classic Gary he would always impinge on other people, their space, their stuff. He overflowed himself, broke his own banks for the sake of a joke sometimes but mostly just for the sake of being Gary Finch. He was a trickster, a compelling pain in the arse to be around like most existentialists, knowing or otherwise.

He had already been expelled from the Ardennes after losing it on a Royal Signals Kayaking adventure which ended up with two locals being hospitalised after a fracas at 'Le Nuts bar' in Bastogne. World War Two tourism was a big draw for the town, given its starring role in the narrative of The Battle of the Bulge; there's nothing more American audiences appreciate than an against the odds surrounded siege story, a victory plucked from the jaws of defeat yarn despite the fact that by Christmas 1944 the German war machine had already been broken. On the walls of the bar (re-named in honour of the American officer who replied 'Nuts!' to a German surrender ultimatum) was an array of 'Bulge' memorabilia, helmets, weapons, flags and photographs tackily displayed at jaunty angles enabling the proprietor to overcharge for the local 'airborne' lager. In one photo by the door, (you only spotted it on the way out), a group of American 101 airborne troops pose like a football team outside the bar on Christmas day 1944, cold, dirty, bedraggled and very nearly beaten.

The legend reads. *They've got us surrounded. The poor bastards.*

A closer look at the photo reveals black and white

American soldiers serving together, the first recorded instance of desegregation in the US Army as units of the black 333 field artillery battalion had been sent to bolster the beleaguered 101st airborne resulting in the first ever citation for a black American unit in combat. Recruits who up till this point been confined to mainly clerical and logistic roles behind the lines; drivers, chefs and latrine duty, you know the drill.

Gary Finch sustained a broken jaw and smashed the knuckles of his right hand on the faces of two Belgian soldiers, who had been working as battlefield tour guides for a group of teenage students from Germany.

Who knows where Gary ended up? What was his destiny? The Legion? God help them. My last impression of him was his manic laughter in the silence of the library head thrown back showcasing his chipped gap teeth behind thin lips, as he charged towards that final deadline.

I don't care what colour you are as long as you go up there and kill those Kraut sonsofbitches. declared General George S Patton in an 'inspirational' address to the 676 men and 30 black officers of the 761 'Black Panthers' Tank battalion.

I like to think of Gary Finch, not as a little Hitler but a little Patton, which suits him better, they probably shared the same heroes and were both expert fencers.

The first ever black tank unit, the 761st was blooded during the battle of the Bulge. This information was part of the tour although there wasn't a monument to their participation. The 'Black Panthers' were ordered into the front line by a reluctant General Patton and saw 183 days of continual combat. These 'Negro Tankers' never convinced him despite their combat record Patton being a typical racist of his time. Sadly he did care what 'color' his soldiers were, he couldn't help himself.

The climax of the Panthers contribution to the war effort came breaching the Seigfried line and celebrating the end of hostilities with advance elements of the Soviet 1st Ukrainian army in the Austrian town of Steyr in May 1945. Has anybody ever seen these photos? Photos of these black/white handshakes, hugs, toasts, exchanges of tokens? Dif they make the papers, were they printed anywhere? In schoolbooks? Did anyone teach this history?

Did they fuck.

Jackie Robinson, the iconic post war American baseball player was in the 761st but never saw active service due to a court marshal for refusing to sit at the back of an army bus. By all accounts it was the battalion that hit a home run and The Brooklyn Dodgers took possession of one if it's finest hitters, rescued (and by the same token emasculated) by racism from a frozen hole in the ground somewhere in Europe to become the first negro to break the colour bar in American Baseball.

You can't make this shit up.

Now. I doubt any of this history was the reason Gary Finch started the fight in Le Nuts bar, but I would put money on it that he called the two Belgian soldiers 'French cunts' before landing the first punch. He wouldn't have distinguished them as Belgian, cunts or otherwise.

The clash of civilisations was coming to an end, one side had worn the other down without it realising. Like the uneven wear on the instep of a shoe it affected the way we all walked. Big ideology was running out of steam on both sides. It was time to jump ship, time to change shoes.

ESCAPE VELOCITY

The city took us in, dealing us to its four corners, reclaiming natives and absorbing graduates of the provinces without missing a beat. What did we seek there? Money, fame, fortune, girls, boys or just a good time? Whatever the desire, however inchoate, London provided the answers and posed more questions. The city proved to be the best vantage point from which to gauge the rest of the world; It rushed us in a totality of smell, taste, people, food, ideas, protest and opportunity, an emotional, intellectual and sensory overload we sifted through with indiscriminate abandon.

For all of these things and whatever else we would develop a hankering for, London supplied the rhythm and routine, the roadmaps for ways of living to suit all ambitions or lack thereof. After the congeniality of University, of campus life, of shared accommodation, of the calendrical tempo of the academic year not to mention the full grant payments we lived off, all most of us could do was to hang on for dear life.

First port of call was East Ham. An inauspicious arrival, sneaking into the city by way of the A13 a toe more than a foothold from which to clamber up and out of or languish in. Late 80's East London was... Random violence, inside/ outside, on the street, in the mind, mostly domestic in small flats above parade shops, hard drinking pubs, cash economy optics, women not walking home alone at night, snatched purses, the kindness of strangers, cigarettes, mugs of tea, betting shops and stubby pencils, Indian restaurants with automatic locking doors, red plush walls and small bars in the dining room serving pints to quench your thirst, to douse the heat of the off menu special curries they reserved for regulars. Violence delivered by fists, boots and bottles, pool cues, chairs, kitchen knives and crockery.

We got around on one day tube and bus passes, used, shared and resold, crisscrossing London is search of work and play. Dive bars in Soho, shebeens on estates, pool halls, pub after hours, house parties, blues and street corner drink ups, six packs and screw tops on park benches, twenty Marlboro lights replacing the red bands and roll ups, big city fags.

Those with the most energy dragged the rest of us along for the ride, working in pubs, clubs, entertainment promotion or on building sites, at the post office sorting office, as housing officers or other low level, low stress civil service jobs which held great opportunity for graft, or in recruitment consultancy, in 1990 the new game in town along with telesales and property development. You got jobs through mates, careers you applied for in *the Guardian* and never got a reply, not a one. There were leaders and the led, risk takers and routine seekers, high expectations, no expectations, the jammy, the focused, the job creators and the jobsworths, the clocking on and offers, the double shift workers, the schemers, old friends, new acquaintances, one night stands, longer term lovers and soul mates. The relaxed, the anxious, the laid back, the edgy, the passive, the aggressive, the hard workers, the lazy, the jealous, all the things we never knew we could be until we became them. Did any of us change? Did we want to change? What does change mean? Was it possible to change? I want to be richer, yes, who didn't think that? I want to be more assertive, that too? To take more risks? Is that desirable? Perhaps, but there was contentment to be found at all levels, how could there not be and still have a society that by and large got by. Or did it? We fight our corner but only see degrees of the world from that angle. A city made up of seemingly infinite, brilliant corners.

A summer of smoking spliffs in the park with our books and four packs of lager, Red Stripe, Breaker or Stella. The rest went to work, meeting up afterwards, us already stoned, who resented who the most who the winner who the loser, but still for now friends and flat mates.

Slow time, thick time, no time, time on your hands, timeless, contingent, loops of time, time flies, repeating time, endless change, all of this we lived through, each passage as discrete as a Bach variation, accompanied by the cosmic hum if only we listened hard enough to hear it, like Glenn Gould hunched over his piano keys grunting along to the music of time.

For a few weeks I got a job (through a friend, otherwise I would never have heard about it, let alone wanted to do it or indeed get it) at the 'Mars group' (generic holding title, nothing to do with the chocolate I don't think, it might in fact have been spelt with two R's; Marrs.) It was a cold calling hard sales job. You had to 'hit the phones' 9-5, setting up site visits for *our* sales people to install and demonstrate hot and cold beverage dispensers into the new office spaces that were mushrooming across the city. (Once you got the sales team in the door the conversion rate was impressive apparently, they were that good.). On our desks were a collection of phone books and business directories. These were our leads, bible like slabs of opportunity, every page a parable of potential riches. Each time we made an appointment we had to ring a little gold bell that hung on the wall facing us, our desks, like in school all facing the same way. The bell had a short red tassel hanging from the clapper which you tugged to ring it.

We worked in teams, with competitive goals and targets. There were also individual rewards, both within teams and in the wider Mar(r)s group itself. Who knows where the time goes? These fuckers did. It was the 90's. No shame, just gain. I left after my team which comprised both men and women, sprung a surprise birthday celebration for me (I'd been there two weeks, fast friends for fast times) in the pub where a stripper took my glasses from my face and rubbed them in her pussy before putting them back on my nose and grinding herself on me. In those day nobody resigned from jobs, you just left, either you walked out or were fired, without even much hostility, *it was just the case* in the Wittgensteinian sense; nothing to discuss, both sides of the equation working in alienated spaces, passing over each other in silence. Either way it cut down on paperwork and I was back on the dole the day after, if I had even signed off.

The best of us started teacher training or worked in the NHS but they don't feature in this story.

Our friendship group met up Thursday evenings in the pub, for gigs and clubs at the weekend. Subgroups of this wider circle would also meet up after work, depending on location and proximity; the disparity of income between us marking out new boundaries and routines for friendship and generating a surge of individualism that made a mockery of our ideas and passion for a lived socialism. We became atomised, sand blasted, abraded by the scars of envy and self-doubt and cloaked in an almost sensual self-loathing. Death by a thousand comparisons. Not being able to stand your round in one of the fancy wine bars that were popping up and closer to home not being able to pay your share of the weekly food shop or on a Friday night all pissed up in the Pink Rupee not having the money to pay for your curry but ordering nonetheless, thinking somebody else would pick up the tab, the friends with way more money than you, who went to work five days a week, if not more. The incremental shame of that.

Money. Cash in hand, benefits, scabbing off friends, hand to mouth from job to pub to bookies, career paths for other people, never you.

And this rump becoming a smaller and smaller number, denoting fewer and fewer 'people' soon to be the left behind.

We would supplement our benefits and day labour with doing the rounds of pub quiz machines, hitting them at the right time, on the right day, rinsing them like we did the honesty boxes in the common rooms of University departments but this time on a grander scale. But these windfalls, however regular, did not make up for a disparity which sprung up between us, separated us out, graded us like vegetables some wonkier than others. And it was not talked about and this is how people move apart. There are other reasons for sure but this is the root of it, water always finds a level at the lowest point and so do people and we find these levels in silence. We seek out those who earn the same money as we do because it's easier. Keeping up with the rest is relegated to lacklustre reunions that diminish over time.

Those of us in the right kind of jobs took solace in the unions and the social clubs from which Tall Paul had come to us in the first place. I realised then that the power of a union was a design for life within a shared concept of time, an escape from the ever present now, a rhythm of life with a horizon.

In a wider object domain friends drift apart and some of us become closer. There are new friends and also the rise of the life partner. We grow older, habit predominates over spontaneity. We atomise.

This is entropy.

Whilst things still appear contingent, we flow.

To Harelsden.

Spitting distance from where Paul grew up, a more hardcore version of Kilburn. Harlesden where Irish and black Northwest London rubbed up against each other like grumbling tectonic plates, two heavyweight boxers spoiling.

The Willesden junction pub. The Pink Pussycat wine bar. A tale of two cities.

Old pubs that stank of fags, sweat and beer. Aspirational shop front wine bars that smelled of floral notes and citrus fruit, the first time I had ever smelt a joss stick. Brightly painted shop fronts facing towards a brighter future, possibly American, via the conduit of the West Indies or a fiercely independent Africa. The Pink Pussycat was new. A place for romance and commerce, toasting success in whatever shape it came while the Irish stared down into their pints searching for solace and reaping the bitter harvest of diaspora generation on generation and both groups distrustful of the other, dismissive even. Those that should stand together drank apart. Piss artist and rapist amongst the names they traded shamefully in a bankrupt currency of racism and ignorance.

Being neither Irish or black we travelled between the two worlds back and forth from pub to wine bar, smuggling our non-conformity from one side of the street to the other like dogs sniffing for tidbits of something more interesting, more authentic; from Notting Hill carnival in procession along the Harrow Road to Vince Powers Mean Fiddler right on our doorstep from roots and dub to folk and country, similar even in their music and I would hazard a guess also in their literatures, songs and tales of oppression, exclusion and exploitation, the potato and the yam.

Time moved on, marked on the street by the arrival of West Indian gangs and drug mules onto the streets of London in a story first told by Victor Headley in his novel *Yardie*. Shotgun roars, pistols pops and occasionally semi-automatic gunfire stuttering into the night. Stonebridge Park estate, a no-go area for the police where we went to blues parties in the flats or outside the lock ups, a little scared but no bother. Stonebridge Park alongside so many other estates, each full of stories to tell, stories untold, whole histories of London unread because they were unwritten or written but unpublished, movies lived and imagined but never filmed or perhaps half finished on Super 8 cartridges or rolls of 16mm stored in boxes awaiting completion or forgotten in the hard slog to earn money and live your best life until the advent of smart phones and a younger generation finally able to represent through music and video or through creative schemes of access with limited distribution but shared nonetheless.

The University leftovers, although down to a handful, held out for a few more years like Japanese soldiers on a remote island.

. *It ain't over till it's over.*

MOTHER LONDON

Paul came home. His bedroom felt smaller somehow, he kept knocking into things, banging his head, knocking things off his desk, which he had never done before. Marion was gone, nobody had heard from the oldest sister Margaret and his mum rattled about in the house all by herself. A family home without a family, so his mum was very happy when he told her he had a girlfriend as if that was what he had gone to university to get more than any academic qualification.

As if you'd ever use that to get a job in the real world.

She was less happy when Sarah turned up a week later and announced over tea that she had found them a squat to live in.

As if I don't have the space for you here.

It's just down the road mum.

Sarah watched Paul and his mum talking at odds, a dynamic she recognised. Her own kiss goodbye from her mother had been more of a promise me you won't come back than a see you soon.

Full of bad people always was, Kings Cross, whores, druggies, drinkers and worse. A squat.

She looks directly at Sarah as if she had brought one into the house.

Whatever would…

Sarah walks out.

Whatever would what mum? Dad think?

Well no, but you know what I mean. She's a lovely looking girl Paul, I'm not saying she isn't.

But what? What mum?

Paul grabs his coat. His mother calls after him.

What will you do for work? Can they get you back on the trains?

He gives her a peck on the cheek. She speaks for the sake of it.

Come for Sunday dinner, your sister hasn't seen you in an age.

In the street he catches up with Sarah who slouches against a wall smoking. She puts the fag between his lips, he takes a long drag.

Coughs.

It's not what you think, she's just lonely.

What do I think? Grabbing the fag back.

We can't live in that fucking house.

Moving out is always moving away. Families fall apart like this. Without drama but with a little displaced emotion carried over from elsewhere. It's also how they begin, with a starter kit of displaced or surfeit emotion from growing up, from school, work, from people. Things we never had and everything we did have but didn't want. This was the material we must work with.

Sarah had found them a squat in a block of derelict flats behind Kings Cross station.

Paul turned up the next morning.

There you are, she said without surprise.

Paul looked down at his feet. The same kit bag and suitcase he had taken to university, the same hug goodbye in the hallway from his mum on her way to work.

He had called his sister.

A squat is it? she said.

A drummer came round and hooked up the electricity to the mains outside.

There's no meter, so there's less chance of them noticing. There's two other squats on this row, whole lot has been condemned. Be years before they knock them down. Good luck.

They paid him twenty quid. He said the gas was trickier and that they should use camping gas. He'd heard of somebody blowing themselves up trying to tamper with the mains.

Fuck that for a game of soldiers.

The drummer was a bit deaf and shouted as if you were the deaf one. He had been a replacement tour drummer for Topper Headon of the Clash and had terrible tinnitus. When it got bad he got frustrated that it was only him who could hear it, it was that loud. He would point at his ears and shout

Can't you hear anything?

This was a time of signing on and having a lot of time on your hands. The occasional touch, cash in hand. A few notes peeled off from bigger rolls form you to do something, to take something somewhere, to pick something up, work a shift here and there; the staccato world of job and finish. Removals, deliveries, nights on the door, agency jobs that paid fuck all after they took their slice off the top, hotel and hospital porters, clerking in accountancy firms, photocopying and binding documents at law firms. For Paul these gigs meant reading and smoking in vans and canteens much as he had done at university.

Perhaps this was a symptom of depression, a mental come down in the wake of 'the event' a sense of anticlimax, except that this just wasn't true. Paul and Sarah had found each other. That was the event and it made them happy. Their life was lived inside it.

His sister Marion said that going to university had given him funny ideas. Even funnier than the ones he had had before. She had got together with the son of the guy who owned the launderette where she worked. Paul had met him one Christmas morning down the Three Crowns, probably Christmas 1983. He'd had four pints and noticed that his sister and her man had been nursing just the one gin and tonic. Christmas where everybody in the pub bought rounds for each other, for their friends and even for their nodding acquaintances. Buying somebody a drink was saying happy Christmas and good luck to you. There was a language in buying drinks for others, for accepting them back, for saying thank you, for reciprocating, for sharing. This was the language that Paul had grown up in. He spoke it.

I wonder what sister Marge is doing for Christmas? He drawled.

Marion snorts, drinking I imagine, just like you. What they teach you at university anyway?

Manners.

The boyfriend stares out of the window.

Come on Marion, it's Christmas.

Paul stubs his fag out and looks at their empty gin and tonic glasses on the table.

Christmas, yes it is. Buy you a pint Steve?

It's Richard, I'm o.k. for drinks, thanks.

Richard, that's it. Sorry. What's wrong with a pint mate?

Richard shrugs,

I'm fine.

For fucks sake. Sis?

Marion shakes her head.

Full of learning you are.

Not good enough for you anymore? Is that it?

It's you Paul, always was too clever by half for people like us.

Paul snorts.

But I am people like you.

Don't be thick.That's my point.

 Well I'm getting another pint.

Mum will have lunch ready for 2pm.

I remember. Dad would come home from the pub round about that time.

Shut up Paul.

Last time Marge was home for Christmas.

She slaps her brothers face.

Come on Marion. Richard picks up her coat.

Paul lurches to his feet, raises his pint.

Welcome to the family.

Marion had moved into Richard's right to buy council flat in Brondesbury. Near enough to mum far enough away from him. Caitriona couldn't believe her husband was still causing as much damage dead as he had when alive. The resentment towards Paul as a manifestation of his father, the fear he was the same sort of man. Why couldn't everyone just move on? A wedding, grandchildren is what was needed, to mark a new beginning something to bring what's left of the family together. As for Margaret, she'd had little word for five years just the odd postcard so she had to make up a story for for her prying friends and family.

How's Marge doing, Cait?

Marge met a Spanish fella over there yet or what Cat?

When's Marge coming for a visit, Christmas is it?

Another guilty secret, more off-white lies.

A daughter in Spain living the dream, too busy with her new life to visit her mum was better than *I have no idea where my eldest daughter is* which is much sadder, a living nightmare if you stopped to think about it.

Sarah knew none of the details, but felt the pain and didn't pry. Paul kept it to himself and she didn't ask. Besides they were too busy working out how they would live together. She wanted to train as a midwife. She went to a Cuban solidarity night in Farringdon and got all fired up by their mortality rates which had been driven down from 91 per 1000 in 1950 to 6.4 per 1000 mainly due to the community healthcare programme.

In another life I would go and study there, become a revolutionary midwife in Cuba. In this one, well I can do an HE Diploma in Hillingdon.

This lightness of being in the world was what Paul was attracted to. She managed to avoid the potholes of ego and the disappointment and regret that would follow. He had seen it since he was a kid and he saw it in himself. She lived lightly but was somehow centred. She was his revelation about what life could be like.

I'm with her he would think, in so many ways more than one.

Sarah got in touch with her uncle Jerome whom she hadn't seen for years. He took them both out up west to a fancy old school Chinese with signed photos of celebrities including Michael Caine and his wife Shakira on the wall next to one of Bob Hoskins. White tablecloths, a full bar and impeccable table service. Jerome told her about the family problem, why he hadn't spoken to her mum. He had six siblings and the family had inherited a dilapidated hotel on one of the few black sand beaches on the island. Jerome as the eldest had to decide what to do with it. The others wanted to sell to American developers, he didn't.

You hear me? Not over my dead body.

In the aftermath of the invasion it wouldn't look good for the family to be seen to take the Yankee dollar. Not right now. Best to sit tight. They couldn't afford to do it up without investment and the land wasn't going anywhere.

But your mother doesn't understand, so I leave it like that, better wait until things die down.

The food glided past on the Lazy Susan. Ribs, sesame toast, salt and pepper squid, pork and vegetable dim sum. Paul couldn't load his plate fast enough. They drank beer chased with Betancourt rum over ice. When the bill came Jerome paid cash from a huge roll conjured from his trouser pocket. The owner came out and shook Jerome's hand, old friends.

This is Mister Chin, we play cards together every now and then.

'For the last twenty years if I remember correctly. Good to meet you.

Mr Chin shakes their hands.

Jerome shook Paul's hand out on the street. A strong grip. A black man who refused to see colour, even when it saw him. Paratrooper, bodyguard, man about town.

Nice to meet you young man and take good care of my favourite niece you hear me?

London is a city where worlds collide and everything can be connected, woven into its fabric, from the dispossessed to the entitled, their dreams and nightmares entwined.

Paul had a drink with Bob Crow down the union social club. Bob was now the N.U.R rep for track workers. Looking good, how you been, what's going on, you got a job? it was all a bit flat. It all felt a little like 'for old times' sake'. It had been easier to communicate through postcards. They fell back on family, trading updates.

How's your old mum?

For some reason he didn't mention Sarah or that he lived in a squat. He was backing out of a relationship. More than that it was a final disengagement from a life he no longer felt at home in. Why was he feeling like this? On the outside he still fitted in, wore the same uniform, docs, donkey coat, lapel badges but inside he was way more elsewhere than he had ever been, cast out of one life, and not yet fallen into another. The miners' strike had been an ending. It would be Sarah that would show him the way forward. Not Bob.

Bob didn't even talk about the strike now it was all about his members, their pay and work conditions. The dream of revolution had devolved into a street fight for jobs without which Bob was to ask *What do people do?* This was a last-ditch defensive line, he wouldn't fall back any further. His members welfare. The union was everything.

Paul stumbled home. Over the next decade Labour was to lose another two general elections and transform itself into a European social democratic party that wouldn't win a general election until 1997 making enemies of the unions and labour councils alike, the well having been poisoned by Kinnock's visceral (and reciprocated) hatred of Scargill, the red flag being replaced by the red rose, paving the way for Blair, cool Britannia and the invasion of Iraq.

Will the last person to leave Britain please turn out the lights.

MAGICAL
REALISM

The 90's for some were a time and a space that with hard work and a lot of hustle horizons kept expanding. I found an angle, I found purchase. By making the films that sold the idea of the thing rather humping around the thing itself. This came about through happenstance. Almost everyone else had settled into a rhythm of life and career. It was scary being on the outside, so I took my chances. I made a music video for a band I knew, Homeboy Hippy and a funky Dread, backstage at one of their gigs on an old super 8 camera, getting the beer company we worked for to sponsor them if we featured a scene where they drank beer surrounded by sexy girls. Not rocket science. Then I made another video, for another band on the same label. This time it had a simple story instead of a performance. It snowballed from there, shooting music videos on 16mm and eventually 35mm film. The TV and the new cable channels showed the videos every week on the chart show. This drove sales of records and CD's. There was an explosion of bands. Music videos and commercials were all the rage, whipping up a storm. At the top of our road there was a mews where people made porn films. I didn't make any although I was never asked to. Everybody was at it or so it seemed. Fashion, drink, music, film, clubs and bars made up the hustle. The space we expanded into (where all this money was being made) comprised of memorable locations both at home and abroad, hotels, film studios and the reassuring luxury of post-production facilities. One gig led to another, and I found myself and my team on a roll. We were going places.

My political beliefs hadn't changed but the context in which I held them underwent a magical transformation. They had downgraded themselves ontologically further and further into rhetoric. Collapsing in on themselves they became the bones which could no longer carry the body. Intellectually they still held but now served no other purpose. It was only a matter of a few years since I had been on picket lines, printed hand bills, knocked on doors, yet I had come undone.

How do we lose the intimacy between form and substance? Perhaps the question should be how *could we not*. Take political violence as an example. The national liberation movements we supported and raised money for had death by violence at the heart of their lived experience. We were as removed from that experience as we are reading *War and Peace*. It is not our life nor fate. We believed in these causes on behalf of other people yet we had no intimate knowledge of them. We had no skin in the game. Moral authority comes from an obscene intimacy from which we were excluded by our privilege.

Dead bodies.

Somebody I knew had to go to Lagos on business, he worked in oil. Back then Nigeria didn't get a great press. A wealthy independent African country. There had been an odd tension between Nigerians and West Indian students on campus, which involved stereotypes on both sides, but was mostly post-colonial prejudice, re-framing tensions between tribes and countries and the black diaspora.

Going to Lagos for business in the early nineties meant only one thing. Oil. My acquaintance wasn't in the music business, he was a suit, a straight, he was Babylon. Outside the airport he saw a corpse lying by the side of the road and observed other commuters just swerving it. One guy 'carrying a bloody briefcase for fucks sake' stepped over it. He thought fuck this, went back inside the airport and called his boss, telling him he was coming home.

A white corpse story, for balance. Back in the 80's another friend drove a stolen car to the Stonehenge free festival. He arrives after dark and abandons it right by the stage where Hawkwind were in the middle of their set wearing pig's head masks. He gets out, on a pill, and joins a group of hippies sitting around a fire smoking weed. Everybody sheds energy from their bodies like in the Ready Brek commercial, phased to the pulses of electronic sound coming from the stage. He takes a hit off a spliff and goes to pass it to the guy on his right but he just keels over, stone cold dead. Nobody notices, they continue smoking and the band plays 'Sonic attack'.

Far out. Unbelievable.

Reading this back and the guy at the airport in Lagos seems naive. He's read Graham Greene, Daniel Johnson and James Leroy. *We* make bad shit happen. Another software auto-spell. I type James Elroy, the software spells out James Leroy. (I momentarily flash on an imaginary West Indian crime writer that I would love to read.)

At the time the story, well it was a crazy story. A lot more people have to step over dead bodies now. We have seen refugees washed up on the idyllic beaches of Lesbos. A Greek tragedy to match a Nigerian one.

As for hippies, they have always got up to more shit than we give them credit for. Hawkwind, a true cross over band, were more true to the ethos of Punk than the rest, reaching for a cosmic rebalancing of the planet, summoning an intergalactic day of reckoning. We all cum together. Le grand mort.

Guns.

In our world guns are almost as invisible as the corpses they make but our fiction is full of them. In very violent places you might expect the opposite to be true but a fascination with guns and violence is something most of the world shares, a strange communality between places and people that have radically different life experiences of either.

Yet we know so little of the actual physicality of the guns we are familiar with. In the flesh they are of a different order, physical manifestations of a different epistemology. They are strange compelling objects, larger in real life by the same measure that actors are smaller.

How heavy is an AK 47? What does it feel like? How does the safety catch feel under your thumb, how comfortable the trigger under your finger? What does hair line sensitivity mean? The recoil, the smell, does it burn you, (and what do those burns look like?) does the barrel get red hot, does it jam, seize up, can it fire after having been in water?

I have been in close proximity to guns three times in my life for reasons of politics, drugs and make-believe in that order, each a sign of its own time.

The first was on a cold November night in the Victoria

pub off the Holloway road in the early 80's. Deep in the troubles being associated with 'Troops out!' was more likely to get you on a shit list than any pro Soviet activity. Buckets were shaken in the faces of drinkers and 'An Phoblacht' newspaper sellers went around the tables. Last orders and everyone gets to their feet for a rendition of *Amhrán na bhFiann*. A murmur goes through the crowd followed by an odd amateur silence as two masked men take to the small stage (having been bundled in from the street through the kitchen and into the bar to a ripple of cheers and claps when we realised who they were. One of them brandished a small pistol in his fist (it actually looked like an athletics starter pistol). He held it aloft in tableau. The crowd swayed on its feet, fists raised in response.

A ballot paper in one hand, an Armalite in the other.

We sang.

The second time I saw a gun it was in the 90's and I was doing lines of coke in the office of a Lebanese gangster who owned the Zanzibar nightclub on Frith Street, Soho. He reached into the drawer and pulled out a chrome looking pistol and put it on the desk next to the coke. My eyes were dazzled by it as I went by chasing my line. It looked like a big shiny toy, heavy though, like a Tonka toy. He obviously got off on the frisson it created just being out on the table. It set off the coke, framed it, put it in lights so to speak. This was the same night that a girl had asked me if I wanted to sniff coke off her tits outside the toilets downstairs. Guns, sex and drugs. A strong alchemy. Bringing this story down to earth is the fact that a character off Coronation Street was the resident coke dealer at the time.

Those teeth.

The last time I saw a gun was in the naughties on a film shoot for a commercial. We were in Cape Town shooting at a gun range. This was the shot list:

- Hand gun being fired towards camera in close up 25 frames/73k frames high speed camera.
- Slow motion shot of bullet casing being ejected. Also High speed (73k frames).
- The gun bucking in the shooters hand 120 frames.
- Reverse shot on target full of holes, pull focus through hole onto the shooter in the background. 25 Frames.

The firing range guy offered me the gun to hold, gesturing to the targets.

You want a go?

It looked huge and heavy in his hand. A flat, grey, dead weight. I shook my head automatically despite thinking that I wanted to have a go, that it would be fun. I had heard of places in Vietnam/Cambodia/Laos where you can shoot AK 47's and throw hand grenades at water buffalo on your gap year. Kalashnikov rifles had been produced, upgraded and modified for every war since the WW2. Soviet originals had become collectable classics. The much sought-after Makarov pistol was the only East German made Soviet era hand gun. Copied widely it was itself a copy of the German regulation sidearm from Nazi times. All of this information can be gleaned from the sales spiel of market and backstreet basement traders from Kabul to Tirana. This lore, this mythology of weapons has a long heritage, both on and offline.

There are millions of them in the world, handled by millions of people.

In Gomorrah the Napolese gangster dreams of visiting old man Kalashnikov in the city named after him, to pay homage and offer thanks for his gift to the world.

Paul only ever visited America once and there he had his own experience of guns. It is a rare moment of synchronicity in our life stories outside of university. He had a cousin living in Boston, a bad cousin who despite being bad was looked up to, feared not a little and avoided by many in the family. Paul only ever mentioned him once when really drunk out of his mind. On a night where he felt he needed to appear more serious, more worldly and more bloody authentic than a bunch of fucking students he had spent too much time with. I have no recollection of what triggered him to tell me this story, let alone hint at its darker epilogue. In the real world he would never mention either but towards the end of our time at university a certain lassitude of character had set in...

Fáilte go mBoston dheas. Welcome to South Boston, 1980. Whitey Bulger's Boston. The night before the St. Patricks day parade. Back room of 'Whiteys' bar, standing room only. Copies of Republican News change hands and Noraid buckets fill up with bills and change. A bell rings and two masked men wearing leather jackets and balaclavas leap up on top the bar, one of them nearly falling backwards against a wall of spirits.

A handgun salute as the crowd sings...

I was visiting my eldest sister Margaret, she's been over there a while, before she went to Spain, that's another story, not relevant here, but anyway she had fallen in with our cousin, Podraic, who had turned up in Boston just that Christmas, in the aftermath of Warren Point. Said he came by boat. How many had to flee the north after that attack I don't know, more than was involved I imagine, I never asked if he was there, would never ask that. Another story about that one was he claimed his real father was Brendhan Behan, a tall story if ever I heard one, he was the spit of my uncle, reminded me of my father which was why I avoided him.

Well Margaret was working in this bar and he was drinking there amongst friends and we were having a fine old time and he took me outside into the alley for a smoke, although we could smoke inside, perhaps he wanted the fresh air, so I went with him and he reached around behind him and pulled out this pistol and showed it to me like it was, like it was some ancient sword or something, like I should be impressed with him for wielding it, offering it to me and saying go on go on would you and fire it pointing to the bins and I said no fuck off why the fuck would I want to do that, he just stood there not knowing what to do next, his arms flapping at his side, the gun pulling the right arm down, weighing him down, and finally he wipes his nose with the back of his sleeve and shrugged putting the gun back under his shirt tucked into his waistband and I lit him a fag so full of it he was, we smoked and he calmed down and without another word we went back inside and had another round and he started in on the tall stories, things you would never say if they were true. 'Guns, once you pick one up, they follow you.'

Five years later Whitey McGrail was shot dead behind his own bar and 'Whiteys' entered into the Irish mythology of North America. A local bookie, this murder was a 28k hit for an unpaid gambling debt. Stage plays and films followed and the bar became an infamous entry into dive bar culture on the bucket lists of tourists and thrill seekers alike. The Bring your own munchie microwave, endless reruns of 'Law and order' on the TV, the assorted Hustlers, wanna be gangsters and Transvestites that constitute the regular clientele and the all year round Christmas lights amongst the details celebrated on trip advisor reviews.

Thank God we were lost in a fog of booze because what can you say to follow that up? I certainly didn't tell him my Troops out story. No story of mine could match his.

As if by magic some sleight of hand had rendered me inauthentic.

But it got me to thinking, hadn't June's boyfriend Tony in Fuengirola been in two Para? Hadn't Two Para been ambushed at Warren Point the same day they killed Mountbatten? Was that why four years later he was running off at the mouth and drinking himself to death in some Spanish dive bar?

There are many bars around the world where 'people like that' ended up, where the decommissioned, the on the run, the invalided out, the retired, the not dead yet found solace. Corners of the world where the desperate, the junkie, the war addicted, the PTSD veterans would drink in silence or drink and talk into the darkness about what they had seen.

Bukowski's bar in Prague was one of those places. Where journalists and cameramen covering wars would congregate before going in and after coming out to drink and smoke their story away, gird themselves for another assignment or celebrate the night before going home. Or to drink away the fear of going home, of being expelled from the fiction of being at the centre of the story of the world, all of them seeking existential approval by haunting this kind of place, like in Casablanca, Odessa, Kinshassa, Saigon, until the next time they get to play at being mini gods.

These bars, sanctuary from the things they had seen, from the things they had done, from the people they had left, the same loved ones who they would let down on their return.

Anton Chekov is famous for saying if you see a loaded shotgun at the beginning of a story it must go off before the end. The potential energy infuses the story with momentum. Everything moves forward to this point. Fiction is structured to pay off an audience's investment in it. Life is, thankfully, more random, where the causality between things is less clear and we are all capable of making false promises. Guns are both potent symbols and at the same time just guns in the world. The majority of weapons are never fired in war or in peacetime. You can google that.

13 gone and not forgotten, we got 18 and Mountbatten.

Podraic stood and declaimed shaky on his feet from the drink yet his fist still pumping the air and Paul could see the black butt of his gun poking out from under his raised shirt. The chant was picked up by the crowd that filled the bar, Margaret pulling pints as fast as she could, shots on the side, not a care in the world and Paul dragging him down back into his seat, who knows who's listening for fucks sake pipe down. Pod grabs Paul by the collar, chokes him, stone cold.

Pipe down? You're not in bloody London now under the cosh of the tans, this is America.

BLACK CHRIST

Careening back and forth across a road at night, the surface of which was full of melted tarmac ridges and potholes in a taxi from Marrakesh airport with Aswad's manager in the back seat propping the door open with his knee so he could read a fax in the rear seat light, shouting into his phone (the driver eyeing us both in his mirror as if we were aliens) at his assistant about promotion pre sales, money and advances, interspersed by screaming at the phone for its bad reception, whilst drilling me for budget feedback for a music video shoot starring Drummie Zed playing a black Christ, scenes we had already shot up high up on an Atlas mountain pass and in a Berber village, where we stayed the night sleeping in tents, sitting around a fire listening to Sufi drummers and Aswad singing acapella and we smoked hash under stars and all the money had gone out of the window, on top of that the camels we need for the next day's shoot cost way more than agreed, and on top of that the oasis location for Wednesday had fallen through so I needed another fucking Oasis with an abandoned desert Fort in the background as per the storyboard and now this fucker had turned up costing production more money, which you could guarantee he would later chastise me about, just to pick him up and put him in a fancy hotel and take out to fancy restaurants to eat the speciality of the house Pigeon pie and drink carafes of Rose wine whilst a local Gnawa band played and he would be on his shit windows laptop *screaming at the waiters for connection, a wire brought too late to the table and too short to reach his seat because God forbid he would get up and go to the reception area. On top of that the band had fallen out because they all wanted to play Jesus fucking Christ.*

Jesus fucking Christ.

NOTES FROM OVERGROUND

I got on a plane for L.A. in 1991.

This is what I saw from the window of the taxi on the way to Heathrow.

Toy dolls passed off as babies wound onto the chests of begging women at traffic lights, promenading accordion players paid to fuck off by those sitting outside cafes or paid off by worn out commuters on underground trains. Other beggars prone on pavements, no eye contact, scribbled story on cardboard on pavement. Coins proffered, dropped or just palmed grudgingly, willingly or neutrally, a daily tax no more or less, but always taken hungrily, with or without eye contact. The Balkan conflict spilled onto the streets of Britain. The Godless superseded by those displaced by the God thirsty.

What happened next fills another book.

Paul and Sarah were evicted from their squat in '92.

Sarah got her first job at the shiny new Homerton hospital, allowing the Mothers hospital and the German hospital in Hackney to close and be redeveloped into luxury flats. They successfully apply for a two bedroom council flat on the Woodberry Down estate in Manor House.

He worked for a local gardener just as gentrification entered its next cycle. Black working-class streets became white middle-class ones as the Windrush generation sold up from the inner city to the outer suburbs or back home, leaving their families to scrabble for what was left of social housing or brave the margins of the city. White flight East and North replaced by black and brown families in Slough, Hayes, Edmonton, Ilford and Romford. Apparently, a communist lecturer at the University of Melbourne had written 'the six stages of gentrification' back in the seventies. Follow the artists. The poor with the potential to sell their wares to the rich. The poor who have something the rich want other than their labour. Wait for it. It's their lifestyle. People come and people go, they roam, seeking out opportunity, and this basic kinetic activity can be harnessed to the machine. Property developers are attracted to the movement like spice worms. They predict and make it so. For the rest of us, everyday is Groundhog Day, we can't even remember the name of a shop that closedown after being there for years yet we quickly remember the name of the guy who opens up a cafe in the same space.

Morning Jason, Oat milk Cappuccino please.

Our adaptability as a species is 90% forward motion.

Paul spent his days out in the van working jobs across North London. Plenty of fag and tea breaks, thermos flask of coffee in the morning and sandwiches for lunch. Other people's houses and local pubs in unfamiliar places. He kept a notebook and jotted down all the places they had been to, tracing clusters of houses across the city like a General pouring over enemy maps.

Notting Hill had been ahead of the game, a trailblazer, probably at stage four or five by now with Islington and Hackney not far behind, stage two or three. Estate agents and builders set the scene, like sappers laying charges the night before the big push. Plumbers, plasterers, carpenters and later loft extension specialists followed suit as did the attendant architects, designers, interior and exterior make over specialists that created the looks and tastes of a new middle class. Landscape gardeners were needed at any point in the chain. The whole world is a stage and/or a Kinetic machine.

Paul did pick up a spade but it wasn't a shovel. He was digging holes like his father but these holes were full of rich dark earth. Shallow holes you could dig before lunch. Middle class holes.

The rift with his mother had been repaired by family lunches, outings and a holiday on the Costa del Sol where Sarah and Cait finally saw eye to eye, recognising something of themselves in each other over a jug of Sangria much to the relief of Paul who loved both of them. His mum was still rattling around in the family home unable to bring herself to sell it. Surrounded by both good and bad memories, the balance between the two left her undecided. Marion had had two kids by then and well she probably coveted the house herself. Of Margaret there was little sign, a few postcards to Paul about the places she lived, the poeple she knew, the olive groves, the oranges and the beaches, as if to say I'm alive and its not all bad. They described the places and what she did in them. In one she wrote 'I wonder what you are all doing' but didn't include a return address, so she would have to keep on wondering.

Somehow Paul and Sarah missed the christening of Marion's second child starting the next round of family aggravation. They had been trying for a baby on and off themselves and it had become an issue, or rather it was a thing, something between them, this absence of a baby. For the first time it knocked Sarah's spirit. She wished she had been strong enough to not want a child, to live with that fact like she did with all the others, happily and with a sense of humour. She felt let down by her own weakness. Perhaps it was because she was a mid-wife. Which took the shine off the job she loved which now might prove to be her Achilles heel. What's sadder than a midwife who can't have her own child? They had months when it wasn't an issue, but then it came back, a punch to the soul and they tried harder and then didn't want to try at all, didn't want to have sex at all. It wore them down, this cycle wore them down, and other people trying to be sympathetic wore them down.

One of Paul's work mates was Kurdish. A refugee who showed him how to lay bricks by plumb line, which he picked up quickly. Hakan had been a secondary school history teacher in Diyarbakir where he had worked on building sites to put himself through university.

Their boss was an old hippy called Chris with dreads down to his arse. Paul still couldn't believe what a decent bloke he was. Knew how to do a garden as well, knew all the plants, the flowers, when to plant them, decking, all of it. During cigarette breaks Chris asked Hakan lots of questions with such an engaging naivety that he answered freely, not something he was accustomed to. Paul took it all in, chipping in his own questions about Kurdistan, the PKK, their leader Abdullah Ocalan, whose face he recognised on many fly posters all over Hackney. He came alive to it, a fresh struggle to think about after the disappointments of his own albeit sharing the same set of signifiers and participating in similar rituals. Raised fists, bright coloured flags, AK 47 stencils, hammers and sickles superimposed over distant mountaintop outlines, leaders and heroes in military costume, Fidel like iconography, Soviet style logos and banners. A whole new world, yet the same old one. Paul was still in his comfort zone, change for him was best when it looked like this, a struggle that continues regardless.

In the park there was an old punk dog walker who looked like the punks on glossy tourist postcards posing in front of Big Ben. National treasures. Paul was a bit like that, he wore the same clothes as he had done ten, fifteen years ago, from his donkey Jacket down to his dockers. Why change? Same as the Teds you still saw down the pub still spoiling for a fight or the new wave of skinhead girls in the park and on the estates, Oi!, Two Tone, Redskin, New Trojan, black and white 100% working class attitude and period style. Or the odd rockabilly couple you saw in the street, curled bangs and Victory rolls, pompadours, quiffs and low fades. There was a pub in Brighton that him and Sarah liked, the Lord Nelson, just down from the station in the North Lanes. A seedy area like many adjacent to railway stations but enter this pub and it was a time capsule back to the mid-fifties, a snug bar full of immaculate clothes and style, a place for rockabillies to feel at home in. They had been on a couple of soul weekenders down there, enjoyed the scene.

Proper rastas were the same, hold outs against the constantly updating present, representing the ever present I and I. Up on Highbury corner two black twins identically dressed in traditional suits, sometimes tweed, with flat caps or sometimes wearing jodhpurs with riding crops, year in year out part of the street furniture, the fabric of the city, outside the tube or down Holloway Road, local icons, legends, like the artists Gilbert and George (immaculate in suits made by Bangladeshi tailors from Aldgate), their life was their art as they aged slowly, the clothes never changing just a suggestion of grey in their hair and stubble. In the fast moving 90's this type of character brought a little depth to the world, they slowed the flow of the river, added a bass note cadence, obstacles to the loss of memory, subcultural anchors by which to navigate. Like the *faces* you still saw in Soho; the bouncers, the streetwalkers, the club owners, the waiters, the dancers, old pimps, the down and out.

Continuity.

A pale faced rake thin tramp constantly shuffling a route around the streets of Soho in a worn red leather jacket, the only possible sign that he is Danny Kirwan, legendary guitarist from Fleetwood Mac. A latter day and minor key rock star junky, lead singer in 90's band Agent Provocateur, still pretty, cool and friendly, looking for her next fix, both fixtures on the streets for many years.

Life's winners disappear, are rarely seen on the street, in and out of Limos they are constantly elsewhere, fleeing the scene of their success as soon as they make it, leaving behind the stage set and the extras.

We provide their continuity, frozen in time and motion to start again whenever they were 'back in town'...

Perhaps Paul was recognised, almost subconsciously, a minor face on the street or in the pub. He wouldn't mind that but would never consider himself to be like that, it was for others to think what they liked.

Sarah had adapted to the demands and realities of her job. It was hard work, she got tired, the pleasure she got from it was the simple satisfaction of bringing babies into the world but also a very complex thing to have to accommodate in your own life. As that life got more complicated. There was little hint of the punk she had been other than the run of healed over holes in her ears and a liberal use of mascara. She still sang occasionally in a pub and her politics had held up, she still had a union after all. Being a black woman on the streets of Hackney in the 1990's she had skin in the game, she saw the changes, less black faces on streets whitewashed by money.

She did her own thing, Paul did his. Their relationship was as equal as they could make it. Domestically they split the chores, shared the cooking. Paul loved making curry, as hot as you like. Sarah did risottos and all sorts of salads. If they went out it was for Chinese or West Indian. They had a two-man tent from Aldi that cost ten quid used it a few times up in Norfolk and a few times in Epping. History, old cities, films and music were the day-to-day things they shared. Old Ska and Dub Reggae on a stereo with a rattling bass; The Scientist, Skatalites, Augusts Pablo, some jazz and later on dub step if they felt adventurous. They were significant others, but what was the significance they shared? The longer they were together literally the more they had in common, the more bound together they were. Was that enough? This thinking circles the absence of a child, so they back away from it, back into the headspace of work and routine.

Paul had his workmates and there was always a favourite he would go for a drink with. For a while it was Hakan. They went to basement clubs after work and drank cheap beers chased by milky white glasses of Arak. Fuzzy satellite TV played in the background, mostly football, but sometimes news reports, wars, soldiers marching, people demonstrating, bombings, flags waving, as surreal to Paul as the propaganda broadcasts in *Starship Troopers*, one of his favourite movies. If only it were true that the biggest thing to worry about were alien bugs.

Drug wars came and went in North London, Turkish, Kurdish proxy wars, heroin wars, automatic gunfire on streets used to shotguns. Apart from stop and search coppers went awol in the 90's after filling their boots during the poll tax riots.

Belief and ethnicity create their own states of consciousness, seething across the increasingly porous borders of nation states. States of mind, ways of living. Money, exile and ideology create strange brews and stranger, yet still readable maps of the world.

Kurdish refugees include many flavours of identity and loyalty, refracting the existing nation states, Iraq, Syria, Iran and Turkey overlaid by 'Kurdistan'.

Alevi Kurds who are a bit like Sufis, drawn to mystical aspects of Islam, to the incantatory power of music, the spiritual nature of the human voice and the mystical power of poetry. These Quizilbashi are also related to Shia Twelvers, because they believe in twelve (historical) Imams who each represent different aspects of the universe. So far so deep. The double bind of being a Kurd and an Alevi is like being taxed in two countries, add to this the communism of many Alevi Kurdish fighters in the P.K.K. then a triple jeopardy pertains, three levels of exile, three removes of otherness, all yearning for a homeland.

An Alevi wedding in London, bottles of expensive red or black label scotch on each table, guests pinning big denomination notes to the dress of the bride, the dancing, men and women together, the high spirits and emotional intensity of both the union but also the resonance of rituals performed in exile. Keeping home alive in the ways of everyday life. I have a responsibility to exist. Dreams expand, reality contracts. Waking up is exactly the moment of loss. The dream of the impossibility of return. We become slaves to this dream, a hungry mistress that demands to be fed and flattered, a vivid just out of reach promise, how well we perform there, full of vitality and endeavour only to wake lesser men and women. It demands things of us that should never be asked. Blood stain upon blood stain on stone cold altars.

It was a rare day out for Paul and Sarah, meeting Hakan's wife, their two small children running between tables, with the other children, the future, how lucky they were to have a family and a new life. Paul had primed Hakan at work that they couldn't have children, so he didn't have to worry about awkward questions spoiling Sarah's day, which is how you had to roll, even Paul.

Hakan wanted a better life for his family. This is how he had to roll although the cliche of it humiliated him. Only in exile is it possible to pull back the curtain. There are those that can escape these dream states, this slaving of life to memory and longing. Or at least put waking distance between themselves and it.

After twenty years abroad you return home, to the place where you grew up. How will you find it? How does it find you? Does it still feel like home? Why have you returned there? Did you sense it immediately on landing at the airport, a sense of coming home? Is it smell, of a street, a house a city, or taste, a certain flavour that sparks reconnection. Is it the weather, the noise of people and cars, the sounds of the street unchanged. Familiar faces on local TV, on the radio, if not the exact same people but the same shows the same style of media. Or are you unable to reconnect? On arrival you feel nothing except the creeping dread of having made a huge mistake.

These questions constitute the privilege of being able to return home by choice.

The past is another country as are the people in it, those who stand in front of us now and we who stand in front of them all those years later, superimposed by the people we have held in our minds, phantasms who obscure the very real strangers that now present themselves, all of us having shed seven layers of skin many times over, but still something carries over, we are at least the remainder of who we were...

To start with I kept a flat in London but spent my life travelling from shoot to shoot, with a few weeks back home in-between. As soon as work in America took off, I got less work out of London. I spent more time with my Assistant Director than any of my friends back home, work and life blended seamlessly together. Before I knew it, it made sense to lease an apartment on Fountain, a discrete, avenue haunting Hollywood of which Betty Davis remarked when asked about advice for those wanting to conquer Tinsel town 'Take Fountain.' So, I took it and became some kind of exile. When you are constantly working in Los Angeles everything you do makes sense and everything works out. An O1 visa soon followed, sponsored by the lawyers of the production company that was making its lion share of the money 'we earned.' For a while there I was golden.

One night Paul gets back from work to find Sarah sitting at the kitchen table. He takes his dirty boots off in the hall, hangs up his coat. Sarah pours him a glass of wine.

Let me wash up first, I'm filthy.

Sit down Paul. Now, sit down.

What's up? You ok?

He folds himself down into the chair carefully, his back a bit sore. She pushes the glass towards him. He doesn't take his eyes off her, somethings up. She pushes something else across the table towards him, across the invisible border between them. Contraband wine and the plastic lollipop stick he's seen many times before.

What?

He picks it up, carefully, spies a thin blue line.

Pregnant.

It's a miracle.

It's May. 1997.

Things can only get better.

OUR STRUGGLE

2014

> *'No one likes us, no one likes us*
> *No one likes us, we don't care!*
> *We are Millwall, super Millwall*
> *We are Millwall from The Den!'*
> ...*to the tune of 'We Are Sailing' Rod Stewart.*

Dull thuds of horse shat on tarmac, horses biding their time before the Funeral cortege moves off from Snakes Lane in Woodford Green, up the Chigwell Road and down through Charlie Brown's roundabout to Wanstead Station. Charlie Brown (Charles W Brown) was landlord of a pub ('The roundabout') he renamed Charlie Browns (after his father) which was torn down when the motorway was completed in 1972. Charlie Brown senior had been the landlord of The Railway Tavern at 116 West India Dock Road Limehouse that was commonly known (known thereabouts and further afield) as Charlie Browns pub. The old man had the strength of personality to pass on his name, the power to leave his mark long after he had gone, finally coming to rest as the common name for a nondescript roundabout in North East London. Bob Crow would like that, that notion of legacy, of a working man's legacy, and had probably had a drink in one or both Charlie Browns, probably on the house, in fact Charlie Brown would have been one of Bob's favourite characters. Probably...

During the 1912 Dockers strike Charlie Brown had donated large sums of money to the cause and had been made an honorary member of the Stevedores Union for his efforts. After WW1, Charabanc tours of thrill seekers to the exotic East End would stop at the pub for refreshment and plates of authentic cuisine from *Old Friends* Chinese restaurant next door, serving both everyday fare and the more exotic.

When he died in 1932 Charlie lay in state in the Saloon bar under a ceiling hung with sharks' teeth, his coffin framed by walls festooned with 'Tribal weapons' and freaks of nature, whilst upstairs in private rooms visitors gawped at his collection of curiosities from around the world, including Ming vases, Ivory caskets, Inuit bows and arrows, Damascus steel armour and an 800 year old Chinese cabinet. The procession to the cemetery was one of the biggest in the East End and 16,000 attended his funeral at Bow, the streets out of Chinatown packed to pay respects to the uncrowned king of Limehouse. 'Here comes Charlie Brown!' the patrons chanted for the last time, in as many languages.

Charlie had been a regular at *Old Friends* but he would only ever order steak, egg and chips. His wife, family and friends developed a taste for the sweet and sour pork of Jar Jow and the peppery flavour of Chop Suey and quid pro quo the Cantonese chef learnt how to cook the best steak and chips east of Piccadilly.

Eighty years later they came out for Bob Crow, both locals and comrades from all over. The streets were lined with neighbours, fellow workers, friends and comrades, under woven banners and hand drawn slogans, printed posters and flower arranged tributes, 'the traditional east end funeral horse drawn hearse' out of time but in place, a natural fit through these suburban streets. The blue and white plumes of Millwall on the horses, representative of that other religion. Union members, fellow travellers, washed up like survivors of a cult chanting slogans with words that have long gone out of fashion.

Black and white unite and fight, smash the National Front!

If this wasn't a funeral, if it hadn't been Bob's funeral, the raised voices, the exclamations, the fists raised in the air, the snatches of song would probably have sounded self-conscious, apologetic even.

The workers united will never be defeated!

Love you Bob!

RMT. Never on our knees!

Paul rushed out of the tube wearing a black armband on his donkey jacket, late as always. He hadn't seen Bob for ten years, but immediately was spotted by some old faces as he joined the procession, at the back, obviously flustered that people would notice him. A few nods, a couple of handshakes, Paul straightened his tie and polished his dock martins on the calves of his 874 Dickies as the cortege came to a halt outside the Manor Park crematorium.

The crowd swelled forward as the cortege passed, red flags, yellow fists, stemmed roses bouncing off the hearse and family Limos. A two-minute silence. Union banners, the grand gated entrance to the crematorium lined by well-wishers. R.I.P. LEGEND picked out in flowers, the blue and white of Millwall, a rendition of the Internationale...

The peoples flag is deepest red.

No one likes us we don't care.

The workers united shall never be...

Bobs two grandkids pushed by their dad in a double buggy bearing the legend 'RIP Grandad' led the cortege into the private service. The crowd applauds.

At the end of the night there was never any bell for last orders, Charlie just lifted his finger and the piano player stopped playing. Whoever was in, usually stevedores, sailors from around the world, Finnish, Russian, Italian, Lascars and their partners, finished up and in a multitude of languages shouting 'Goodnight Charlie!' as they left the pub quietly...

Footballs made of flowers, BOBPOPS in flowers on the roof of the hearse, wreathes from the RMT, Banners from UNITE, the Socialist party, many branches of trades unions and the NUM, International solidarity from European trades unions, from Cuba, the ANC, the Palestinian solidarity campaign, a condolence book overflowing and a Sky news crew filming the whole bloody lot.

Paul punched his fist into the sky, tears rolling down his cheeks, sang and shouted himself hoarse flooded with the understanding that he had lost, that we had always been defeated. His thoughts unspooled. He was a loser on the losing side and now snot bubbling from his big bloody nose, tears and snot for all of it, for all of the losers all the way back to the spade men, his bastard father included. And he was back in the social club, in that smoky room that he had lost and had never been able to regain. Before losing anything, he had everything to gain; A young man and nobody dead yet on his watch, his life set, his working life laid out in front of him, alongside his beer and his fags, his books, his mix tapes and his union, a place he missed, his home. Up on stage Bob singing his heart out, and Paul chuckling into the foam of his pint at how bad it was, along with everybody else.

Sweet Caroline

Paul stuffed his wet hands deep in his donkey jacket pockets and walked back through the crowd head down. A photo of Bob was propped up on an easel outside the tube.

Goodnight Bob.

Through the automatic ticket gates, (another battle lost), and back home, or back to the pub, all that he felt tamped back down inside, unable to articulate it in words to his wife or daughter, or his family he hardly spoke to anyway, in any words, another failure, impasse. Real people close to him and alive, not somebody he hadn't seen for years and not really known even thirty-five years ago, but somebody famous, somebody to say you knew, somebody who had the power to pass his name down, for it to mean something, at least for some, a name for the newspapers and the television, a small victory of sorts. A man who could raise his finger instead of his voice.

And down the escalator he went, deflated, hollow, standing on the platform, back underground.

Waiting for the self-loathing, an old friend late for a meet up.

ATATURK INTERNATIONAL AIRPORT

My Turkish airlines flight to Kiev was delayed for six hours in Istanbul. I found a bar where four action man lookalikes were getting wasted. It was small and quiet enough for me to hear everything they said as I sipped my litre sized Efes and munched through a tube of salt and vinegar Pringles, thinking did they really make Pringles with bat guano or was that Doritos? Every fucking time I swear this pops into my head.

These Englishmen were all in their mid-fifties, built, with buzzcuts and inked arms, wearing utility outdoor clothes without recognisable labels, and travelling with carry on kitbags stashed under the table. One asked another about what his kids school was like in Gloucester as he was thinking of moving out from Pinner. They were real life mercenaries or similar, ex-army and with the regiment tattoos to prove it.

This was a chance to hear first-hand what was actually going on, behind the miasma of fake news and the emotional narratives of social media. The Efes emboldened me. We were all Brits abroad after all. They budged up and asked me where I was from. I was in, I just had to bide my time, answer their questions before casually drawing them out.

Three of these guys were ex two Para and one of them had been in the Cheshires. From their banter they had all been weapons training Peshmerga fighters in Northwestern Syria. This was half whispered as the Turkish authorities are in effect fighting the same organisation in southeastern Turkey and we were in their airport. The pay was generous; Twenty-six thousand pounds, six weeks on six weeks off. No tax. 'Weapons training' a euphemism for fighting alongside, which was, apparently the only way to teach people how to use weapons.

I was desperate to sneak some iPhone pics at the table, but was worried about the stupid fucking fake shutter sound which I hadn't figured out how to turn off. I would also fumble the volume buttons on my phone, not instinctively knowing which was up and down without conspicuously peering at it. Also, I probably didn't have the balls to pretend to look at the phone and take a snap at the same time, even if I had figured out muting the sound. So I left it on the table alongside the other phones in ruggedised cases. Tonka toy phones compared to my civilian slim case, on whose screens I tantalisingly glimpsed foreign landscapes or family screensavers when they sporadically came to life accompanying text or email notifications. Phones which probably harboured photos to back up (or not) their increasingly far-flung stories.

As the toilet breaks increased exponentially with the rounds of drinks, I managed to corner each of them in turn. During these 'sidebars' I heard the more intimate personal stories behind the banter and camaraderie of the group. The kids at school story, the missing the wife story, the close shave story, the dead body story, the this is how it is on the ground story (lots of these) etc. Things that fighting men won't talk about in a group with an outsider.

A collection of short stories subdivided into sections imitating the organisational structure of the fighting units they had served in.

One of the perks of Peshmerga training for them is that the fighters are women. And these are liberated women. I took their braggadocio with a pinch of salt. Later I googled the whole thing. The female fighters didn't seem to be anybody's fools, or indeed anybody's perks. They fought for their own land but also for the liberation of women at the same time, not afterwards. Their freedom wasn't to follow it wasn't an add on or a promise to be delivered on later. It was now or never.

Ocalan, one of the founders of the Kurdish workers party and de facto 'leader' has been in prison on Imrali island off the coast of Istanbul since 1999. This is where they filmed Midnight Express. It's not a place you escape from. He is on record as saying 'Every man has to kill the man inside him'. This to reboot relations between men and women, to radically alter the course of Islam and world history. Almost a Millenarian aspiration, the world finally turned upside down. Theorised as Jineology, (a Kurdish Neologism for 'woman and life') it places the emancipation of women at the heart of what freedom means for any possible Kurdistan. Having seen his sister virtually sold to a man for food, Ocalan posits this precondition in direct opposition to the subjugation of women as practiced by ISIL. His wider idealism holds up Switzerland as a possible model for an impossible future, his brand of democratic con-federalism to be forged in the heat of war; An ice cube that defies the flames.

I can't imagine this is realistic. Switzerland in the fucking middle east, wake up right? It makes for a great story, but it can't be anything more than a fairytale. What evidence I do have are the hulking men sitting opposite me brimming with piss and vinegar. I believe this fairytale is making men like them a lot of money, and giving them a lot of pleasure, as men.

In war 'we' take our pleasure where we find it, liberation being the climax of war, it's final, but not only orgasm, the course of all wars punctuated by orgiastic moments along the way. Paris, Berlin, London, Singapore, Manila, Saigon, Beirut, Aleppo and Tripoli to name but a few. Sex is at the heart of every war, at its inception, the moment of the desire for war, in its execution as we conduct war, and at the end as part of the celebration of its conclusion, how we finish war, kill the desire for it, although these triumphs, these VE days are nothing more than a little deaths, nostalgic *au revoirs* to arms; until the next time.

The conversation veered again, this time to that of fantastical technology, a fascination for men of action, these soft machines who rely on tech, on constantly upgraded hardware with which to survive the gears of war.

Apparently, the Russians have lent the Syrians 10 of their new top secret tanks (designated T90 but this designation I gather has since been changed.) Observed closely by Ipad Pro clutching Russian technicians, these tanks have EMP technology that deflects ISIS ground to ground missiles (their strongest suit when it comes to armament) literally disabling them in the air by means of an electromagnetic pulse wave. When the enemy has exhausted their missiles, the tanks move in and take them out. Zero tanks damaged, zero loyalist casualties. An aerial electronic blackout means 'our' drones can't see any of this, so myth, hearsay and propaganda must be taken into account when listening to the story, which may be in fact, a modern Russian folktale, Baba yaga wreaking havoc from the skies, striking ISIS with her invisible pestle.

Then they discuss who they think are the best fighters 'on the ground' in Syria and with surprising largess agree that it is the 5000 Iranian Republican guard. I asked them why and they just looked at me for a beat and carried on, my question not worthy of an answer. I wasn't even a sounding board for their opinion by this time.

Who knew if any of this was true? I have always found airports to be full of hot air. In fact this country, *Syria* seems such a porous entity, a place that can't be seen clearly, only spied as if through a miasma of the mother of all anxieties. Barrel bombs, super tanks, drone wars, chemical weapons, white helmets, free Syrian forces, foreign forces, air cover, deserters, freedom fighters and Daesh/Isil/Isis, sleeper cells, cross border incursions, refugees, stateless persons, and increasingly becoming a cross border narco state with Lebanon.

The first time I heard of the Bob Crow Brigade was in this bar, from the mouths of his fellow Englishmen.

Yeah there's anarchists from all over, Yanks French, Spanish, they've even got an English group call themselves the bloody Bob Crow brigade although by the looks of them they've never done a days work in their life.

To be fair Mick, they're fighting fucking Isis nutters with hand guns, give 'em some credit.

Bloody amateurs, get themselves killed and others with them. Would you fight with them, would you fuck?

Peshmerga seem to have integrated them into defence units, fuck it, don't sweat the small stuff Rog, kill the Isis fuckers first then let God decide right?

Wankers dead anyway. Your round Steve. More flags than soldiers that's their problem.

When Steve gets back they're onto Iraq.

Another big story, the classic inside view which you can't really google is the dam on the Euphrates above Mosul. It's structurally damaged and ISIS or the Iraqi military could blow it up, each blaming the other. The flooding could kill hundreds of thousands of people. Italian engineers employed to assess and repair the dam have been unable to access the site due to the war. Is this true? Can it be verified? Or is it just another tall story told by drunk soldiers revelling in their insider knowledge.

I never hear about this dam again, its perilous state still hangs over Iraq like a phantasmic symptom.

Kurdistan is split between Iran, Iraq, Syria and Turkey. Any way you look at it, you gotta think they're fucked.

Steve reaches for his fags, wipes the back of his hand across his nose and top lip.

Bakur, Bashar, Rajalat, Rojava. North, south, east and west in our money, they are the regions of Kurdistan.

He gets up and leaves for the smoking zone.

Steve loves the lingo, it's a whole other world mate, a whole other world. And that's just one of the languages, there's more than four, plus all the dialects, you could draw maps in each one and they would all look different.

Four languages and four religions. A right royal cluster fuck. You got your Sunni Kurds, your Shia ones, then Alevi, and Zaza in Turkey. I think that's a religion? Am I right Trev?

Fuck knows mate. And the Yezhedi, they're Christians. Good luck. Isis cunts don't know who to kill first.

Chuckles all round.

When they launched their Toyota blitzkrieg it was brutal. Kill the men, play footy with their heads, rape the women, move on to the next village.

Don't forget fill up with petrol.

Steve sits back down, settles himself into the conversation.

Keeping their supply lines open.

What they don't tell ya is that probably no more than twenty-four peshmerga, mostly women saved 30,000 Yezedhis from the bastards up on that mountain, Mount Sinjar. Held them off between airstrikes.

And they're all communists, right?

Mid pint silence.

Damn, I forgot to keep my mouth shut.

Fight first play politics later is what I tell them. Keep it simple. Focus on that and you might stay alive.

I had to play dumb in the university of life.

To be fair Mick the way they fight is Commie isn't it, or anarchist what have you.

I was all ears.

When you're hugging the last remaining wall of the local Mosque your face eating the fucking bricks to avoid incoming, 40 degree heat for two hours without moving until somebody orders you to take the next poxy last remaining wall, all you got is the shit in your pants and the simple animal reflex to follow orders. Only thing you think about is will my fucking legs work or turn to jelly.

Yeah but that's another level mate, In Iraq we would discuss tactics with our officers and non coms, nobody was going to put his head on the line without being happy with the plan, Commie or not, it just wasn't talked about openly. This lot as you say are some kind of communist. Fuck it. We get paid, enemy of our enemy is our friend and all that. Then you get to like them, see their point of view for what it is, and it gets more difficult.

That's how it is. 40 million Kurds split between four of the most fucked up countries in the world and they gotta look after themselves, because who would you trust over there? The yanks? Russians? Assad? That's a rum hand of cards.

No friend but the mountain.

Inshallah Bismillah.

They clink glasses.

Two of them get up for another fag, leaving me with Trev, who hasn't said much so far.

Smoking will kill you, mate, mugs game.

Beat of silence, then it's my turn to laugh.

Way I see it is the Turks are the real problem. I read this book see.

He leans into the table, speaking softly, conspiratorially.

They fucked everyone out of what was once called Anatolia. Like the yanks and the Indians. There was tribe upon tribe of people, Greeks, Armenians, Coptic Christians, Asyrrians. All of them kaputt.

He draws a finger across his throat.

Kurds are the last ones standing. Half of that 40 million is in Turkey and they've got their top boy Ocalan locked up as tight as a nun's cunt. But get this, he's still pulling the strings. To fuck him over the Turks allow ISIS the run of the country, well at least down on the border with Syria. Whole towns flying the black flag. We met a CNN crew down in Kobani where fucking ISIS tanks were driving past columns of Turkish ones exchanging greetings turret to turret like on a fucking parade. Film that I told them. No chance, they'd be out of the country in a flash. Doesn't serve their purpose to tell that story. News is big business mate.

Their flight is called. Trev gets up and pats me on the back.

The others return, grab their bags. Our moment out of time had come to an end.

He been boring you shitless with his politics?

I shake my head.

Nice to meet you mate

Handshakes all round. Firm, gripping hands, theirs not mine.

Enjoy your time at home.

A lame, potentially obscene riposte.

The school run, village cricket tournament, can't wait to get back. Lovely jubbly.

The four of them laughed like drains, hoisting kitbags onto shoulders and sauntering off to their gate.

I wasn't going home, I was going to Kiev to shoot another mobile phone commercial. Sober, I would have been confused, but drunk I thought I saw the connections, that I held a clear picture in my mind's eye.

YGA, PYD, P Jack, (the Kurdish for Life Party in Rojava), all of these acronyms swirled confusingly in my mind. KDP, TAK, HPG, Kurdish names for Arabicised cities, maps on top of maps, American airstrikes protecting Kurdish troops on the ground whilst fellow NATO member and ally Turkey sponsors ISIS on the ground against the Kurds. Another beer, another two beers. The Kurdish Stalingrad that was Kobani. A city flattened but ISIS pushed out. A city destroyed at the point of victory. Another little death. 2014. Now two years later a side-by-side photo shows us the amazing human ability and resourcefulness to rebuild. New roundabouts and mosques. You knock us down, but we get up again. Shit Khazakstani MDMA powder from the night before had given me a terrible headache, that plus the six beers I'd had with Britain's Finest made me feel distinctly un-chipper. Finally, my flight was called and I cold sweated my way to the gate.

FROM THESE HANDS

2016

Rosa had spent her summer holiday in Lebanon, learning to restore the stonework on a Mamluk Hammam in the old port city of Tripoli. She also picked up passable Arabic. At night she would hang out in the bars of El Mina, where locals mixed with the aid workers and black market currency dealers, drinking and trading stories in a polyglot of Arabic, French and English. She would buy fish in the market and get it grilled next door, eating fish and chips on the seafront. El Mina 'City of waves and horizon' was a mixed neighbourhood, full of quiet squares, busy souks, and a long corniche along which Christian and Muslim families stroll at dusk eating ice creams, riding bikes and dodging seagulls. Everyone rubbed along together, Mina was laid back and almost sleepy in atmosphere, in a way that second cities can often be more relaxed, even more confident than their bigger brothers. Beirut felt a lot further away than 50 miles. Being overshadowed has its upside, and being seen as a backwater in a country as troubled as Lebanon was probably a blessing. In one of the bars Rosa also finally found a driver who was willing to take her across the Beqaa valley and into Syria. A young man eager to impress a foreign woman, Eli had grown up in the village of Ksara halfway between Beirut and Balbek, home to Hezbollah and also the oldest winery in Lebanon, where his family had worked for generations. Rosa embraced the contradictions that found a common enemy in Isis, for this fragile alliance would, *'nshallah*, see her safely to Rojava.

Ranged against them would be the anti-Hezbollah 'Free Sunnis of Balbek' brigade, The Abdullah Azzam Brigade, the Ziad Al Sarah Battalion, Jund Al Sham, the anarchy of the self-defence militias that ISIS nurtured in order to gain influence and oppose the nation states of the region to make way for its own caliphate. This was to be her education on the road, told with a surreal animated passion by Eli, as his subject matter passed by at speed. He was only twenty-two years old but steeped in the lore and language of conflict, a diversity of confessions each with their own comet tail of injury, slight, massacres retold and feuds remembered.

El Mina *Forget me not and come back soon*, was to be Rosa's staging post, her horizon was set on Syria and a 340km drive to Kobane.

Her dad would later call this her destiny.

Rosa would have disagreed.

Destiny is a load of phallocentric bollocks, dad.

At which they would have both burst out laughing.

A tragic demise wasn't her goal, she didn't frame her life within any trajectory, she wasn't fettered by what had come before her, nothing aimed her, pre-ordained her actions. She hadn't chosen to be named after Rosa bloody Luxembourg.

My mum and dad are so lame, Christ the predictability of that. Being named after anybody is pathetic, branding you for life with their bullshit. In fact, nobody should be given a name, we should all wait until we are old enough to choose our own.

Soon she would be asked to take a new name. Names stick, whether you like them or not.

She was drawn to things that had no precedent, she always sought out the parameters of possibility, however obscured by the cynicism and self-interest of those around her. Rosa felt her way along, and always towards what she sensed was right, but also what gave her pleasure, for are they not the same thing? Your senses, your instincts are indeed a guide for life.

Rosa Luxemburg was murdered in Berlin, beaten and shot to death by fascists, her body thrown into a canal. That hadn't been her destiny either. Destiny can be used retrospectively as a threat, a cheap and hollow compliment after the fact. In reality it is a veiled warning to others, in many cases women, if you do that, this is what will happen to you. Destined for disaster, doomed from the outset, starstruck lovers marked for death. How many times have children been told they are riding for a fall; control of the narrative; manifest destiny means you can't escape it and that's why it's useless, is literally nothing. Rosa Luxembourg had always looked up towards a brighter future, not down into the filthy waters of a city canal.

Rosa thought that the future should be built simply, one day at a time, each holding the same thought, the same idea of what a future could be and if you placed them correctly you would build something of value. Just like that she would say this, without self-awareness, without argument, she was expressing something she intuited about life in words, however they may sound or be perceived, they were the words she had to hand, but what she wanted to say as simple, as matter of fact and every day as climbing up a ladder, one foot after the other.

Destiny be damned.

99 BLACK BALLOONS

Discombobulated by the proximity of war and commerce I found myself sitting in the restored/reimagined art deco bar of an old cinema in what is now chic Kiev, sipping gin cocktails that taste vaguely of cucumber and talking to a Jewish journalist who claims to be the spokesperson for the Azov civic corps.

I seem to have stumbled from one war into another. It was like falling out of orbit and back to earth. This was the day the Azov brigade had blown up a Russian power station in occupied Crimea.

This guy, balding, in his fifties, with Lenin specs and small needle like teeth, sports a heavy rock T shirt with the logo of a band I didn't know and lots of jewellery. Bangles and necklaces, silver skull rings, he jangled as we shook hands. This was the style of the counterculture in the Ukraine. Part hippy, part grunge, wrapped up in 70's rock and roll. Now I remember that T shirt in more detail, or to be more precise, recalling the sound of his jangling handshake brought the T shirt back into focus. It just looked like a heavy metal logo but was in fact an Israeli Defence Force symbol in the style of a heavy metal one, stretched across his flacid man boobs.

Do you know that the brigade is mostly made up of graduates from the Kharkov University history department?

He shouts across the table, happy in his possession of such arcane knowledge.

I don't know what to do with that information, so I order another round of drinks. I was introduced to him by his much younger Ukrainian girlfriend Kseniya who is my executive producer on a commercial shoot for *Kyivstar* a local mobile phone company.

Hey, you gotta meet my boyfriend Andrey, you two would really hit it off.

I agreed, in this city where I find myself agreeing to almost anything. A sex, drugs and rock and roll city mainlining pure energy cut with simmering violence. I had only known her for six hours but she had figured me out as much as I had her. You have to get to know people quickly in production, you land the job, arrive on location, meet the team, bond with them (or not), problem solve and shoot all within the space of ten days at most. Fast times, faster friends. This trip seemed even more crazy and off kilter than most. Just off the plane from Istanbul I buzzed with vertigo.

The three of us entered the smoking room for a cigarette and some privacy. Behind the glass window we must have resembled figures lost in fog.

Andrey lent in conspiratorially, smoke exhaling from one nostril only, which was off putting, the other must have been blocked.

It's my job to persuade them that anti-semitism serves no purpose for their cause, that in fact it binds them to the old polarities of east and west, of Russia, Germany the events and aftermath of the war in the east, the war in which we in fact were extinguished as a nation, so in effect antisemitism is the undoing of Ukrainian independence and to be true nationalists they have to jettison this conditioning, and that yes, Jews, and yes even Israel itself will support them in their fight against the Russian devils.

And then he says, You want to meet the boys? They're back in town, at their clubhouse here in Kiev!

Everybody wants me to meet everybody else. It's the price of being 'a director' in the zero sum game of television commercial production. Mostly my opinions sound brittle up against so much lived experience but if I drink enough I will voice them nonetheless.

Yeah why not?

I extinguished my cigarette and groped my way to the door.

Outside I drew ragged breaths to tamp down on my building anxiety, that feeling of something about to happen I was addicted to. Kseniya hailed us a taxi.

Kiev for fucks sake and not for the first time.

The city passes by in a low wattage blur. The Azov brigade, why the romance of that word? Brigate Rosse, the light Brigade, the Belfast Brigade, the International brigades, brigade a word that slips the mooring of its usage, crosses the line servicing both sides in most wars. All of these brigades ripple through my mind, to a soundtrack of horse hooves, tank tracks, revving getaway cars and the slap of boot heel on tarmac; A seductive word. In the back of the taxi I crave the stringent local taste of horseradish vodka, the double burn of root and grain.

The producer was so full of life the first thing she did in the cab was open the window and ask the driver if it's ok to smoke. He agrees and she lights up. Oddly he doesn't light one for himself.

So fantastically Bohemian, in a way I think only Eastern Europeans can be now, in the sense that they fulfil the grand traditions and criteria of European Bohemia, (by this I mean singing for your supper, drinking like vikings, living hand to mouth, a milieu consisting of painters, writers, artists, singers, through feast or famine, danger, art, integrity, war, performance art, music festivals, occupation, late nights, black outs, impromptu gatherings, early deaths, happenings, work, travel and tragedy!)

All of this 'bohemia' worn like a lucky charm bracelet on steroids, jangling with life each trinket a passion, a memory, a conquest and a tall tale. A word that has become so devalued elsewhere and co extensive with privileged western cultures that there had to be something interesting or good about this man, his girlfriend and their connection to what I had thought up to that point were dangerous right wing nationalist scumbags. That night, and many others from that period of my life in exile, I was to experience the authentic bohemian lifestyle of the wild east.

As we got out of the taxi in what looked like a deserted parking lot Andrey told me that a free democratic Ukraine had to rid itself of all of this crap. I assumed he meant racism but I wasn't sure. Kseniya grabbed by arm conspiratorially and pulled me towards what looked like a giant Portacabin in the corner of the car park under some railway lines. There were no lights on because the cabin had no windows. I pretended this was normal.

Kseniya pounded three times on the door with her gloved hand. It looked like a set up, but this this wasn't a code to get in like in the speakeasies of Lvov where you needed the password of the week, 'Let's eat and let's jazz' or more darkly I had heard a rumour of a hipster bar in a dingy basement, where 'Death to Jews' or 'Slava Ukrayini' whispered through a peephole gained you entrance.

This was Kiev, you knocked and if you're face fit you got in.

They expanded to the size of a regiment during the defence of Mariupol, having started out as a gang of Ultras called the Right sector.

Andrey filled in the backstory as we waited to be let in. I felt his bad breath on the back of my neck.

The metal door opened and after a few terse questions in Russian, we were ushered inside. The man on the door smiled at Kseniya, nodded at Andrey and blanked me.

A green neon glow emanated from behind the bar. The place was full of smoke and men, mostly men, all in the semi combat wear of militia everywhere, Camo trousers, rock T shirts, skull and cross bone neckerchiefs, head torches and bandanas, Doc Martins or local copies, a few high top trainers, a mixture of heavy duty coats, North Face, or more military, probably Russian or Ukrainian army issue. It made me flash on the things you steal from the people you kill; silver cigarette cases, a good pair of boots, a padded jacket, gold teeth, some such nonsense from Sven Hassel. For who else would spring to mind in this company.

A few hand guns (my fourth, fifth and sixth) on tables next to flasks of vodka and cooked sausages on plastic plates, some radishes and cucumbers and throwaway cartons of mustard. Busy hands, the clink of bottles, the low thud of men hugging, sporadic greetings and laughter. They had just come from blowing up a power station in the Crimea which would be out of action for at least a month. The room sizzled with post combat chemicals.

What the fuck was I doing in this room? Getting drunk and aiming to get drunker. It was like being backstage at a concert or an after party for the cast and crew, a special place for special people, the people of the story.

Not me.

I listened, smoked, drank, ate a sausage, all of this titillating, but there was also a sense of familiarity. The way these men were behaving was familiar, our bad habits had bled into the new century. The deja vu felt like a performance.

Slava Ukrayini.

Some cheap coke appeared from Kseniya's coat pocket. I sniffed it.

Come on let's introduce you to Maty.

Kseniya grabbed me by the arm, which was how she guided men to do her bidding.

Sergey Korotnikh was their leader and he sat at the head of a long trestle table at the back of the room. His nom de guerre was 'Matyvta' after Ivan the terrible's henchman. I had never heard of Ivan the Terrible's henchman but he must have had a reputation.

Watch out he hates people who take drugs.

Kseniya had whispered helpfully into my ear just before I sat down.

Matyvta was sitting opposite me with a handgun (7) on the table, a row of vodka shots and beer chasers in front of us and his hand reaching across the table to shake mine

He smiled muttering 'Blood before Empire' as he shook my hand. On the wall behind him was a drab olive grenade launcher covered in stickers and what looked like signatures. Signed like old school broken arm plaster casts at school. This launcher had been used during Maidan and was now a prized possession, relic, totem of this event, this revolution.

Maidan, an Ottoman word for square, now also a

Ukrainian word for square.

He still gripped my hand.

A soldier and a scholar.

He was keen to tell me in bullet points his 'position'. How educated he is and how animal like the Russians are. He understands thanks to Alexei that gays and Jews are not the enemy, that this hatred alienates some of the people he wants to protect and is indeed wrong in itself. I see him struggling with his own argument here, as he distracts himself, or distracts me from his poor performance by raising his glass in another toast, to another fallen hero, dead comrades from the past years fighting. I clink glasses with him.

He's telling me about 'Born' a gang of thugs who murder torture and film themselves doing it to foreign, mainly Tajik workers and migrants in Moscow. They fight for their city block by block, street by street. His point being I think is he has to be as strong as his enemy. But the relish with which he tells the story confuses what he is for and who he is against. Blood is stronger than empire now makes sense.

The 'Born' leader Ilya Goryachev was jailed for life for beheading a Tajik worker. Born being the acronym for the 'combat organisation of Russian nationalists'.

Not as snappy as Right Sector

I can't help interjecting.

His English is not so good so after a beat, a moment of confusion/internal translation I think he thinks I offered up a toast to the Right Sector. Andrey has taken a seat next to me and now nudges me in the ribs. I offer up my glass which is clinked and vodka spills down my forearm inside my shirtsleeve, I shake it out.

Andrey rescues the conversation.

Born also hate gays, see them as pedophiles. Another vigilante street gang pompously called 'Restruct' carried out campaigns against gays, prostitutes and drug dealers luring them online, beating them up and humiliating them on camera which they post to YouTube as warnings to the rest. These are the people we are dating with.

I'm bored, zone out on the coke.

I flash on a modest statue of Isaac Babel I once saw in Odessa, a man, a Jew, a red cavalryman whose stories of the Jewish underworld in pre revolutionary Ukraine had intoxicated me with the power of the story and wondered if he was here now would he snap his pen across his knee, or fill his notebook with ink, eyes sharp on his interlocutor, hand rushing in neat lines across the pages or would he draw his sabre?

I was no longer tethered to the here and now. Vodka poured into glasses and bowls of steaming pirogi were passed around. Kseniya was now singing a Ukrainian folk song accompanied by guitar and accordion. I could barely see her through the fog of cigarette smoke and I was vodka drunk and coke edgy enough to experience her performance as if it were already a memory. Who knows what she sung, but it sounded like folk music the world over, a melody of loss, betrayal, love. Love of country or love of a person rendered much the same by the sentimentality of the medium.

I take a bite of gherkin and a slug of horseradish vodka which burns my throat and my eyes well up. All the pain of one hundred years in this pitiful room, date of birth 1917. My eye caught the odd green stubby tube of the Maiden square rocket launcher hanging on the wall not six feet away. A Momento Mori which amplified the performance, an umbilical chord to the reality of war in a modern age. Kseniya's voice soared over it all, the right and the wrong of it, the only pure and good thing in the room. At that moment the absurdity of being in Kiev for the production of a TV commercial brought me crashing back to earth with an an attack of the giggles which thankfully coincided with a roar of applause as the song came to an end, followed by more toasts.

Kseniya came and rescued me from the table, Andrey and Sergei were by now deep in conversation, they barely acknowledged us as we left, girlfriends and foreign commercials directors surplus to the moment. I hadn't challenged him once on his fake conversion or bullshit politics.

She would be dead within the year, a heart attack whilst diving into the river after a night out clubbing. How many bright shining lives are snuffed out like this so randomly? Her energy deducted from the world just like that.

At one of the many parties held to mark her passing, and there were many because she was very popular and had touched many peoples hearts and lives throughout the world, because the world passed through Kiev as it ever has done, from Mongol to Ottoman to Russian, Soviet now American and British, each of us leaving some words, some traits, some spirit and this time round, this gyre of the wheel, it was advertising and film people who come and go and she had passed through the world in turn through social media, amplifying her souls presence. At her funeral party they released ninety-nine black balloons into the sky over Kiev. Black balloons, what could be more fitting for this city? Kseniya. A true free spirit, singer, producer, actress. A liberated Ukrainian woman. When I saw she had died on facebook I thought of the black flag of the anarchist cossack Nestor Mahkno, conjuring a sentimental link arcing in time between two Ukraines, across the almost infinite, or so it felt, distance between the two, then and now, except she had just folded herself quietly into the past, bridging the gap in the blink of an eye. I only knew her for that week I was in town. But I knew that this gesture was at least part of who she was. Fuck you world and all your rules and hypocrisy, because here is love and light to be weighed against all of that.

ARE WE DANCER?

'Enough Mother, I want to be a revolutionary.'
From a YPJ ballad Kobani 2015.

No shit.

I didn't skip school to come all the way here to go back to the classroom. But our teachers tell us to be patient, that before we are taught how to fight, we have to learn why.

The male has become the state. In order smash the state we must destroy masculinity, the hierarchy of control it exerts, its love of war, of hate and the slavery of women.

We read 'Liberating Life' by Ocalan which sounds like a culty type book, but is more like he's channelling Andrea Dworkin, that she has somehow migrated into his brain! I keep this to myself, behind every man, even the good ones...

> *Sakine Cansiz! She was the first female fighter. She taught Ocalan the true value of women! Murdered in Paris. It was her protest funeral I saw one night in Hackney, a symbolic, empty casket asking the question. Who killed Sakine Cansiz?!*
> **Notes from Rosa's Journal, recovered 2018.**

The history of Kurdish struggle. On a blackboard. The worlds craziest most fucked up map, all chalk arrows, circles and front lines, these in red chalk, dotted lines, sweeping arrows with tails, different colours for different groups and combatants. The IFB, the PKK, the YPG, the YPJ, PYD, TEV-DEM, so many acronyms, my head is spinning, how do you even pronounce them? With a fake Kurdish accent, learnt from our translator? The teachers here all have aliases, usually including the place where they come from. The Arabic names sound cool, places like Raqqa, Idlib, Afrin, Kobani, but what I should I call myself? I come from Hackney, perhaps this sounds better heard by Kurdish ears. The names serve to guide the fighters ultimately home, where we want to go back to, to make revolution, to export the radical democracy we are taught the practicalities of here before we fight for them. I can't imagine my return home, primed to wage the same war in London, but I am not yet a fighter.

From outside I smell wafts of cinnamon, boiled with tea leaves. Cinnamon reminds me of apple strudel from our local bakery. A flick of a switch somewhere in the cosmos jolts me with vertigo. My hand touches the doorjamb, I hesitate in the doorway. This exotic smell floods me with memories of home. Dad always used to spill strudel down his shirt, drove mum crazy. Should be in a highchair being spoon fed she mocked. Too fucking oozey he would reply.

The moment passes, I step outside.

Every morning we drink copious amounts of Chai Kurdi with sugar cubes which we munch on as we drink. I am surrounded by people with sweet and blackened teeth and imagine mine will soon follow suit.

Enclosed are some delicacies from the famous Hallab in Tripoli. My secret pleasure! It reminds me of a fancy sushi restaurant but instead of fish they make sweet shapes made from honey, dates, walnut and pistachio, these are Maamoul, my favourite. The box the packaging is so cute. Miss you both and will hopefully come home with all my teeth still intact. Lots of love, your Rosa x.

The last letter I sent.

Lunch is bread, cheese and spicy olives and for supper it's usually soup and potatoes, also spicy. Coffee is dark and bitter. We drink this in the afternoon. I want to lose some weight and gain some muscle. We do boxing training in the early evening, pads and gloves, jabs, crosses, hooks and upper cuts, to prepare us for what lies ahead. It's all footwork and swivelling your hips, really exhausting.

I aim to become combat fit. We skip with a long rope, jumping in and out, taking it in turns to swing it for the others.

Originally the area was home to nomadic Kurdish tribes. A ramshackle village grew up by the railway line populated by refugees from the Ottoman genocide against neighbouring Armenians and local Christians. The Kurds named it Kobani after the German company who operated the Baghdad railway. A foreign name for foreign people.
We Kurds have to atone for our role in the Armenian genocide.
Apo Ocalan

I never knew any of this.

We are surrounded by sand and scrub, sand in the air as well as underfoot. Sand blows in and out across up and under. Before bed it falls out of your pants. We live under wide pale blue skies, most of the cars and trucks are white, as are the houses. So many buildings are made from breeze blocks and everywhere there are piles of rubble. The streets are wide and full of people, In the background there are grain silos and cypress trees, set amongst dirty brown scrub, and everywhere greasy black smoke stained concrete and holes, so many holes in walls at every level. Holes from which the Kurds fought back, victory holes.

I learn that Turks colonised Anatolia. Turkish maps are an expression of this colonisation, their names erase the names of others; Armenians, Assyrians, Coptic Greeks all of them homogenised as Turkish. The Kurds are the only ones left as a political force. They were promised Independence after World War One and the end of the Ottoman empire.

Even though I am here the war has moved on taunting me with its traces. In the ruins of Kobani there are still black ISIS stencils on the walls, a few tattered flags now just rags to wipe down gun barrels with. How will I cope with fighting proper? All these new people to let down if I fail, seize up somehow, or even run away. I try not to think beyond tomorrow.

The next day a fighter from Raqqa came to talk to us. She told us what it was like to live under Daesh. The Hizbah (religious police) arrested her for not wearing her niqab properly. First, they took all her money and jewellery before throwing her in jail. Then she was sentenced to 1500 lashes. Three men delivered 500 lashes each, the task shared by three men so that they wouldn't tire. She survived by thinking about her revenge until she lost consciousness. Many people die from less than a hundred lashes. The skin on her back had been stripped back to the bone. The translator caught her breath, she was visibly upset, the woman hugged her apologetically before continuing. I didn't blink, I couldn't blink. For a moment I was sure she was going to show us her back but thankfully she didn't, I blushed with shame for thinking she would. The first time she saw an armed woman, a female fighter she burst into tears of joy. The gun was the opposite to the niqab, it was her answer, and why she was here today taking to us. The woman and her translator embraced. We sat in silence, until one of us started clapping and we all joined in. Her war name is Raqqa's revenge.

She was my answer to the question *why are you here*. If anybody was asking other than myself. It is what I will tell my parents when I can muster the courage to tell them.

As she got up to leave, she took her rifle and said one last thing to us.

'Everyone who is armed is equal.'

On the front-line Kurds rely on air support from both the Americans and the Russians. ISIS can't move during the day without being targeted, but at night, or under heavy cloud cover they send their suicide squads of trucks and people with belts. As the fighters push towards Raqqa I am sure we will see them in daylight.

One day I may be able to say *we* un self-consciously but not until after I have swallowed the whole history of Kurdistan it seems and move on to weapons training and eventually combat. The history will give me context, birthing me into the struggle.

I'm fine with that. Like dad says, knowledge is power.

Ocalan was in Damascus in the 80's and 90's protected by the regime but the PKK agitation for autonomy in Rojava led to unease in the government. Who would the Kurds fight for in a civil war? Ocalan was once again on the run. For ten years he travels the world from one temporary sanctuary to another in Russia, Italy and Greece. In 1999 he is captured in Nairobi by Turkish Intelligence operatives with the help of the CIA. Apo is now the only prisoner on Imrali Island. 1000 guards for one man. Condemned to death, he was reprieved when capital punishment was banned In Turkey (A sign of modernisation we are told, of a modern west facing Turkish state.) Ocalan speaks and thinks in Turkish. Here they say, 'but he dreams in Kurdish.'

At night we sit on the roof of the village Mosque smoking and watching the stars. The sky is teeming with pin pricks of light against an inky Bible, Koran, or Anarchist black, the alternatives pass through me. I didn't smoke much before, but I can't think of being here without smoking, it is part of our everyday ritual, like tea. These old fashioned American Arden Cigarettes have become intimate tokens of friendship. Rojava is organised according to the principles of democratic confederalism, which boils down to lots of committees, communes and sub committees debating the everyday organisation of food production and distribution, women's rights, industrial development, which is from what I can gather a single cement factory. Military operations are split between the peoples' protection units, the male YPG, the female YPJ and the IFB which consists of mixed male and female volunteers assimilated into the YPG. In the push from Kobane to Raqqa the SDF are in overall strategic command.

Under this sky my Insta feed uploads instantly. At night it looks as if a pane of very thin glass is all that separates us from the cosmos. Here we are at the centre of the world. This food distribution centre, this warehouse and these hands are powering this human corner of the Universe. I hear Italian, German, Swedish, Arabic, Kurdish, American, Turkish, Scottish, I hear French, Spanish, Portuguese, we have built the tower of Babel in our spare time. I bunk with six others, four men and three women in a house assigned to the IFB. Two committed Marxists, one libertarian communist and the rest vaguely anarchistic, and me, winging it with my advocacy of women rights and self-determination within the nation state. Every night the state itself is unpicked in front of me much to my comrades relish, yet everyday I point out to them our actions are the building blocks of just such another nation state. This is the flux we live in, and we are to train and fight also in the literal rubble of the ideas we debate.

After school we go to work, six hour shifts at the relief warehouse. Heavily guarded we are told these distribution centres are targets for the enemy.

One can of cooking oil. Check.

One bag of rice. Check.

One bag of couscous. Check. (If it's yellow its couscous, white its rice. Check.)

One bag of beans, black or white. Check.

Three tins of chopped tomatoes. Check.

There are 35,000 refugees in Kobani.

One of the other Brits says that post modernism kicked us in the balls. Obviously a bloke but I think what he means, is that we were immobilised by so many clever words, it allowed us to avoid taking responsibility.

Somebody had a copy of *The Handmaid's tale*. Why read that? It is happening HERE. Which is why this middle of nowhere feels like the centre of the world, the nut of it, stripped bare of its fictions. Isis is what happens when the mask slips but the face is always the same, it is always a male face.

And then this same British guy told me he had *fidelity to the transformative power of the revolutionary event* which sounds like to me the seduction of words all over again. Just different ones. In sixth form we all read Mark Fisher who said the problem with the left was that they couldn't see past capitalism, couldn't imagine what a victory would look like, so we were just all focused on the end of something that we couldn't defeat because we didn't have a vision of what was to replace it. He called it the erosion of the future.

The future is bursting with possibility. It is miraculous. One of our more serious teachers told us:

Freedom crowns the heads of the free, but only slaves know its value.

Whatever. Get on a plane, on a train, get a bus, walk, run HERE.

Here words are spoken. Spoken with the purpose of making decisions and then acting on those decisions collectively. In meetings, discussions, endless debates about rights, food, protection, pay, flags, names, elections, action tagged with words, words signposting action.

Jineology. The science of women. A new revolutionary society founded on gender equality and the liberation of women from all forms of oppression and exploitation.

Statist power is born from the enslavement of women. The male has become a state

Dworkin would have embraced this because it was territorial. Women protection units. She would have set these up in New York, in London in anywhere. To physically build safe territory (not nebulous head spaces, but actual bits of land) for women.

Men will not bring us our freedom, it is not to be gifted.
Kurdish YPJ fighter, July 2017 on the road to Raqqa.

Now they teach us the three sexual raptures. Is he dreaming of women in his solitary confinement? Is this where the ideation come from? Are we fighting for a fantasy, for a man dreaming of woman?

We will protect you as if you were our own eyes.
Yezehdi Fighter August 2017 Raqqa.

In liberated Kobani, Kangreya Star, the star congress for women. No forced marriage. A campaign against domestic violence. They have established women's centres in each refugee camp, in each village.

The most fierce war is ideas, the most powerful war is ideological.
Apo, Ocalan.

A man's idea, a man's conversion. But does it matter Dworkin learnt everything she knew from her father, she says so! Does that make her any less radical? What she did was not her father's doing. Does Ocalan being a man have any bearing on what happens here? Can ideas transcend gender? Can his words liberate themselves in the action of women? A man in prison for twenty years is no longer a man, he fades as a man but grows as an idea or a collection of thoughts, a cloud of ideas that rain down on us, for us to sow or plant them, take them make them ours whilst he fades away as an actual man.

Masculinity must be killed to kill power.

I think his release would be a terrible anti-climax, a backward step in this Jineology, my fierce Kurdish teacher tells me this, tells me Apo is exactly that, an uncle, a distant uncle, the ultimate exile who can't ever return to undo all of his good work, to destroy the mystery, the power of the man in the iron mask.

Self defence is the defence of a woman's body from the customs and rituals that favour men. Forced marriage is rape. These self-defence groups are my home, but the only language we share is that of our bodies.

Kobani.

The murals tell the story of the siege, like the Bayeaux tapestry. We honour the dead. Women have become fallen heroes. Macho shit is now the same for us, we have become macho shit. How is it to fight like a woman? How do we measure? Are we better snipers like the Soviet female snipers in the Second World war, are we crueller, crazier in combat, more incandescent in our anger like Phoolan Devi the bandit queen? Or are we the same? Or are we lesser?

Or are we dancer?

I play The Killers on my phone. I sing along. it rouses me,

makes me feel epic, it always did as a child and still works now. So desperately uncool I know.

New and old bridges, the bridges that survived, the new bridges of victory and new born babies are now called Kobane. The Kurds very own Stalingrad, celebrated in song and dances around fires, painted on walls and in TV montages of the dead.

After a month working in the warehouse, we start our military training at the YPG International academy, which is based in a half burnt out farmhouse surrounded by a few scattered outbuildings. Mostly drills, exercise and small arms tactics. We sit in a circle and are encouraged to talk about why we are there, what our faults are, what our strengths are. Who annoys us, why they annoy us and if we think we have any bad habits. Also, what are our best traits? Simple stuff but it works if the aim is to forge bonds between us, thankfully English is the Lingua Franca of the unit, that is until we can speak enough Kurdish, so I get by.

Breaking down an AK blindfolded. Losing my temper trying to re attach the firing pin. The laughter of my comrades, fingers fumbling bullets into the magazine.

Finally, weapons training. Old Chinese AK 47's, newer AKM's with taped up magazines. Two heavier Draganov sniper rifles. These are the guns we get to know. How they work, how to break them down, how to sight them, how to breathe when sighting them, how to live with them. At the shooting range (a field behind the farmhouse) you are given nine rounds per weapon. Three standing, three kneeling and three prone. At night our guns line the walls of the communal sleeping rooms, we always know where our own one is, we can get up, grab it in the dark and fall in without thinking. You do not touch another fighter's weapon.

On cold mornings I tuck my hair under the seam of my first Keffiyeh. It is cobalt blue with red tassles and pearl embroidery. Wearing this makes me feel like I fit in, more than anything else it marks me out as a female fighter. It includes me.

Our Kurdish trainers make us a last supper and there is a graduation ceremony where we swear allegiance placing our hands on the Kurdish flag and repeating after our commander the following oath parroting the Kurdish, amplifying it into the sound of a chorus. (We have read a translated photocopy of the words, so we know what we are saying.)

Based on the paradigm of a democratic society, an ecological society and freedom of ideas irrespective of religion, language, ethnicity, group or party, to take into account the idea of self defence based on the regulations of the YPG and YPJ on this basis before Kurdistans fallen heroes by the people of Kurdistan and my brave comrades in arms, I swear, I swear, I swear, I swear.

Not one of us older than 21. This feels like a blood oath, the words repeated in our mouths raise the hairs on my arms, I am dizzy with the rhythm of them.

Pick-up trucks come to take us to our first postings to the villages of Churas, Boxaz and Zerik, south towards the Euphrates and the frontline. Dawn breaks and I am bouncing around in the back of a Toyota speeding through the outskirts of Kobani. As we pass fighters on motorbikes pull up alongside us with a whine of acceleration and flash victory signs at us and we shout back.

Woman, life, Freedom!

They overtake us, white teeth, wide smiles, the pure joy of speed, a game, a celebration, a defiance.

Woman, life, Freedom!

After two weeks of quiet 'village life' we get our first posting. Guard duty on the M4 motorway that connects Afrin to Manbij. 74 Km north of Raqqa. On the third night terrorists attack at 4am. Small arms fire, no RPGs. We hold them off. Daesh have been told they will go to hell if they are killed by women. They are scared of us, so we shout, 'Women's bullets!' to keep our spirits up. I fire my weapon into the darkness, the first time and I manage to do my part, what was asked of me.

At sunrise airstrikes force them back. Usually, Daesh time their retreat just before the planes arrive. You can have hours of firefight without serious injury, usually just stone or wood splinters. We hardly see anything. One morning we spotted an enemy truck travelling on an unseen road along the horizon. Our commander came up and ordered the heavy machine gun to fire a few rounds at it. The gun was mounted on the back of a truck, so the driver, an old man who loved trucks and could repair any engine, we called him Papa Kurdi, drove it up the berm which protected our position from direct fire. A fighter sighted the guns, which sat behind twin plates of steel armour and fired a few bursts towards it, by slapping down on the firing Mechanism with the palm of his hand. Everyone cheered and ululated but we didn't hit the truck. The sound and the smoke was a spectacle more than anything. The truck stopped moving as soon as it came under fire and retreated. We cheered some more.

Everyone is so focused on not getting shot, on both sides. If you imagine ISIS are crazy and reckless then you will be disappointed in facing them. They hold their lives as dear as we do ours. Suicide bombers aside, their fighters were like us. Scared 99% of time reckless 1% after two hours of cowering being a wall, or just shooting off indiscriminately above your head you will get to the point where your superiors gets serious or somebody on the end of a walkie talkie wants to see some results.

On the horizon we can only ever see the two-story schoolrooms the regime built all across Syria, the highest look out points are on their roofs. Both sides occupy them. There are also water towers we use for vantage. A single thermal scope is shared between three units along the M4. No point holding a water tower if you can't see anything. Isis gamble on which tower will have the scope on which night. That is after they figured out we didn't have enough scopes to go round. So it's cat and mouse, trying to be counter intuitive in our battle order and distribution of resources. Their goal is to mine the road not to take our positions.

The theory we were taught on a blackboard; New recruits always hold the centre. The veteran units operate pincer attacks either side of a target and we hold front and centre. The back door is open, so they can retreat, as long as we push them back and together, we can push towards Raqqa, where all the rats will end up in a barrel.

Offensive!

Seven of us take cover in the folds of low hills that line either side of a remote road. For hours. Our packs cut into our shoulders, our weapons sweaty, dusty, I constantly clean mine, wipe it down, check its mechanism, double check the safety catch, all of this as a way to pass the time. The veterans amongst us move with much greater economy, they don't fuss with themselves at all, not even to slap away insects. They smile at our discomfort, or at least I imagine they do. We look over towards the radio op to see if he has any news. Nothing. It's forty degrees. I glaze over and my mind wanders despite this being my first offensive action. The waiting and the heat have leeched the adrenalin, normalising the fact that I might die or get horribly injured like in the war films I have seen, hands holding in guts screaming medic.

The desert of Northern Syria. A bandana instead of a helmet, soaked with sweat, now dried as the sweat has run out. A sand coloured scorpion scuttles across my Doctor Martins, my legs scissor as I worm my way backwards in disgust. A round of Shushes from my comrades. The radio crackles to life and the adrenalin floods back, this is it. We are waved forward and down the incline towards the sliver of road. Up ahead the two veterans shoulder their RPG's as a white truck comes out of the dust on the road below us. I never thought I could summon this much focus.

I stumble and gash my knee and scuff my AK in the dirt. My knee oozes blood but I'm up and running doubled over as we have been taught, low profile, a skill I am still pretty crap at because it makes me dizzy. The whoosh of the RPG which misses the swerving truck. There is sporadic returning fire, firecrackers taken by the wind. The truck passes before I reach the road and aim my rifle for the first time in anger at its taillights. I slow my breathing and pull the trigger, letting off a burst of five bullets just as the second RPG scores a direct hit on the back of the truck and it swerves off the road into a low sand berm. A flash of heat on my face, in my eyes, fresh beads of sweat. I flick the lever to automatic and offload as many rounds as I can into the smoke and fire ahead of us. The commander screams for us to cease fire but I only do so when the magazine is empty, the barrel burning my hands, I dangle it by the wooden stock, clumsily changing the magazine. We approach the vehicle step by step as if it was a sleeping monster. One of the vets, creeps up and kicks open the passenger door and a body falls out onto the road. I'm right behind him and bite down on vomit to save my honour as a headless body lies at my feet. The driver is dead in his seat. Whatever was in the back of the truck has been destroyed by the grenade and burns with an acrid stench. We sing a song of triumph, one we have learnt from the Kurds amongst us, and in return as we disappear back into the hills we sing, 'Bandera Rossa'. In the sky above us hazing into late afternoon, American fighter jets zoom past on their way to fulfil another mission against the same enemy. Maybe this is all a post-modern joke? Dad would point that out I am sure.

This is my 2017. In a Toyota, south of the M4 highway running across northern Syria, on the road to Raqqa, tearing up sand berms, hanging off a rusty, squeaking heavy machine gun faring, blaring out the Killers. It is our version of the Beach Boys in an old Spike Jonze movie.

Fuck yeah as the Americans can't help themselves saying. It was sunset, we were speeding and the western girls are all singing...

Are we human?

Or are we dancer?

PLANET OF THE APES

Paul perches on the edge of his daughter's bed, surrounded by the bright colours, angry bookshelves and alternative celebrity pin ups of a late teenager, a young woman. He slumps. His sitting has become a slump, like when he was a kid.

You've got sleep in your eye.

He licks the corner of his hankie and leans in.

Urgh that's disgusting dad!

Rosa shudders.

Keep still.

He delicately wipes it away.

How can there be sleep in my eye? I've just been asleep, now I'm awake.

Paul shrugs his shoulders.

That's just what it's called.

But it's more like an eye bogie, isn't it?

I don't know Rosa, I don't look at bogies.

They both giggle.

Come on, you'll be late for school.

Late for breakfast you mean, I'm hungry!

Another day same Rosa.

Dad, You think that story is true?

That a gang of monkeys set up a roadblock to steal water

from aid workers during a drought? No, I don't think that's true. It's a good story though.

Monkeys don't form gangs they go about in troops.

Paul raises his eyebrows.

That's just words Rosa, it's just a convention to call them a troop. Like, like a murder of crows. It's just words.

Rosa looks concerned.

But is it possible?

Is what possible?

For chimpanzees to organise like that, like humans do? To hijack something?

Perhaps. But it would be spontaneous, not organised in the sense you're thinking of.

Well maybe you are being naive dad.

Maybe. Now get some sleep. Goodnight, Rosa.

Goodnight.

Still frowning she turns off her bedside light, pulls up her duvet.

PIECES OF ME

A marine patrol came into the village we have just taken to co-ordinate with our commanders and share intelligence. They also dropped off some medical supplies. I shared a smoke with a young marine. He had a crumpled soft pack of white tip Marlboro Lights, the best of America, unlike the Arden crap we usually smoked. He couldn't believe I wasn't army trained, that I was even here. I was like a discovery for him.

Why the fuck was he here I asked him?

He shrugged.

Daddy was a marine. I grew up with his stories. Wanted some of my own.

Which sounded like a soft sell from a recruitment video. No hard luck story, no drugs or broken marriages, no sports team analogies. I was disappointed.

He asked to take a look at my Kalashnikov. I handed it to him. He sighted along the barrel, dug the wound fabric stock and checked the magazine. He handed it back. This was flirting.

Fucking respect! Fuck.

He gave me a well-used copy of *Starship Troopers* by Robert Heinlein. Said it was on a list they got from their commander. He said the officers got *All quiet on the western front*. Which was a bum deal for them.

I smiled in return. In his eyes I saw it was a fair exchange, playful overtures in the ever war between men and women.

You seen the film?

Starship Troopers? I nodded, smoking vigorously it was one of my favourite movies. I felt light headed.

Take it easy girl. This here ain't a film or a book.'

Sir yes Sir! I smiled, caressing the blood red cloth of my rifle. To be honest in moments like these I feel like I'm in both.

He handed me the rest of his packet of lights. Our fingers brushed. A payment of sorts and with that he got back into the Humvee and *hightailed* it out of there.

15th May 2017

As the push on Raqqa intensified more journalists arrived with their fixers through Iraq. One of them was here to do a story on foreign fighters. The guy looked like a Euro rich kid with an expensive camera, a blonde haired and blue eyed war junkie handing out dollars to get to the front line. Our unit leader pointed to the three of us and winked as she sent the man over. The SDF had been told to tolerate reporters, as we needed the world to witness the moment Kurdish fighters defeated ISIS, proof of our autonomy. Foreign fighters were rarely on the frontline as not speaking Kurdish made us something of a liability. I have picked enough up to follow orders and the rest is the language of being a woman in this hell made by men, something all of us share with humour, toiletries and the solidarity of struggle.

The photographer was Swedish I think, a pampered Viking, ravishing us with his camera.

You speak English?

I nodded, biting my tongue not to follow this up with *a little*.

Where are you from? Are you Muslim?

(Asked because I am mixed race?)

Why are you here? What unit are you with? Are you a combat fighter?

Questions, questions as he clicked away with his camera. I fended them off.

(None of your business, No, why do you ask? That's classified information. Not yet...)

I hear there are lots of foreign fighters on the other side, in Raqqa, some Brits too.

This man was really charmless.

I looked at the shiny gold camera around his neck. His eyes followed mine. A Contax T3 35mm film camera from the 1990's.

He raised it to his eye.

To break this bad karma spell, I put my rifle down and started dancing, like I was back home at a festival, we out here or secret garden party.

He lowered his camera.

Ah that's a bit odd, dancing...

It's a silent disco for one. You're not on the list.

He didn't get it, just smiled and shrugged. To get rid of him I gave him want he wanted. A great shot. I posed with my AK raised above my head, bathed in the orange glow of a Northern Syrian sunset.

No, no, maybe that's too much, can you hold the rifle lower like this?

He makes the gesture of cradling a baby. A woman who cradles a gun instead of a baby. Fucking wanker. I shrug, lowering my arms. I think and try hard to make what I'm thinking visible.

I am a non gendered human being!

He blanked that and took his photos. My mind wandered. Seriously, what if the man I have to kill or be killed by is a British volunteer, for example a Pakistani working class man. If he kills me in battle and pulls the Keffiyeh from my face who would he see? Me? All the doubt floods back. Stupid wasteful thoughts that limit me, gnaw away at my commitment to this struggle. This very specific revolution. All of the things my parents will never understand: how I cried for every last thing, every last thing I believed in and we never won anything, it was all taken away, we were always being defeated. I couldn't live to be as old as them and have that disappointment bearing down on me. I wasn't that strong.

...but it was never easy, shutting down doubt, the doubts in my head, and my fear, my love of myself to the exclusion of...so I must understand what it means to face a British ISIS fighter, a fighter of colour but from a different background and from a religion, a world view, where all I have is my instinct to question all world views. It sounds weaker than what he has. But it boils down to a simple opposition; I am fighting for women, for some kind of probably messy socialism and he is fighting for a fascist patriarchy. So, he has every right to fight me and I him.

After the photographer left (I didn't speak to him again, not one word, I didn't even take the inevitable pack of cigarettes he offered), a group of British volunteers arrived in a truck, on their way to positions on the outskirts of Raqqa. They were the Bob Crow brigade who we had heard of. Typical British blokes, all the way out here in the Syrian badlands.

My dad knew Bob Crow, was all I could think of to say.

At least it was true. I remember when dad came back from his funeral. He was very quiet. It was the first and last time I ever saw him cry. Mum put her arms around him when he came in the door. There seemed to be less of him somehow, like he had been totally vanquished. He went to bed and she stayed up crying. I went out, couldn't be around that.

The press loved the Bob Crow Brigade and the story had social media cut through. Banners, logos all made up and some slogans, words from comrade Bob, which to me seemed a bit obvious, a little old fashioned, the kind of bland rhetorical internationalism which had let the left down since forever. What do I know? *Vice* love the story, it has granularity, whatever that is. The Bob Crow brigade, not even up to brigade strength to be honest but I am nit picking, in fact part of the awkward squad, smaller than a brigade but... Anyway, I had my photo taken with them, why not? I was a Londoner after all and my dad used to be a tube driver with Bob Crow so maybe it will be a story and I'll be famous and my dad will be so proud of me and the Bob Crow brigade.

What do people do? That's what Bob asked wasn't it dad? I came here...

We move out, south east towards the Euphrates and the city of Raqqa.

May 28 2017
Smoke rises on the horizon from all points of the compass. One village east, one west, north and south, linked by the arrows of invisible roads. In summer haze smears these simple contours, in winter the flat light delineates with such clarity it smarts the eyes. We advance and retreat

like opposing sand dunes. Our villages, their villages and villages caught between the two. A few houses, a petrol station, some times a mosque, some farm compounds, a market. Some friendly, others suspicious. We witness and we watch as we wait.

I have been granted so much time I never thought I would have.

When we first arrived the Kurds cooked kebabs and special dished for us as guests. As time went on we ate the same as everybody else and had our share of going without. When they handed out American MRE we shared the excitement of something different and devoured the sweet nourishment from our wealthy benefactors. This was how I became one of them, through what we did or did not eat. Our shit smelt the same. A biological fact, a fact of carbs and protein, second helpings and hunger.

The terrorists fall back as we come south but progress is slow in each village we find and clear mines and the villagers return. When the roads are busy with them is the most dangerous time for suicide attacks and mortar fire. They disappear across every horizon. We follow. In their wake they send more suicide vehicles along the veins, the tracery of roads in the sand, the rock and rubble of the plains that lead to Raqqa. Mines, booby traps, other IED's, an endless inventiveness of death slowing us down. We sit, walkie talkies from unit leaders bark, go silent bark again, we sit on ridges flanking villages being assaulted, waiting to intercept reinforcements or cut off escape. We perch on ridges spying through lopsided optics of binoculars, touch screen pads prodded to plot and plan a route forward, a coordinated advance. Our war, uploaded to Instagram, plotted on whatsapp groups and debated on Twitter. No pressure then.

Mortar fire pins us down for what seems like ages. Nobody is in a hurry to move. Nobody wants to get killed or injured. The enemy sights on vehicles, the only things visible to their spotters. We drink tea, veteran fighters try and flank the mortar truck if it is near enough to us and far enough from their village. If it is in the open, they can get within its minimum range. We drink more tea.

June 6 2017

Magically the city appears in the distance, like it had come to us rather than us crawling towards it. As if we had moved with our eyes shut and now, all of a sudden, opened them to see it. After so many flat horizons with villages somehow below our eye line, these modest outlying neighbourhoods brought with them vertigo.

I have been reading more Dworkin.

'*Am I rounded, existentially and publicly? Who is ever and anywhere rounded, and is it necessary to be complete? And rounded in order to live in a complete and rounded way? Unbelievable idiocies!*' I am not believable as a person. Is anyone? I might do something, and for a moment be believable in that action. Make breakfast, toast, jams, butter, orange juice, strong coffee. I appear at a rally, I speak there. I turn up to meetings of a committee for some kind of justice, I appear in the minutes of that meeting. These fragments of me, these pieces are believable. The rest? No I don't think so, none of us are, the totality, the big picture of who you are is a falsehood, falsehood you either participate in or its on other people. be a fragment, put yourself in the clear on a daily basis is my advice, don't play the adding up game. Don't create a penis out of yourself...'

SNAKES AND LADDERS

In July 2017 I was in Dalaman Turkey shooting content for a TUI holidays 'All Inclusive Mahoosive' resort. All you can eat (buffet) all you can drink (local brands) all the attractions, kids club and family excursions, for one price. Premium Chalets had a shared pool around which six or seven units were arranged and there were three huge common pools with slides, wave machines and pool side drinks service. The beach was at the end of a walkway. It was empty.

'Blue Resort' was exclusively for Brits. It was adjacent to a similar resort reserved for Russian guests and maybe some other northern Europeans. There was a shared reception area which branched off into the two different, for want of a better word, sub hotels, or regional Holiday wings.

You can tell who the Russian guests are because they don't have many tattoos, as until very recently it was still associated with criminal organisations and prison. The Brits were head to toe covered in tats. Cars, kids, towns and cities, football clubs, mums and dads, births deaths and marriages for ever family legends, Army tats, trade union tats, Thai tats, brand tats, the variety was as impressive as its repetition. Tattoos had colonised not only the torso but every extremity of the male and female body, across at least three generations. Hands fingers, toes, backs, heads, faces, necks, calves, tummies, you name it, they tattooed it. All of the bodies real estate was up for grabs. In fact the most interesting person I met there was a somebody who's nickname was 'the King of Poland'. He was the on-site tattooist, leasing his parlour directly from the hotel, who took a cut, bypassing TUI. Every summer he took home 35k a month for four months. Do the maths. For the rest of the year he was the king of Poland. Brits booked their holidays at this specific resort so they could book an appointment with him. His shop was in an odd arcade tucked away behind one of the onsite buffet restaurants, where there was also a shabby gaming hall, a souvenir shop and a launderette. A little piece of home, fake heritage on the Turquoise coast, almost equidistant from Istanbul and the Syrian border.

Passing through customs at the modern, just completed glass and steel Dalaman airport, we saw another film crew getting hassled by security. The big boss had been called and in the meantime the customs officials were taking a fag break. An irate producer was flapping his carnet about but to no avail. The camera boxes had been hauled off the scanner and emptied out on the shiny marble floor. Embossed on them (in bold 'raised' red lettering) were the words 'Red Weapon'. Which is the name of the camera. The viewfinder was called the 'Red bomb'. It had its own embossed box. Great marketing from the people who brought you Oakley sunglasses. We sailed past with our Prosumer Sony A7 cameras slung over our shoulders, Go Pro's stuffed into our pockets as if we were on holiday.

The free booze was so watered down yet the minor buzz it created by volume gave the whole place a vibe of serenity. I didn't see a single fight or even a face off. Like everyone had been medicated. Proper drinkers got wise after the first few days and stumped up the extra cash for the brands they knew, or went to the bars in town and got pissed and possibly into fights.

It helped the holiday go smoothly, although rumours of domestic abuse and elderly guests dropping dead after too much to drink in the constant heatwave that was August were flatly denied by the tour guides and local hotel staff. Perhaps silent ambulances came and went at night. I wouldn't put it past this place, this resort. I was here to help sell its version of the great summer holiday.

The 'Red Weapon' film crew appeared at the resort three days later, they must have got their camera back. They had arrived to shoot a big budget television and cinema commercial for TUI Holidays. I was there shooting content for the TUI social channels and corporate video for their annual conference. That night in the bar the young director arrived with his Art director and met the rest of the crew, high-fiving them. He briefly looked over colour swabs for wardrobe, held numerous mobile calls with the agency, the room now energised by all the hustle and bustle of the night before the first days shoot of a big job.

He was what I had been. A commercials director on his way to the top.

That night it became apparent to me that I was a snake who had slithered to the bottom of the ladder.

How was this the case? What mistake had I made? What had I done wrong? What decisions had I made that were this bad? That led to this humiliation. I, who had flown transatlantically first class, had been one of the winners who had turned left getting onto the plane, I had been in the room! At the table! However briefly. And was now being shown the door, or indeed was showing it to myself. A tourist class flight to a package holiday destination. I drank another generic beer and chased it with no label vodka. Confused (by alcohol), all I could ask myself, pathetically, was 'How had it come to this?'

Later I worked out this was the same week that Paul's daughter Rosa fell in the battle for Raqqa.

HARMOLODICS
Nº 5

Andrea crouched in the Quasr al Banat, the palace of the maidens. She snorted when somebody told her the name of the now mostly destroyed building they had just occupied, fingers burnt and bloody from loading and unjamming her hot tired almost worn out machine gun. Hugging what walls were left, eyeballing her female officers for signals to move, forcing herself to become a kinetic response unit, her intellectual life behind her, shredded like a snakeskin. She had become pure ancillary.

Overhead another American airstrike gave her pause to think of that fucking cock in the sky, to almost chortle at it as it spewed death a few hundred yards either side of her, in ruins explored millennia ago by Getrude Bell no less. Andrea, breathing hard, biting down on the blood metallic taste in her mouth and crazy ringing in her ears, her thoughts returned, momentary inaction allowing her mind to recapture, occupy her tortured body once again, terrifying her into immobility. Stiff with fear and horror only repeated jabs from her officers AK barrel got her up and moving, ancillary once more, out from the shade into the heat, sunlight and smoke of the city, firing into the nothingness that had been spunked from the skies to cover her. She sensed movement and unloaded her ammunition into what remained of the enemy, screaming 'Woman, life, Freedom!'

GAME THEORY

I saw the ruin of Grenfell tower from the plane. There was anger in the air, the resignation of having just lost an election reignited by the outrage of such an avoidable tragedy. In the pub with some old friends everyone was talking about it, somebody asked me if I wanted to go to a Labour party meeting. Power corruption and lies never closer to the surface of our national conversation. Oddly this energy, this engagement with events felt like home. I remembered my old communist party membership card with its row of squares, to receive stamps from the branch secretary (or treasurer?) marking dues paid, and a room of elderly men and women having their cards stamped as badges of an honour they still coveted. After two years of attending party meetings in which the membership was regularly reduced by old age and death, operating more like a bereavement counselling service than an active political party, I had joined the Labour party. One of life's minor disappointments.

The following week I went to my first Labour party branch meeting in twenty-five years, above a pub.

Where else.

A London University media studies lecturer was giving us a pep talk about the impact digital media had had on the general election. How Corbyn's Labour party was being transformed by its use of social media channels to connect them with the electorate.

He wore a pork pie hat.

He brought to mind the word Polytechnic.

An elderly party member timidly asked him a question about the efficacy of all of this new technology at our fingertips as we had just lost a general election.

No no no. He said,

You don't understand.

She had posited the opinion that without feet on the street, talking to voters face to face all of this social media buzz was unsustainable. He shook his head, she was the latest in a long line of morons who didn't understand. Roused from my stupor I interjected.

You can't talk to people like that, her opinion is as valid as yours.

To which he thousand-yard stared me and the rest of the room looked elsewhere. Even the old cow I was sticking up for kept silent.

For the rest of what passed for a meeting I watched him closely. Every time somebody else spoke he either closed his eyes or worried his phone, totally disinterested in their contributions.

All those in favour raise your hand.

A motion was passed unanimously in support of the victims and survivors of the Grenfell tower fire. The meeting was wound up.

I shit you not. All of the reasons I had gone to America so many years before, in one room.

My two friends left after a couple of pints and some

pleasant political banter about the direction of the leadership 'going forward'. I stayed, partly because I had nowhere else to be but mainly because I wanted to talk to the pork pie hat wearing poly lecturer type arsehole. I spotted him at the bar on his phone and offered to buy him a drink. He hesitated for a beat then nodded.

London Pride please mate, I'm Richard.

We shook hands. I didn't tell him my name which didn't seem to bother him in the slightest. I was fascinated by the existence of such a monster.

I discover he had also been to Essex University, as a postgraduate. He was fifty odd, and had a three year old boy. Read into that what you will. He was *into* game theory and ludic strategy in the service of the party (He told me). He had John McDonnell's ear (ditto), which I couldn't stop thinking he meant literally, like singeing the Spanish kings beard and he kept talking about Guy de Bord, as if this was a magic name, an angelic or divine talisman that validated the shit he was talking, a word he repeated in lieu of listening, a heartless repetition, a knowing self-regarding enchantment.

His nasal estuary twang, giving him the air of a self-taught fraud who had come across aspects of French post structuralism in a second hand bookshop and had been stringing them and us along ever since. He told me about a game he had developed, an app called 'Corbyn Run' in which you (playing as JC) hunt bankers whilst baddie Theresa May throws champagne bottles at you from a helicopter. Over the course of the election it had been (he told me) downloaded 1m times.

A game changer.

There was not a shred of kindness in this ghoul, he

was fiendlike in his didactic obsessions. His breath stank. (a familiar trait in bores and frauds of all stripes). He shamelessly bought himself another pint without returning the round, forcing me to do the same. I was really enjoying this, in my mind I begged him to continue talking.

He was already (again) preparing for power. His glassy eyes couldn't power a gokart. Mr zero watts, man not on fire, a soulless zombie, yet I was transfixed by him, more precisely by the set of conditions that allowed him to exist and operate 'on the left'. He was living proof of the systemic failure of our struggle, how we consistently let the wrong one in. California flooded back through my senses, for a place that had so quickly forgotten me, edited me out of its story, it had never felt so appealing as in the aftermath of this man's company . The beach called to the whale inside me. I had never felt so 'ornery'.

After he left, after I think he made some oddly racist remark about Diane Abbott, the local MP, a woman more sinned against than sinning if ever that phrase had value, another party member filled me in.

Yeah Richard, he's a bit self-obsessed, his dad was a professor.

His dad was a professor? Fuck me if I hadn't fallen for his Dick Van Dyke accent, I had been away too long, accustomed as I was to west coast fakery. I was out of tune. This creature was middle-class and had played me for a fool. Media studies. Guy de Bored. Laclau and Zizek seemed as remote now as Marx and bloody Engels had then. Paul would have decked him. Well, the Paul I remembered would have. Why did he spring to mind, somebody who probably wouldn't even recognise me if we bumped into each other, and perhaps neither I, him. Why had I summoned this perennial sounding board to my own inadequacies? I couldn't help myself. Was he still like a vulture, stick thin with heroin chic jowls, or was he just worn out and sporting a pot belly?

My immunity had been weakened, leaving me wide open to the opportunistic infections of nostalgia, which is why I had never come home, desiring like all good expats to live my best life unencumbered.

Paul would visit elderly members of the community, his paper round, as he called it, was the most run down of blocks on the estate. Fag and chocolate runs from the newsagents, a couple of trips a week to Paddy Power or Bet Fred the bonus king, or ordering online nine pairs of the same slippers in different colours, so Auntie Babe in number 422 had a choice and she smiled, remembering her favourite colours from her youth, emerald green and ruby red, her mind boggled at what Paul was able to do on his phone, the whole idea of try before you buy as foreign to her as English had been the day she arrived here, less than a mile from the flat she had lived in since the 1950's, after Stan had died, sprawled on his tailors desk, scissors in his hand after his third and final stroke, aged 47.

Colour is as important as comfort babe.

At which they both chuckled as she poured him a cup of tea, muttering in yiddish still and forever her mother tongue.

After moving to L.A. I hardly stayed in touch with anyone back home. LA was a place for new friends, for constantly changing the patterns of your social life in tandem with what you were working on. One serviced the other. In between times I was always out of town. Other than a few drunken or drugged late night Whatsapps or Facetimes with who we imagined were old friends, peppered with do you remember when's and promises of we must catch up soon. Even these petered out as I travelled more often in different time zones further delimiting my social group to that of the changing faces of crew and random hotel assignations. In effect I came home to nothing much. Hook ups replacing relationships the older I got. Like people you meet on holidays, except we never promised to stay in touch. Other than Facebook updates from family which I always replied too late if at all. I think I saw my parents twice in seven years. By the time I came home they were almost strangers who I had to get to know (again?) before I buried them. We had enough in common to enjoy an occasional meal and the rhythm of regular short telephone calls about work, weather and our respective healths. Not having grandchildren took a big chunk out of the things that most parents had to say to their adult children, after years of worrying about this it eroded into just another silence.

If you don't immerse yourself in life you become aware of the simulacrum, the game of life rather than the thing itself.

I rented a flat in Clerkenwell, drank in the Three Kings minutes away from the house Lenin stayed in in 1903. This is the fix I needed from my hometown, to pick up on some continuity beyond the biological confines of my own body and lifetime.

A pint of Harveys or Pride and a packet of pork scratchings.

I never went to my graduation ceremony. None of us did. I never said goodbye to the people I cared for because we all went to live in London together. Our goodbyes came later and were more complicated. Capitalism loves nostalgia, extracts surplus value from it. It made you judge yourself against (not with) the rest who had more money? Who had best looking wife? Who the best job? All these anxieties played into the status quo. Look at prom nights and class reunions for bookends of the same continuum. Life™. Our rites of passage hijacked by the death cult of late capitalism, loaded dice rolls in the craps of life.

MOTHER/ COURAGE

The Happy Man pub closed. The site was waiting to be demolished as part of phase three of the Woodberry down redevelopment project. The one hundred- and fifty-year-old plane tree was also scheduled to be destroyed. Protestors had built a treehouse in its branches from which to occupy it. '#Save the happy man tree' was painted in red on the hoarding outside the pub, it had 1,092 followers on Instagram at its peak.

Paul sat on the bench in the park. It had cost two hundred quid. She hadn't used the park much but now there was a bench with Rosa's name on it, her legend. Once a week, after work, he would bring some flowers. Sometimes cheap petrol station flowers, other times more expensive ones. Paul didn't think Rosa had a favourite flower; he couldn't remember.

Rosa Feeney. January 6 1998- 5 July 2017. Our daughter the Lioness.

Sarah had only come once to the bench (as far as he knew) the first day, almost six months after her death. 'Why did we get married, such a conventional thing to do, Rosa was the only one of her friends not to have a double barrel name.'

Wouldn't have fitted on the bench would it? A smile interrupting their tears. Sarah's family name was Butler

Samuels. A servants name on top of a masters her mum had always joked, shaking her head at this double misfortune.

Today Paul had brought some roses from a man at a traffic light. A deeply tanned man with a terrible limp, almost a jump and shuffle gait to his walk as he threaded himself through the traffic. *Cut flowers are such a waste dad.* He replaced the dead ones tied to the armrest.

I sat down next to him took my gloves off and offered him my hand. He looked at it, then up at my face holding his gaze for a long time searching for a sign that he either knew me or didn't.

Remember the day you came out of Severalls?

Paul hesitantly took my hand, shook it.

Cold as fuck, just like today.

I told him my name.

Fuck. How did you find me?

What must he look like to other people? Did he care? He had become that person. Somebody you felt sorry for. One of them, the left behind. Not able to settle, to move on, stuck in a loop of grief and memory. Years ago, a young woman had hung herself from a tree in the park at night, her body found by a park keeper the following morning. Ever since her father had haunted that tree, made it his own. He placed framed photographs of his daughter around its trunk and hung plastic butterflies from its branches, perhaps something she had had in her room as a child. Perhaps recreating her childhood bedroom on and under the tree. Teddy bears, trinkets, a pair of her shoes and a T shirt also. The tree became a shrine to her memory. Flowers being replaced regularly, the whole paraphernalia of grief and remembrance tended to by the father. You never saw anybody else there, definitely not anyone who could have been her mother. And then it became a memorial to his grief. A pain which dominated the memory. Erratically replaced flowers and photos, following a private rhythm, the ebbs and flows, the surges and flat lines of his despair. Although technically illegal the council turned a blind eye. Eventually the activity of grief around and on the tree became less, became 'normalised'. Perhaps it had subsided into being a thing with normal proportions. On the anniversary of her death, and also her birthday what remained was replenished, sometimes embellished with lanterns, fabrics and other meaningful objects. School photos, a graduation one I think, poems, the tree stood as a raw representation of a woman's life curtailed. All of this kept up over years. Instead of an expected atrophy of grief, the fathers resistance to it was heroic. Paul had always wondered what her actual grave must look like, was it neglected in favour of this tree? In the past they buried suicides at crossroads. But all resistance finally gives way and now staring at the tree it was once again just a tree, with nothing to show what had happened there. Perhaps the father had died? Paul could not imagine himself being like that but also had no idea what the rest of his life might look like after Rosa's death. The only thing Paul had was this bench. This might be it. He never thought he would be the sort of person that needed somewhere to go. Was it his Catholic background? Sarah felt awkward with it, with him sitting here. It wasn't him. He wasn't Paul anymore. It would probably ruin what was left of their marriage but he didn't seem to have any agency over his behaviour, he had given himself up to quite a conventional undoing.

One day Sarah had come off shift one Thursday afternoon and found him drinking on the sofa when he should have been at work.

Now listen to me Paul was just the start of it. When it could have been the end of it. But Sarah was strong. She sat him down in front of the computer and read with him everything she could find about where Rosa had gone, about Rojava. After four hours of this Paul asked her.

I know where she went. But I don't know why.

Why? Because that's what she was compelled to do, because she grew up in this house, because she was open to the world, just like we wanted her to be. She grew up with us as her parents, she lived with all of these books and the endless bloody wonderful talking and ideas and anger, she lived in the world. She was a woman of colour in the world. And we know what happens in the world.

But why didn't she tell us?

Now that, that, I can't answer. I thought she would have told us.

And what would you have said, if she told us what she wanted to do? Would we have stopped her?

Sarah shook her head.

Perhaps that's why she didn't tell us because she was scared we would talk her out of it. We would pour water on her fire because our fire had become extinguished. Because we still had that terrible power over her.

Paul opened his mouth, but nothing came out. They held hands.

Paul called Hakan who put them in touch with people in

Kobani. The situation had got worse and now it looked as if Turkey was going to invade Rojava. Communication was difficult. They received condolences about their daughter the martyr, one of the immortals of the struggle. This isn't what Paul wanted, so he replied bluntly, How had she died? Where was her body? Had she been buried? Whilst Paul and Sarah waited for the answers they scoured the internet, looking for more, there was so much of it as if the internet itself had made space for this story, for Kurdistan, granting it a premature independence online. There were many Facebook pages, websites with alternative news, German, Italian anarchist pages, left wing media sites like Novara, Plan C, YPJ YPG portals and Instagram and Twitter feeds from individual fighters, commanders, volunteers and politicians. Endless threads to follow, away from the well-trodden paths of western media and back into the once familiar territory of their own beliefs and passion from their own youth. Watching Al Jazeera, Russia Today and even Press TV gave you news, stories and opinions a parallel universe liberated from the perspective of the American world view.

The spectacle of the American domestic news cycle was muted.

Slowly the story of what was happening in Rojava became part of their story. The struggle for national liberation, and in this instance, beyond that, a struggle for confederalist emancipation, in effect the emancipation from national aspirations that had up till this point doomed the Kurdish struggle to failure.

Killing the state one piece at a time. Allowing it to wither away. Making it redundant step by step, devolving power into granular bite size pieces.

There was a shortage of water in Rojava and Paul started fundraising for that, with a few old union mates they set up a Kickstarter and had raised 20 grand in the space of a few weeks. They spoke to Rosa's commanding officer via Skype. She sat behind her desk, with a photograph of Apo looking down benignly behind her and a YPJ flag draped next to it. She informed them that Rosa had been killed on the 7th July taking part in the final YPG assault on the Palace of Maidens in Raqqa old city. Assault rifle rounds to her head and torso. Her body had not fallen into enemy hands. She died at the moment of victory. The men that killed her had themselves been slain in turn. Her body had been recovered and buried according to her wishes in the martyrs cemetery in Kobani. She held up a photograph of a coffin surrounded by many people draped in the same flag they saw behind the commander, an all-woman guard carried a coffin carrying what they assumed was the body of their daughter. She told them she would forward the video of her funeral which had attended by hundreds of comrades in arms. Rosa would live forever. They would both be welcome as honoured guests in Kobani at any time. The YPJ intended to name the water well they were digging in memory of Rosa.

Is that what she would have wanted? Paul turned away from the screen.

Sarah shrugged.

To die and have a well named after her?

I mean the cult of the personality, was she..

She was nineteen for fucks sake.

Yeah, I know that.

Sarah turns back to the screen.

Sorry, this is a lot of information for us to take in, we need some time...

The commander nodded.

My memory of Rosa was somebody who knew her mind, she was stubborn but principled. She came here to fight, to learn why she was fighting but also to grow as a human being. But she knew who she was, and where she came from. She never took a Kurdish name, most of the volunteers do, even though she spoke the language better than most of the other volunteers, she was always just Heval Rosa, from London, as you say, a Londoner.

Thank you. Thank you.

Later Paul read out the facts of the battle of Raqqa from Wikipedia to Sarah.

On the 5th July US artillery destroyed 25 metres of the old city wall allowing the Kurdish fighters to gain access to the neighbourhoods of the old city where they encountered fierce resistance, concentrated on the ancient Palace of Maidens.

They looked at photos of a city destroyed by war. None of it sunk in.

Paul turned the computer off.

Strange to think she managed to learn Kurdish when she hadn't done any languages for GCSE.

Paul was back at the bench talking to Rosa.

Mum's in New York. can you believe that? There's a book launch of photos by a Swedish photographer, you must of met him, because you're on the cover.

He smiles, another cheesy joke for her to roll her eyes

at. He speaks quietly, deliberately, sitting there bolt upright. Paul rummages in his knapsack for the photograph and sellotapes it to the back of the bench.

She's going to be the guest of honour, they paid for the flight, hotel, everything. Your mum.

Paul stares at the photo.

Rosa cradling her rifle like it was a baby. She was wearing camouflage trousers and jacket. Her blood red Kefiye framing her face, an embarrassed smile, but flashing eyes, staring harshly at the camera, as if she would rather be elsewhere, doing something else. Behind her was an open field with what looked like Olive trees in the distance.

What's up here? You don't look so happy, I know that face.

In the first discarded photograph, (it probably exists somewhere as a negative in the photographers archive) Rosa dances like at a rave, or a beach party, the shutter captures her with her feet off the ground, levitating against a backdrop of mountains (not photoshopped, but they could have been), her Keffiyeh like a sail haloing her head and her eyes shut. In the adjacent negative in the archives we would find Rosa with her AK raised in defiance above her head, her eyes open and a smile on her face. An image that shouts *everybody is equal who has a gun.*

The picture on the cover of the hard cover Linen cloth coffee table photographic art book 'Lions of Rojava' (150 hand printed large format portraits, worldwide shipping available $250 plus postage and packing) was a portrait of a woman as a fighter, and not a fighter who happened to be a woman. A woman who was compelled to be fighter, a human unit (as Rosa would say) who was compelled to take up arms. No, this image of a female fighter, taken by a man, was always already inscribed with ideological meaning the photographer and his viewer were always already powerless to resist, around the spectacle of violence; connotations of gender and sexuality.

We can't help ourselves in this war of position.

The camera always lies.

Images of female fighters in Rojava proliferate on Pinterest and Getty images, downloadable for a fee without the burnt in watermarks.

At the drinks reception after the launch (slide show, speeches) Sarah sedated herself with champagne. A young woman introduced herself. Kimmy somebody, who sounded American but was Canadian. She had just returned from Rojava (she was a medic) and had something to give her. Sarah backed off. She didn't want to see what a medic might give her. Another photograph, she was sick of them, sick of looking. She took the envelope just to get rid of her, the survivor, the hero, the smug one full of life and purpose still, and not the dead one, the lost daughter on the cover of a book.

'Only by 'being fighters' or more simply fighting can we attempt to win the war of manoeuvre. A new hegemonic bloc will only come about through the seizure of power by way of a war supported before during and after by wide reaching cultural hegemonic struggle.'

So serious, so young, so earnest, so changed.

Inside the envelope a photograph of her gravestone with an inscription, which must have been Rosas choice, she had first read it at school and it had inspired her and must have given her courage.

The gravestone, a wooden marker with painted letters,

or maybe they were written in nail varnish, a deep purple colour, in a field of many others.

> *How can we expect righteousness to prevail when there is hardly anyone willing to give himself up individually to a righteous cause? Such a fine, sunny day, and I have to go, but what does my death matter, if through us thousands of people are awakened and stirred to action?*
> **Sophie Scholl, Berlin, 1942. Age 19.**

Dead people are much easier to value, because we can sum them up. There is nothing more of them to add. Now that they are finite they can satisfy the infinite. We pour ourselves into them, replacing who they were with who we are not.

I stood up and said goodbye. Paul had been talking for at least an hour, some of it to me. Talking had kept him warm, I stamped my feet. Thirty-five years had passed since University and most of his life had happened in the last twelve months. Mine had played out differently, not that he asked. Why would he?

And what would I say? That I had kissed Sarah in a pub thirty five years ago whilst he was locked up in a loony bin and she had laughed it off as a bit of fun and for some reason I hadn't. Why would I say that. He'd probably punch me out. Not that I wanted him to, which is why I had no intention of telling him. My problem was why was I thinking about it? Was my life so stilted, morose, lost in the past? Or was it because I had come back home and all of this flooded back as if waking up from cryogenic suspension. Now my memories present themselves too vividly for things that happened so long ago, time collapses in on itself disoreintating me.

There's no biological/reproductive reason that so much physic energy is channeled into the preservation of memory. Where I was a kid my social worker told my mum I had an overactive imagination. I remember that. My mum was non plussed. How do you fix that?

In science fiction you come back to earth years later still young whilst everybody else has aged. So even thinking about the time I kissed Sarah was literally childish. I was not even sixty. What did we have in common? Me myself and I. An unholy trinity. My struggle had just started.

Death to the Samovar!

EPILOGUE

1985

At an Anglo Soviet friendship society event in the Student Union party room we talked to a pasty faced Russian in a cheap suit. The wonders of linear programming in a supply led economy didn't manifest themselves in this Soviet mannequin who did lame James Bond impersonations to request, as we stood there wearing our plastic Lenin lapel badges on grotty moth holed cardigans, drinking cheap red wine from crumpled plastic cups.

There was little sense of the clandestine about this event, which observed the rules of the (late) cold war. The third man had come and gone. Mutual surveillance had kept the world safe enough for both sides to shoot themselves in the feet. There were few moves left in a game that was winding down.

A week later I used a phone box to call another phone box in London when I arrived at Liverpool Street station. Now they use burner phones and Telegram. End to end encryption. Personal enigma machines in every hand. My cold nervous fingers clasped a fat 50p piece. An hour later I was sitting on a park bench in Hyde Park. My Mohican got funny looks from the young nannies pushing prams and the old posh couples walking their dogs. I blew into my fingers and lit a red band, hot and bitter. After ten minutes a heavyset, middle-aged man slumped onto the bench beside me sucking a lollipop. I thought Kojack, but this man had a full shock of black hair. I looked past his shoulder, then in the opposite direction. He looked at my mohican whilst sucking. He waved the smoke from my cigarette away from his face and disdainfully pulled out a manilla envelope full of cash and chucked it into my lap. I put my coat over it, I started to sweat.

Relax. The revolution will not be televised. He smiled to himself, a Cheshire cat smile underlined by two chins.

Gil Scot Heron?

The man shrugs. Remember, the money is for posters and hand bills. Anything else and I'll know about it.

He got up and walked off. My one and only contact with Soviet Intelligence. He'd left the sticky lollipop stick on the ground next to its wrapper. Chupa Chups, from the verb to suck in Spanish.

I took the five grand and we printed 2000 posters, 7,000 handouts demanding the release of all miners and their supporters from prison. The rest was anonymously donated for food parcels (I never heard from my contact, he was all bluff.) I kept enough back for a night in the pub. London prices! Fuck you very much comrade. A few weeks later the strike was over and the Miners had been humiliated. Within ten years everything Arthur Scargill had prophesied about the industry had come true and a few years after that the Soviet Union had gone too, its passing marked only by a few bullets and a handful of suicides. The only top-down revolution in history.

Off with our head.

Much like the controlled rituals of carnival, we may have been co-opted into a societal pressure release valve, no different from its medieval counterpart. King for a day, the world turned upside down. It was a game, kicking that pigskin up and down the high street, rolling the wheel of cheese down the steepest hill, head over heels, topsy turvy down, all of us prime suspects in the locked room mystery play of the end of history. In the face of history in the making I faded. Like rent a ghost I haunted my own funeral.

Exile on market street is what Paul called himself as a grumpy old git in the months leading up to his daughter's death, stalking the aisles of Stamford Hill Morrison's for prices held bargains.

Psychoanalysts would call the Miners' strike a psychotic delusion of the left. A little unfair, but probably true for those of us involved who weren't actual miners.

Theory brooks no defeat, for you can weave all of this history back into itself, working the fabric of life into ever more finely woven and intricate shapes and patterns. Workers and students, the high altar of post '68 left theory, the radical contingency of each and every contested issue throwing up unlikely alliances, popular fronts and solidarities in the face of, in the margins of the mainstream tribalism of liberal democratic societies. Unlikely bedfellows were the warp and weft of leftist theoreticians. Feminists, the unwaged, sweatshop workers, the South African liberation movement, Californian anarchists; fantastical moments of opposition. Hopping from one of these moments (euphoria and defeat) to another was to be how we spent the next ten years in opposition.

Paul sent two postcards to Bob Crow during the strike, one at the beginning and the other when it was all over. He got this one back, dated February 16th 1985, which read:

Don't sweat the small stuff comrade, this is history and we are invincible!

Clearing out the boxes under his daughters bed he found this postcard in a New Balance trainer box. He couldn't remember what he had written to illicit this response. What had been the small stuff that he shouldn't have sweated about? Paul remembered those trainers, a Christmas gift when she was fifteen. Green trainers with a white logo.

Box Fresh.

> *Well, come along! I've got two spears,*
> *And I'll poke your eyeballs out at your ears;*
> *I've got besides two curling-stones,*
> *And I'll crush you to bits, body and bones.*

The long game. Unlimited billy goats gruff. And always, always only one troll.

Our struggle continues.

Rest in power Rosa Feeney
Our compassionate and courageous friend
we miss you greatly xx
Written on a classroom blackboard in chalk.

KURDISTANSOLIDARITYCAMPAIGN.ORG

Andra tutto bene
– graffiti, Italy, 2020

ABOUT THE AUTHOR

Wayne Holloway is a novelist and film maker from London.

He is the author of the novel *Bindlestiff* (Influx 2019) and the collection *Land of Hunger* (Zero 2016). His latest film, From These Hands was released in 2021 and he is currently writing his next book set in Liguria, Italy.